SPECIAL DELIVERY

What he saw hit him like a physical blow to his stomach, and he almost gasped, a convulsive wave of nausea rising from deep within him, his face flushing hot and clammy in the same instant. It was a photograph of himself, a radical and shocking departure from the others. He stood in his raincoat, one hand in his pocket, the other holding his trilby.

But there was more.

With a black felt-tipped pen, a smoothly arcing, dotted line had been drawn depicting the trajectory of a bullet crossing from the left side of the picture entering Haydon's head through his right eye. A red felt-tipped pen had then been used to draw the resulting blast. But the explosion was not just a quickly tossed-off jumble of scribblings, rather it was a curiously stylized effluence of curlicues, tiny starbursts, spirals, and sparks, wedges of bone and tufts of hair flying from his skull in moist and graceful patterns.

IN THE LAKE
OF THE MOON

David L. Lindsey

BANTAM BOOKS
NEW YORK · TORONTO · LONDON · SYDNEY · AUCKLAND

This is a work of fiction. Names, characters, places, and incidents are either the product of the author's imagination or are used fictitiously. Any resemblance to actual events or persons, living or dead, is entirely coincidental.

This edition contains the complete text
of the original hardcover edition.
NOT ONE WORD HAS BEEN OMITTED.

IN THE LAKE OF THE MOON

A Bantam Book / published by arrangement with
Atheneum Publishers

PRINTING HISTORY
Atheneum edition published 1987

Excerpts from The Florentine Codex, Book VI, *are reprinted by permission of the University of Utah Press, copublisher with the School of American Research of Fray Bernardino de Sahagun,* A General History of the Things of New Spain, *trans. Charles E. Dibble and Arthur J. O. Anderson (Salt Lake City and Santa Fe, 1969), 197*

Bantam edition / February 1990

ISBN 0-553-28344-8

Published simultaneously in the United States and Canada

Bantam Books are published by Bantam Books, a division of Bantam Doubleday Dell Publishing Group, Inc. Its trademark, consisting of the words "Bantam Books" and the portrayal of a rooster, is Registered in U.S. Patent and Trademark Office and in other countries. Marca Registrada. Bantam Books, 666 Fifth Avenue, New York, New York 10103.

PRINTED IN THE UNITED STATES OF AMERICA

O   0 9 8 7 6 5 4 3 2 1

para Elena
la otra mujer dentro de la mujer

The steps a man takes from the day of his birth until that of his death trace in time an inconceivable figure. The Divine Mind intuitively grasps that form immediately, as men do a triangle.

—JORGE LUIS BORGES,
The Mirror of Enigmas

Prologue

IT SEEMED TO SATURNINO BARCENA THAT THE ENTIRE WORLD WAS shrouded in clouds and rain. His flight's departure from the smoggy Benito Juárez International Airport in Mexico City in the late afternoon had been delayed by a sudden deluge, a caprice of the rainy season. When the plane finally received clearance to take off after half an hour's delay, it roared down the tarmac in the bruised light of a sodden dusk, its windows streaked with blasted water as it rose into the nether zones of a night storm, climbing steeply to clear the volcanic mountains, heading north across the Tropic of Cancer.

He sat in a seat next to a window, the overhead light turned off, while the two women to his left read silently in the bright shafts from above their seats, leaving him alone in the dark pocket of his own solitude. For a while he stared at his reflection in the glass, trying to be detached, trying to see himself objectively: a man in his early forties whose wavy, black Mexican hair was receding slightly toward a widow's peak above a high forehead, a man whose cedar-brown eyes were prone to hooded lids, whose hawk-nosed good looks were passing into middle age without appreciable damage. He saw a professor of anthropology with a modest professional reputation, but with no professional ambition, a man who had never married, who slept with his women students, who lived alone. He saw a man who had never achieved what might have been expected of him, a man who had been deceived and cheated, whose entire life had been wrenched and twisted by someone else until it had become the perverted thing of others, not his own.

Barcena's thoughts could easily fester in this vein for hours at a time. After all, he had spent most of the past year coughing up the concentrated bile of perceived injustices that he had accumulated over a lifetime, a year in which he had dredged up every pain he had ever suffered, every malefaction, and placed the blame, not on goats or gods as in the past, but on a single man.

He refocused his eyes and for the rest of the flight peered out into the vast blackness, sometimes seeing nothing, sometimes seeing indistinct movements only inches from his face that might have been mists or the wraiths of old grievances. And sometimes, when the plane moved through towering ranges of cumulonimbus clouds, he watched far-off threads of lightning jerking in glyphic patterns with a purpose he could only imagine. And he did imagine. His mind was fecund. That was why he had begun the journey.

He remained silent during the three-hour flight, keeping his face turned to the window, spurning a complimentary drink, declining dinner, gnawing instead upon the strong spice of a rankling obsession that he earnestly yearned to bring to resolution. For nearly a year he had thought of little else, incessantly bedeviled by a single ruling passion that gradually had turned his days and nights into distortions, that had shifted the borders of reality and had transformed his life. In the end, Saturnino did not shrink from his final conviction that at the heart of things, the life of another man had been the cause of his own puzzling misfortunes. Nor did he flinch from the severity of his final judgment: that nothing less than the other man's death would assuage the agony he had endured.

If Saturnino Barcena saw any inequity in what he was about to do, it was only that it had taken him a lifetime to discover the provenance of all his misery. And it ate at him like an acid that the discovery itself had been accidental, that the secret had been deliberately concealed from him in an inconceivable act of the worst kind of betrayal. Without the intervention of unreasoning fate, he might never have known, might never have understood the queer ways of his own heart.

Suddenly he was surprised by a shift in his equilibrium, and then immediately he realized that the heavy body of the plane was tilting gently forward, beginning its long descent to the Houston Intercontinental Airport. The flight had seemed only a moment. Symbolically, for he was a man keenly attentive to symbols, he removed from the lapel of his suit coat the marigold he had bought from an urchin on Truentos Street and absently twirled it by its stem between his fingers. He held it to his face and let the bright yellow petals feather over the surface of his lips as he gazed out the window. He suppressed a shudder of excitement, a recognition of the stalking tension that rose inside his chest as the plane plummeted through the night sky, hurling him toward the act that would unriddle his past and rectify the ache of the mordant years. It would be a satisfaction that too long had been denied him.

======================================= *Chapter 1*

HAYDON STOOD UNDER THE BEL AIR MARQUEE WEARING HIS RAINCOAT and trilby as he watched Chuck Nagle splash across the street in the rain, his plastic slicker pulled up over his head. Nagle stamped his feet as he approached Haydon and reached into a hip pocket for his comb, which he quickly ran through his damp hair, feeling for the part. Nagle was a young detective, tall, husky, good-natured, and baby-faced, working with an old hand named Sid Lynch who had bad teeth and a worse disposition, and who sat across the street in the dry car, looking at them.

"She still in there?" Nagle asked, turning down the collar on his slicker. He looked down at his soaking feet. "Shit." He stamped them again.

"She's sitting in the audience now, watching the film," Haydon said. "About six rows in front of the projection booth in the center section."

"You get a look at the guy?"

"Not his face."

Nagle grinned crookedly. "He's the projectionist?"

Haydon nodded. "Apparently." He had just had the first real break in the investigation of a young widow who was the primary suspect in the murder of her middle-aged husband two weeks earlier. The case belonged to the punctilious Pete Lapierre and his partner, Robert Nunn, but three teams of detectives had been assisting them with an around-the-clock surveillance that had begun three days before. Within the last hour, just at the end of his shift, Haydon had followed the woman to the movie theater, where he had discovered her in a rainy-afternoon tryst on the floor of the projection booth with her boyfriend, whose existence they had not been able to confirm until now.

Nagle snorted. "And I was beginning to believe you guys were wrong."

"Has Dystal called Lapierre?" Haydon asked.

"Yeah. He's on his way down here."

"And Gilbert is taking Balkin's place in the cab?" Balkin was Haydon's temporary partner on the surveillance, operating out of a taxi.

"Already has. Balkin's on his way back in."

"Fine. Then I'm going to leave it with you, Chuck," Haydon said, slapping the young detective on the back as he moved away. "See you tomorrow."

He stepped out into the rain and strode across the street to his car, parked a couple of cars behind Sid Lynch's. Sid's round white face peered at him passively through the foggy car window. He nodded at Lynch as he unlocked the car, but Lynch simply looked the other way, seemingly pissed off at having to be there and at the weather in general. Haydon crawled into the car, started the motor, and flipped on the air conditioner. He laid the trilby crown down on the seat, pulled away from the curb, and drove off without looking back.

He didn't want to think about the lubricious widow anymore, and gladly put her out of his mind as he turned onto Kirby. At the Southwest Freeway he merged with the inbound traffic and settled back, determined not to fight the uneven flow of cars and vans and pickup trucks.

He listened to the rain drumming on the roof of the car. September in Houston was a frustrating season. Because of the subtropical influences of the Gulf Stream waters, extreme high or low temperatures were rare in the city. However, the effective temperature—the way the temperature feels to the body as a result of a combination of temperature, humidity, and wind—was the highest in the United States. And at no time was it worse than in September, one of the wettest months of the year as well as one of the hottest, when the oppressive swelter of July and August did not let up but hung on tenaciously, unabated by the rains and turning the month into an equatorial ordeal, one day melting into the other monotonously, endlessly.

But this year it had resembled a true monsoon. It was only two weeks into the month and they had already received more than double the monthly average precipitation, and the forecasts continued to be gloomy. The entire city was beginning to smell fusty, and the trunks of the trees were sprouting a fine, linty pelt of Kelly-green lichen. Every color exposed to the weather was two shades darker from the incessant moisture, and the city's traffic plowed sluggishly through the glazed streets, headlights burning day and night. The bayous had risen and stayed up, and some parts of the city flooded every few days when heavy storms passed through the already darkened skies. The rain seemed interminable, and Haydon believed he was the only person in the city who really didn't mind it.

In the clean sweep of the windshield wipers he let his eyes follow the beaded file of ruby taillights as they curled gracefully into the soaring acropolis of downtown that loomed ever larger as they approached, like an immense galactic outstation hovering in a hazy alien atmosphere. Thousands of columns of lighted windows ascended into the low-hanging banks of clouds and fog, their brilliance fading as they rose into the upper reaches of the drifting rain until they were totally extinguished. Haydon always had thought of this phenomenon as a gigantic exhibition of magic—the disappearing city, a metaphor for the place where anything could happen. It was an idea in which he took little comfort.

After emerging from the interchange onto the Gulf Freeway, he was skirting the western edge of downtown, coming up on the exit to the police station, when he caught among the scratchy transmissions on his radio the West Texas drawl of Bob Dystal's baritone calling his code number. Haydon answered, and Dystal, sounding thick-chested and detached, said that he would like Haydon to stop by his office before going home. Haydon answered that he would, and the radio fell silent again. Slightly irritated, he began looking for an opening in traffic to move into the right lane. He had intended to go straight to his own car after dropping the department car off at the police garage, avoiding the main building altogether. Balkin had already agreed to handle the day's supplemental report. Now . . . well, it didn't matter. He shrugged, and exited the freeway.

When Haydon walked into the squad room, he stopped at the coffee table and filled a Styrofoam cup from the fresh pot that was frequently made at the beginning of the evening shift, especially when the weather was as nasty as it had been during the last two weeks. He added a packet of artificial creamer, a dietary absurdity he no longer disdained, indignation having given way to senseless habit, and swirled the off-white powder into his coffee with a plastic stirrer. The squad room was relatively busy with the changing shifts, but Haydon kept to himself as he walked toward the back, where for the last four months he had shared his small cubicle with Josef Balkin, who had been using what Haydon still thought of as Mooney's desk.

"Hey," Balkin said, looking up from the computer terminal where he was typing in the supplemental report. "I thought you were long gone."

Haydon threw his overcoat and trilby onto a chair between his desk and the wall and nodded as he raised the coffee to his mouth and blew at the steam. "Dystal called on the radio, wanted to see me before I left."

"Tough luck." Balkin grinned and returned to the terminal. During the fourteen months since Mooney's death a number of detectives had done stints in Haydon's office, which didn't particularly affect him one way or the other, since he had been more or less responsible for the rotation. He would have preferred to be alone, but no HPD detective had ever had that luxury, so it wasn't something Haydon even considered. Though he had easily adjusted to the changing personalities with whom he had shared the tiny office during the last year, Haydon was a man who put a high premium on privacy, and he did not, with one or two exceptions, form friendships that extended beyond the hours his job required. He did not participate in Happy Hour drinking, did not belong to a softball or bowling league, did not volunteer to work for any of the department-related charities, and did not belong to either of the unions. But those who knew him well enough liked him, and those who knew him only by reputation respected what they had heard.

Dystal was sitting behind his desk, hands clasped behind his head and a booted foot propped across an opened drawer as he talked with Walter Kramer, an evening-shift lieutenant. When Kramer looked around and saw Haydon coming toward them across the squad room, he began winding down their conversation. Haydon spoke to him as they passed outside Dystal's door, and then stepped inside.

"Stu, come on in," Dystal said, bringing his hands down but not budging from the chair. His tie was undone, and his desk was littered with papers and crime-scene photographs that had come from a manila file folder on the corner of his desk. "You might as well shut that thing," he said, pointing a blocky thumb toward the door.

Haydon was immediately alerted, but closed the door without any reaction. He sat down in the chair in front of Dystal's desk as he had done hundreds of times before, and tried to read between the lines of the lieutenant's attitude of day-end fatigue. He wouldn't have to wait to learn the purpose of the summons. Their long-standing friendship meant that small talk wasn't necessary; they understood each other.

Bob Dystal had been Haydon's lieutenant for six years, but their friendship went all the way back to their rookie years when they had first worked in plainclothes on special duty assignments. A stout bull of a man, Dystal had grown up in the ranch country of West Texas and had played Southwest Conference football at Texas Tech University with enough raw grit to be placed in the front ranks of the NFL's draft choices at the end of his senior year. Characteristically, he had rejected that career possibility and used his petroleum engineering degree to obtain a position with an oil exploration company headquartered in Houston. The bearish ex-lineman who had never been farther from home than his college campus spent the next two years traveling in Latin America, Southeast Asia, and the Middle East. On returning to Houston he unexpectedly quit his job and incongruously entered the Houston police academy. In later years he claimed, rather unoriginally, that it had seemed like the right thing to do at the time.

Much like Haydon, Dystal was a man who liked to play his cards close to the vest, though he had the kind of inquisitive mind that invariably wanted to know about others what he was unwilling to reveal of himself. Although he had long passed that point in his life when he had lived in the city more years than he had in the country, he had never lost the basic values and mannerisms of a country boy. For the most part he was a straightforward man, unpretentious, and with a reputation for watching out for his men. He smoked generic cigarettes when he was in the office and chewed Tinsley's red tag tobacco when he was out; listened to country music on KILT; had a proclivity for chocolate-brown double-knit suits (he had three identical ones); wore handmade cowboy boots which he kept polished to a well-buffed luster and resoled again and again until the bootmaker said he had to have another pair; and drank the strongest coffee any living man could tolerate, which he brought to work in a wide-mouth thermos jug that was so old and dented that Haydon guessed it must have been one of the first of its kind.

"So the little widow has a libido after all," Dystal said with an amused expression. "That's good. I think ol' Pete was getting a little antsy about her."

"I don't blame him," Haydon said. "I would bet she still has a few surprises in store for him."

Dystal dropped his big boot to the floor with a heavy thud, closed the drawer, and rolled his chair up to the desk. He picked up his yellowing Lucite ashtray, in the shape of Texas with rattlesnake rattles imbedded in the bottom, dumped the old butts and ashes in the trash, and set it out of his way on a stack of papers. His shirt sleeves were rolled back from his log-sized wrists. He interlocked the thick fingers of both hands and placed them in the empty space in front of him as he looked at Haydon from under his dark eyebrows.

"The captain wanted me to talk to you again," he said. "About this partner business."

"And about the lieutenant's opening," Haydon said, suddenly understanding why he was there.

Dystal grinned. "Yeah, and about that too."

"I had heard Stimson was taking early retirement."

"Yeah, he is."

"So if I go ahead and take the lieutenant's position, Mercer will solve two problems."

Dystal nodded wearily, still grinning. "Yeah."

Following Mooney's death, Haydon had asked for a special consideration, and it had been given to him. He had requested that he not be assigned a new partner right away but be allowed to work alone, as far as it was feasible, on the cases he and Mooney had been investigating. Considering the stringency of departmental regulations, that was a big request. But it was done, and he gratefully did not ask how it had been arranged. He had had several "conversations" with the departmental psychologist—as per division regulations—and was well aware that his request that the assignment of a new partner be postponed was viewed with suspicion by some members within the administration. It didn't seem like a move toward a healthy adjustment.

On the other hand, Haydon's "floating" status was not viewed as a bad thing by everyone. Of the 105 detectives in the homicide division, he was now among the ten or twelve with the most seniority, and was arguably the best detective in the division. This was a long-standing topic of informal discussion among some of the senior officers, and their criteria were stringent. Though a detective's investigative abilities might be above reproach, his performance-to-potential ratio was always suspect (though not officially) if it was known that he considered alcohol too much of a good thing or found women too much of a temptation. If he had to struggle to keep his marriage together (and the nature of the job meant that many did), it was noted. If he cut his shift short one time too many, it was noted. If he was obsessed with his work, it was noted. If the tension showed, it was noted.

For the most part, Haydon came off well under this kind of scrutiny, and was given the highest marks for investigative intelligence. But on three occasions when one of the rare vacancies for lieutenant had opened up, he had turned down the opportunity to be promoted—one of the positions ultimately had gone to Dystal. And that wasn't the sort of thing that was done without attracting attention. It was suspect behavior, and only added to the talk in some quarters that Haydon was just a little too independent for his own good.

He sipped his coffee, looked at Dystal, and put the cup on the edge of his desk.

"I'm surprised they've let me go this long," he conceded. "I hadn't thought they would."

Dystal nodded. "It's been long enough, Stu."

"I know that." Haydon stared at the edge of Dystal's desk. He could hear the faint, tinny strains of country music coming from the red plastic Hitachi radio that sat on top of Dystal's metal filing cabinet. He never turned the radio off and never turned it up, keeping the volume so low that at times you weren't sure what you were hearing. "Will I have any say about who it will be?"

"I imagine Mercer will give you a chance to put in your two bits' worth," Dystal said. He leaned back in his chair again; its wooden frame creaked as if it were approaching its stress limits, about to explode under his weight. After his long day in harness his military haircut with its Brylcreem finish was slightly rumpled where his beefy hands had run through it in occasional moments of distraction.

He smiled reminiscently and said, "Stu, we've been working together a pretty good while now, long enough to have stored up some things to look back on. We've done each other some favors, stuck our necks out a few times, had some disagreements. But for the most part we've gotten along, and we're friends. I've learned a hell of a lot from you. You've got your peculiar ways, and I know damn well you know that yourself. You don't always look at things the way other people do, and sometimes your intuition is downright spooky." He grinned again. "Which I like."

Dystal hesitated, letting his smile subside, then went on.

"I'll tell you straight out, you're the best man I've ever seen in this business. Best by a long shot." He held up both thick hands, palms out. "Honest to God. It's a fact. And I trust you like my own bud, Stu, I really do."

Haydon was surprised to see that Dystal was looking at him with an expression of undeniable mellowness, even a sense of affection. Whether it was meant for the memories or the friendship he had no idea, but it was definitely an uncharacteristic demonstration of feeling, however restrained and subdued. That expression, as much as what Dystal was saying, sharpened Haydon's attention.

Dystal leaned forward once more in the creaking chair and put his hands on the edge of the desk to support himself as he jutted his bulky neck forward, and started slowly shaking his head as he added, "But I'll be damned, Stu, if I understand just what in the hell it is you got against being a lieutenant in this police department."

Haydon was touched by Dystal's short but uncommonly personal disquisition, and by his old friend's effort to set the stage for what was undoubtedly going to result in Dystal's delivering to Haydon a hard departmental fact.

Having said his piece, Dystal regarded Haydon silently, his brawny shoulders hunched up on either side of his neck as his crossed forearms supported him on the desk top. The air of expectancy he had introduced would not bother him in the least; he could remain immobile and silent indefinitely, leaving Haydon the responsibility of moving the meeting forward.

However, Haydon didn't know how to respond. In the uncertain silence that followed he thought at first that Dystal was actually going to wait for a reaction from him, and then in the next instant he thought Dystal's last remark had been a rhetorical statement that required nothing from him whatsoever. But the curious part had been Dystal's obviously sincere preface.

"Have they grown a little impatient with me?" Haydon smiled, trying to give Dystal an opening to ease up.

"I guess that's about the size of it," Dystal said, sighing hugely and shrugging.

"Then what do they want?"

"You know how it works," Dystal said. "We never had this little conversation, it never happened. The fact is, you're getting a new partner. Maybe you'll have some say in it, maybe not. But what's more important, it seems to me anyway, is that they're going to come to you one more time with this lieutenant's opening that Stimson's leaving behind. If you turn it down this time, rumor is you'll never get another crack at it. All unofficial, of course," he repeated. "Nobody asked me to talk to you. Well, Mercer did say why don't you talk to Stuart, but that was all he said. But he knew I knew what he meant."

Dystal stopped, to let that soak in, Haydon supposed, and then he said, "You gotta decide how you want to spend the rest of your career in this business, Stu. If you're ever gonna get off the streets, this is the time to do it."

Haydon took the Styrofoam cup off the edge of the desk and sipped the coffee again. It had cooled, and tasted terrible. The evening shift's criteria for what made a good cup of coffee were even worse than the day shift's. He crossed his long legs, trying to formulate his thoughts. He deeply appreciated what Dystal was doing, and knew that his old friend deserved an explanation, however awkward.

"That's an interesting development," Haydon said, honestly surprised. There was a burst of laughter outside in the squad room, but neither man paid attention to it. "How did it come about?"

"Oh, come on, Stu." There was a hint of exasperation in Dystal's deep voice. "You've been so sidetracked by ol' Mooney's death. . . . Maybe some of those boys up in administration are getting chapped about you throwing that promotion back at them every time they offer it to you. Ever think of that? They got people standing in line for it, but you always get first crack at it because you keep taking the damn exams and always come up with the highest scores. And then what do you do? You turn your nose up at it like it's bad tuna. Why the hell do you take the exams if you aren't going to accept the promotion? They don't *have* to offer it to you every time, you know, and I guess now they've decided they're not going to. Maybe some of them are saying, hell, he don't ever want it, fine, he won't ever get it. It's not all that hard to understand, Stu. This time they want you to either piss or go blind."

Dystal could be depended upon not to dance around a subject too long before he went straight to the heart of it with a tart colloquialism, and though you might not be familiar with the idiom, you weren't likely to be in doubt about its meaning.

"And I think they've got a point," he added bluntly.

"Okay. Look," Haydon said, glancing out into the squad room and crossing his legs the other way. "You're right and they're right. I can understand how they could feel that way. But I want *you* to know, Bob, that there wasn't anything calculating about my turning down those opportunities."

He looked at Dystal. "The truth is, the first time I turned down the promotion it was a simple decision. I just didn't want to leave the streets right then. I was a lot younger. That was a long time ago, and I liked what I was doing. It wasn't a complicated thing at all. And I told Captain Mercer that." He put the cold coffee on the edge of the desk again. "The second time . . . well, at that point maybe I thought there were certain principles involved. I thought what I was doing was valuable, that being a 'manager' of detectives wasn't the same thing as being a detective. I liked the immediate payback of being actively involved. I told *that* to Mercer." He paused, and made a conscious decision not to get too wrapped up in his explication. "The last occasion . . . it was just bad timing. I wasn't in the proper frame of mind. I was disgruntled with some of the administration's changes about that time, and I just didn't want to get involved. I kept taking the exams . . . so I would have the option of getting off the street if I finally decided that I should. But I kept backing away from it at the last minute. Maybe I haven't been thinking it through as well as I should have."

As badly as Haydon wanted to say the right things for Dystal, to honor the confidence his friend had proclaimed in him, he couldn't bring himself to be more open than that.

"It hasn't been any great scheme," he said. "I've just let it happen each time. That's about it. It's got nothing to do with politics, with my wanting to make any kind of statement. It seems to me I've gone out of my way over the years to stay away from that kind of thing. The decisions were personal, very personal."

Dystal was nodding, listening, assenting, and when Haydon stopped, he said, "*I* know that, Stu, but you've got to play the game a little. You've got to give them a reason, not be too tight-lipped. You know damn well some people think you're a little . . . uppity anyway, and how you go about your business—never explaining yourself, never, you know, loosening up—doesn't help your case any at all."

"The people I respect know me better than that," Haydon said. "And the others—and I could count them on one hand—don't matter."

"Hell, that depends on what you mean by 'matter,'" Dystal retorted. "That's just what I mean, dammit. Right now it's that handful of people who're in a position to cause you some trouble. Let's be honest. You've never needed the job, so you've always had the freedom to tell those little generals to shove it. All these years you refused to play those damned little ol' games—which we all hate, but most of us go along with 'em a little ways, except you—and now you're paying for all that independence in spades. They're giving you an ultimatum, Stu, and because *they've* been playing the game all these years they're now in a position to make it stick."

Dystal stopped, his eyes settled on Haydon with the steady assurance of a man who knew what he was talking about, who understood the convolutions of a system and had long ago decided to do what he had to do to survive in it. After a pause he asked, "Well, how do you feel about it this time?"

"When are they going to announce the opening?"

"Monday. A week from today."

"I'm going to have to give it some thought."

Dystal shook his head, as if he had known that Haydon wouldn't make a simple decision, that he would have to drag it out, agonize over it. Then he began to nod. "Yeah, you give it some thought," he said. "What're you going to tell Nina?"

"I'll tell her what's happening."

"What do you think she's going to say?"

"You know how she feels about it."

Dystal nodded again, and chewed on the inside of his jaw, regarding Haydon. "You gotta consider her this time, Stu," he said, his voice low and personal. "I mean, more than you have before."

Haydon accepted that mild admonition. It was sincerely spoken, and he knew it was more than justified.

HAYDON STOOD IN HIS FATHER'S LIBRARY—EVEN AFTER ALL THESE years he still thought of it as his father's—and looked out through the small panes in the French doors. In the pale afternoon light, the pools of water on the slate terrace reflected a dull lacquered image of the house and its darkened windows, emptiness looking back at emptiness. He guessed it would be another couple of hours before Nina would be home from the studio. She had told him the night before that she had a three o'clock appointment with the Cassells, who were coming over to review her new sketches for their beach home, an ordeal which somehow always took longer than she anticipated. Gabriela had left a note on the small hall table where she always put the day's mail; it said she and Ramona had gone shopping. He was alone, which was fine with him. It suited his mood.

He looked out to the lowering September skies under which the city had been cloistered since before the beginning of the month. Haydon liked rainy weather, and every day since this had begun he had come home from work and gone straight to the library to read, or listen to music, or simply gaze out the windows as he was doing now. At times, amid thundering, the rain would blow in sheets across the sloping lawn toward the lime trees, whipping the flamboyants and scattering their frail ruby blossoms. Sometimes it would fall straight down, heavily, without respite. At other times there was only mist and fog. But always rain, unceasing. Time in legato, a seamless progression of wet days merging one into the other in a damp, unending dusk.

He looked through the mizzle to the high rock wall at the far end of the lawn where purple and red passionflowers hung from limp vines. Low on the wall he could make out the stained limestone tablet, and beneath that the small grassy berm of Cinco's grave. The old collie had not endured the long hot days of the previous summer, and Haydon was still unaccustomed to his absence. He would not have been startled to catch a glimpse of Cinco's white paws passing among the dripping hedges near the greenhouse.

His eyes moved back to the water-polished stones of the terrace, where a slight drizzle stippled the reflected sallow light, and the bright cerise firebursts of bougainvilleas overflowed the terra-cotta urns that stood against the balustrades.

Haydon breathed deeply, smelling the books that lined the walls, the wood and leather of furniture, his breath making wavering ghosts upon the rain-cooled panes of the door. He thought of his conversation with Dystal. It didn't matter how hard he tried, it seemed impossible to remain aloof from the long tentacles of departmental politics. He thought that no one had been more determined over the years than himself to remain detached from the manipulations and power plays that were an integral part of any organization. He wasn't any good at it, never had been, and he had been willing to pay the necessary price of a stalled career to remain independent. It was a luxury he had thought he could afford.

When he had entered the police academy nearly eighteen years earlier, there were a few who had made grousing predictions that Webster Haydon's son had ambitions, that by "starting at the bottom" he was simply admitting the necessity of political cosmetics, and that one day with the help of his father's money and influence he would try to go all the way to the top. Early on it seemed as if their predictions were on target. The political players laid their bets and watched as Haydon graduated from the academy near the top of his class, and spent less than a year in uniform before he received his first plainclothes assignment. Within two years he was a detective sergeant in homicide. But there his career stopped, though it seemed to be of no comfort to his detractors, many of whom had advanced past him in the natural course of events, that his static position within the department was a direct result of his own choosing.

Turning from the French doors, he faced the library. He had not turned on the lights, and the large room was illuminated solely by the soft, silver luster of the overcast afternoon. A subtle light muted the room's colors to the fading hues of an old film and threw a dull sheen on the glossiest surfaces: thin spines of books, the crescent curve of a lamp globe, the cambered edge of a walnut chair, the rail-straight border of the mantel, the gilded motifs on the picture frame at the far end of the room.

He looked at the picture, a portrait of his father of which he could see little except a reflective smear across the varnished surface of the canvas. But he knew the image by heart. Maybe his father had been right to be disappointed in what Haydon had chosen to do with his life. Haydon had been the first son in four generations who had not become a lawyer, and though Webster Haydon himself had been something of a noncon-formist, leaving the family firm in Boston and seeking a different way to put his life together outside the structure of the clan, he had been significantly disappointed in his son's departure from the profession, and from the possibility of one day joining him in the practice he had begun in the early 1940s. It had been impossible for him not to see Haydon's decision as a form of rejection, but he had not been so blind that he couldn't see the parallel to his own behavior many years earlier. The pain of Haydon's decision had healed long before the old man had died, but Haydon now wondered if his father hadn't sensed, far in advance, how unsatisfactorily it would eventually end for his son many years later.

A faint electronic clicking came from the small speaker mounted on the wall near the library door, interrupting Haydon's thoughts. The room was darker, though there was still a dull-pewter light outside, and Haydon realized he had been lost in thought for a good while, staring up at his father's obscured portrait. The clicking signaled that one of the remote controls was being used to open the front gates.

Turning away, he leaned over the long old refectory table near his desk and snapped on the green-shaded lamps. Nina always looked at him oddly when she found him sitting in the dark. Though she had gotten used to this habit over the years

and never said anything about it, he felt that she still considered it one of his strangest penchants. If he wasn't too far lost
in thought, he sheepishly tried to avoid getting caught at it.
His eyes landed on the stack of mail he had brought in from the
hallway earlier and had not bothered to open. There were
several letters and an envelope. Whatever they were, they
could wait.

Stepping out of the library, Haydon crossed the entrance
hall to the front windows and glimpsed the station wagon
turning off the oval brick drive to the servants' entrance. He
walked down the corridor, went into the large utility room,
crossed it, and opened the outside door just as Ramona was
opening the door at the rear of the car, where he saw half a
dozen sacks of groceries. Gabriela was a little slower about
getting out of her seat on the passenger side, clutching a
shopping bag from Lord & Taylor.

"Looks like you had a good day," Haydon said to her,
holding the car door as she steadied herself. The old house-
keeper was pin-neat, as always, in a canary-yellow dress that
enriched her Latin complexion. He smelled the same inexpensive powder she had worn since he was a boy, the name of
which he had never known, and caught a sweet whiff of Juicy
Fruit chewing gum, which she carried in half-pieces in her
purse to give to the children she met when she was shopping.

"We almos' drowned a coupla times," Gabriela said, rolling
her large black eyes. "The rain, my God, the rain is not ever
going to stop again." She paused, tilted her head of thick gray
hair at Ramona, and grinned at Haydon. "We went to a ladies'
chop. This girl, she has got *some* very good things . . .
sostenes de encaje negro." She drew out the words in a slow,
sultry voice as she winked at Haydon and lightly fluttered her
pretty tapered fingers over her heavy chest.

"Sssss, Ga-beee!" Ramona hissed, glaring at her from the
back of the car.

Gabriela laughed, and the two women chatted back and
forth in Spanish while they got their packages out of the car
and Haydon began carrying the groceries into the kitchen. He
set the sacks, which smelled strongly of damp paper, on the
heavy old butcher's block in the middle of the kitchen. While
Gabriela and Ramona took their packages to their rooms he
rummaged around in the sacks and found a bundle of green

onions. He took them to the sink and cleaned them, cut off the ends of several, and put them on a salad plate with a few slices of cheddar cheese and some olives. He poured a small bistro glass of white table wine and began to eat the snack as he leaned against the cabinets, waiting for the women to return.

He enjoyed being in the kitchen when they were working, a habit from boyhood. When his parents had died six years earlier, Gabriela had stayed in the home alone until Haydon and Nina could arrange to move in. There was never any question about whether she would remain with them, as she had with his parents. She had been in her early twenties when she moved with Webster and Cordelia from Mexico City to Houston in the early 1940s, before Haydon was born. Having grown old with the family, she watched over the household as if it were her own, with a benevolent authority that Nina, whose even-tempered nature was rarely thrown off balance, tolerated with graceful patience. So protective was Gabriela of her duties that it had only been within the last year that Nina finally had been able to persuade her to allow Ramona Solis, a Colombian student at Rice University, to assist her in running the large old house. Gabriela had quickly formed a motherly affection for the girl, who eventually moved in as the fourth person in the household.

Haydon was pouring another glass of wine when the security panel in the kitchen indicated the front gates were being opened again. He took another glass out of the cabinet and filled it too, returned the bottle to the rack, and then carried both glasses through the dining room and out into the long hallway that stretched from the terrace in back to the front entryway. He opened the front door and watched Nina's black Vanden Plas come along the glistening driveway and pull under the porte cochere. He went down the steps, balanced the two glasses in one hand, and opened the car door with the other. She swung her legs out of the car, smiled up at him, stood, and kissed him.

"I smell onions," she said.

He smelled Je Reviens. She took a glass from him and sipped, looking at him past a wandering strand of cinnamon hair that had floated away from her temples where it was swept back in a tight chignon, the way she always wore it at the studio to keep it out of her way when she worked at the drawing tables. "You're terrific," she said, and kissed him again.

"Ramona and Gabriela just came in from 'chopping,'" he said, resting his arms on top of the opened car door. "They'd stopped by the grocery."

"And you sneaked the onions out of the grocery sack."

He nodded.

"You always do the same things," she said. A few yards away, at the end of the porte cochere, the rain was falling steadily again. "Did they have a good day?" Nina asked, taking one more sip from her glass before she turned, put it on top of the car, and bent down to get her briefcase from the front seat.

"Ramona bought some black lace bras."

Nina looked back at him from inside the car.

"Gabriela was teasing her about it," he explained.

"In front of you, of course."

"It wouldn't have been any fun otherwise."

"Here, take this," Nina said, handing him the leather briefcase as she stood again. "I've got some drawings in the backseat."

She opened the rear door and reached in to get them, the silk of her emerald dress sliding easily over her stockings, revealing the backs of her knees, and a little more. He loved the backs of her knees. No one had ever had prettier legs.

They went inside the house, and he followed her up the long curve of the marble stairs carrying her briefcase, listening to her talk about what the Cassells had thought of her drawings, and watching her hips. In the bedroom she threw the rolls of drawings on the bed, and Haydon laid her briefcase on the small sofa under the ceiling fan near the windows that overlooked the lawn. He stood behind one of the armchairs and leaned against its back sipped his wine and watched Nina undress, listening to her describe the changes the Cassells had wanted, what they had liked, and what they were reconsidering. She stood in front of the mirror, the olive contours of her shoulders interrupted by the thin green straps of her bra, and began taking the pins out of her hair. Haydon studied her, wondering how many times in their fourteen years of marriage he had watched this process. Though she was not as thin and rangy as a model, Nina was a little taller than average, and long-limbed, and she possessed a refined manner that was not practiced but entirely natural; she was one of the least pretentious persons Haydon had ever known. She was entirely accepting of herself, neither deceived in her shortcomings nor conceited in her graces. At forty-two she seemed to Haydon to be at her best, both physically and emotionally; her good common sense and uncondemning heart that had been the stabilizing forces in their marriage from the beginning were still intact, still the core of her personality.

He turned and looked outside, where night was creeping from the murky corners of the lawn, from under the lime grove, and darkening the stone wall that surrounded the grounds. A mist was hanging over the trees, settling over everything like a shroud of heavy smoke. Details became less and less distinct until he saw only a Whistler painting of dusk.

"Stuart?"

He looked around. Nina's back was still turned to him, but she had fixed her eyes on him in her mirror.

"What was I just saying?" she asked, jerking the brush through her long hair with a quick stroke.

"You were talking about the Cassells, about your drawings for them, and what . . ."

"I knew you were somewhere else," she said. "No, I was asking you what you were thinking about staring outside like that."

He grinned at her.

"You're out of your mind." She laughed, taking a short-sleeved silk blouse off its hanger and slipping it over her head. Then she stepped into a pair of pleated linen pants, which she buttoned at her waist as she put her feet into woven leather sandals. She shook her hair out, came over to Haydon, and sat down on the sofa opposite him. "Okay," she said. "What's bothering you?"

He nodded at the briefcase sitting beside her. "Did you bring home a lot of work tonight?"

"Nothing that can't wait." The lighthearted expression on her face was beginning to fade.

"I had an interesting discussion with Bob this afternoon," he said.

"About?"

"A couple of things. They're going to assign me a new partner." He studied his glass. "And there's going to be another lieutenant's position opening up next week."

Chapter 2

SATURNINO BARCENA STOOD AT THE GLASS-LOUVERED WINDOW OF HIS room and looked through the horizontal openings to the gloomy overcast afternoon. He lighted a filterless Pall Mall and watched the smoke hang still in the air. There was not even enough breeze to pull it out through the louvers. He looked out at his mud-spattered rental car parked at the end of the short sidewalk, its windows opaqued with an oily film of humidity, and then let his eyes drift up to the two ragged palm trees that marked the entrance and the exit of the semicircular asphalt drive pocked with potholes. The trees leaned toward each other with shaggy, glistening fronds. Between them a neon sign half their height stood at a right angle to the street. On the side of the sign visible to Barcena, a neon palm tree bowed gracefully in an imaginary tropical breeze at the same angle as the real ones. It had green fronds and a red trunk that repeatedly bled to a quivering pink, sometimes going out altogether until a surge of electricity caused a momentary resurgence of its former brilliance before it faded once again to a tremulous pastel. The words "Rio Courts" glowed flame-blue in happy letters below the perpetually disintegrating palm, and beneath them the word "Vacancy" vibrated in an excited commercial yellow. The sign was the only bright spot in an otherwise dreary landscape.

The small motel was on South Main. A professor of his ranking, even though he taught at the National University, did not make the kind of money that would allow him to stay in a first-rate hotel, and this time he would not be receiving an honorarium to cover his expenses. No, everything was coming out of his own pocket, and considering the astronomical disadvantage of the exchange rate, he had spent a great deal of money on this venture already. Although he did not want to deplete his funds before he had accomplished what he had come to do, the mere lack of money would not stop him. It was not a matter of money; he would gladly spend every peso he had in this pursuit, and he would gladly swallow his pride one more time and borrow from the old woman if he had to. After all, it would only be poetic justice if she had to finance what he was about to do. Barcena grunted to himself. Why hadn't that thought occurred to him long before? He wished it had; that would have been much the better way to do it.

Barcena's "bungalow" was number five of nine, situated exactly in the center of the curved drive and directly behind the flat-roofed motel office, where he sometimes could see the owners, a carbuncular alcoholic who wore shapeless, stained jumpsuits and his wife of harried mien and desperate eyes, moving back and forth behind their screen door, which was backlighted by the dull sky showing through the plate-glass window at the front of the office. The office and all the bungalows were stucco, and Barcena supposed that at one time they had been white, though now they had turned a smutty gray from the dead mildew of too many soggy Septembers. His own room and tiny kitchenette smelled as if they had been moldy for decades, and even though he had cranked open the glass louvers as far as they would go, it was of little help, since the air that seeped in was as warm and muggy as steam. He had forgotten how oppressive the change in altitude would be. Coming from the dry, thin air of Mexico City a mile and a half above sea level, he found the rancid dampness of the Gulf Coast almost too thick to breathe.

He flipped the cigarette through the louvers into the rain and turned back to the kitchenette. Normally conscientious about his appearance and particular about the cleanliness of his surroundings, Barcena was now oblivious to the fuggy odor that issued from the toy-sized refrigerator as he took a bottle of Tecate from the rows he had stacked on the rust-speckled wire shelves. He took no notice of the roaches that scuttled into the filthy cracks where the narrow counter of chipped lemon-yellow tile joined the wall as he stepped to the cabinets and used the bottle opener that dangled from a dirty string tied to one of the cabinet doorknobs. He paid no attention to the carious grout crumbling from between the tiny tiles on the countertop where he used a large butcher's knife to shave thin slices of lime onto a saucer. He didn't look twice at the tartar-colored enamel of the tiny gas stove, its vents slogged with gray fuzz and the nicotine stains of old grease, as he held the beer and saucer of limes in his hands and bent over the stove's burner to light another Pall Mall. Such incidentals had paled to insignificance against the singular focus of his preoccupation.

Returning to the vinyl-upholstered dinette chair at the windows, he set the sweaty Tecate bottle on the cinder-block sill along with the saucer. He pulled thoughtfully on the cigarette as he looked out the window and sipped the beer. From time to time he would pick up one of the translucent slivers of lime and eat it, rind and all.

He thought of the long months of anticipation that had brought him to this point, to the very brink of the event. It had begun in Mexico City seven months earlier, when he had made the discovery. Like a stunned initiate he had reeled helplessly under the weight of this new knowledge that had explained everything, changed everything, and shifted his world on its axis so that nothing ever could be the same again. He had sent a message to his superior at the university that he was sick, and he did not set foot on the campus for two weeks. He had stayed home, sometimes not getting out of his pajamas for several days at a time, his mind consumed by the revelation he struggled to understand, now feeling an exhilarating liberation, now plunging into black despondency. When he eventually did dress and go out, he wandered the meandering streets of Coyoacán for hours on end, suddenly finding himself on a back street or a plaza with no idea where he was or how he had gotten there.

Then one day, on an afternoon of high, hazy clouds and with the ubiquitous dust of the dry season hanging in an opal sky, he took a taxi downtown and walked into the offices of the American Chamber of Commerce of Mexico on Lucerna Street. He located the reference section and found the Houston Yellow Pages. Surreptitiously he tore out three sheets under the heading "Detectives," put them into his pocket, and walked out. That had been the very beginning, and he now supposed that deep in his psyche he had already worked it out, though he only remembered the plan occurring to him one step at a time.

It had taken quite a few long-distance telephone calls before he located precisely the right investigator—Ira Swain, "Experienced, Skilled, and Discreet Investigations"—one who didn't flinch at being asked to gather information on a touchy subject, one whose scruples shrank in direct proportion to his increasing fee. After three separate telephone negotiations, they agreed upon fees, terms, expectations, and an advance-payment schedule. Then Swain went to work. Over the next seven months, careful to work at a cautious pace, Swain had managed to compile a modest dossier, which he sent to Barcena piece by piece, bit by bit, whenever he came up with substantive information.

Barcena's initial interest had been something akin to voyeurism, a prurient curiosity about the way Haydon lived. Being visually oriented, he had wanted photographs, and Swain was able to gather a variety of these from newspapers, including pictures of Haydon's home, his wife, the cars he drove, the Houston Police Department. Swain soon learned that no detail was too small to be dismissed by Barcena's voracious appetite. Each photograph was accompanied by a typewritten memo on Haydon's relationship to the subject. The memos ran from a single page to half a dozen pages and contained factual information as well as gossip and hearsay that Swain had wormed out of casual conversations with any number of sources. On numerous occasions the reports were accompanied by a letter from Swain on his letterhead in which he reminded Barcena that he was having to move slowly, be careful. Haydon was a private man, and persons who had dealings with him—the mechanic at the garage where his cars were serviced, the clerk at the dry cleaner's, his barber, his tailor, etc.—did not easily divulge even the most trivial information about him. Since Haydon was a police detective, his entire employment picture was out of reach, as was any information that might be gleaned from his accountant. Just one question too many to any of these sources, Swain claimed, could make them suspicious and Haydon would be tipped off.

Two sources provided more than any of the others: police reporters, one at each of the daily newspapers, who had become professional Haydon watchers. There was plenty of gossip here, and the reporters—a man and a woman—were clearly fascinated by Haydon's reputed eccentricities: his tightly run investigations and his dislike of media attention to the same, his hostility at being photographed, his incomprehensible devotion to a relatively low-paying job despite his considerable financial independence, the rumors of his struggles with chronic depression, his reclusive private life, his beautiful wife. The speculation ran wide, sometimes so wide that it was difficult to distinguish between a truly eccentric personality trait and something elevated to myth. But whatever the truth, it was clear that Stuart Haydon had a reputation that went beyond the boundaries of his profession, a fact that made him all the more jealous of his privacy.

Barcena sucked the last drop of Tecate from its bottle, thought a moment, and then blew softly over the smooth lip of its small opening, making a haunting moan that was lightly accompanied by the dripping of the rain from the eave of the bungalow. The sound made something flutter in the pit of his stomach, and he glanced over near the foot of the bed to the narrow wobbly desk, its mirror covered with a pillowcase and Haydon's dossier scattered over its surface. Near the edge of the desk a cheap vase of fresh marigolds glowed in the dimness, a few of their slender petals lying on the papers. As it was with most things now, Barcena saw a sign in these images. He remembered the words of the Aztec midwife as she bathed the newborn and offered prayers to the goddess Chalchiuhtlicue on the child's behalf:

Lady, our lady . . . the commoner has arrived. . . . It is not known how he was arrayed, the nature of that given him in the beginning, the nature of that which he came bearing, the attributes with which he came wrapped, with which he came bound. But behold, perhaps he cometh laden with evil; who knoweth the manner in which he cometh laden with the evil burdens of his mother, of his father? With what blotch, what filth, what evil of the mother, of the father doth the baby come laden?

Indeed, who knew?

Satisfied with this conclusion, Barcena got up and lighted another cigarette from the stove. He stood with his hands in his pockets drawing the hot smoke into his mouth, sucking it into his lungs as he let a mental image of Haydon form in his mind, an image he remembered from one of the newspaper clippings in the dossier. The image wavered, but Barcena held it before his mind's eye while he considered it. Haydon. He did not even know that Barcena existed, but before the end of the week he would be willing to trade his fortune simply to talk with him. In the end Barcena would grant him his wish, though he would require more than Haydon's fortune for the privilege. But first there were a few more calculations to be made, additional manipulations to be effected. Before they could meet face to face, Barcena must go about the delicate task of fastening the strings, securing the action of limb and joint so that, like the smiling *calaveras* that children puppeteers amuse themselves with on the Day of the Dead, Haydon would jerk and leap at Barcena's pleasure.

Chapter 3

HAYDON LEANED AGAINST A WINDOW FRAME, ONE HAND IN HIS pocket, the other holding the bistro glass, as he told her about his conversation with Dystal. Occasionally he glanced out to the dying light of dusk, but always his eyes came back to Nina, who sat on the small sofa, a leg tucked under her and her long hair falling loose around her face. Haydon watched her closely, hoping to read her reaction, to gauge the temper of her thoughts. She did not interrupt him, though he several times provided calculated pauses to give her the opportunity, but let him relate the information in his own way and in his own good time, between sips of wine. By the time he had finished the story he had finished the wine too. He sat the glass on the table in front of the sofa.

They looked at each other, neither of them saying anything, Haydon seeing nothing in her eyes that helped him interpret her feelings about what she had just heard.

Finally she said, "Stuart, have you been wearing that suit coat ever since you got home?"

It took him a second to follow the comment, and then he smiled at her. "I guess I have." He pulled off the coat and tossed it over one of the armchairs and then came over and sat down beside her.

"Come on," she said, reaching around and loosening his tie.

He unbuttoned his collar and then bent down and unlaced his shoes and kicked them off, because that was what she would tell him to do next. He leaned back on the sofa and propped his feet on the table in front of them, crossing his ankles.

"Therapy," he said, settling in against her and laying an arm across her thighs, thinking how good she felt.

"Right." She set her wineglass on the table beside the sofa

and linked her arm through his. They were quiet for a while, watching the rain move across the dark treetops.

"You've been brooding over this all afternoon, haven't you?" Nina said, lacing the fingers of one hand into his as it rested on her knee. "You sat down there in the library, probably with the lights out, your coat buttoned up properly, brooding."

"I wouldn't call it 'brooding,'" Haydon said, knowing that was exactly what he had been doing.

"How would you describe it?" she asked, turning her face toward him. He could sense her eyes on him, could almost feel them as he was now feeling the warmth of her body through their clothes, as he felt her breast pressing against the side of his arm. At moments like this she was so much a part of him he couldn't imagine life without her. To lose her would be the beginning of a long, sure death for him. He took a deep breath of her fragrance, grateful for her ability to penetrate the web of isolation he seemed compelled to spin around himself, almost against his will.

"I'd call it 'thinking,'" he said lamely.

"Oh, that's a good word for it," she said as if she were humoring a child who had given a wrong answer but whom she wished to encourage.

Haydon smiled at her sarcasm and rubbed his socked feet together, massaging them.

"Let's say I resign," he said. "Then what?"

"You're only forty-three, Stuart."

"Meaning?"

"It's not as if you were being put out to pasture. You're being liberated. Go back to law school. Or read all the books you keep adding to that library down there, but never have time to read. Start working on one of the dozens of books I've heard you say you'd like to write some day. You're sitting here with a master's degree in literature and two years of law school behind you—and you have a very comfortable independent income. Remember all those things you've always wanted to do?"

"What about the other scenario?" he said, ignoring her question. "Let's say I take the promotion."

"Okay, let's say that."

"How would you feel about that?" All of this was a diversion before getting to the central issue. He knew Nina realized that, but the psychological feinting seemed necessary to him, a kind of preparation for the unavoidable confrontation.

"Wonderful. At least I wouldn't have to worry about getting that late-night visit from Bob Dystal bearing news of . . . something dreadful."

He thought there was perhaps a hint of terseness in her manner and tone, as if she were impatient with the way he was going about this.

"There's the third alternative. That I stay where I am."

Nina did not speak, but Haydon felt her supple body stiffen. Even without turning to look at her he knew that her face had changed, that all animation had drained away, leaving the cold sternness of an old anger. This was not a subject she could discuss with dispassion.

"I don't feel any differently about it than I used to," she said flatly.

"You mean that in a more perfect world I'd be out of this business altogether," he said, expressing her feelings for her. "And the next-best thing would be for me to get off the street, behind Stimson's desk, or anyone's desk."

"Damn you."

The words separated them like a cleaver, creating an immediate distance between them that widened in the ensuing silence, surprising both of them with its decisive effect, with its sudden potential for alienation.

"I can't walk away from eighteen years—"

"No! Just a minute," Nina snapped. She jerked her arm out of his and moved away from him, turning her back to the corner of the sofa to face him squarely. "I do *not* want to have this conversation. Have you any idea how many times we've done this? I know your arguments, you know mine." She held up her hand, trying to control her temper. "I really do not believe either of us wants to do this."

Haydon waited, not looking at her, feeling like a heel for going about it the way he had. He could have saved both of them some agony by simply telling her what he wanted instead of initiating this inept probe of her feelings, which, as she had already pointed out, he understood perfectly well. From her perspective he was only pretending that her feelings would make a difference to him, and the farce infuriated her. And it should have. The truth was, however, that her feelings did make a difference, but in this matter, he regretfully had to admit, there had never been any evidence of it. In the final analysis, his decisions on this subject had always seemed to disregard her feelings, and he knew that she expected this time to be no different.

"I know how you feel about it, Stuart, this work," she said suddenly, bringing her voice under control, but only barely. "You feel an obligation to do it. You would never admit it, but you have an old-fashioned sense of responsibility, a personal sense of obligation to right wrongs. You may have intellectualized it in your own mind, you wouldn't use my terminology, but that's what it is. It's at the very heart of what motivates you. And it's an honorable instinct; I admire you and love you for it."

She paused, then added, "I don't understand what attracts you to that kind of excitement. I wonder if you even understand it yourself. But I've watched those men in homicide come and go over the years and I've seen what it does to them, how it affects different men in different ways. For some it's destructive; it is for you." She shook her head, frowning. "I don't know why. Maybe it's your refusal to be as detached as you should be. Maybe you try to crawl inside those people's minds too much, become too intellectually engaged. I don't know."

Nina hesitated, raised both hands and ran her fingers through her thick hair in a gesture of uncertainty, then seemed to set her mind to go ahead. "But that's not the only thing, it's not all. I'll tell you something. It took me a long time to put together what I was seeing day after day, month after month, for so many years. It took me a while to comprehend that this is the single, most potent influence in your life. You know, I used to watch you and your father playing chess in the library. Both of you bent over that board for hours, plotting, maneuvering, stalking each other. Well, this . . . business is the real-life extension of that game, isn't it? Except now the stakes are infinitely more compelling. In this contest somebody dies at the beginning, and you play the moves backward in time until you somehow arrive at the beginning again. The hours have become years—eighteen of them—and you're still absorbed in the stalking. More than that. You are clearly *inspired* by it."

Nina stopped again. Night had fallen while she spoke, and now the only things visible outside were the silhouettes of the trees against the ashen fog illuminated from the reflected lights of the city. When she spoke again, her voice had once more recovered its natural mellow timbre.

"For you it's destructive," she repeated, as if she were picking up a dropped idea, regaining her train of thought. "That's not a theory, it's a fact. I know it. Bob knows it. That's why he called you in. You think I don't *understand* what's going on, Stuart? I'm aware that detectives in homicide don't stay on the street this long. They transfer out to other departments, they take promotions, they retire, they quit . . . they don't stay out there *forever*. Right now you're holding the record on that score."

Nina stopped. Her voice had risen again, and she was trying to regain control. He was afraid to look at her. He didn't want to see the anger, he didn't want to feel guilty for what she was going through.

"The work is valuable," she continued slowly, not even trying to hide her effort at self-control. "But honest to God, Stuart, right now I'm not concerned about the larger issues of law and order and one's responsibility to society. I'm concerned about you and what *that* job does to you . . . to us. I know it sounds selfish, but the way I see it, you've served your time on the front lines. And, for that matter, so have I. There's nothing left to prove."

The telephone beside the sofa rang softly, the intercom signal. Neither of them moved, as if they needed time to extract themselves from their intense involvement of the last few minutes. When the telephone rang a second time, Nina turned away from him and answered it. In the following silence as Nina listened to Gabriela, Haydon listened to the soft drumming of rain on the slate roof and watched the water falling in rivulets from the deep eaves of the house. He had no idea how to respond to Nina's resentment, but deep inside he knew they were at a turning point. He thought Nina believed that too. It was clear that this time she was not going to play the long-suffering wife, a part he had selfishly let her assume in the past. He had been grateful, yes. He had loved her all the more for it, yes. But ultimately, each time, it had been Nina who had compromised. Haydon had gotten what he had wanted and Nina had adjusted. He did not believe she was willing to do it again.

Nina spoke to Gabriela in mixed phrases of Spanish and English, the familiar polyglot language of the border. Years ago, before they were married, when Haydon had first begun bringing Nina to the family dinners on Wednesday nights, it had been this ease with which she conversed with Gabriela in mixed tongues that had first endeared her to the old house-keeper. In the intervening years, Gabriela had come to love her with a devotion even more unguarded than the love she had had for Haydon's mother.

After a few minutes Nina hung up the telephone and turned back to Haydon. "They'll be serving dinner in twenty minutes," she said, her voice neutral and flat.

Everything was wrong between them now, and awkward-ness intruded like the unexpected arrival of an old lover from the past, separating them with resurrected doubts and new suspicions. Haydon could think of nothing to say or do that seemed natural. He was angry, at himself, at Nina, at the whole wretched dilemma. Nina waited.

Finally he said, "Let's give it some time."

"I've given it all the time I'm going to," Nina said. She was neither bitter nor antagonistic. "You're the one who has to make the decision. You have to decide what's most important to you."

DURING DINNER GABRIELA TALKED ABOUT THE DAY'S SHOPPING, ABOUT the price of everything, about the treachery of the flooded streets through which Ramona had bravely maneuvered the station wagon. Nina asked Ramona about her courses for the new semester, if she had gotten the professors she had wanted, if she had any scheduling problems. Since Ramona had come to live with them, the Haydon household had become her family. Her concerns became their concerns, and they were as protective of her as if she had been their daughter. Although she ostensibly had been engaged to help Gabriela keep house, in reality she served more as a companion for the old woman, who gradually had slipped into semiretirement, her only real responsibilities being those related to preparing the meals for the four of them and overseeing the maids who now came in to do the housecleaning.

When they had finished eating, Gabriela brought a fresh pot of dark Honduran coffee to the table and poured cups for everyone except herself, having recently resolved to forgo caffeine in the evenings. Haydon took the large chunk of bitter chocolate that was also on the service and used a sharp knife to shave some into his cup. He stirred it until the chocolate dissolved, and then added cream as he listened to Nina tell Ramona and Gabriela about a ring that Mrs. Cassell had been wearing when she came to the studio. It was set with a sapphire and diamonds, and there was a story behind it, but Haydon lost the thread of it as his own thoughts wandered. After a few minutes he excused himself and took his coffee across the hall to the library.

With the phrases of Nina's earlier frustrations still disturbing his thoughts, Haydon idly stepped over to his desk and looked at the new volumes of Mandelbaum's translation of the *Divine Comedy*. They had arrived on Friday, and he had put them there to read in the first free evenings available to him. But he was in no mood for it now. The rain beyond the French doors brought to mind one of Bach's few chamber-music sonatas. He had started to turn to the record cabinet when his eyes caught the stack of letters that still lay on the refectory table under the green-shaded lamps. He had forgotten the day's mail completely. Moving to the old table, he set down his coffee and pulled out a chair. He flipped through the envelopes. There were a few household bills, a bill from Anton Busch for a small red Conté drawing by Odilon Redon that Haydon had bought the month before, an announcement of a book sale at a store where he had an account, a note from a detective in El Paso, and a manila envelope.

Haydon set everything aside except the envelope, which he frowned at with increasing curiosity. There was no return address, and no postmark canceling the stamps. When he received mail with any visible irregularities, he automatically took special note and examined the envelope with more care than otherwise. Superstitiously, he felt that an unopened envelope still "belonged" to its anonymous sender, and carried with it a special fragile identity that was inexplicably destroyed once he had broken the seal. It seemed to him that if he examined the packet closely before opening it, he might discern some detail, however minuscule, that would enable him to intuit something of the original owner, a detail that might disintegrate instantly if he opened it, like the fabled archaeological artifacts that crumbled to dust when the vaults containing them were opened after millennia of darkness. He wouldn't have admitted such a strange notion to anyone, but he thought of it nonetheless, and watched what he was doing. After turning over the envelope several times, he used the letter opener to make a clean cut in the end opposite the flap.

He buckled the heavy manila paper and looked inside. He saw what appeared to be a single sheet of heavier paper wrapped in white tissue. He carefully pinched the edge of it and pulled it out on the table. Through the single layer of tissue he could see the photograph of a man. He tore the tissue loose where it had been taped to itself to protect the photograph and pulled it away. In front of him lay a black-and-white photograph of an oil painting, a portrait of a young man.

With his eyes on the picture, Haydon reached for his coffee cup. He sipped the dark, chocolate-accented brew and then replaced the cup on the saucer. The portrait itself appeared not to be recent. That is, the young man's hairstyle seemed to be of the 1930s, closely barbered, shaved around the ears, combed with pomade, and cleanly parted on the left. He sat in an old baroque chair, his long legs crossed at the knees, his double-breasted suit buttoned properly, his eyes looking directly at the artist. His left arm lay casually on one of the heavy wooden arms of the chair. His right arm, holding a half-smoked cigar in his long fingers, was poised across his chest just below the top button of his suit coat. The background was vague, but interior, perhaps a hint of a sun-flooded window to the right.

Haydon turned over the photograph. There were no identifying marks. Kodak paper of a current grade. He looked again at the portrait. The young man was not smiling, but his large dark eyes seemed to regard the artist with interest. He was completely at ease. There was a casual, assured elegance in the way he sat in the chair, as if he were used to having his portrait painted, and fully expected to be satisfied with the results.

Again Haydon reached for his coffee cup and held it in both hands as he sat back in his chair and regarded the portrait. He sipped the coffee and listened to the occasional spray of rain that reached the French doors and pecked at the panes like the

tappings of small fingers. He frowned at the portrait of the
stranger as he studied it. It was in the young subject's posture,
really, more than in his face that Haydon first sensed an
intimation of something familiar. It was an odd awareness that
centered on nothing in particular, but rather grew out of the
image as a whole. The portrait itself elicited the illusion that he
had seen it before, though he had absolutely no recollection of
it. Even so, he had the vague impression that he was seeing it
again, after having forgotten it from a long time in the past.

NINA CONTINUED CHATTING WITH GABRIELA AND RAMONA IN THE
dining room for a while and then came across the hall and
leaned into the library door to tell him she was going upstairs
to work through her notes on the Cassells' drawings. Normally
she would have brought them down to the library. He
understood. He remained at the refectory table, having lost
interest in the anonymous portrait, and began paging through
the Dante volumes with their strange and unsettling illustrations. But he was unable to focus his attention and eventually
found himself staring out to the soggy darkness, his hand idly
flicking the edges of the pages as his thoughts ranged across
time and back again, without purpose. After a while he stood
and prowled among the books, moving along the shelves,
pulling down a volume here and there as he looked for a quote
that had come to mind. When he finally found it, it didn't seem
to be exactly as he had remembered, and with a sense of
dissatisfaction he decided to put on the Bach sonata after all.
As the low, soothing strains of the cello filled the library, he
retreated to one of the leather wing chairs and let his thoughts
drift back to his conversation with Nina earlier in the evening.
   It was late when he went upstairs and found Nina already in
bed, her back turned to him, asleep. He wasn't surprised. She
had the wonderful and amazing ability to disassociate herself
from agonizing stresses and, when it was clear that no amount
of masochistic torment would provide any real solutions, to
will herself to sleep. It was an intelligent method of disengage-
ment from senseless worrying, a technique he had never been
able to accomplish. He lay awake for more than an hour,
hearing the long strokes of midnight from the black slate
mantel clock before he finally gave in to an uneasy sleep.
   The alarm went off at five-thirty the next morning. It was

Tuesday, and since he had drawn alternating weekends during September he was one day away from his "weekend" on Thursday and Friday. He got out of bed and went over to the windows. In the darkness he could see a thin rain peppering the shiny surfaces of the puddles on the terrace. He turned away and went into the bathroom. After a quick shower, he shaved and dressed and went downstairs without waking Nina. For years he had worked the day shift, seven to three, and since Nina didn't open the studio until nine, Haydon always let her sleep. Gabriela woke her with coffee and a light breakfast around eight.

Haydon was a habitual early riser, even when his work hadn't demanded it, and since boyhood he and Gabriela had enjoyed breakfasts together, sometimes eating on the old butcher's block in the center of the large kitchen, sometimes in the sunroom between the kitchen and the terrace. He enjoyed this quiet beginning of his day, and loved coming into the bright kitchen when the rest of the house and the world outside was dark and seeing Gabriela in her dressing gown with her thick gray hair, not yet put up for the day, falling down her back as she busily cooked *migas* or *huevos rancheros* for the two of them.

This morning as he came into the kitchen Gabriela was squeezing oranges, pouring the juice into two small glasses sitting on the cabinet. The kitchen was filled with the tangy fragrance of the citrus fruit and the *migas* cooking in the skillet.

"Good morning," Haydon said. He walked over to the cabinet and poured a cup of coffee.

"Is Colombian," Gabriela said, jerking her head toward the coffee pot. She looked at him with a sideways glance as he took his first sip.

"Colombian?" he asked.

Gabriela laughed. "I put a tiny little bit of vanilla in it. You like it?"

"It's good," he said, and sipped again. "I like it without the vanilla too."

"Well, of course." Gabriela shrugged. "But you never know till you try it some other way, huh?"

"Right," Haydon said. He leaned against the cabinet and watched her squeeze oranges. Though Gabriela was nearly seventy-three, her Indian complexion was only now beginning to show the darker tones of age around her eyes. Her jet hair, thick and coarse, had always been long, and more often than not was worn up in braids. Now it was mostly gray, and silver in places, but still streaked with jet. As a boy, he used to look at her and think how finely drawn were her Indian nose and lips, the high, almost haughty, cheekbones that seemed to symbolize the inner character that he had come to recognize in her. She had her own standards, and she lived by them. Though she had not grown heavy with age, the feminine lines of the younger woman he had known were less distinct now, and the high, firm breasts that he had been coddled against as a child had taken on a decidedly matronly bulk. But her hands had remained young, with small tapered fingers and strong white nails that she still massaged nightly with the pulp of a lemon before going to bed. And her eyes were the same, the eternal eyes of the Indian, as dark and deep as the *cenote* of Xlacah.

"*Bueno,*" she said, pouring the last of the juice into the glasses. "Why don't you put those over there," she said, nodding at the butcher's block. "I don't want to eat in the sunroom . . . there's no sun, and I've seen enough of that rain to las' me awhile." She moved over to the stove and stirred the *migas*.

Haydon did as he was asked, and then took the silverware and napkins out of the cabinet drawers and set two places while Gabriela was taking up the *migas*. She set them on the butcher's block with a covered bowl of hot tortillas. They sat down opposite each other, and Gabriela sipped from a fresh cup of coffee that Haydon had poured for her. She tasted it carefully, thinking.

"Maybe the vanilla is better for after dinner," she conceded. She smiled. "But is pretty good."

Haydon knew their mornings together were also special to Gabriela, and it was one of the reasons he continued the routine. For her it was a ritual link to the old days, when Haydon's parents were still living and Haydon was at home and they were a family. Having helped Haydon's mother rear him from birth, having looked after him in nearly every way until he moved away from home as a young man, Gabriela had long ago lost sight of that nebulous boundary between nurse-maid and mother. She loved him with unabashed devotion, and Haydon treated her with unfailing deference. For her part, the old woman never presumed too much, though she could have presumed infinitely more than she did. Still, she was not hesitant to stand her ground with him when she thought it was required, as a mother would. They understood each other well, held no illusions about one another's saintliness, and were unafraid of the affection that had cemented their relationship for so many years.

After they had eaten for a few minutes in silence, except for the splashing outside on the terrace, Gabriela said, "Well, how is everything going?" She continued eating, spreading butter on a tortilla with innocent unconcern.

Haydon smiled to himself. He knew immediately what she was fishing for. Last night at the dinner table he had noticed her casting furtive glances at Nina and then at him when she thought they would not notice. She was very sensitive to tensions, and she suspected that something was amiss between him and Nina.

"You mean in general?"

"Whatever." She took another spoon of *migas*.

"In general everything is fine," he said.

"Tha's good." She nodded.

He didn't expect her to go any further than that right now, but she would be watching them. Gabriela was very protective of Nina, in whom she found no fault, but she was not always so forgiving with Haydon. He sometimes felt embattled in this house of women, though he would not have had it any other way. He always had been far more comfortable with women than with men.

Gabriela began talking about the conflicts in Central America, which she fretted over and followed in the news with the conscientious attention of someone who had a vested interest. She empathized with the peasants caught in the middle of ideological conflicts they did not understand, and worried about an entire generation of children who knew nothing but the tragedy of killing and being killed. By the time Haydon stood to pour her a last cup of coffee before emptying the rest of the pot into his thermos, they had once again reviewed the countless causes and potential remedies of what Gabriela called the "tragedy of the little wars."

He left her sitting alone at the old butcher's block, her last cup of coffee steaming at her elbow as she began the contemplative ritual of braiding her hair while she hummed the familiar, melancholy refrain of an old Mexican *cantilena*.

It was a long morning. Haydon sat in his car under a somber canopy of pecan and oak trees, their limbs sulking under the heavy burden of rain, and watched the widow's house nearly a block away through a gray drizzle. He sipped cup after cup of Gabriela's coffee and thought about Nina. When they had married fourteen years ago she had been a young architect at a new firm that was expanding rapidly. It was in the mid-seventies, the years approaching Houston's building boom, and the excitement of a burgeoning economy had created a heady atmosphere, and the opportunities had seemed unlimited to her. But after seven years, Nina's down-to-earth temperament had grown impatient with the gamesmanship that became an increasingly larger part of her job as the corporate competition heated to a frantic pace. More and more she had found her personal perspectives and aspirations at odds with the firm's ambitions.

Then, in 1981, Haydon's parents were killed in a plane crash and he and Nina moved into his family's large old home and assumed the obligations that came with Haydon's inheritance. Both of them suddenly found most of their spare time taken up with their new roles, Haydon overseeing his father's investments and Nina managing the operation of a much larger home. Changes had to be made, and in her sensible and pragmatic manner Nina set about making them. Within a few months she had resigned from the architecture firm and established herself independently with only one associate, and gradually she began adjusting to a new kind of life. That had been seven years ago, and since then Nina had deliberately limited her work to private residential design, accepting only a single commission at a time so that she was able to control completely the quality of the designs and to work with her clients in an exclusive relationship. In the long run her selectivity had worked to her advantage, and she had gained a reputation that ultimately attracted some of the most prestigious commissions in the city.

It was knowing that Nina had a true talent for turning a critical eye on life, for cutting through its superfluities and simplifying its complications to reveal the essentials, that made him replay their conversation of the night before. He knew she was right, about all of it. It hadn't been only recently that he had let the job take control of his life, not just since Mooney's death. He had always found it too easy to become obsessive about it. He did take it too personally—not the career part of it, he had never given a damn about that, but he invested himself too seriously in the personalities of the "actors." Every good detective did that to a certain extent, tried to understand the minds of the men and women they pursued, but a sensible detective also knew when to disassociate himself, when to walk away from it. Haydon never had.

He looked out the beaded window next to his face to the empty street, to the widow's house where a young murderess slept a cool dreamless sleep late into a pale morning. After a moment he shifted the focus of his eyes to his distorted reflection in the glass and remembered Nina's words. She had said two things that had especially caught his attention. She had said that throughout his career he had "refused" to be detached, that he tried to "crawl inside those people's minds too much." It was one thing to become preoccupied with a case—they all did it from time to time when something about a particular killing lifted it above the routine of cases, touched a nerve in you and wouldn't leave you alone until you had taken it right down to the wire and had all the answers, had achieved whatever kind of justice could be achieved for an essentially irreconcilable act. But for Haydon these kinds of cases had been the rule rather than the exception. He never had allowed the pressure to ease up. He had refused.

Studying his distorted face in the refracted glass, he remembered the second thing she had said that had caught him up short. Even after all these years, she had said, he was still absorbed by the stalking, in fact, he was clearly "inspired" by it. Never had he been so jolted by such an uncommon application of a word. That word, which was so inherently positive and religious in connotation, suddenly seemed perverse. Not only did he find the idea unsettling, but he also found it disturbing that Nina actually believed it. Had he taken it that far? Did it really seem to her—was it in fact the truth—that he was animated by homicide, by the people who committed it, and all its ramifications? Had he himself become such a deformity without ever having gotten a glimpse of what was happening to him?

He was suddenly startled by a burst of static on the radio. Balkin, a few blocks away in his taxi, was wanting to know if Haydon would like him to pick up sandwiches at Butera's delicatessen. Haydon looked at his watch, surprised to see that it was noon, and told Balkin what he wanted. Twenty minutes later Balkin pulled up beside him and handed over the sandwich in a Styrofoam box. They exchanged a few words before Balkin drove away to resume his post. As he began eating, Haydon took a cassette of one of the *Brandenburg* concertos out of the glove box and put it into the player. This was one of the advantages of having his own car on a stakeout. He didn't want to think anymore, and he concentrated on the music. The rain picked up, and he fiddled with the windows, trying to get the air to circulate without letting in the rain. He turned on the windshield wipers to slow pause, getting a clear view of the widow's house every few seconds.

Three hours later, numb and lethargic from sitting throughout the entire shift and having played every tape in the glove compartment to keep his thoughts from wandering back to the conversation with Nina, he turned over the stakeout to Nagle and Berry and started home. On the way, seeing the west side of the Rice University campus through the trees to his right, he made a spur-of-the-moment decision to go by Nina's studio, which was not far away. The rain was only a drifting mist again as he slowed the Jaguar and turned into a side street near the studio, which was located on the top floor of an art gallery near Bissonett. He stopped the car across the street and looked up through the rain at the lighted windows. The studio consisted of several large, open rooms with hardwood floors and skylights, and from where Haydon sat he could see several people standing and moving around in what he knew to be the conference room. He looked down at the parking area in the drive and recognized the Cassells' car. He should have known he wouldn't find her alone. He pulled away from the curb and drove home.

He had completely forgotten about the photograph he had received in the mail the day before until he stood in the entryway unbuttoning his dripping raincoat and looked down the broad hall to the small marble-topped table across from the library where Gabriela always left the mail. Even from where he stood he could see a large manila envelope sticking out from beneath the white letters. He hung his coat below the trilby, wiped his feet on the mat, and walked straight down the hall to the table. He took the letters and magazines in one hand and picked up the manila envelope with the other. It was identical to the first, except this time there was a cancellation mark on the postage.

Haydon continued examining the envelope as he walked into the library and turned on the refectory-table lamps and then those on his desk. He tossed the mail on his desk and sat down at the refectory table with the envelope. The opened envelope from the night before was still there, and he laid them side by side. The penmanship was the same, the same slant to the printed characters, the letters themselves remarkably uniform in size and style, the same black ink—he guessed it was a felt-tipped pen. The stamps were the same, the standard issue of the American flag. He turned the envelope over. The tines of the brass clasp on the back were splayed out through the hole in the flap, and a wide strip of Scotch tape had been placed over them to keep them from snagging in the mail. That had not been done to the first envelope.

Picking up his letter opener, Haydon slit the end of the envelope opposite the flap and saw another photograph wrapped in tissue. He pulled it out on the table and unwrapped it. A second portrait of the same young man. In this printing he was dressed informally in white trousers and white shirt with the sleeves rolled in a loosely wadded fashion to the elbows. His hair seemed to be tousled by a breeze as he sat on the wall of a balcony or terrace, one leg propped on top of the wall showing his white canvas shoe and bare ankle, the other hanging down out of the picture. There were mountains in the distance behind him. He frowned slightly in the sunlight.

Immediately Haydon felt the same peculiar sense of remembrance, the same vague sense of understanding. Then suddenly he was stunned, his face flushing hot, then cold. Incredulous, he reached for the first portrait and placed the two side by side, looking from one to the other, comparing, concentrating on the youthful features as if to see beyond them, to see more than was told in the oil and canvas. How could he have looked at this first photograph without having seen it instantly? Over the sharp bright eyes of the youth his mind superimposed the hooded, murky eyes of a much older man. He looked at the straight, even line of the youth's mouth and tried to see intimations of the slacker lines it would acquire in old age; the sharp clean jaw would take on a heaviness not hinted at in these portraits. There was a taut energy in these portrayals of youth that Haydon had never known in the man himself, a cavalier manner that had been translated into a posture of greater calculation in old age. Haydon was stricken by the amazing visual paradox, the folding of time. Here was a familiar stranger, a man he had known intimately, but a youth he had never imagined, this young man who once had been his father.

Chapter 4

SATURNINO BARCENA LAY ON THE DAMP SHEETS IN HIS BUNGALOW AT the Rio Courts and blew the smoke of his Pall Mall toward the louvered windows, toward the sound of rain that seemed willfully to hurl itself out of the sky in its eagerness to irritate him. He wore only his boxer shorts, and every time he moved, his gummy skin dragged at the limp sheets, wadding them around him so that he was forever having to straighten them.

He had already run his errand for the day. He had done that early, just to be sure. Then he had returned to the motel and bathed, shaving in the cramped, moldy shower, feeling his way over his face like a blind man, because he couldn't use the medicine-cabinet mirror over the sink, since it was covered with a towel. When he finished, he had made breakfast, an omelette with sautéed bell peppers and onions—again—and then he went through the dossier—again. He did this every day even though he had long ago memorized the sequence of the pages, every word, and every image. Still he made himself turn through it the way a devout Catholic tells the rosary, perhaps with a wandering mind but faithfully, without fail, out of a sense of duty, or perhaps more accurately, out of a superstitious fear of what might, or might not, happen if he faltered in his obligations. Then he had smoked and looked out the window. There was nowhere to go, nowhere he wanted to go, and time passed slowly.

Now it was noon. He fried bacon for a sandwich and ate it sitting on the edge of the bed, staring out the windows and sipping Tecate. Afterward he smoked another cigarette. Having had a restless night with little sleep, he finished the cigarette in a nodding fog, the incessant downpour thrumming in his ears. He stirred enough to grind out the butt in a tin ashtray and then lay back on the clammy sheets, his arms away

45

from his body, his legs separated to keep from sweating. He shouldn't have.

He went to sleep and then rose from the bed, straight up without having to bend his legs, levitating forward as if his feet were hinged to the sheets. It was raining in the room, but he was dry, the only thing in the world that was dry. The iguanas were everywhere, listless and inscrutable reptiles on the windowsills, on the yellow-tiled cabinet with their long tails hanging stiffly over the edges, on the stove where a large brackish-colored one sat with a low-lidded, placid stare while his hindquarters sizzled and smoked in the flames of the gas burner, on the desk where their short stubby legs scrabbled over the soggy pages of the dossier while blue ink flowed from between the leaves of paper and ran down the legs of the desk in indigo rivulets; two iguanas danced in the bathroom sink, standing on their hind legs and embracing in an awkward saurian samba, the smaller of the two reaching out occasionally to swipe at the towel over the mirror, which was just barely hanging, about to fall, a sight that filled Saturnino with dread. And the capuchin monkey was there like a humped and hooded little priest, perched on the top of the opened door, his fur matted by the rain, his long child's fingers inserted in the sides of his mouth to pull back his elastic lips in a horrible rictus directed at Saturnino. The rain drummed steadily. The iguanas watched him from their various soggy vantage points. The capuchin watched him, its tongue sometimes darting out obscenely. Then the deep roar of the rain developed a faint rhythm and Saturnino began to sweat and the pounding rain throbbed like an omnipresent pulse . . . whump . . . whump . . . whump . . . the pounding horror of the approaching Night Ax and an iguana on the desk swished its stiff, heavy tail in the rain, nearly brushing the pillowcase off the mirror above it, and Saturnino's heart leaped in his chest and began to beat in the same rhythm as the rain and then he knew he had to stop it because this was only the beginning and if he didn't stop it now he would die and so he opened his mouth as he would do later only this time he screamed . . .

He was flat on his back, naked. He didn't know how his boxer shorts had gotten off, because he was still lying in the same position. Drenched in sweat. His throat tight, almost closed. His heart rocking in his chest. Outside it was raining hard, and he lay there listening to it, waiting for his pulse to regain a semblance of normalcy. He tried to think of routine things, not wanting to reflect on what had happened. When did he have to buy more food? What kinds of food? Besides his daily errands, what else did he need to do? One more thing. Only one more thing before he returned to Mexico City in five days. He had one more request of Swain, something Swain would have to do tomorrow or the next day for sure.

Suddenly he had a disturbing thought. What if he couldn't reach Swain? Barcena hadn't corresponded with him or spoken with him in weeks. What if he was out of town? That could easily be. What if he had gone out of business? It happened. They had made no arrangements to stay in touch, because as far as Swain was concerned the last time Barcena had sent him a check their relationship had ended. Swain had no idea Barcena would ever come to Houston.

He sat up and swung his legs over the side of the bed, found his shorts on the floor, and stood to put them on. His arms were weak, trembling, as if he had slept through a fever. Damn the dream. It was getting worse, more intense, more real, and even though he seemed to be gaining some degree of control over it now, he wasn't sure if maybe that, too, wasn't a dream. Did he really wake just now because he willed it, or did the dream merely release him, capriciously, mocking him? Christ. What a madness.

He sat down on the bed again, took a cigarette from the damp pack on the windowsill, and lighted it. Then he picked up the telephone and dialed Swain's agency number, which he had memorized. It rang four times, and Barcena began to imagine the worst. On the fifth ring someone picked up the receiver.

"Hel-lo."

Barcena recognized the flat, almost nasal voice of Ira Swain.

"Mr. Swain?"

"Who's calling?" Detached caution.

"This is Saturnino Barcena from Mexico City."

Pause. "Well, I'm damned," Swain said, recognizing Barcena's voice. "So it is." There was another pause, then Swain added, "Mr. Bar-ceno, you don't sound like you're long-distance anymore."

Swain always divided Barcena's name in half, putting the

emphasis on the wrong (first) syllable, and making the *a* at the end an *o*. Barcena had corrected him several times when the detective first began working for him, but Swain stupidly persisted.

"That's right. I am in Houston."

"Well, that's interesting," Swain said, sounding interested. "Business?"

"There is one other thing that you could do for me," Barcena said.

"Uh-huh."

Something in Swain's manner alerted Barcena and made him suspicious. Could Swain be tracing his call? Could he have that kind of technology? Barcena knew nothing of electronics, and it was a risk he didn't want to take. It had been foolish to call him from the motel anyway. There would be a record of that, and he didn't want Swain to know where he was staying.

"Can we meet somewhere to talk about it?"

"Whatever you want to do, Mr. Bar-ceno," Swain said accommodatingly.

"I don't know the city well enough to suggest a place, but I have maps," Barcena said. "Why don't you choose a restaurant where we can have a cup of coffee."

"You want to give me a general idea where you're at? This's a big city."

"I'm used to big cities."

Swain snorted. "Yeah, I guess you are. Okay. There's a coffee shop on Alabama that's an all-nighter. May be good for future reference, too. It's not far off the Southwest Freeway and not far off the West Loop."

Swain gave Barcena the name and address, and they agreed to meet there in an hour. Barcena put down the telephone, thought a second, and then lay back on the bed. He felt prickly with perspiration, or was it the humidity? God, what a city. He reached over to the chair on the other side of the bed, where he had piled newspapers, a couple of magazines, and the maps. Using the street index, he quickly located Alabama and the tiny red street numbers which gave him the general vicinity of the coffee shop. It wasn't that far. He had plenty of time.

He lay back on the pillow again, lighted another Pall Mall, and looked out the louvers to the three palm trees, the two real

ones and the one on the motel sign, which continued relent-
lessly to disintegrate and rejuvenate. He had stared at the
neon palm so much that he knew the rhythm of its peculiar
death and rebirth, and followed this endless cycle with the
same inner cadence with which one attends to a familiar song.
Perhaps in his random selection of this particular motel on the
night of his arrival, he actually had been guided by his
subconscious, guided to the sign of the palm, an age-old
symbol of victory. Now, as he watched this neon metaphor
persistently triumph over its own destruction, he embraced it
as an omen of his impending success. Musing on this, he
smoked his cigarette to the end.

The place was called the Koffee Shop, with that peculiar
phonetic spelling North Americans seemed to think was so
clever on retail signs. It was twenty years past its prime, the
sort of place most people would pass up to go to the newer,
brighter Denny's that was sure to be sitting just off the main
expressway a few blocks away. As Saturnino pushed open the
front doors he cringed at the sandpapery surface of the handle
where the chrome plating had worn away and millions of
sweaty palms had rusted the underlying metal.

Inside, he stopped beside the cash register and behind a
sign that advised him to wait to be seated. For some reason,
which seemed not to bother the management, a dozen or more
dead crickets lay scattered on the floor around the nearby
cigarette machine, reminding him of the little licorice crickets
he used to buy in the candy store at the corner of Chapultepec
and Orizaba. This thought distracted him, and when he
returned to the present he was still waiting. He took in the
coffee-shop-generic decor, plastic upholstery in three shades of
orange, a variety of booth arrangements next to the plate-glass
windows on three sides of the restaurant, and a long counter
for nighthawks who wanted to be closer to the waitresses and
maybe strike up a conversation if things slowed down.

Swain had told Saturnino that he would recognize him by
his small mustache and beige plaid sport coat. Wanting to be
careful, Saturnino had arrived at the restaurant early in order
to have the advantage of looking Swain over as he came
through the front door. When a waitress came up to him with
a plastic menu, he asked her if he could sit at one of the booths
next to the windows, only a few of which were already

occupied. She said sure and took him halfway to the back and tossed a menu onto a table as she jerked her order pad out of the waistband of her apron. Barcena took the side of the booth that allowed him a good view of the front door, handed the menu back to the waitress, and asked for coffee.

She promptly returned with his order, set it down in front of him with a glass of water, and wrote out his ticket, leaving it on the edge of the table. Saturnino pushed his coffee cup to one side, took several napkins from the chrome holder, and dipped them into the glass of water. He wiped the sticky spot he had discovered as he slid into his seat and then he wiped the entire area in front of him, and dried it with another wad of napkins.

As he sipped his coffee he looked around at the other customers. Most of them were also only drinking coffee, the drizzly afternoon almost justifying an otherwise purely social convention. Notable exceptions were an older woman and a small boy who were eating pie, and a chunky sandy-haired man sitting in the first booth inside the door whom Barcena had noticed as he came in because he was wolfing down a large plate of pancakes, fried eggs, and ham—an incredibly heavy, warm meal for a muggy afternoon.

Even though he had come early, Saturnino had to wait longer than he had expected. He had three refills, shifted over in the booth to get off a stiff piece of plastic tape placed over a tear in the seat, and watched four customers walk up to the cash register, pay their bills, and leave. Swain was overdue, and Saturnino was beginning to feel uneasy. The man with the pancakes who faced Saturnino over the backs of three booths tended to his food, cleaning up his afternoon breakfast and then ordering apple pie and ice cream, which he dispatched with equal diligence. Occasionally he looked out to the rain as he chewed, but mostly he kept his attention on whatever food was on the plate in front of him. The older woman and the boy paid and left.

Barcena checked his watch, thought about leaving, thought about calling Swain's number from the pay telephone at the front of the shop. The chunky man ordered a glass of milk. He drank it as soon as the waitress brought it, all in one breath, then leaned over sideways to get to the change in his pants pocket, which he tossed on the table with a loud jangle. He eased out of the booth and stood a little stiffly, grabbed his raincoat from his seat, and took his bill to the cash register. He paid, asked for a receipt, and took a toothpick from the dispenser and chewed on it while he watched the waitress write it up. When she finished, he smiled and thanked her, and then turned and walked straight toward Saturnino, his eyes locked unblinkingly on Saturnino's until he stopped beside the table. Then he seemed to wince.

"Mr. Bar-ceno. Ira Swain." He threw his raincoat in ahead of him and slid into the booth across from Saturnino. Swain was perhaps a little shorter than Saturnino, he had no mustache, and the only plaid he wore was his open-neck sport shirt under his dull-gray suit coat. The handkerchief pocket of his suit coat bulged with a plastic case for eyeglasses, the kind with the magnetic flap that hung outside the pocket. He wore a Masonic insignia ring on his wedding-ring finger, and the cuffs of his suit coat were dingy from infrequent cleaning.

"Where is the mustache and plaid coat?" Saturnino asked. He was angry about the lie.

Swain grinned sheepishly, shrugged, and shifted the toothpick to the opposite side of his mouth with a sweep of his tongue.

"Could I see some identification?"

"You bet," Swain said congenially, unoffended. He rolled sideways, took a fat, overstuffed, and badly worn wallet out of his hip pocket, and held up an official-looking license with his picture on it. Saturnino recognized the same button nose tending to spread in middle age, the same low hairline, the taffy-colored hair combed back with a high part.

Saturnino nodded, and Swain put away his wallet.

"You don't look much Mexican," Swain said, talking around the toothpick. "Except your hair. I didn't know what you'd look like." He caught the waitress's attention, and crooked an index finger as he tilted his wrist to indicate a cup of coffee. He turned back to Saturnino. "I never did anything long-distance like that before. Worked out pretty good though, huh?"

"So far," Saturnino said circumspectly.

Swain grinned, letting Saturnino know that he knew Saturnino was pissed about the lie. The waitress brought the coffee, which Swain promptly doctored with large quantities of cream and sugar.

"So, what now?" he asked, bringing the cup to his mouth. He flinched; it was still too hot, and he set it down.

"Do you have a Polaroid?"

"You bet."

"I need half a dozen pictures of Haydon. I need them by the day after tomorrow, Thursday."

Swain considered this a moment, suppressing a belch. "Any old pictures?"

"Yes. Something of him outside. On the sidewalk, crossing a street. Something like that."

"You want close-ups?"

"It needs to be obvious that they were taken outside, without his knowledge."

"That's it?"

"Yes."

Swain nodded, thinking, and looked out the plate glass to the fine rain drifting across the street.

"May be tough to do it in the time frame you're talking," Swain said. "Depends on his schedule, his routine. Sometimes they don't go out much. They do a lot of paperwork. I'll have to check about his days off. If he's on a stakeout or something, forget it." He looked at Saturnino. "I don't know."

"What about when he leaves home or comes home?"

"He'd be in his car then," Swain said. "And once he gets inside those iron gates and behind that wall that goes around his place, there's no chance." He thought some more. "It's gotta be a Polaroid?"

Barcena shook his head. "No, I just thought that would be easier for you to know what you have."

"I use my cameras I know what I have."

"Fine. However you want to do it, whatever you want to use."

"This is a bit touchy, taking this man's picture," Swain said, cocking his mouth to one side and squinting one pale eye. "I mean, I'm messing with the man's professional nature here. This kind of shit is his business, and he knows it inside out. I get caught snapping him we're screwed. He'd get my license jerked for sure. Man's got some pull. Ve-ry touchy. This's big-league, Bar-ceno."

"Which brings us to your fee?"

"You bet."

"More than the usual?"

"Oh, you bet. I could do without the risks I'm gonna be running here. Man's not to be messed with. You could say I'm risking my business here." Swain looked outside again and tugged at his plaid button-down collar to perk it up around his jowly neck. In profile Saturnino could see that Swain needed a haircut.

"How much?"

Swain, still looking outside, shook his head, kept shaking it, his eyes fixed on something unspecific as he thought about the prospect of what he had been asked to do. He kept it up so long that Saturnino began to feel that Swain wasn't even thinking of the job anymore, that maybe his mind had gone on to something else equally engrossing and that Saturnino was only of incidental interest. Someone in the kitchen dropped a plate that exploded like a gunshot. Saturnino flinched, but Swain appeared not to have heard it.

Finally, still looking away, Swain said, "Whether I get the pictures or don't get the pictures I run the same risks." Then he turned to Saturnino. "So we need to look at it this way: you're going to pay me for running this kind of risk. Two weeks' fee at the same rate we been using. That's cash in advance. I get the pictures, whether it takes me two days or an hour, that's another two weeks' fee when I deliver." Swain nodded as if that sounded right to him. "That's nonnegotiable. I could do without this one, easy."

Saturnino suppressed his anger. It was an outrageous fee, already high because Swain had claimed in the beginning that investigating a police detective was hazardous duty. Still, this was the end of it. Saturnino couldn't balk now.

"I don't have that kind of money with me," he said stiffly. "I'll have to go to a bank tomorrow and arrange to have it transferred."

"Whatever."

"I'll call you when I have it."

"You bet." The muddy mixture in Swain's cup now had to be lukewarm, but he lifted it to his lips anyway and drained it in a single breath just as he had the glass of milk. He wiped his mouth. "I'll get the coffee," he said. "You go ahead."

Chapter 5

HAYDON LEANED OVER AND TURNED OFF THE LAMPS ON HIS DESK AND then those on the old walnut refectory table. He faced the gauzy gray light of the afternoon as it came in through the French doors that opened onto the terrace, where a heavy downpour had slackened to a thin blowing drizzle. The bougainvilleas were sagging from the pummeling of the heavier rain, and the water that had been caught on the terrace was now rushing through the drains along the edges and spilling over the top step to the wide stairs that led down to the lawn. The lime trees were black.

He knew of only one portrait of his father, and if he turned around he would see it hanging at the other end of the library. It had been painted when Webster Haydon was fifty-one. That was in 1961; Haydon had been a sophomore in high school. He remembered the artist coming to the house to make sketches and take photographs, and he remembered several preliminary studies quickly executed in oils. His father had not seemed particularly affected by the fact that he was having his portrait painted; his mind was most likely elsewhere, as it often was. But Haydon himself had been painfully self-conscious about it. In the sixties, when the tenor of the times was rebellion, it seemed to him an extremely egotistical thing to have one's portrait painted, even though he knew that it was his mother who had insisted on it. Still, his father had not protested, and in the righteousness of adolescence Haydon had faulted him for that. It was not until years later that he realized his father's quiet acquiescence had been far less pretentious than if he had protested while continuing to go ahead with it. Above all things, Webster Haydon had always tried to be honest with himself, even about his vanities.

And now here were these portraits, paintings from a time in

his father's life when Haydon could have had no claim to judgment, however presumptuous, about how they had come to be executed. It was disconcerting, this resurrection of his father as a youth, rather than as the older man Haydon had remembered. Here was a young man he had never known, with memories he could not imagine.

Haydon looked down at the pictures. The portraits seemed to have been painted at about the same time. How old had he been? It was difficult to say, the styles of the time had given to young men an appearance of maturity they lacked today, but surely it was safe to say he was in his twenties. Perhaps his mid-twenties. Since his father had been born in 1910 it was easy enough to calculate a projection: 1935. What did Haydon know about 1935? What was happening in the world then; what could he remember? History. Hitler . . . gaining strength, repudiating the Versailles Treaty, forming the Luftwaffe. The Curies were awarded the Nobel Prize in chemistry. Roosevelt was president . . . signed the Social Security Act . . . Huey Long assassinated in Louisiana. What else? Literature. T.S. Eliot wrote *Murder in the Cathedral*. Thomas Wolfe, *Of Time and the River*. He cast about in his mind, but there was nothing else. That was all he knew of 1935. It was still three years before his parents would marry, almost a decade before his own birth.

Where had his father been? He tried to remember the stories. Born in Boston in 1910, the third son of four, to a father who was also one of four sons. Prepped for Harvard Law School, where his grandfather, father, and uncles all had earned law degrees and where his brothers would eventually earn theirs. But Webster rebelled—the first of a series of rebellions that would eventually separate him from his family—and insisted on going to Columbia, where he earned his law degree in 1934. Instead of joining the long-established family firm he persuaded his father to use his influence with friends at Standard Oil to secure him a position with Royal Dutch Shell in London. It was done, and while he was there he studied British law, met and married Cordelia Temple, then moved to Mexico with Royal Dutch Oil in 1938 just as President Cárdenas was expropriating the oil companies. Remained in Mexico to help the Cárdenas administration organize the government-owned petroleum industry, then moved to Houston in 1943 to begin his own private practice.

That was roughly it. And it placed Webster Haydon in London at about the time the portraits were painted. If that was the case, the background of the second portrait was completely fanciful, for it definitely depicted distant snow-capped mountain ranges, and though he could not really identify the vegetation, it had something of a subtropical feel about it. He supposed it was an artistic contrivance, much like the backdrops of Italian gardens used by the turn-of-the-century photographers. Still, it seemed a curious choice of landscapes.

But to Haydon it seemed much more important, at least more immediate, to ask who had sent him the portraits, and why. And would there be others? Why had they been sent anonymously, and why now? But the answers to those questions, he suspected, would not be forthcoming until the sender wanted them to be known. He would have to have patience.

He listened to the water dripping from the copper gutters onto the flat stones of the terrace, his eyes focused on the opposite edge of the refectory table where the dark polished wood reflected a border of smoky light. In the six years since his father's Centurion had gone down with both his parents in the stark Glass Mountains of West Texas, Haydon had relived his life with them thousands of times through long hours of recollections that from time to time had commanded his attention to the exclusion of everything else. His memories of them were, he realized, from an intensely singular perspective. Having no brothers or sisters, he had never seen his parents through the eyes of a sibling who had had to share them. There always had been only the three of them. He was a part of them, and they of him, in so special a way that for years he had been unable to view their relationship with any kind of real objectivity. And though he had eventually gained a less biased perspective, much of what he had come to understand about his parents had been learned in retrospect, after their deaths. The sad irony was that it had been with Haydon as he often had observed it to be with others: he had achieved the deepest understanding of his parents, had gained his greatest intimacy with them, as a result of that irrevocable event that had separated them forever.

After he and Nina had moved into the family home, it had been a long time before Haydon could sit in the library alone without feeling an almost physical sense of his father's presence. The old man was so indelibly established in the room that death was far too slight a force to banish him. During the first months after the funeral, the gloom of loss had been so intense as to be disorienting, and Haydon's longing to have just one more conversation with his father threatened at times to overwhelm him. But there were delicate balances in one's memories of another person, slight nuances of psyche that determined whether the memory was one that haunted or comforted. In the end, Haydon had come to the latter.

The library itself held a central position in Haydon's remembrances of his father. As a boy he knew it as the place where he could always find him, either at his desk or standing straight-backed in front of the bookshelves, where he had the habit of pulling down a volume and then standing there reading it, forgetting, presumably, all the rest of the world, or even to sit down. It was the only room in the house where Haydon's mother would permit Webster to smoke his cigars, which he often did with the French doors open to the terrace, when the weather was cool enough.

Haydon suddenly remembered a particular early-summer afternoon when he was a boy, one of the countless afternoons he spent lying on the grass under the lime trees, daydreaming. The severe heat of the season had not yet arrived, and he had been surprised to hear the singular, solitary rasping of the first cicada, harbinger of the furnace-hot days that were soon to come. He had looked toward the sound, in the direction of the house, and had seen his father, tall and lean, standing in the opening of French doors flung open to the terrace, his white shirt in brilliant contrast against the dusky interior of the library, where Haydon could barely make out the old refectory table, his father's desk, the green-shaded lamps, and fainter still, the rows of books. His father had been looking toward him, looking at him he thought, but when Haydon waved there was no response. His father remained motionless, one hand in his trouser pocket, the other bent at the elbow, holding the cigar. At first Haydon believed that his father, lost in thought, simply had not yet seen him lying in the shade, that soon his eyes would focus on him and he would return the wave. But it didn't happen. They stayed that way, facing each other for what seemed like ages, Haydon looking at his father and his father looking at him but giving no indication that he was seeing him. Then in the numbing shock of a single moment it had occurred to Haydon that his father *was* seeing him, and that his refusal to acknowledge the boy's innocent wave was a strange, stoic effort to convey to him something profound about their relationship. Lying there in the shade, he sensed that his father's motionless gaze was an unspoken sign between them, a telling look that for Haydon fell abysmally short of its intent. Though he recognized that something momentous was happening between them, his boy's mind could not fathom it; he did not understand. Even now, he still remembered the empty nausea of bleakness that overcame him, a numbing aloneness as if he were out of time, in another realm of existence apart from his father's. The pall of isolation had paralyzed him, and he had lain there afraid to move, as if to do so would be a grave mistake with consequences so awesome, so final, that his mind could not conceive of them. It was then that he had wondered, for the first time in his life, if that was what it was like to be dead.

With a pounding heart, Haydon returned to the present. He felt claustrophobic. He stood, turned his back on the photographs, and looked at his father's portrait hanging on the far side of the room, dimly visible. Though he couldn't see it clearly, he really didn't need to. With each passing year, he had practically become a replica of the portrait himself. The resemblance between father and son was so distinct that even as a boy Haydon himself had been able to see it. By the time he had passed through adolescence it was clear that even his physique would be like his father's: six feet in height but seeming taller because of his lean frame and longish face. They had the same dark eyes, with flecks of amber that glinted like pyrite when they were angry, and though Haydon's sable hair had begun graying at the temples much earlier than had his father's, by the time the portrait had been painted it was a distinguishing feature of his father's appearance.

Webster Haydon had been an easy man to be acquainted with, but he had not been an easy man to know. It was not that he was aloof, he was in fact congenial, but he had a way of using his impeccable manners to hold himself in reserve. Not many people became his close friend, but no one had ever felt slighted by his acquaintance. Webster and Cordelia were well known for seldom accepting the social invitations that inevitably came their way. He had been responsible for that, not Cordelia, who had a far more accessible personality. He was not disdainful of society gatherings, only disinterested. Yet in his own way, Webster Haydon was amiable. Gentlemanly reserve was the starting point of his relationship with anyone, but once he became comfortable with you—and the circumstances in which that might happen could appear entirely capricious to everyone but Webster himself—there was no greater warmth of companionship. His curiosity was potent and eclectic, international law being only the starting point of his interests. In later years his profession actually had commanded less and less of his attention, so that by the time he died his library contained volumes on everything from the *Kama-sutra* of Vatsyayana to abstruse theological treatises on Origen's theories of *apokatastasis panton*.

The extraordinary moment Haydon had just recalled from childhood had not come to mind in years. It had been a strange occurrence, especially in light of the kind of relationship he and his father had actually had. They had not been "buddies"—his father hadn't been that sort of man—but they had understood each other in such a way that intuition had played as great a part between them as any other kind of communication. Haydon had inherited his father's wideranging mind, something the elder man recognized early on, and cautiously encouraged. As Haydon grew older and began his university studies his father had urged him toward law. Haydon had studied literature, taking a master's degree before entering law school. But after nearly two years he had dropped out and entered the police academy. Webster Haydon had swallowed his disappointment.

Yet from that time on their relationship developed a new dimension. Haydon, living on his own by then, continued coming home on Wednesday evenings for the family dinners that had been a tradition since he was a boy. It was something his mother had established during their more hectic years to ensure that the three of them had the opportunity at least once a week to be together without interruption for an entire evening. The meals, prepared by Gabriela, were leisurely, and there was never a lack of things to talk about. All of them looked forward to it.

It was to one of these Wednesday-evening meals that Haydon had first brought Nina to the house and watched his parents, and even Gabriela, fall in love with her. After their marriage, the tradition continued. And it was after these Wednesday-evening dinners that Haydon and his father frequently found themselves back in the library, drawn by his father's habits and a new desire on the part of both men to share ideas and hear each other's opinions. These discourses, often rambling, sometimes involved, sometimes speculative, created an even more tightly woven bond between father and son. Though he always had thought of his father as a man who was traditional by his very nature, more than a few times Haydon had been surprised by his father's ideas, surprised at the strong strain of unorthodoxy and independence that ran like a steady, refreshing stream through all his thinking. It was not until after his parents' deaths that Haydon had fully understood what rare and wonderful things those nights had been. During the last six years he had wished countless times for just one more evening like the many he had taken for granted.

"STUART."

The single word of his name spoken in the mellow tones of Nina's voice interrupted his thoughts like one dream intruding into another. He was brought to the threshold, a spectator rather than a participant, aware of the mist hanging in the dusk and settling among the lime trees across the lawn, aware of the leaden light that came through the glass panes of the French doors and cast a ghostly patina on the old refectory table.

"Stuart."

He turned around and saw her silhouetted in the doorway of the library, several rolls of drawings tucked under one arm at skewed angles, the other hand holding her briefcase. She was stepping out of her high heels, kicking them a little bit to get them out of her way.

"You all right?" she asked, coming into the room. She set her drawings on one end of the refectory table as he reached over and switched on the two lamps, the monochromatic evening jumping into full color.

"Sure," he said, rubbing his face as Nina laid her briefcase beside her drawings. "Just feeling uninspired." He smiled halfheartedly. "I spent the entire shift today parked at a curb waiting for something to happen that never did. A lot of time to think."

Nina came over and kissed him. "And what did you think about?" she asked. She stepped to his desk and turned on the lamps, then walked over to the armchairs and turned on others. Like the man in the short story, Nina liked a well-lighted place. She always had been that way, and it seemed to Haydon an extension of her positive personality, the compatibility of optimism and luminosity. He guessed too that because she was an artist whose work relied on a lambent setting, that light had become a habit with her. Even the designs of the homes she had done were marked by the recurrence of atriums, tall windows, courtyards, high ceilings, all providing brightness and light. It was probably the major reason why she was so suspicious of his own gloomy tendencies. She saw no profit in darkness.

"I thought about as much as I could," he said, turning around in his chair to watch her.

"I'm sure you did," she said. She was wearing a champagne silk charmeuse blouse with padded shoulders and a straight black skirt that came below her calves, a style that seemed a reflection of her strong-willed personality. This was the first time they had spoken since last night, and Haydon studied her, trying to anticipate her feelings.

"Can you be more specific?" she asked, sitting in one of the leather armchairs and crossing her legs. She bent forward and massaged one of her stockinged feet. "Are we going to talk about last night?"

"Do you want to?"

"That depends."

"On what?"

"Have you decided anything definitely?"

"Had you expected me to? I would have thought it would require some more . . . discussion."

"I don't think I want to get into it again unless we can be more specific than last night."

"I thought you were pretty specific," Haydon said.

Nina bent her head and looked at the foot she was massaging. He thought he saw her smile.

"Yeah, I was," she said, looking up. "You were not."

There was a brief silence, then Haydon said, "I'm not sure I know how to get specific about it."

"That's all I need to know, then," Nina said. "Let's leave it at that." She straightened up and leaned back in the chair, stretching her legs out in front of her.

"You brought more work home," he said.

"The Cassells are wanting to pick up the tempo. They're reaching that stage where they want to see the hard line drawings faster than I can complete them. They're really getting excited about it."

"It's going well, then."

"Very well."

Haydon nodded. "You see Gabriela when you came in?"

"Yes."

"I haven't seen her."

"She said she looked in on you, but you seemed preoccupied and she decided not to disturb you."

Haydon shrugged.

"What is it that's bothering you?" Nina asked. She reached down to her side and unbuttoned the waist button on the skirt and began pulling out the tail of her blouse. "This lieutenant business, or is it something else?"

"Nothing's bothering me. I told you it was a depressing day. Wasted time." His eyes fell to the table. He looked at the two pictures and at the two envelopes. Then unexpectedly he said, "But something interesting has been happening." He scooped up the two pictures and walked over to a second armchair near Nina and sat down. He reached out and handed the first picture to her. "Ever see this fellow?"

Nina sat up in her chair, and he watched her face as she held the portrait in her lap and looked it over. After a minute she shook her head. "No. He looks like he was thirty years ahead of me."

"I think you're right," Haydon said, handing her the second portrait.

She looked at it. "Same man?"

Haydon nodded.

She held the pictures side by side and compared them.

"Well, he's handsome, rather proper it seems to me, even in the casual one here. But I don't believe I've ever seen him."

"Yes you have."

Nina looked at Haydon. "Okay, don't be coy. What's the deal with these?"

"Think about it just a second."

Nina gave him a puzzled frown and looked at the two pictures again, tilting her head to one side, thinking, then shaking her head slowly. "No, sorry."

"When would you say these portraits were painted?" Haydon asked.

"The thirties, sometime around there, judging from the clothes."

"That's what I guessed. Now, imagine this person fifty years older. A little heavier, all the features more pronounced."

Nina was still, staring at the photographs, then she looked up at Haydon. "Is this a joke, or what?"

"What do you mean?"

"They look like you."

Haydon smiled and shook his head. "No." He raised an arm and pointed to Webster Haydon's portrait hanging on the library wall. "Him."

Nina's eyes widened as she turned around in her chair, and glanced back and forth from the pictures to the portrait.

"This is Webster? I'm not sure . . . I would have . . ." She held the two photographs at arm's length in the direction of the portrait on the wall. "Well, yes, I can see him in this," she said tentatively. "The eyes. The shape of the face . . . and the mouth." She began to nod. "Yes, I can see it. How odd."

"Very odd," Haydon said.

Nina turned back to him. "What do you mean? Where'd you get these?"

"They came in the mail. One yesterday, one today."

"The mail?"

Haydon nodded.

"Who sent them?"

"No idea. They came in envelopes with no return address. The stamps on the first one hadn't even been canceled by the post office, which means, I suppose, it was hand-delivered to our mailbox. The second one did have a cancellation mark on it, from here in Houston."

He stopped. Nina was looking at him with increasing interest.

"And . . . ?"

"And nothing," he said. "That's all there is to it."

"But you've never seen these before?"

Haydon shook his head. "Had no idea they existed."

"Well, for Pete's sake," Nina said. She looked down at the photographs in her lap. "He was a dashing thing, wasn't he. Had that inimitable style even as a young man. Of course, I remember family photographs from his university days, but this was after that, I guess." She smiled. "Quite continental."

"It's my guess they were done in Britain," Haydon said. "The mid to late thirties would have put him in London working for Royal Dutch Shell. Maybe before he met Mother, or about that time."

"You think so? The mountains in this one, and what I can see of the architecture of this terrace or whatever it is, don't seem British."

"No, you're right, I noticed that too. But the chronology puts him in Britain."

"They're really quite well done, aren't they?"

Haydon nodded again.

"What an intriguing thing," Nina said pensively. "Then someone living in Houston has these? The originals?"

Haydon shrugged. "One of them was mailed from here. That's about all I know."

"And someone hand-delivered the other."

"Apparently."

"Strange."

"It'll be interesting to see what comes next."

"Next?"

"Well, whoever's doing this could very easily have sent both photographs in the same envelope, but chose not to. That suggests to me there was a specific purpose for doing it this way. Maybe they're trying to tell me something. Maybe they're trying to build suspense toward some end. Whatever the reason, I don't know what it is, which means they haven't accomplished it yet."

"What do you *think* is the reason?"

"I can't imagine."

"Maybe they have these old paintings in an attic somewhere

and this is a buildup toward asking you an extraordinary price for them, supposing you would want them for sentimental reasons."

"It's a peculiar way to approach me."

"I can't wait to meet them." Nina paused. "You haven't shown these to Gabriela? Maybe she knows something."

"I doubt it," Haydon said. "This was certainly before her time. Besides, I imagine this thing will answer itself in a few more days. But they've definitely got my attention."

He stood, took the pictures from Nina, walked back to the refectory table, and slipped the photographs into their respective envelopes. He opened one of his desk drawers, put the envelopes inside, and closed it. He was facing the French doors, and the lamps in the library were throwing splashes of brassy light on the terrace flagstones glistening in the rain.

"I actually didn't recognize him in the first one," he said quietly. "Just like you. I went to bed last night having no inkling of who he was, not giving it much thought. There's a kind of melancholy irony in that. As if he had come back as I had wished so many times he could, and I didn't even recognize him. Makes you wonder. And then today, when I opened the second one I still didn't know for sure who it was. It was an extraordinary sensation, almost like seeing myself without realizing it. And then when it hit me . . . it was breathtaking, a tremendous jolt. Memories flooded back, vivid ones." Haydon shook his head. "Very powerful."

When he stopped, the rain was coming down so hard it sounded like a strong wind beyond the glass panes. Nina had come up behind him and slipped her arms around his chest and laid her head against the back of his shoulders. He was grateful to her for the gesture, and for the empathy he knew came with it. They stood there, neither of them speaking, for a long time.

Chapter 6

BY THE NEXT MORNING, WHICH WAS WEDNESDAY, HAYDON HAD NOT heard from Dystal or Lapierre regarding the stakeout at the widow's. When he went downstairs for breakfast, he stepped into the library, where he kept the radio when he was at home, and called in to the station. Rick Mays was the night-shift lieutenant.

"No, they called it off," Mays said. Haydon could hear the crinkling of cellophane as Mays unwrapped a piece of peppermint. He kept a large bowl of the little red-and-white pinwheel candies on his desk, filling his office with their aromatic scent. "When Lapierre took over from Nagle last night the little widow was already at the movies," Mays explained. Haydon had noticed that everyone was referring to the woman as "the little widow." He guessed it would become known as the little-widow case. Detectives loved a case tag. "But she hadn't gone into the projection booth yet. So everybody was there, Lapierre, Nunn, Nagle, Berry, a couple of electronics guys, all with their ears glued to the 'phones, when she finally got up and slipped in there after the last feature got rolling. The bug worked like a charm. They blabbed to each other like a couple of schoolgirls at a slumber party, him wanting to move in with her, her putting him off, him saying after all he'd done for her she wasn't treating him too good, her asking what was he complaining about he'd gotten paid good for it, him saying yeah but the only reason he'd killed the guy was because he loved her, not for the money, she could have the money, he wanted her, she was the best thing ever happened to him. Then they started wrestling. The guys stayed on the 'phones for the whole show.

"Anyway," Mays concluded, smacking his lips around the peppermint, "Lapierre went on home and this morning he's going down to the DA's to double-check his position before he goes ahead and picks them up. That's it."

Haydon was relieved. He had been on the stakeout for four days, and there were other things on his desk waiting to be done. There were a number of people he needed to talk with regarding cases that weren't progressing well, and after being cooped up in a car for four days he was looking forward to getting out and moving around, even in the bad weather.

He drove to the office and checked in for the morning review, visited awhile with Balkin about the little-widow business, walked over to the crime lab to check on serum tests in a rape/homicide and while he was in the building checked with ballistics regarding evidence in a recent cab-driver killing. Back in the office, he called the firing range to schedule a qualifying shoot, and then walked across to the garage and checked out a department car. By nine-thirty he was on the streets heading for an apartment complex off Memorial Drive to interview a groundskeeper about his statement regarding the description of a man he had seen leaving the complex the morning a female tenant was strangled to death.

Standing under a cabana beside the deserted swimming pool, Haydon listened to the groundskeeper give essentially the same description he had given earlier, according to Haydon's notes, except this time he thought he remembered a funny way the man carried himself. He demonstrated, but Haydon couldn't determine if he was imitating a limp or a seizure, and it seemed so dramatic a physical characteristic that he wondered how the groundskeeper could have failed to recall it in the first interview. Upon closer questioning the man conceded that maybe it wasn't quite that pronounced and that he wasn't really sure if it was a limp either, but it sure as hell wasn't a regular walk, that was for sure. He knew that much.

Haydon thanked him and got back to the car just as a fresh downpour fell out of the dark fog that had moved in while they were talking. He sat in the car a few minutes filling in his notes, and then started the car and made his way out of the network of apartment-complex drives back to Memorial. His next stop was a condominium development off Westheimer where he wanted to talk to the sister of a middle-aged man who had been killed by a single gunman who walked up to the man's car when he stopped at a drive-in grocery, put the barrel of a Smith & Wesson .38 to the man's left eye, and fired twice. The shooter then had turned and walked to his own car nearby and driven away. The only witness was a derelict who had been drinking wine on the sidewalk under the pay telephone outside the convenience store. He had described what had happened, but beyond that he was useless.

By the time Haydon got to the West Loop his suspicions that he was getting occasional whiffs of an odor that indicated someone had recently thrown up in the car were confirmed as the inside of the car warmed up. The air conditioner did little good, so he rolled down the window as much as he could without getting wet and began casting about in his mind for a car service center somewhere in the vicinity of Westheimer.

The manager of Mitch's Car Center told Haydon he would have to pay the same to have the interior cleaned as he would to have the whole thing washed, so he might as well go ahead and have it washed, it was all part of the same package deal. But Haydon told him to forget the wash, just clean the interior and be sure to get rid of the smell. The manager said he would have his people spray the inside of the car with an "odorless scent" after cleaning, which should do the job. Haydon said that would be great, and stood in his coat at the plate-glass windows of Mitch's Car Center staring out at the sluggish traffic, wondering who the hell had returned the car to the garage in that condition.

It was eleven-thirty by the time he got to the condominiums where the victim's sister lived, only to learn from an elderly "second cousin" that the sister had gone out with her daughter-in-law but should be back any minute. Haydon thanked her and drove two blocks back to Westheimer, where he found a franchise seafood restaurant and ate lunch sitting in a Formica booth and watching high school kids in buccaneer costumes serve more than two dozen lunches without once offering a smile. After a while he turned his attention from the kitchen to the street. He looked at his watch. It was almost twelve-thirty. The mail was usually delivered at home between one and two o'clock. In a little while Ramona would put on her plastic raincoat, get an umbrella from the entry hall, and hurry down the curved brick drive to the gates, where she would open her side of the mailbox set into the thick wall that surrounded the property and take out the letters and magazines. When she hurried back to the house she would be carrying another manila envelope.

He left the restaurant and drove back to the sister's condominium, where the elderly second cousin apprehensively gathered the collar of her dress in one veiny, liver-spotted hand and said she didn't know *where* the sister was, but she was sure she would be back any minute. Haydon told her it was all right, he should have called first. He left his card after asking the elderly cousin to tell the sister that he would call later, that it wasn't anything urgent.

At Chimney Rock Road, Haydon cut across to the Southwest Freeway and headed back downtown. At the office again, he sat at the computer and typed in the supplement to the groundskeeper's peculiar statement, and spent some time reading through the file on the convenience-store shooting looking for a detail he had remembered, checking to see if he had remembered it correctly. His thoughts kept straying back to the mail, to the manila envelopes, and he repeatedly had to backtrack and reread several sentences. Three o'clock arrived at last, and Haydon left the squad room without speaking to Dystal, glad that Dystal had given him enough room to postpone any follow-up discussion of the proposed promotion. Now he had two days off. Enough time to distance himself from the problem if he could, and maybe gain a new perspective.

He pushed the Jaguar through the rainy streets, his mind now completely occupied with the anticipation of opening the third envelope. A block away from the house, he activated the remote control on the wrought-iron gates and swept into the brick drive almost without slowing, braking hard under the porte cochere. Hurrying up the front steps, he barged inside the front door and hastily removed his trilby and coat, once again recognizing a manila envelope across the hall on the small table.

Not even bothering to look at the other mail, Haydon tossed it aside as he sat down at the refectory table and examined the envelope. The sender was nothing if not consistent. The uniformity of the lettering was so precise that it almost seemed as if it had been stenciled. There was a cancellation on the stamps, Scotch tape on the tines of the clasp on the flap. Again using the letter opener on the opposite end of the flap,

Haydon cleanly cut open the envelope and looked inside. This time there were two tissue-wrapped photographs. He pulled them out onto the table one at a time.

Eagerly but carefully unwrapping the first print, Haydon saw yet another black-and-white photograph. But it was not a portrait, though it had been taken inside an artist's studio. The indirect light coming in from a series of massive windows was adequate to have made a good picture, but the old film and camera had not been equal to the task, resulting in a picture of dark tones and ambiguous content. A woman, seen in profile, was working at a canvas mounted on a large easel. The contrast was so poor that Haydon could discern no distinctive features, would not have been able to identify her if asked to do so. Most of the objects in the open spaces of the studio were distinguishable only by their dim contours—jars with paintbrushes crammed into them; an empty easel; canvases leaning against the wall; a long table stacked with a miscellaneous jumble of things, perhaps tools for stretching and framing canvases, jars of turpentine and odd rags, something that looked like a small human sculpture, the graceful silhouette of a vase, a stack of books. The room was large, and in one place there was a dull reflection from the time-burnished surface of the wooden floors. Haydon recognized nothing, though he pored over every dim object, cursing the coarse film that had captured so tantalizingly little. He got his magnifying glass from his desk top and moved it slowly over the photograph, confirming his first impressions, but discovering nothing new.

He turned to the next photograph, tore away the tissue from the black-and-white print, and saw a street scene. This picture was bright and clear, a tree-lined sidewalk crowded with people, obviously dressed once again in the fashions of the thirties. A young woman who appeared to be in her early twenties stood on a street corner, conspicuously the focal point of the photograph, smiling unself-consciously at the photographer and leaning against an ornate iron streetlamp that also served as a street sign. The words on the two panels mounted above the woman were easily readable: "Londres" and "Florencia." Behind her stretched a long file of palm trees in the median of the boulevard.

The surprising intrusion of Mexico City was momentarily confusing. The young woman was standing at the traffic

intersection known as the Ángel *glorieta*, where the famous
Monument of Independence, surmounted by a golden angel,
stood in the island of a traffic circle on the Paseo de la Reforma
in the Zona Rosa section of the city. Assuming all the
photographs had been taken at about the same time, this area,
in the Colonia Juárez, would have been in its heyday, one of
the city's most aristocratic neighborhoods. At that time it was
the downtown residential sector for Mexico's wealthiest families and a coterie of international entrepreneurs who were
then heavily involved in Mexican politics, finance, and industry. Though he could not tell if the young woman in this
picture was also the artist in the shadowy studio photograph, it
was clear that she was Mexican, and that she was extraordinarily beautiful.

Without any clear justification for his reaction, Haydon was
immediately wary. He didn't know what he had expected—
perhaps another portrait; certainly something directly and
unmistakably linked to his father. But these photographs,
especially the second one, implied a complication he had not
anticipated. When he had seen the artist's studio, his thoughts
had immediately placed it in London, and he had thought he
was looking at the place where his father had sat for the
portraits. There was nothing in the studio picture to cause him
to doubt his assumption. Though he had not thought it
through, his gut instincts had told him the studio photograph
fit into the puzzle of the portraits. The details and manner of
that fitting would have to be explained, but it offered no
disturbing incongruities, it set off no alarms in his mind.

But the second photograph was discontinuous, and therefore disturbing. First of all, the young woman clearly played a
part in whatever story the other photographs were telling.
Second, Mexico City's role in Webster Haydon's life was not to
come until several years later, after Haydon's father and
mother had married and moved there in the early months of
1938. If this picture had been taken then—and certainly the
styles and fashions of 1935 and 1938 were not so different that
Haydon could distinguish between them—then what part had
this young woman played in the life of a newly married man?
The presence of the woman and the city were discordant
factors in all that had come before them. Was the studio
picture in Mexico City or London? Haydon had assumed

London, but in truth, there was nothing in the picture to confirm that. It could just as easily have been Mexico City. If it was Mexico City, why was his father having his portrait painted so soon after his marriage, and again, what part did the woman play? Obviously the artist in the studio was a woman, but was she the artist who had painted the portraits, or was she the woman on the street corner? Or were they the same?

Haydon could not know the answers to these questions, but he did know that his sixth sense throbbed like a tuning fork when he looked at the street-corner photograph. The young woman's manner did not bespeak a professional relationship, but a personal one. Her smile was too capricious, the pitch of her hips too graceful, and even the way in which an innocent highland breeze caught the thin material of her dress and lifted it in a harmless billow above a poised knee seemed collusive.

He leaned over the photographs, kneading his temples with his fingers, frustrated at his inability to discover a logical relationship among the four prints, and impatient with his inability to disregard a persistent qualm. Yet, on the face of things, there was nothing in the photographs that provided cause for apprehension. There was only Haydon's intuition, an imprecise but unmistakable inner resonance warning him that in these photographs he was being shown more than he was seeing.

Chapter 7

THE DAY HAD BEEN PROTRACTED AND DISCONCERTING. HE HAD, IN
fact, been forced to call Chabela at the old woman's villa in the
San Ángel section of Mexico City. Though he had not communicated with her in more than six months, when Chabela
answered the telephone he began speaking to her as if they
had temporarily broken off a conversation only a few minutes
before, no greetings, not identifying himself, launching right
into the business at hand, curtly, with no courtesies. He
informed her of his overdraft at the Bancomer in Coyoacán and
told her (didn't ask her) to cover it for a couple of months until
he could get it straightened out. She didn't ask him why he was
overdrawn, of course she wouldn't, but said she would take
care of it immediately. And she didn't ask him why he was
calling long-distance, though she must have known he was, or
where he was calling from. Chabela had her faults, her
insufferable piety in her devotion to the old woman being the
most irritating, but she was totally reliable and nonjudgmen-
tal. For years now she had been his only real link to the
wretched old simian, and on those rare occasions—times that
still made his gorge rise when he thought about them—when
he had had to ask for money, she had arranged it without
question and without delay. She knew the score, and she
wouldn't have denied him fifty times that amount. He didn't
know if the old woman ever knew. He supposed that Chabela
told her, but whether she ever *knew* was another matter.

All of this had taken time, and it was midmorning before he
had been able to call Swain to tell him he had the cash. But
there was only a recording at Swain's office asking for a name
and number, neither of which Barcena would leave. He stayed
in the fusty bungalow all day, calling Swain's number every
thirty minutes and smoking anxiously, killing roaches with

rolled newspapers, watching the rain stop and start, and as the day turned toward afternoon, cursing Swain. Barcena had wanted the photographs by noon the next day, at the latest, and if Swain was waiting for his deposit before he began then it was clear he wasn't going to get them in time. He supposed it could be done differently. Would a couple of days' delay really make a difference? Probably not, but he had dwelled on this plan for so long that it seemed to him to be the only "right" way to do it. He had established a momentum, and Swain was screwing it up. He had been careful, conscientious of detail so that as the plan progressed it would establish a rhythm, a pendular regularity that would eventually translate into a sense of the inexorable as it assumed a life of its own, moved of its own will, and became an inescapable fate. Cursing the chunky detective, Barcena looked through the glass louvers at the disintegrating neon palm.

By four o'clock the gray light of day was rapidly fading and Barcena had already begun to develop an alternate plan using one of the photographs from the file. It hadn't rained heavily for several hours, but a soupy mist kept the water dripping from the eaves in a steady tempo, the drops falling in muddy puddles outside the windows in a three-note score of excruciating monotony. Noticing the time, Barcena picked up the telephone and dialed Swain's number, more from habit than hope, and waited for the recording.

"Hel-lo."

Barcena tensed.

"Hel-lo."

"Where the hell have you been, Swain?" Barcena snapped hoarsely, seized with a sudden fury.

"Bar-ceno," Swain said in his flat, toneless voice.

"I've called you every half hour, goddammit."

"Yeah, I was out," Swain said reasonably, sounding unconcerned. "I've got what you wanted. Right here. I'm looking at them."

"What?" Barcena was incredulous.

"I said I've got what you wanted."

"The photographs."

"You bet," Swain said, dragging out the last small word reassuringly.

"But what about the deposit?"

"I figured you were good for it," Swain said as if it was the most natural thing in the world for him to change his mind without consulting Barcena. "So I went ahead on. Why don't you meet me at the Koffee Shop about seven-thirty. Bring the money and we'll do some business."

The weight of Barcena's anger, the sputtering frustration that had swollen to the bursting point during the long afternoon of waiting, was suddenly lifted, and he experienced the weightlessness of immense relief. Exultant, he felt the regaining energy; the plan was intact, the rhythm reestablished. Perhaps this thing had generated a life of its own after all, something that could not be destroyed by the likes of Swain, or anything else.

Appeased, but his nerves still taut, Barcena walked to the refrigerator and took out another Tecate. At the cabinets he used the opener on the string and left it swinging as he went back to the window and the pack of Pall Malls. He was smoking too much, but he didn't give it a second's thought as he lighted another cigarette. This was the fourth day, but it seemed like the fourth week. He had never known such a seamless string of days, without dawns or dusks or high noons. There was only gray, dark gray, and light gray. And rain. It was maddening.

He did not go out except to buy food, to run the daily errand, and that one time to meet Swain. Otherwise he mostly read newspapers and sat by the windows smoking, drinking the Tecate, and now, today, watching the iguanas in the rain. He had seen the first that morning just as it was light enough to recognize it for what it was. Once again he hadn't slept well, had sat on the edge of the bed smoking since an hour before daylight, looking out through the opened louvers. Actually, he had noticed it for quite a while in the lightening dawn before he realized what it was. It had been stone-still, something the iguana does beautifully, on the hood of his rental car, like a Rolls-Royce angel, like the stylized rocket on the old Chevrolets, like the amber Indian on the old Pontiacs—the iguana on the rental car. It hadn't surprised him. He only thought it was funny that it was precisely where a hood ornament would have been.

After he had made breakfast and eaten, and had gone back to the dinette chair by the windows, he saw two more. At first he wasn't sure, they blended so well with the shabby landscape, like the child's game in which there is a drawing of a jungle where one was supposed to find a variety of animals hidden in the dense forest. These iguanas were the same. They were there and then they weren't, and then he would find them elsewhere. Another talent of the iguana. Now, in the afternoon, there were six: the one that had been on the hood of the car was now under it, just behind the front tire, and another lizard was on its back in the same position. They were still, like an Olmec black stone carving. There were two in the fronds of one of the palm trees and one in the other, all three glistening in the rain, stoically ignoring it. The sixth iguana, the largest one, was on the sidewalk outside the bungalow. It faced the screen door, and there was something about it, perhaps its color of tarnish, or its warty, leathery hide, or its ringed eyes, that made Barcena believe that it was old, very old. It hadn't moved, it hadn't even blinked, since it appeared there.

Barcena felt a mounting tension, a growing anxiety. He wondered if Haydon could sense it too, that it was almost the hour of One Death, the time of the Mocking God. Of course he did. How could he not, a man like him. And that was precisely the way it should be.

He listened to the rain. He looked up to the sign above the Rio Courts, where the neon palm was pulling itself together again. Everywhere there were paradigms and symbols.

"I DON'T KNOW," NINA SAID. "THIS IS REALLY STRANGE." SHE SAT across the conference table from Haydon, looking at him over the scattered jumble of paper napkins and the small cardboard boxes of carry-out Chinese food. She had pulled off her shoes and propped her feet in an empty chair that she had turned away from the table. Rolls of drawings and magazines had been shoved to the far end of the table to make room for the Chinese food. The two photographs Haydon had received in the same envelope were lying next to each other in front of her.

After opening the mail in the library at home, Haydon had sat at the old refectory table poring over the photographs with a magnifying glass, growing increasingly uneasy with what he was seeing. The more he had thought about what was happening the greater the possibilities became, and he was driven to pacing restlessly about the library, sitting in an armchair for a while, moving to his desk for a while, and then pacing the room some more. Finally he called Nina at her studio and told her he had received two more photographs and wanted to bring them over. She had told him that Margaret would be leaving around six o'clock and suggested he go by Paoshan's and pick up something they could eat there. As he was putting the photographs back into the envelope, he heard the piano in the living room, and stopped by to tell Ramona that he and Nina would not be home for dinner. Then he grabbed his raincoat and trilby and left.

Haydon nodded. He had told her nothing of the vague sense of uneasiness that had come to him with these last photographs. He tried instead to present a natural curiosity, though not an overly concerned interest. He wanted a gut-level reaction from her, uninfluenced, so far as possible, by his own feelings.

"What do you mean, strange?" he asked, stabbing the last shrimp in his box with his plastic fork. He had tossed his suit coat over an empty chair and had turned back the cuffs of his shirt. His gold cufflinks lay on the table among the paper napkins and carryout boxes.

"I mean strange," she said, leaning over the table and pouring each of them a little more beer from the Tsing Tao bottle that sat between them. She tucked a wayward strand of hair into her chignon. "I don't see the point. I thought this was going to be a question of art, of portraits, of someone from Webster's years in London coming up with those paintings and deciding to proffer them to you for a steep price. Maybe an odd way to go about it, but that's what it seemed like. Now these. It doesn't feel like that's the direction it's going in now." She shrugged, picked up the photograph of the woman under the streetlamp, and sat back, looking at it. "I don't know."

"What direction is it going in now?" Haydon began picking up the dirty napkins and stuffing them into the empty cartons.

"Oh, I don't know," Nina said. "I don't like this sort of thing. It's devious. I get the impression they want you to believe they're revealing something, but at the same time I have an equally strong feeling that what's more important is that they're also hiding something."

"Maybe it's blackmail," Haydon said, leaning his elbows on the table and nodding toward the pictures. "If these were

photographs of someone else's father, and I were a disinterested party, I would have to suspect an involvement with this
woman. An illicit involvement, or there wouldn't be any point
to it."

Nina looked at him over the photograph. "You can't be
serious."

He didn't say anything.

"I couldn't believe that."

"That was a long time ago, Nina."

"What's that supposed to mean?"

"Do you think the young man in those portraits possessed
the same convictions, the same standards, the same common
sense and good judgment, as the old man you knew?"

"Stuart, your parents were already married when they went
to Mexico. *Newly* married at this time," she said, holding up
the photograph. "Knowing him, yes, I would look for some
other explanation before I jumped to the conclusion that all
this was about an affair he had had within a year of his
wedding."

"We can't assume that kind of chronology," Haydon reminded her.

"Well, it was something like that."

Haydon leaned back in his chair. He twisted his neck,
pulling at the muscles that were tightening, wishing he had
taken a couple of capsules of Fiorinal before he left the house
when he was already feeling the first dull tensions at the base
of his skull. Above them the rain beat on the long glass panels
of the skylights. He eased his head down on the back of the
chair and closed his eyes, smelling the Chinese food and
occasionally the ever-present resinous pungency of rubber
cement and wood shavings that pervaded the studio. His
thoughts drifted.

Nina said, "You're more than a little curious about the
photographs." Haydon didn't move, but heard her pick up the
second picture. "What is it I'm not seeing here?"

He didn't answer immediately. "I see exactly what you see,"
he said, his eyes still closed.

"No you don't," she insisted. "What is it?"

Haydon raised his head, pulled his feet out of the chair
where they had been resting, and sat up, leaning his forearms
on the auburn wood of the conference table.

"I've been thinking," he said, looking at the photographs in her hands. "Actually, it's not at all unusual that I didn't know about the portraits. And it's not unusual that I didn't know about this woman, whatever ties she may have to all this. These were things of my father's past, his life before my life. Maybe they weren't even secrets, just things I didn't know about." He looked away, thinking. "No person can know everything about another person, especially a child about his parents. They were another generation, a different world. Even in families where there's a tradition of reminiscing, where children hear stories about their parents' own childhood and youth, volumes must be left untold. There have to be things they owned or cherished or feared, things they did, that will go to their graves with them, that their children will never know existed. Maybe not necessarily because it was deliberately kept from them, but simply because it was never told, never recorded because of forgetfulness, or lack of opportunity, or because there was never enough time. These things pass out of memory, out of existence. It's impossible to convey the whole of any person from one generation to the next, even if you wanted to."

He looked at Nina. "Of the countless things I didn't know about my father, someone has selected a few to reveal to me. I have to believe that there is a continuity to the selection, and that their interrelatedness constitutes a kind of guide, or code. What disturbs me is the mind behind the code. What am I supposed to be gaining access to? What if that mind overestimates my abilities? On the other hand, what if that mind itself is not up to the task, misjudges, provides too few symbols, too few keys to decipher the code?" He reached out and took the photographs from Nina and turned them around on the table in front of him and looked at them. "The pictures themselves are innocuous," he said. "But I have to agree with you—I'm beginning to believe there's something about the way this is being handled that implies something more serious than the offbeat actions of an eccentric."

IT WAS TIME NOW, HE THOUGHT, TO PAY MORE ATTENTION TO IRA Swain. The chunky detective had been an important and integral part of the plan from the beginning, but he was destined to play a more central role than even his own wormy mind could imagine. Barcena understood men like Swain. Mexico City, with its beggared millions living in desperate poverty, its strangling economy, its rampant crime, and inescapable graft, was a breeding ground for crafty men. Swain was smart, but he was not smart enough, and he lacked the one essential ingredient that would make him a truly dangerous obstacle: passion. Cold calculation would lose to passion every time; it simply wasn't capable of generating the heat that was necessary to challenge and transcend the constraints of logic. Barcena understood the liberating potential of passion.

He arrived in the parking lot almost an hour early, the headlights of his rental car piercing the dark rain as he pulled into one of the spaces on the left side of the restaurant that angled into a low brick wall separating the coffee shop from a service-station driveway. He got out of the car, quickly locked it as he humped his shoulders against the weather, and then hurried around to the front door of the restaurant. Going inside, he stopped beside the cigarette machine and scanned the booths and counter just to be sure. When he didn't see Swain, he walked around the end of the counter to the door that led to the restrooms and went through. In a narrow hallway that smelled sweetly of disinfectant there were three doors, one marked for men, one for women, and a third unmarked. Barcena went to the last door, pushed it open, and found himself outside the back of the restaurant, where the stench of sodden trash dumpsters quickly cleared his nostrils of the cloying scent of disinfectant.

Turning up the collar of his coat against the drizzle, Barcena walked briskly toward the alley, where he turned left and circled the service station, following the sidewalks and curbs until he was across the street from the front of the Koffee Shop, seeking shelter under the shallow porticos of half a dozen darkened storefronts. He carefully judged the vantage points of several doorways and settled on a shoe-shop entrance as his post. It afforded a deep shadow from the streetlight on the corner and provided a clear view of the coffee shop's two small parking areas. The portico was just deep enough to dump a steady stream of water onto the sidewalk barely out of splashing distance from his feet. He took a wrinkled pack of Pall Malls from his coat pocket and lighted a cigarette.

There were five white cigarette butts melting on the

sidewalk in front of him when Barcena saw a muddy tan Buick pull into the Koffee Shop parking lot and slowly circle the restaurant until it came around to the side where Barcena's rental car was now sitting between a pickup truck and a small sports car. The Buick pulled into one of the slots farther back and cut its lights. After a few minutes, Barcena saw Swain get out of the car, slam the door, and start toward the front of the restaurant. He walked casually, despite the rain, with both hands jammed into his raincoat pockets and with the slight roll of a fat man. As he was approaching the rear of Barcena's car, he glanced around quickly, brought one hand out of a baggy coat pocket, and squatted and reached up under the rear fender. He was there only a second before he stood again, put his hand back into his pocket, and continued around the end of the building to the front door. Barcena was surprised that Swain knew which car he was driving, but realizing that, he was not surprised at what Swain had done. He looked at his watch. The chubby detective was nearly fifteen minutes late.

Hurrying across the street, dodging puddles and having to stop once for traffic, Barcena entered the front door of the coffee shop just as Swain, standing by the cash register, was figuring out that Barcena wasn't there.

"Swain," Barcena said, and the detective turned to him with a cold look, a defensive expression intended to hide his surprise.

"Hey," Swain said casually. "You just get here?"

Barcena knew what he must be thinking. "I was over at the service station looking at their street maps."

Swain glanced down at Barcena's empty hands. "Get one?"

Barcena shook his head. "I already had some like those."

Swain studied Barcena's face a moment, measuring what he thought Barcena might have seen or not seen, whether he should believe the explanation. His own face, with its button nose and small round eyes, was only a tense twitch away from a frown. Then suddenly he smiled. "Maps," he said, and laughed softly.

When the waitress came to seat them, it was clear that Swain was a frequent customer. She smiled and spoke to him familiarly, and as she turned to walk them to their booth Swain leaned into her and asked if she would give them the round booth in the back, because they needed a little privacy. She seated them as he asked, the two of them alone at a large banquette, and Swain ordered coffee, pork chops with green beans, carrot coins, mashed potatoes, and an extra dinner roll. Barcena ordered coffee. As the waitress walked away, still writing on her pad, Swain looked at Barcena.

"How long you figuring to be in town?" he asked, studying Barcena.

Saturnino flinched inwardly, suddenly cautious. Hadn't he brought the photographs?

"Just a question," Swain said easily, sensing Barcena's reaction.

"Not long."

Swain nodded. "You always lived in Mexico City?"

"I was born there," Saturnino said, taking out his Pall Malls. Apparently he was going to have to endure a little conversation before he got the pictures.

"Never been there," Swain said. "I hear it's . . . crowded."

Barcena lighted his cigarette. "It is a dirty place now. It didn't used to be."

"You speak good English."

Barcena nodded and looked at Swain as he picked a fleck of tobacco off his tongue. "Do you speak Spanish?"

"Nope." Swain grinned.

Barcena didn't bother to blow his smoke away from the table.

"You in business of some kind?" Swain leaned back as the waitress brought their coffee. He poured in a lot of cream and a lot of sugar, stirred vigorously, pinged the spoon on the side of the cup, and laid it on the table. He picked up the cup, tested the coffee, which apparently had been cooled considerably by the large amount of cream, and drank half the cup before he set it down again.

"No," Barcena said.

"Independently wealthy." Swain chuckled.

"I teach anthropology at the National University," Barcena said. It didn't matter how much he told him now.

"Anthropology," Swain snorted, seeming surprised, a slow grin slowly spreading over every centimeter of his pudgy face as if he were enjoying that information enormously. "Professor," he said, and twisted his head a little before picking up his cup and gulping the rest of the coffee.

Barcena watched him set the empty cup on the saucer and shove it away. He noticed that Swain's face was beginning to flush.

"Where'd you learn your English?" Swain asked. Suddenly his complexion was excessively florid, and his expression gradually sobered, as if he knew what was happening. Barcena wondered if he had drunk the coffee too quickly or if this was something to do with high blood pressure.

"I went to a Catholic school," Barcena said, exhaling a stream of blue smoke and casually studying Swain's peculiar alteration. "The nuns were from the United States."

Swain once again twisted his head with a slight jerk, and reached for his water. His fingers gripped the sweaty glass like little sausages, and he took in several huge mouthfuls. He yanked a paper napkin from the aluminum holder and wiped at the perspiration that had popped to the surface of his forehead. Barcena could not take his eyes off the bulging arteries that now stood out on either side of Swain's engorged neck, which was already as thick and jowly as an old boar's.

The waitress suddenly appeared at the table with Swain's order of steaming chops. He raised his empty coffee cup to her as she put down his plate, and she took it and filled it from a pot at a nearby hotplate. Whatever had come over Swain began to subside, and before he picked up his fork he pulled a manila envelope from inside his raincoat lying beside him on the banquette, and laid it on the table in front of Barcena. Without saying a word, he turned his attentions to his plate of food.

Barcena quickly reached for the envelope, and took out the photographs. He turned through them briskly. There were six of them, Swain not being the sort of man to throw in an extra print even though Barcena knew that the odds were he had taken a lot more than just these. Swain obviously had used a good telephoto lens; the quality of the photographs was excellent. While the detective plowed through the oily pork chops, Barcena savored the photographs, this time going through them more slowly, studying each print, considering its potential, believing the selection of the right one was of critical importance. Which of these had the most force, or would have the most force when he was through with it? Which one, when seen from Haydon's perspective, would have the greatest impact? Which one had the potential of conveying more than its face value to a perceptive viewer? Barcena knew his man. Where Swain saw one thing, Haydon would see five.

"What," Swain said.

Barcena looked at the detective, who was looking at him as he pushed the last bite of green beans onto his fork. There was only the stripped pork-chop bone left on the plate, sitting in a thin, runny juice beaded with grease.

"What," Swain said again. "They're what you wanted, right?"

"Yes, they are," Barcena said, watching Swain wipe his mouth on a fresh paper napkin. He had used three napkins, all of which lay wadded and greasy beside his plate.

"Good."

Barcena looked at Swain.

Swain shook his head. "You give it to me out in the parking lot. We'll walk out together." But he made no move to go. "Is this the last thing? You gonna get in touch with me again, or what?"

"Nothing else," Barcena said. "This is it."

Swain's hands rested on the table, doing nothing, as he let his eyes float languidly around the coffee shop, with no other intention, it appeared, than to give his enormous meal an opportunity to digest. Apparently this was the routine he followed after every meal, and he wasn't going to deviate from it just because Barcena was there. It seemed he had nothing else to say and felt no need to give Barcena a clue to what might happen next or how long they might remain in this after-dinner hiatus.

Barcena was now in no rush either, so Swain's indolence did not make him nervous. But he was offended by the detective's boorish manner, and was not entirely sure it was not meant to be deliberately insulting. He was thinking about this when Swain reached over and got the bill, grunted under his breath as he rolled sideways and grappled for change in his pants pocket, and then tossed the coins onto the table without even looking to see if he had thrown down dimes or quarters or pennies. He began scooting around the banquette, pushing his raincoat before him until he got to the end and stood up beside the table. Without saying a word, he headed toward the cash register. Barcena followed him.

Swain paid, took a toothpick from the dispenser beside a March of Dimes poster while he waited for his receipt. When he got it, he walked out the front door of the restaurant, struggling to pull on his raincoat. Outside in a drifting mist, Swain headed for the cars. He walked past Barcena's car and stopped at the rear end of the pickup and turned to face Barcena.

"Okay," he said.

Barcena pulled a white envelope from his coat pocket, a small packet, because the bills were large, and handed it to the detective. Swain shoved it into his pocket without checking it.

"You know my number," he said, extending his hand in the mist.

Barcena shook it, feeling the tight swollen flesh. "Thank you," he said.

Swain nodded, showing no sign of even a polite smile, and walked away.

Barcena drove out of the parking lot and headed east, knowing he needed to get on a stretch of well-lighted streets. Off to his right he could see the dazzling cluster of skyscrapers he remembered as Greenway Plaza rising up in the night rain and turned in their direction at the next street, which was Timmons. Careful to drive the speed limit, he watched his rearview mirror as he switched into the left lane. When he got to Richmond he turned left and drove through the heart of Greenway Plaza, its soaring towers of light flanking the wide, bright streets. He saw nothing in his rearview mirror until he was almost at the Buffalo Speedway intersection, and then, five or six cars behind him, he saw Swain's Buick glide through a pool of misty light. Fine, he thought. Fine.

At Kirby Drive he turned right. He didn't know where he was going, except in general terms, but he knew what he was looking for. He would drive until he saw it, but would have to be careful not to meander too much or Swain would grow suspicious. He had to make it look as if he had a specific destination.

He drove until it seemed as if he would never find what he wanted, every once in a while catching another glimpse of the tan Buick a little way behind him in the traffic. The rain had stopped, but a thick mist on the windshield required an occasional swipe of the wipers. Just when he thought he would take a perpendicular turn and try his luck in another direction, he came to a bayou, a wide canal-like waterway flanked on both sides by streets that followed its serpentine path. Barcena crossed the bridge, turned immediately, and drove along the bayou. This was looking more like it, but the houses here were separated from the bayou by the street he was on, while on the other side he could see smaller streets that came down into the greenbelt of the bayou itself. That was even better. At the next intersection he turned right and crossed over to the other side of the bayou, then turned right again and again until he entered the shallow curving residential street he had seen a few minutes earlier. He slowed, watching the density of the foliage around the houses on his left as well as in the greenbelt that led down to the bayou on his right. When he saw what he wanted he crossed the street and stopped in front of one of the houses, choosing one without a porch light.

He quickly got out of the car, slammed the door, and started running back in the direction from which he had come, being careful to keep behind the hedges and clumps of shrubbery that shielded the homes from the street. Twice he slipped on the soggy grass, but he scrambled to his feet again and kept going. When he was three houses away from his car, he turned and looked back. It was almost out of sight around the curve. One more house. He ran across a drive, breathing strenuously, his lungs sucking desperately at the muggy night humidity, trying to wring oxygen out of the mud-laden odors that hung in the heavy bayou air. Finally he stopped, falling down on one knee behind a clump of something that looked like pyracantha. His chest was heaving, and he felt a brief light-headedness. He put a hand down on the grass to balance himself and realized he was soaking wet nearly up to his knees. His soggy pants legs clung to his calves, and his shoes were heavy as lead, caked with mud imbedded with twigs and grass.

He was taking stock of his condition when Swain's Buick slowly nosed around the corner. The headlights were out, but Barcena could see the mist flickering past in front of the orange parking lights. He was ten feet from Swain when the Buick idled past, Swain's face faintly visible from the greenish glow of the dash lights and the blipping monitor on which he was reading the signal from the bug he had slapped under the fender of Barcena's car. Swain stopped ten or fifteen yards past Barcena, hitting his brakes only once before he cut the motor. Barcena couldn't believe his luck, that it was happening exactly as it should, as if Swain had agreed to cooperate. He needed Swain to do one more thing, and he had no doubt that he would.

Barcena waited. All around him was the sound of dripping, every leaf, every limb, every vine was dripping, and when he moved his foot he could feel the waterlogged soil sucking at him from underneath the grass. Then Swain, the clever, second-guessing, calculating, street-wise detective, rolled down his window.

Suddenly Barcena was at the car door, unaware of how he had crossed the fifteen yards, not knowing if he had crawled or run like a mad animal, but he was there, drawing his hand from his coat pocket and shoving the well-worn butcher knife from the bungalow kitchenette into the soft jowl of Swain's throat, his perceptions heightened so that he experienced every tactile sensation as if he were the blade itself, feeling the uneven resistance of tissue and cartilage, the easy penetration into the hollow trachea, and again the resistance of cartilage on the opposite side until the knife was buried up to its wooden handle and Barcena could feel the bristles of Swain's prickly beard pressing against the back of his thumb.

Swain's right hand flew up robotically and gripped the steering wheel as if he were going to drive away, while his left hand shot up beside the door and clamped Barcena's wrist. For a startling instant they were grimly locked to each other and to the car, Barcena's left hand clutching the outside mirror for leverage. Then a bizarre thing happened. The explosive energy of Swain's terror gave him extraordinary strength, and, mewling and gurgling, he seized absolute control of the knife in his throat by his grip on Barcena's wrist. Barcena stared helplessly at Swain, whose mouth was frozen into a wide yawn as he gaped at Barcena from the corners of his rolling eyes. Swain could have pulled the knife out, but in his stupefied horror he forced Barcena's hand in the wrong direction, and in a burst of unreasoning desperation thrust it forward, cutting his own throat.

Chapter 8

HAYDON OPENED HIS EYES TO THE PEARL LIGHT OF THURSDAY morning coming in through the tall bedroom windows. He lay still with Nina cradled in his right arm and guessed the time, then raised his left wrist and saw that it was eight-thirty. He had missed it by forty-five minutes. The house was quiet. Everyone slept relatively late Thursday mornings, the first day of Haydon's "weekend." Ramona had been lucky at fall registration the week before and had gotten all of her classes on Monday, Wednesday, and Friday, allowing her to sleep in on Tuesdays and Thursdays. Nina didn't go to the studio till noon on Haydon's days off, and Gabriela easily adapted to whatever schedule was necessary.

He slipped his arm from around Nina's neck and eased out of bed. Running his fingers through his rumpled hair, he headed toward the bathroom, glancing outside at a heavy mist drifting across the grounds as he passed the windows. He stood in the shower, letting the water beat against his bowed head, and thought about the mail. This would be the fourth day, and he was beginning to feel like a newly caged animal who was quickly learning the importance of the arrival of the man in uniform; all his thoughts and concentration were increasingly focused on the anticipation of that one daily event.

He finished showering and toweled dry, then stood in front of the mirror and combed his hair. Deciding against shaving, he splashed cologne on his face anyway and walked to his armoire, where he pulled out a pair of casual linen pants and a clean white shirt. He put them on and tucked in the shirttail as he stepped into a pair of old espadrilles with the toes almost worn through. Nina stirred, and Haydon stopped and watched her, her cinnamon hair and long olive arms lying on the white percale sheets. In a moment she resumed her even breathing, and he walked across the bedroom and went downstairs.

Gabriela was already in the kitchen making coffee, and Haydon pitched in to help her after calling Yost's bakery to have sweet rolls and breakfast breads delivered. He sliced and squeezed oranges while they visited, deciding not to mention the photographs yet, preferring to wait until after the day's mail. When the buzzer to the front gate rang he pushed the remote control and went out to the service entrance to meet the Yost truck, which was always driven by one of Earl Yost's five sons, who would hand him the box of bakery goods and the morning papers he had picked up at the gate.

By nine-thirty Nina and Ramona had finally crawled out of bed and the four of them were sitting around the sunroom table scattered with jars of jams and jellies, reading the papers and talking as they ate. By eleven o'clock Nina had left for the office, Ramona and Gabriela had gone their separate ways, and Haydon had climbed to the third floor, which was mostly used for storage, though it could have been a complete third living area. Haydon's father had finished it out when he had built the limestone house in the early forties, and the floor plan was roughly that of the second floor, though it had been left largely undefined so that it could be adapted to any number of uses. But the family had never had a need for it beyond the obvious one of storage. Haydon found the room where he had put all the family records and let himself in.

After his parents had died he had spent weeks going through the family's picture albums, the boxes of letters, and the trunks of mementos Haydon's mother had stowed away in this top-floor room. Like the keepsakes of many families, they had been stored haphazardly, though Cordelia had made periodic promises to herself that she would one day get up there and straighten it all out. But it had never gotten done until Haydon did it himself during those months following the funeral. He had organized everything chronologically—the picture albums and the boxes of loose photographs that had not found their way into albums; the negatives; the letters; the newsclippings, mostly about his father up until the time Haydon had joined the police force and made detective. After that, there were also the articles his mother had saved about every case he had worked on that had made the papers.

Because he had been meticulous about the chronology, there wasn't much for him to go through now. The letters and photographs in Webster Haydon's possession that dated from those years between the time he left home for England in 1934 and married and moved to Mexico in 1938 were surprisingly few. Haydon had known his father to be a conscientious letter writer. While Haydon was growing up there had been a number of times when he and his mother returned to Edinburgh, Scotland, to visit her family for several weeks at a time when Webster's work prevented him from going along. During those visits Haydon's father would write every other day, letters to both of them, letters to Haydon which, when he was a child, were decorated with eccentric drawings and the "tracks" of curiously named animals that Webster had made by putting various parts of his hands and fingers on an ink pad and pressing them onto the page. When Haydon got older the letters were filled with the antics of their collies—of which there had been several over the years—which his father described in thoroughly human terms, perfectly portraying their personalities.

The letters to his mother, many of which he had never read until after their deaths, contained some business, some questions he wished her to present to her family about someone's health or someone else's legal affairs, much of which he handled for them gratis. But his letters to her also demonstrated a deep affection. Haydon had noted at the time he was organizing this family memorabilia that these letters never seemed trivial, as letters of this kind often did when read years afterward by a third party. As a detective, it was not uncommon for Haydon to find himself reading such letters, usually with a feeling of embarrassment and sorrow that emotions so genuinely and deeply felt should be so unskillfully expressed. But his father seemed to have avoided the pitfalls of maudlin sentimentality, and his letters to Haydon's mother were articulate expressions of endearment.

And always, the letters were written on his father's special stationery, always in ink—he abhorred ballpoint pens—and in his characteristic thin, forward-leaning style that seemed to have been learned from those practical self-improvement books popular in the nineteenth century and intended for the "common man" who wished to enhance, among other things, his penmanship.

But there were few letters in Webster's own hand to be found here among the drawers containing the material from the years 1934 to 1938. Most of these were received by Webster in London, not written by him. They were from his family in Boston, surprisingly stern correspondence from his father, perhaps reflecting the tensions still felt there because of Webster's "defection," often dealing with finances and social proprieties Webster was urged to observe with those persons in London who could prove influential for him in the future; and warm, mollifying letters from his mother who was more apt to show concern for his health, and tried to get him to commit to a date when he would return home. There were a couple of letters from an older brother who urged him to take advantage of all the opportunities he could, and to enjoy himself, a counterbalancing male voice that seemed to want to soften the unrelenting and humorless tone of their father's.

There were a few courtship letters addressed to Miss Cordelia Temple, Edinburgh, that apparently Haydon's mother had saved. They were formal. There were one or two letters from the Haydon family about the time of Webster and Cordelia's marriage, discussing the legal implications thereof, and wishing them the greatest happiness. There was a letter and a cablegram from the Mexico City office of Dutch Royal Shell confirming Webster's new position just a few weeks before they sailed.

There was little else.

The photographs were even fewer, mostly of Webster and Cordelia in Edinburgh with her family, some of their home in London, a few with friends along the Thames. Nothing that shed any light at all on the existence of the portraits or the photographs Haydon had been receiving in the mail.

The files for the Mexico years, 1938 to 1942, were considerably larger, especially the photograph albums. Haydon lost track of time going through these because much of what he saw here was familiar to him, though from later years when he and his parents returned to Mexico City for their annual visits during the summer rainy season. There were the earliest photographs of a young Gabriela smiling shyly in front of a giant maguey, pictures of Webster and Cordelia under the towering *ahuehuetes* in Chapultepec Park, on the broad and grand avenue of the Paseo de la Reforma, in the lush floating gardens of Xochimilco, on the beaches near Ixtapa decades before it became a resort, and in a countryside villa near Cuernavaca where they frequently vacationed. There were dozens and dozens of pictures, but none of them having to do with artists, or portraits, and only a few in which there were persons Haydon did not know.

He was still sitting by the windows, poring over the pictures, when something caught his attention out of the corner of his eye and he looked down to the drive to see Ramona hurrying out to the mailbox in the front wall. He looked at his watch, laid the album down in the chair, and went downstairs.

Ramona was just coming through the front door as Haydon reached the bottom of the stairs, his eyes immediately seeking and finding the manila envelope among the assorted packets in her hands. He asked her for only that one, thanked her, and turned back to the stairs, which he climbed slowly, examining the envelope as he went. It was so perfectly and consistently addressed that he easily could have believed he was receiving the exact same one every day, like a recurring dream. When he got back to the top-floor room, he returned to his chair and sat down. Meticulously, he began tearing off the very tip edge of the envelope opposite the flap.

It was the artist's studio again, but the subject was startling. There was only one person in the photograph, a woman he quickly recognized as the smiling coquette with the breeze-blown dress on the palmy Florencia Boulevard. The film and camera had performed perfectly this time. The print was not cropped, and the edges of the negative were in place to prove that the framing had been done through the viewfinder. This photograph itself was something of a portrait, seeming to have been taken with an artist's eye, and perhaps with a camera of better quality than the more popular ones of the time. She was nude, and reclined on an Empire *lit en bateau* in an oblique shaft of sunlight that came from one of the studio's ceiling-high windows. She lay on her right side against a bank of white pillows, one leg extended full-length and the other propped up against the back of the narrow bed, openly revealing the dark triangle of her pubic hair. Her youthful skin was taut and smooth, and the natural light had been used to its greatest effect, falling on the swells and shallows of her body, evoking all the erotic mystery of an Ingres odalisque. She was not smiling, nor did she appear self-conscious of her nakedness. Nothing of her body was hidden from the camera, into which she gazed with frank collaboration. And there was something else in her expression, too. Something anticipatory. It was, he thought, that brief moment of inhibition he had seen before in women's faces, a spark of commitment to an unbridled emotion, of laughter, or rage, or passion.

Haydon sat holding the picture in his hands and looked out to the lawn and the oval drive. It was quiet, and occasionally the silence was broken by the harsh cawing of a solitary crow from a flock that had moved into the oak trees along the wall. From time to time one or two would leave the high margins of the trees and sail over the front lawn through the gray mist, black eidolons, gliding from one world to another, traversing a vast, bleak emptiness. Haydon felt an affinity with that image, as if he too were crouching on the cusp of one world, listening, listening to his father's past as it beckoned to him from another, from the far side of a great, murky distance of time, knowing that in the next instant, or the next, he would leap into that unsure span and begin the long crossing.

AS SOON AS HAYDON HAD UNWRAPPED THE TISSUE FROM THE PHOTO-graph of the odalisque, he had known he would have to show the pictures to Gabriela, and by now he had a lot of questions to put to her as well. But he wanted to wait; he needed time to put this latest revelation into perspective. Though he now found it more difficult to concentrate on the task at hand, he eventually finished going through the family's pictures and papers from the Mexico years. He jotted down questions and noted a few more that came to mind as he went through the albums and letters. Now more than ever, he was convinced there was something menacing behind the orchestrated presentation of the photographs, though he still had to acknowledge that there was nothing menacing in the content of the pictures. But he felt a keen urgency to learn more, everything he could, about the young woman who had become the counterpart to his father in whatever story was being unfolded.

Haydon spent the rest of the afternoon in the library, considering the possibilities, taking notes, and reconsidering the possibilities. Because he was convinced that Gabriela would know the woman in the pictures and, to some extent, would be able to elucidate what had been happening, time passed slowly through the long, gloomy hours.

In the late afternoon Nina called and asked about the mail. He told her there had been another photograph, and when she asked him what it was, he told her that he was going to show all of the pictures to Gabriela that night, and he would like Nina to wait and see it for the first time with her. She didn't ask why, and he wouldn't have known what to say if she had.

Ramona had a date that night, so only the three of them ate Gabriela's dinner of redfish *veracruzano*. When they were finished, Nina got up to get coffee for herself and Haydon, and when she returned Haydon decided it was time.

"Gabriela," he said, stirring cream into his coffee, "how did you meet my father?"

She looked at him as if she thought she hadn't heard him correctly and then cut her eyes at Nina, who was also looking at him over her cup.

"Mr. Haydon?" Gabriela asked, squinting at him.

"Yes, right."

She looked at him a moment. "Your mawther introduced me, of course," she said.

Both women were looking at him.

"Then you met Mother first?"

"Of course," she said again, as if everyone knew it couldn't have been any other way.

That surprised him, though he didn't know why. He had always assumed that his father had hired her. When he thought about it, he didn't know why he should have had that impression.

He looked at Nina and then back at Gabriela. There was no point in putting it off any longer.

"I've got something I'd like to show you," he said, and he related to her the story of how the pictures had arrived over the past four days. He didn't describe the subject matter, only saying that he thought they were related to his father's past during the Mexico years. He watched the old woman closely. At first she seemed to be truly puzzled and interested in what had been happening, but by the time Haydon finished her attitude had changed, though Haydon couldn't say exactly in what way.

Gabriela was quiet, and then said, "Okay, fine. Where are these pictures?"

"In the library."

"Let's see them," she said.

They stood and walked across the wide hallway to the library, where the green-shaded lamps were still burning on the refectory table. The photographs were lying on the table in one stack, a piece of paper covering them.

Haydon pulled a chair out for Gabriela, but she shook her head, her eyes already locked on the blank sheet of paper. She seemed to have assumed an attitude of determination, as if she were bracing herself for some ghastly review at which she was staunchly refusing to show weakness. She folded her arms under her breasts and waited. He picked up the photographs and laid only the two portraits down on the table in front of her. Much to Haydon's surprise, she stood stock still and looked at them, not only with recognition, but with what he thought was an expression of profound sadness. Then, almost imperceptibly, she began nodding her head, lost in thought.

Haydon watched her, waiting.

"Mr. Haydon," she said gently. She unfolded her arms and bent over the table and picked up the first picture, tilting it toward the lamp. "I have never seen these ones before," she said. "He must have been so yowng," she mused softly, laying down the first and picking up the second. She put her left hand alongside her face and nibbled on the fingernail of her little finger. "So yowng," she repeated wistfully.

"You said you hadn't seen *these*," Haydon said to her. "Have you seen others?"

Gabriela didn't answer for a minute, and Haydon had the distinct impression that she was not thinking about the portrait now, but rather was trying to decide how to answer his question.

"No. No, I never seen no others," she answered. Then she motioned behind her to the portrait on the library wall, but she didn't look at Haydon. "Jus' that one."

Haydon didn't believe her, but he knew it wouldn't do any good to challenge her now.

"Why don't you both sit down," he said, pulling out a chair for Gabriela. "There are three more. And you might want to use this," he said, putting his horn-handled magnifying glass on the table. "I had to use it to see the details on some of these."

They sat down, Gabriela noticeably apprehensive now. Nina, sitting beside her, pulled the second portrait over in front of her and looked at it more closely. Haydon watched Gabriela as he laid in front of her the next picture, the poorly exposed photograph of the artist's studio, the woman sitting at an easel, painting. Gabriela's delicate hands rested on the table on either side of the photograph. She looked at it without moving, without leaning over to see better, without using the magnifying glass. She was immobile, looking at the picture. After a minute she shook her head and gave a slight shrug. "*No sé*," she said, and using her left hand shoved the picture over to Nina.

Haydon laid down the next one: the beautiful young woman on the busy street corner smiling at the photographer, Londres and Florencia. Gabriela did not pass this one on to Nina so quickly. She looked at it without expression, and then Haydon saw a slight tremor of her right hand, and he thought she was going to pick up the magnifying glass. But she didn't. When she finally shook her head again, it was a mechanical action and seemed to have little to do with the fact that she might not have recognized the young woman.

"Don't you know where this is?" Haydon asked.

Gabriela shook her head more forcefully, a stubborn refusal to acknowledge the obvious.

Haydon reached across and put his finger on the street sign. Gabriela shrugged.

"Mexico City," he said.

Gabriela tilted her head a little to one side, as if to say "Maybe," or "So what?"

For him her reticence was tantamount to recognition. All spontaneity had drained from her, and she was now playing a role that did not suit her.

"When would you say this was?" he asked, looking at Nina. She looked at him, then realized he wanted her to repeat what they had already discussed. She leaned over and looked at the picture in front of Gabriela, who sat with squared shoulders, not moving, looking at the picture as if being forced to do so.

"The thirties, I'd guess," she said.

Haydon nodded. "Yeah, that's what I thought too." He placed the last photograph in front of Gabriela: the studio again, the nude odalisque on the chaise, her unabashed gaze fixed on the lens of the camera, the lines of her body rising and sinking in the soft light.

Gabriela looked into those eyes that had not closed in fifty years and unconsciously placed her right hand on the black edge of the photograph where the negative provided the natural framing. Her left hand rose slowly and almost stopped at her mouth, but went on and distractedly tucked a loose strand of hair behind her ear. With a weak motion she pushed the photograph away to Nina, and fixed her eyes on the night rain beyond the windows. "I do not know," she said mechanically.

Nina had leaned forward to see the new photograph and seemed oblivious to Gabriela's reserve. "My God," she said with surprise. "She's gorgeous, really extraordinary."

Haydon's eyes were on Gabriela, whose forearms were resting limply on the table as she faced the darkness. In the short space of a few seconds her shoulders had lost their determination, and she seemed dispirited. He sat down in the chair beside her, his eyes tracing her profile. He knew she was aware of him looking at her, but she didn't turn to him.

"I don't know these people," she said, her eyes straight ahead. The tone of belligerent denial of a few minutes before was gone, replaced by a note of unmistakable nostalgia. "They do remind me . . . of those years . . . in Mexico. But this girl . . ." She pulled down the corners of her mouth and shook her head slowly. "I do not know this woman." Then, as if she had thought of something, she turned to Haydon. "This is all? You have no more of these pictures?"

"These are the only ones."

Gabriela opened her eyes at him. "So? What is this, then?"

"I told you, I don't know. I don't understand anything about why they were sent to me."

"Must be a crazy person," Gabriela said, her eyes studying her fingers now. She was touching the fingertips of her hands together, ten fingers lightly touching. "I don't understan' why you stay with this business anyway," she said, growing petulant. "There is enough misery in this worl', let me tell you. You do not need to go looking for it." She lifted her chin toward the photographs. "This is a crazy person. You should have nothing to do with this crazy person."

She said this without energy, touching together her fingers, her thoughts not entirely on what she was saying.

"I didn't 'go looking' for this," Haydon answered. "I don't have any idea who's sending these, or why."

Gabriela was silent. Then she put her hands on the edge of the table and pushed her chair away. "I got to go clean up the kitchen," she said, as if she had no more time to waste looking at old photographs of people she didn't know.

As she got up, Haydon stood too, and watched her walk out of the library. He was watching her slumping shoulders as she crossed the hall to the dining room when Nina said, "What's going on here?"

She had turned in her chair and was looking up at him, still holding the last photograph. "What was that all about?"

Haydon sat down again. He took the photograph from Nina and looked at it. "I think all of these pictures were probably taken in Mexico City when my parents were living there." He nodded toward the doorway. "She knows something. I think she knows the woman in the photographs."

Nina gaped at him. "Gabriela?" She looked down at the picture and then back at Haydon. He thought she was about to ask another question, but instead she said, "Oh, this is strange, Stuart." She picked up the photograph of the nude woman. "This is the same woman who's at the easel in the studio?"

"I don't know."

"Maybe not. Maybe the young woman was the artist's model."

Haydon shrugged.

"Do you think this woman at the easel painted Webster's portraits?"

"Possibly," he said. "I don't know."

"But you think Gabriela knows?"

"I believe she does."

Surveying the pictures on the table, Nina said, "What in the world is the point of all this?"

Haydon didn't answer. His mind was casting back through the years, gathering the images of another night fifteen years ago when he was still dating Nina and had been in homicide less than six months. He had been working the evening shift with an older detective, long since retired, and they had been called to a scene off Memorial Drive not far from St. Mary's Seminary in an upper-class neighborhood of secluded, expensive homes.

He remembered the fragrance of pine trees that had filled the air on that mild May night as they walked past the squad cars and coroner's van, past the patrolmen milling around in the yard and up to the front door, where they encountered the first blood: a heavy, rust-colored splatter of it in the surprising location of the lintel, and then a fine spray trailing down one of the doorjambs to the floor. They followed the bloody handprints and smears on the entrance-hall wall, past a bright splash where the woman had been hit again, and then much more blood, the footprints on the Italian tile floors showing clearly how she had struggled to keep her balance while slipping in her own gore as she fled to a sunken living room, where she lay facedown with her head in the fireplace. There it appeared the assailant had beaten her head beyond recognition and then had gone to considerable effort to rake cold ashes into her blood-clotted hair, mixing and patting it into a dreadful mud that formed thick, ropy plaits. In this condition, her head seemed not to have been a part of her at all, but a separate thing, a small, mangled animal of some kind lying lifeless above her shoulders. Her wispy nightgown had twisted around her in the struggle until she was bound tightly, one arm pinned within its windings, the other stretched out on the hearth, the white palm of her hand wrenched upward. One leg was wrapped completely, even the foot; the other was naked up to her buttocks.

Haydon remembered the details vividly, because when he followed his partner into the kitchen where patrolmen were waiting with the assailant, who had called the police himself and was now sitting at the breakfast bar drinking a glass of water, Haydon had suffered one of the deepest shocks of his early career. The man on the bar stool turned around and Haydon looked into the flat, empty eyes of one of his father's oldest friends. He was a prominent lawyer in his late fifties, a man whom Haydon had known since he was a kid, who occasionally had been to their home, and whom Haydon's father had considered not only a superb probate lawyer, but also a man of integrity.

Seeing the shock on Haydon's face, the man said, "It's all right, I've called Raymond," referring to another friend of the family who was a criminal lawyer.

Speechless, Haydon nodded, and turned and walked out of the room, leaving the formalities of the interview to his partner.

He had called ahead, but it was nearly one o'clock when he drove through the iron gates of his parents' home and was met at the front door by his mother, dressed in her housecoat, her face grim with the effect of the news he had given them. She took his arm and they talked quietly as they walked together along the wide hallway to the library. At the door, his mother gave his hand a firm squeeze and let him go in to his father by himself.

The French doors were thrown open wide to the cool spring night, and Webster Haydon was standing just outside on the terrace in his silk robe and pajamas, smoking a freshly lighted cigar. Only one of the lamps was lighted on the refectory table, and two moths flitted around its green globe, occasionally hitting the glass with a soft tap. Haydon walked across the room and through the French doors to stand beside his father, looking down across the lawn to the lime grove. They stood in silence for several minutes before his father stepped out to the terrace balustrade and leaned against it, turning to Haydon, half of his long face lighted from the single lamp in the library, the other half obscured by the darkness.

"What was it?" he asked. "An affair?"

"It had been going on for over a year," Haydon said. "The two families were longtime friends. He lived only a few houses down the lane from her. It was an absolute surprise to both spouses. Neither of them had had the slightest hint of it."

His father looked at him without emotion. "She was wanting to break it off?"

Haydon nodded.

"Damn fool," his father said. There was no bitterness in his voice, no condemnation.

"I didn't handle it very well," Haydon told him. It was almost a confession, and he had made a great effort to subdue his anger, an anger that had smoldered with a steady and growing intensity ever since the initial shock of walking into the kitchen. "I couldn't talk to him."

"Was it bad?"

"It was overkill . . . vicious." He heard the hard edge to his voice, felt instant regret that he hadn't been able to avoid it.

They looked at each other, Haydon unable to read anything in his father's expression, though he knew the agony the older man must be feeling. Haydon had turned away and leaned on the limestone, looking out over the dark grounds. His father held his cigar in the long fingers of his left hand which had rested on the balustrade, his other hand thrust down in the pocket of his robe. An occasional rising breeze carried the cigar smoke away from Haydon and brought with it the earthy odors of spring.

"Are you trying to reconcile the man and the act?" his father asked.

Haydon shook his head. "I don't feel any need to do that," he had said harshly. He recalled the shapeless mess that had been the woman's head, her bloody hair deliberately matted with ashes. "I think this is something I can understand without agonizing over it."

His father raised his hand and pulled on the cigar. For a long while he was silent, and Haydon could feel him studying him, could feel his eyes, the same color and shape as his own, regarding him with thoughts that Haydon was inwardly frantic to hear expressed.

Then his father said, "It's a mistake, you know, to believe a man is only one thing. The human personality is too complex for that kind of thinking."

"I don't have any trouble with that," Haydon said, almost too quickly. He was irritated at the remark and, irrationally, at his father's emotional equilibrium. He breathed deeply of the night air and then straightened up and took off his coat and laid it over the balustrade, still avoiding his father's level gaze.

After a minute Webster turned too and rested his forearms on the balustrade, the two of them side by side, looking at the night.

"It is a rare man who actually is as he seems to be," his father said. It was an observation, almost as if he were talking to himself, reasoning it out. "Most men are either more or less.

Sometimes men willfully deceive us in this, sometimes we deceive ourselves. In fact, I think we are by nature inclined to self-deception, not wanting to see the reality because it's invariably complicated and we prefer to keep things simple, if at all possible." He paused, and for the first time Haydon was conscious of the crickets. "It seems to me," Webster said, "that it's an error of pride to believe we can fathom the absolutes of any situation, or of any man."

"I don't know what you're driving at," Haydon said.

His father ignored his petulant tone and touched the end of his cigar to the edge of the limestone, dislodging a gray cylinder of ash that fell into the darkness.

"You've chosen a hard profession, Stuart," his father said. "You're going to see a lot of peculiar behavior that you won't understand, and you'll see it so often you'll get to the point you can predict it. And then you're going to believe you *do* understand, and you'll want to pass harsh judgments. But the reality is that we can never really penetrate the truth of why some men do the strange things that they do. We can only view such men with pity and compassion, and remind ourselves that none of us are exempt from error, sometimes serious error, from playing the fool. When you look at these men try to temper your judgment with humility, with a modest nod to your own ignorance of the uncertain ways of the heart."

Chapter 9

THEY LAY IN BED TALKING FOR A LONG TIME, WATCHING THE RAIN ON the dark panes across the room. When there were intermittent downpours they unconsciously stopped talking and listened to it, each left to his own thoughts until the rain slackened and one of them picked up the thread of their conversation. Nina lay close to him, her head on his bare shoulder, an arm across his chest. The ceiling fan turned slowly, and he could smell her freshly shampooed hair. Sometimes he would move slightly just to be able to feel her body in a different way against his own.

She was worried about the photographs. He admitted that it was an odd occurrence, but insisted that it would be silly to interpret it as something ominous. He was sure Gabriela had her suspicions about what was happening, and if she had thought it was something threatening she would have said so. At worst, he guessed, the episode hinted at a family embarrassment of some kind. Maybe a scandal from the past that someone had reason to resurrect, thinking perhaps that Haydon would pay to have it kept quiet. He wasn't worried about the blackmail, he said, but conceded that he was more than a little curious about who was behind it all.

Nina wasn't fully convinced, but after a while she began to talk about how she couldn't conceive of his father having been involved in anything "scandalous." Such a thing was entirely incompatible with the man she had grown to love as her own father. Though the photographs did seem to suggest a relationship, even an affair, it was only a suggestion. Webster and the young woman weren't even directly linked. In fact, she said, it really was a weak association. She didn't see how anyone could expect to extort money on the basis of what they had seen so far. It was ridiculous. There wasn't even the appearance of Webster being compromised.

That was fine, he thought, listening to her, as long as she was thinking in those terms rather than in more foreboding ones. He, however, felt as if he were dealing with another dimension. Had Gabriela sensed anything ominous? It was difficult to imagine what she had felt as she looked at the photographs. He was convinced she knew the young woman, who, considering the approximated dates, couldn't have been much older than Gabriela herself. If she knew the woman, knew how she fit into the context of his father's past, did she also know, or suspect, who had sent the pictures, and why? Haydon could not believe Gabriela would remain silent regarding these possibilities, especially if she suspected malice was a motivating factor. It was going to be difficult for him to be patient with her silence, and if his suspicion that the next photograph would be considerably more explicit proved true, then he would no longer be able to allow Gabriela the luxury of coming forward with the information in her own good time.

He didn't know how long he had lain there pursuing his own ideas, but Nina hadn't said anything for a good while and her breathing had assumed the measured tempo of deep sleep. The insomnia that so readily plagued him was foreign to her. At the worst of times she might not sleep well, but she slept. Haydon simply lay there, watching the rain that trickled down the windows cast nebulous, drifting shadows upon the ceiling.

Moving his arm from around Nina's shoulders, Haydon gently pulled away from her. He lay still until her breathing regained its rhythm and then he got up. He stepped into his pajama pants and tied the drawstring as he walked over to the windows and looked out over the treetops. There was nothing to see but a vaporous darkness. He would have liked to have a cigarette, but it had been almost ten months now since he had quit, this time for good. Actually he had quit a couple of years ago, but had continued to smoke cigars occasionally, and now and then he had bummed a cigarette off whoever was nearby when he was tense or needed something to do with his hands while he waited. There was a lot of waiting in what he did. But now he didn't even have the occasional smoke. He was through.

His eyes dropped down to the terrace, and his heart

jumped. A splash of light glistened on the wet surface of the slate, like a thin, crinkly sheet of gold foil. It came from the library. He turned and grabbed his robe from the back of the sofa and slipped it on. Throwing a glance at Nina as he tied the sash, he gently opened the bedroom door and stepped out into the hallway. Hurrying to the head of the stairs, he paused, listened, then started down, the marble smooth and cool under his bare feet. When he got to the bottom he turned to his right and followed the broad hallway that stretched toward the terrace in the back. Halfway there, he saw once again a thin blade of bright gold cutting across the marble floor from the crack in the library door.

Approaching the door, he slowly eased it open and saw what he had expected: Gabriela, sitting in the light of a single lamp with the pictures scattered in front of her on the refectory table. She sat in profile to him, wearing a nightgown, her long brindled hair combed out full and wild over her shoulders so that the lamp behind her made him think of her as a figure in a Mexican *retablo:* an aging Madonna surrounded by the heavenly nimbus of her lighted hair. As he stood there, Haydon realized she was not looking at a picture now, but thinking, her head tilted a little forward as she rested her forearms on the table, her hands clasped together.

"Come. Sit down," she said to him without looking around. She reached out to the chair next to her, gave it a nudge, and patted the seat with her small hand.

Haydon did as he was told, not surprised that she was not surprised that he was there.

They faced each other, and he thought how pretty she looked. He was reminded of those bedtimes when he was a boy and she would come into his room looking just as she did now and sit on the edge of his bed, smelling of lemons, to tell him stories. It had been a time he relished, because Gabriela's stories were not the same ones his mother told from her own childhood in Scotland, nor were they like the stories he had read in the books his parents had given him. Gabriela's stories were more hauntingly exotic, even mysterious, about creatures and gods and places he had never heard of, and could hardly imagine: there were names like Daybringer, Cacao Woman, Blood Gatherer, One Monkey, Master of the Close and the Near, Seven Thought, Snatch-bats, and Yellowbite, who lived and roamed in the far regions of Broken Place, Bat House, Place of Advice, Red Road, Thorny Place, Region of Wings, Xibalba, and the Great Abyss of Carchoh.

Those nights he thought she was the greatest storyteller in the world. Her accented voice and expression of wonder fired his imagination and inspired him to conjure fabulous colors, sounds, and textures that he was sure he would never have known without her. She had been the myth-spinner, the dreamer of dreams, the keeper of strange flames. And now she was beside him again, looking as she had looked then, transformed once more into the fabulist from whom he awaited yet another story.

"I should have looked at them in the dark," she said of the photographs, smiling wanly at the weak joke. Her eyes turned to him. "I did not fool you, huh? Ah, *hijo*, you are too much for me."

She chuckled to herself, in a rueful way, it seemed to Haydon. He glanced at the pictures. Which ones had she wanted to see again, and why?

Gabriela must have read his thoughts. "I wanted to see them all again," she said. "You will understand. I know that much about you, anyway."

She turned to the pictures, surveyed them all in general, and sighed a shallow sigh. "You want to hear a story," she said. "About these." A hand opened, palm up. "Well, they were so long ago that maybe they were only a story to me, too. I think to myself, maybe I did not know this woman. I look at the pictures of her. I look at her eyes. I look at her smile. I even look at those beautiful breasts and naked legs. Did I know this one?" She nods slowly. "Of course I did. I knew her better than I wanted to."

All of this was said in a low, pensive voice, Gabriela swimming in the deep waters of the past, her hushed voice hovering over the rippling surface, soft as the lapping margins.

"Her name was Amaranta de la Sierra," Gabriela began. "After she married she was Amaranta Sarmiento de la Sierra. But that was later. The *amaranta*. Flower that never fades. Dark red, purple, like wine. Of course, you can see for yourself that this *amaranta* was a great beauty. God was with her mother when she carried that girl." She touched the photograph of the naked Amaranta. "But her father, he was an unlucky man. When he lay with her mother the devil gave him a wild seed. It was part of that girl from conception. There was nothing she could do about it, you know, just as she could do nothing about her beauty. A blessing; a curse. What could she do?" Gabriela shrugged. "*Ni modo*.

"Amaranta's father was very wealthy. I do not know how. He was with a bank or something, the government. She was educated at the National University. This was 1933, '34. She was very modern, and whatever Amaranta did all of the smart young people of Mexico City's high society wanted to do also. She was the gayest of them all. And the most elusive. There was no young man who did not have his eyes on her, but she would not give them any satisfaction. Because her family was wealthy, she had the luxury of doing what she wanted, and what she wanted was to be an artist. And, of course, she took lessons from the most famous teachers. Frida Kahlo, about the time she married Diego Rivera. Private lessons. Siqueiros. Artists were always in need of money, and she paid well.

"But that cannot be held against her. In fact, she was very talented. And these famous artists quickly proclaimed her a great discovery. Soon she was at the center of the artistic community, just as she had been at the center of the high society. She mixed the two worlds together. The family had a home in the heart of the old city, now the Zona Rosa." Gabriela tapped the photograph of Amaranta on the street corner. "Near here. They had another home in San Ángel, south of the city, and another one in Cuernavaca, which was then at its most famous as the weekend and holiday retreat of the city's society people. At different times Amaranta lived in each of these homes, and sometimes she even had homes of her own. Whatever she wanted."

Absently Gabriela moved the photographs of Amaranta side by side, aligning the corners of the three pictures, matching their edges, touching them for slight adjustments, her mind elsewhere. The rain had stopped outside, but a drip from one of the gutters was spatting with an even measure on a window ledge. There was no other sound. The entire house was waiting.

"It is too bad that these pictures are not in color. This way you do not see Amaranta's most striking feature. Never were there eyes like hers. Emerald. They would take away your breath." Gabriela smiled to herself, then looked at Haydon. "You know, the thing about Amaranta was that she was . . . in *color*. When you look at people, usually something strikes you about them. Some feature catches your eye, the shape of the face, something beautiful here, something not so pretty there. With her, you saw *color*. Green eyes, hair like cinnamon with streaks of the sun in it." Gabriela's delicate fingers came up to her face and moved airily. "Skin so . . . wonderful . . . so smooth and clear with, you know, places where it was a little bit different shade as if God had colored her himself, and sometimes you thought you could see into it. I remember, sometimes I could see, very faintly, a small blue vein near her mouth. It seemed just right, you know, like a clever beauty mark that Amaranta had thought of all by herself." She gave a little laugh. "I wonder if she ever knew that I would look at her so closely. Everyone did. You could not help yourself. Amaranta was created to be looked at."

The expression of pleasant reminiscence on Gabriela's face gradually disappeared as she looked at the pictures. She lifted a hand and began to massage her forehead, her elbow resting on the table. It was evident that either she did not want to say what she was going to say next or she didn't know how to say it. Clearly she wasn't finding it easy to begin.

"I just do not understand *why* you have these pictures," she said, frowning and cutting her eyes sideways at Haydon. "There was no letter, huh?" There was an accusatory tone in her question. "No little note or small something?"

Haydon shook his head. "Nothing."

"I do not know . . . for me this is not making too much sense." She shook her head. "I see no purpose for this."

Haydon remained quiet. There wasn't anything he could do to make it any easier for her even if he had wanted to, which he didn't. He wanted to hear what she had to say, and he knew she would find it next to impossible not to go ahead now. She was one of those persons who couldn't tolerate silence when someone had asked her a question and was waiting for her to answer. All of the coercion to talk came from within. It was in her own psychology.

"Well," she said after a while, "maybe I was not all the way honest tonight when you asked me how I met Mr. Haydon. It is true that your mother introduced me to him. That was exactly true. But, well, the truth also is that I had seen him before." She paused, looking at her hands where she was kneading the palm of one as if she were rubbing in lotion. "I had seen him many times before." She tucked her chin in as if she were holding her breath to go underwater. "In San Ángel . . . in Cuernavaca . . . in Coyoacán . . . in Mexico City . . . in all the houses where I had been a maid for Amaranta."

HAYDON WAS TAKEN ABACK, BUT HE SAID NOTHING. IT WAS BECOMING increasingly apparent to him that he was going to be traveling passages that up to now had indeed been secret. And he was beginning to grasp, uneasily, the fact that some of these corridors were going to conceal old bones, bones that he might one day wish he had never disturbed. Gabriela's restiveness was a warning that twisted in his stomach.

She shifted in her chair, tucked her nightgown around her more tightly, and sat up a little straighter, gathering new strength for her story. She looked at him as if she were waiting for his questions, and when he didn't ask any she looked down and moved one of the pictures a little. Realizing he was waiting for her to continue, she threw open her hands in an equivocal gesture and then dropped them to her lap and faced him a little more squarely as she rubbed the thumb of one hand over the fingernails of the other as if she were wiping something off of them.

"Well, I do not know," she said with a little lift of her shoulders. "There's so much that . . . where, you know . . ."

"I've got to admit," he said, hoping to put her a little more at ease, "that I'm surprised you'd worked for someone else. It's natural that you did, but it's interesting that I'd never thought of it before."

"Oh, yes, of course," Gabriela said quickly, relieved to have somewhere to begin. "I had my first domestic job when I was fifteen. All of us, my sisters and me, started at fifteen. Many of our friends began working much younger, but Papa was against it. At first I worked for a family who lived on Colima Street, near the parks on Cuauhtémoc, which was only ten blocks away from where we lived. So I walked to work in the mornings and then back at nights. Not too bad. But then I got a better job, with a family on the Avenida Chapultepec near

Insurgentes." She paused. "It was at this second home that I
first saw Amaranta. One of the daughters of that house had
been a classmate of hers at the university, and Amaranta
occasionally came to dinner.

"I remember that I had just turned nineteen at that time.
One day Amaranta came to the house and I answered the door.
I told her everybody was gone, and she said that was all right
because she had come to see me. Well, what happened was
she offered me a job. Twice the money to be *her* maid. I could
not believe it. You see, at this time Amaranta was, maybe,
twenty-three. She had completed her studies at the university
and was for the first time setting up her own house, living away
from her family. This was at the time when Frida Kahlo and
Diego Rivera had moved into their new, very modern—and
very strange—home in San Ángel. They were so famous. Frida
and Diego, nobody ever used their last names. Amaranta, of
course, had to live in the neighborhood too. So it was there
that I went to work for her in a wonderful old colonial house
that was the color of a faded pink rose. It was surrounded by
high walls that you had to enter through iron gates, and it had
a lovely courtyard and fountain. For me it was a dream. I lived
there too, since San Ángel at that time was still a little village
far out on the edge of the city. I went home for two days every
two weeks."

Gabriela paused, her head down and a slight smile on her
lips as she remembered. "Amaranta had such parties there.
Sometimes my sisters would have to come and help me. We
saw so many famous people. Writers, painters, photographers,
political activists. The poor little crippled Frida, so proud and
colorful, came often, and sometimes the toad-eyed Diego
came too. Juan O'Gorman. María Izquierdo, Lola Álvarez. I
saw Dolores del Río there. Amaranta had her studio on the top
floor, a large airy room where the artists would gather and talk
all night, smoking and drinking, playing their parts like
children. That is where I first saw your father."

Again Haydon was caught off guard, and this time Gabriela
saw it in his face. She nodded at him, waiting for the obvious
question.

"When was this?" he asked.

"1934."

"But that was before my parents married."

"Yes." She looked at him squarely.

"But I thought he had moved to Mexico City after they married, that he had been transferred there by Royal Dutch Shell from London."

"Yes," she said, nodding; then, shaking her head, she added, "But that was not the first time. He had lived there before he went to London, at this time that I am telling you about."

Haydon was bewildered. How was it that he had never understood this? Over the years he and his father had talked many times about those early days in Mexico, and somehow it had never been made clear that it involved two separate occasions. Had he been that unobservant? Or had his father deliberately deceived him? He really didn't see how he could have misunderstood, unless it had been meant that he should. What could have been so . . . wrong during that time that his father had wanted to conceal it?

"What was he doing there?"

"He was with the oil company."

"Then his father had gotten him the job with Royal Dutch Shell in Mexico first, not London?"

"I do not know the details. I guess so."

"How long did he live there, the first time?"

"Almost two years."

"From 1934 to 1936?"

Gabriela nodded.

Haydon couldn't believe it. He thought of the letters he had so carefully arranged in chronological order. It was true, he remembered no references to Mexico before his parents' married, and no letters to his father addressed to Mexico until after the marriage. How could he have failed to notice a two-year gap, or at the very least, an eighteen-month silence that had occurred between his father's graduation from law school and his move to England? He had noted that the correspondence was thin for the years he thought his father had lived in England, but what he had not observed was that the volume of the correspondence must have been sparse as a result of a total absence of communication during one particular segment of time: from the fall of 1934 to sometime in 1936. Whatever correspondence there might have been during that time had been removed deliberately from the family's papers.

"He never told me," Haydon said.

"It was a beautiful time for him, and very painful."

"What happened?"

"He was in love with Amaranta." Gabriela looked wistfully at the two portraits. "And she loved him. But she was not a simple woman to understand. She was almost . . ." Her voice trailed off and she stopped, sidetracked by a memory.

"What came between them?"

Gabriela looked at him. "Amaranta's wild seed. She would always do something that would hurt her, even when everything was going well for her, she would do something to bring it all down. The girl was emotionally . . . not unstable, maybe unpredictable is the way to say it.

"I saw Mr. Haydon for the first time at a big party in the rose house. All people from the art world and the high society. Amaranta's mixture. My sisters and I were always busy in the kitchen and going back and forth with food and coffee—they drank gallons of coffee—but we had such big eyes and ears. I saw many of these people as they came and went during the week, and I learned who they were. At the parties I would tell my sisters who was this, who was that. It was like watching movie stars.

"Your father caught my eye not only because he was a new face, but also because he was so . . . *elegante.* Ahh, he wore his clothes like a patrician, you know. Always since he was that young man he knew how to wear clothes. I do not know who he came with that night, but I think Amaranta did not invite him personally because I clearly remember seeing them introduced. From that very moment you could see they belonged together. I remember it exactly."

Gabriela was quiet, and then she got up unhurriedly and walked around to the French doors. She stood there with her back to him looking out to the terrace, and he heard her tapping idly on one of the small panes.

"They began an affair almost from that very night," she said, turning around and folding her arms. "But you have to understand about Amaranta. She had many, many men who wanted her. In those days it was not like now. To be intimate without being married—well, it was more rare. But in the artistic community maybe it was less rare than elsewhere. There were *intrigas amorosas*, some very complicated relationships. Amaranta was not promiscuous, but she was fiercely

independent and if she wanted to have someone then she had
him. She was a woman who denied herself nothing. Even
then, everything was on her terms. If she wanted the pleasure
of bed, then she had it, but that was all it was. No one really
possessed Amaranta.

"Until him. With him it was different, I think it was
his . . . *gravedad* that attracted her. He was such a kind
young man, but so serious. He was not a man who enjoyed
large parties, which Amaranta loved. She was radiant at
parties. Always at the center of attention, like the largest ruby
surrounded by little jewels. You could walk into a room and in
a glance you would find her. Mr. Haydon would never be in
those groups. He had a great disdain for that kind of fawning.
He visited quietly with this man or that woman, always a little
to himself." Gabriela shook her head. "Socially they were not
suited to one another. But when the last light went out, only
the two of them remained. Maybe it was because he was so
different from all the other men she had known, not a Latin
personality, I don't know. But Amaranta became very much in
love with this *norteño*. And yet, aside from the fact that they
both were very beautiful people, I could see nothing they had
in common. Whatever it was between them, it was private.
Whatever they talked about, whatever they did when they
were alone, it was *that* that bound them together. Only that.
But I can tell you, it was a fierce bond."

She came back around the table and sat down again, looking
at Haydon as if she wondered what he was thinking.

"How long did this go on?" Haydon heard himself ask. He
could not define what it was he was feeling. Gabriela's words
had created a swarm of reactions.

She thought. "Maybe a year, a little more."

"Did they live together?"

She shook her head.

"What came between them?"

Gabriela looked at the pictures on the table. "This I do not
know. I can tell you they were very happy. Until the bad
times. Of course, I am telling you this through the eyes of a
young girl. I do not know what happened out of my sight, but
I can tell you that their coming and going was happy. Then one
day, for maybe a few weeks, Mr. Haydon did not come to the
house. Amaranta was restless and short-tempered. When he

finally returned there was a little formality between them. But it soon passed and things returned to normal. Except now, every once in a while, there were arguments. I could hear them in the studio. After one of these I would see him leave, silent, very determined about something it seemed to me, and Amaranta would brood in her studio all day. Many nights after they fought she would go out to parties. Defiantly, you know. Sometimes it seemed that her anger was maybe against herself as much as against him. She was a person who offered herself many torments.

"I remember something else, too," she said solemnly. "It was after maybe their second or third big fight, at the beginning of the bad times. She had gone out again, but before she left she told me that if he returned to the house I was not to answer the door. And of course, it happened. When I heard the bell at the gates I hurried up to the studio, where there were very big windows looking over the street. I stood then in the dark and watched him at the gates, pushing the button, then looking through the iron grille into the silent courtyard. He looked up at the studio, but I stepped back. Finally, when no one answered he turned and walked away, passing under the street lamp, following the cobblestones down to Frontera Street. I felt such terrible anguish over what I imagined was his sadness."

She sat with slumped shoulders, thinking back. "That happened on three or four occasions. By this time their affair was a torment for them both."

She picked up the two photographs of Webster's portraits and held them in her lap.

"She painted portraits of him," Gabriela said. "Quite a few. When he left for England she went crazy. I do not think he told her he was going. A woman, another artist, whose name was Ada, came to see Amaranta one day. It was summer, and they were upstairs in the studio. They had been there only a short while when I heard Amaranta screaming and then there was a great commotion of things being thrown around. Suddenly I saw paintings falling past one of the downstairs windows into the courtyard. I watched her burn the portraits at the back of the courtyard, her green eyes flashing as tears ran down her face, her beautiful hair in tangles as she stabbed at the fire with a stick. It made a terrible black smoke. I thought she had burned all of them." She shook her head. "These two I never saw."

"They're not signed," Haydon said.

"Ah, I did not notice," Gabriela said without interest.

"But you think she painted these?"

"I think so, yes. I do not know why she did not sign them."

Haydon looked out at the terrace balustrades, glistening in the dark as if they were finished in lacquered ebony. The mantel clock struck once. He was always vaguely aware of the hour, since the mantel clock chimed the proper number of times on the hour and then once on the half hour. When it chimed once he didn't have to look up at it because he normally remembered what the hour had been. But in the middle of the day and the middle of the night he could be deceived: twelve-thirty, one o'clock, and one-thirty. All received only one chime, and he had to look, as he did now, to know the correct time. It was one o'clock.

"Mother knew about this?" he asked, without looking at Gabriela.

"Aha, you have hit upon a very interesting part of this story."

Haydon dropped his eyes from the clock to Gabriela. She was smiling with a decidedly amused expression. She lifted one of her hands from her lap and held an index finger up between them as if making a point.

"One day, a couple of years after Mr. Haydon had gone to London, Amaranta came to me and told me that she was going to move into a large home in Cuernavaca with some other artists. There were, I think, four of them. She would not be needing me anymore, she said, because there were already arrangements in Cuernavaca. She wrote an address on a piece of paper, an address north of Chapultepec in the very exclusive section of Polanco. She said the woman there needed my services, that she knew my reputation already and was waiting to interview me.

"Since my family still lived in the city, I packed up and went home for a few days before I called on the lady. I met her and we talked. She was very kind, not used to having servants, I think. We agreed on my pay, on my hours. She told me to come at a certain hour the next morning to meet her husband. When I arrived I visited with the lady in their front room. She brought me coffee and treated me as if I were a guest, not the maid she had just hired. In a little while her husband came in and I stood as she introduced me to your father."

"What?" Haydon was incredulous.

Gabriela chuckled. "I do not know. I do not know how it happened. While I was new with them I did not think it was my place to ask into the reasons of how this had come about. Later, it did not seem to matter. Our lives became the habits of a new household, your parents were very sweet to me, and the past did not seem important."

"No one ever said anything?"

"No one."

"Surely he recognized you from Amaranta's."

"He must have, yes."

"How did he conduct himself when he met you?"

"Kindly, as was always his manner with everyone."

Chapter 10

IT WAS NEARLY TWO-THIRTY BY THE TIME HAYDON GOT TO BED. NINA
stirred when he crawled under the covers, but did not waken.
Sleep was impossible. He lay in the dark, listening to the rain,
listening to the mantel clock chime the hours and half
hours, moving in and out of a state that confounded dream and
reality. Each time the clock chimed he was thrust into another
scene of his father's youth as narrated by Gabriela; sometimes,
omnisciently, he followed his father through the crooked,
cobbled streets of San Ángel, watched him with the green-
eyed Amaranta, watched him sitting alone at the smoky
soirées, watched him watching her from a distance, watched
him grow ever quieter and withdrawn as they were
pulled apart by their own divergent personalities despite the
enchantment of passion; and sometimes he became his
father, feeling the real and potent greed from the naked
odalisque, feeling the contradictory pains of attraction and
alienation, feeling the pull of his own identity that drew him
away from her, feeling the pain of loving what he could never
fully possess. There was soon no difference between himself
and his father; the rules of chronology and geography collapsed
and Haydon and Amaranta lived in a city where simply
walking around a corner or looking out a window could make
a difference of fifty years and a thousand miles. Nothing made
sense, and yet, for the first time, Haydon began to have the
initial glimmerings of understanding.

When he opened his eyes on Friday morning, he woke with
the same feeling of deliverance one normally hopes to find in
sleep. Even though it was midmorning, he felt as if he had
slept only a few stolen minutes. He was not surprised to see
that Nina was not in bed. Dragging himself from under the
covers, he showered, dressed, and went downstairs. Only

Gabriela and Nina were in the sunroom, the morning's papers scattered on the table as Nina had already turned her reading to the new copy of *Progressive Architecture* that had come in yesterday's mail. Gabriela, looking tired, was eating a croissant and staring out across the foggy grounds.

"I thought you were going to sleep all day," Nina said, looking up from her magazine and pouring him a cup of coffee from the pot on the table. "We've got a lazy household this morning. Ramona's still sleeping, and Gabriela just got down here. Did I miss something last night?"

"If you did you're lucky," Haydon said. "I don't think I slept half an hour all night." He didn't know how Gabriela would be feeling about last night, so he played it cautiously. He would tell Nina about their conversation when they were alone.

"It was not so good for me, either," Gabriela conceded, somewhat subdued. She ate the last bite of her croissant and wiped her hands on her napkin, then got up and went over to a large watering can she kept filled with rainwater near the back door. Quietly, she started watering the ferns and potted palms scattered along the glass walls.

Haydon felt Nina's eyes lingering on him before she picked up her own cup and refilled it as he buttered a croissant. He could depend on her to keep her suspicions to herself until later. They continued in silence, Haydon scanning the headlines in the two Houston papers and then reading the *New York Times* with the same superficiality. After a while Gabriela finished watering the plants, took her plate off the table, and went into the kitchen. Nina took advantage of her absence to nudge Haydon with her foot and frown quizzically at him. He shook his head, putting her off, and they both quickly returned to their reading as Gabriela came back in and got the coffeepot to make a fresh serving.

The telephone rang on a small table close by, and Nina picked it up. Haydon rarely answered the telephone when he could avoid it. The call was from Margaret, who was having trouble with a model. Nina discussed the problem with her in some detail, eventually agreeing to go in early to help her work through the rough spot, glancing at Haydon to see if whatever was going on was something she should stay home for. He shook his head again, and Nina told Margaret she would be there within the hour.

"Well," Nina said, hanging up. "Gotta go shower." She took one last sip of her coffee and picked up her magazine, pausing to look at Haydon. "Is everything all right?"

Haydon nodded. "I'll call you."

"This business with the model doesn't require any great concentration, but I've got to be there," Nina said. "If you get a chance, why don't you come by."

"I will," Haydon said.

Nina stood and kissed him, and walked out through the dining room.

When Gabriela returned with the pot of fresh coffee, Haydon put down his paper and looked at her.

"Have you got a minute?" he asked. Gabriela's face was mulishly impassive, as if she thought that if she pretended hard enough the whole awkward subject would go away. She didn't say anything, but gathered her skirt and sat in one of the chairs at the side of the table, not leaning back but sitting forward in a posture that indicated that this was only a temporary distraction from a busy schedule. Her gray hair, wavy at the temples, was pulled back in a loose bun. Cautiously she wiped her hands on the cotton apron around her waist and looked at him.

"I've got to go a lot deeper into this business between my father and Amaranta."

"Why do you have to do that?" she fired back suddenly. "Because of those pictures? What is going on with those pictures?"

"I told you: I don't know. But someone wants me to know something about all that. I don't know why whoever it is is going about it so . . . peculiarly, but there's no way I'm going to ignore it. I'm telling you right now I intend to find out as much as I possibly can about what happened to my father during those years. I want to know what's going on, too."

Gabriela looked at him, searching his eyes. He watched her face change, and for a moment he thought she was going to cry. She closed her eyes, put her elbow on the table, and rested her forehead on the base of her opened palm. He was surprised at this reaction, that she so quickly found herself in the position of trying to control her emotions. At last she put her hand down on the table and looked at him.

"There is more to this than you are telling?" she asked.

"I know nothing beyond what I've told you," he said. "But my gut tells me there's more. A lot more, and I think it's serious."

Tears quickly sprang to Gabriela's eyes, but she didn't give in to them, though it took her some time to recover as she looked away.

"Is Amaranta still living?" he asked.

Gabriela showed no surprise at the question, her eyes looking out to the dreary morning. "I don't know," she said.

"Is her husband still living? Sarmiento?"

"No. He died."

"Did she have any children?"

Gabriela nodded.

"Where are they?"

"In Mexico City. A girl and a boy."

"By Sarmiento?"

"By Sarmiento."

"Have you met them?"

"No."

"Did my father have any long-standing quarrels with anyone? Anyone who might have held a grudge over all these years?"

Gabriela shook her head.

"But you actually didn't get to know him well until after you both left Amaranta."

"That is right."

"Whoever is sending the photographs is mailing them from here in the city," Haydon reminded her. "Do you know anyone who lives here now who lived in Mexico during those years?"

Gabriela didn't respond immediately, but picked up the edge of her apron and began running its seams through her fingers, back and forth, back and forth.

"You should ignore these things," she said suddenly, dredging up one last burst of anger. "Leave it alone. This is a crazy person."

"How do you know?"

"Anybody ought to know that," she said testily, turning to him. "You have nothing to do with things that happened before you were born."

Haydon waited, watching Gabriela fighting tears again, seeming angry, and sad and fearful all at once. Finally she

snapped, "Mrs. Engenio Venecia. You go see her." She stood
abruptly and picked up the coffeepot, her attitude seeming to
soften as she did so. "Nothing good will come of this," she said.
"Nothing good ever came from Amaranta." She looked at him
with sad, tired eyes, and walked out of the room.

MRS. ENGENIO VENECIA'S NAME WAS IN THE TELEPHONE BOOK. SHE
lived near the eastern edge of River Oaks on a little street
called Troon, just off Kirby Drive. Her home was a large
Spanish-colonial affair on the high side of the street with a
sidewalk that led from the curb, climbed six or eight steps,
leveled off, and then climbed six or eight more steps to the
house. Haydon parked the Jaguar in front of the house and got
out in a driving rain. He took the sidewalk steps two at a time
up to the house and huddled under the shallow arch over the
front door as he rang the bell. It seemed a long time before a
black maid in a white uniform opened the door and gave him
a guarded frown.

"My name is Stuart Haydon," he said, automatically reaching into his coat pocket and pulling out his shield. "I'd like to
speak to Mrs. Venecia, please."

The maid hesitated, her eyes questioning. She looked a
second time at the shield and then reluctantly stood back to let
him step into a small entrance hall dominated by a tall gloomy
Spanish-colonial painting of a goateed grandee. The portrait
was laden with a heavy baroque gilt frame. She asked him to
wait and then disappeared through a living room furnished in
the colonial style, massive wood furniture and more gilt frames
from which brooding faces peered out through a veneer of
yellowing varnish. At the far end of the room, the smoke-
blackened mouth of a head-high fireplace presented a cold,
sooty backdrop.

Shortly the maid reappeared, approaching from the far end
of the living room.

"Mr. Haydon, if you would like to wait in here, Mrs.
Venecia will join you shortly." The maid's Spanish pronuncia-
tion was perfect.

He followed her into the living room and sat in one of the
elaborately carved high-backed chairs that she indicated for
him, and then she disappeared again through another doorway
that had not been visible from the entrance hall. Now he saw

other paintings, many modern ones hanging on the beige plaster walls. There were a few abstract pieces, and a striking Art Deco portrait of a woman he did not know, though he recognized the unmistakable style of the painter, Tamara de Lempicka, the exotic Polish artist who had spent the last years of her life in Houston and Cuernavaca.

He didn't have long to wait before he heard something that sounded like the jangling of a small chain against metal. It stopped, then jangled again. Stopped, then again; stopped, then again. From the doorway where the maid had exited, a small, elderly woman emerged with her hands firmly gripping an aluminum walker, which she lifted slightly and moved along in front of her. A long necklace of silver beads swung in front of her and made the jangling noise against the aluminum each time she leaned into the walker. She had a hunched back and peered up from a craned neck like a small, curious bird as she negotiated her way through the islands of bulky furniture.

Haydon stood and waited for her. She wore a black dress that fitted strangely because of her shape, and her short, gray-streaked hair seemed to have a mind of its own, drifting aimlessly in the general direction of the right side of her head.

"I'm not as old as I appear," she said, working her way to him. "I haven't had good luck these last years." Her voice was precise and softly accented, and her drawn face displayed an asymmetric smile. She stopped in front of another chair near Haydon's and looked at him.

"I'm Stuart Haydon," he said, stepping forward and extending his hand.

She studied him, still smiling, and offered her own frail claw. "I can see that," she said. "It's quite clear." She sat down on the soft cushion of the old wooden chair, but kept the walker in front of her, her hands resting on it, her face looking over the top. She wore a huge pearl ring on one hand, and an equally large amethyst on the other. His presence did not seem to be a surprise to her.

"I should explain . . ." Haydon began, but the old woman interrupted him.

"Gabriela called me," she said. "She explained, in a way, though somewhat breathlessly."

Haydon hesitated. "Well, she didn't explain much to me. I

don't really know your connection to all this, why she sent me to talk to you."

The old lady tossed back her head and laughed without making a sound. "Ah, I love it," she said, genuinely amused. "So . . . so typical of everything that has happened in this story. Not even death allows them any peace or clarity." She looked at Haydon, smiling still, her head nodding. "Before I married, my name was Suárez, Ada Suárez. I was a good friend of Amaranta's."

Haydon looked at her. "Ada," he said, remembering the name. "You're the one who told Amaranta that my father had left for England?"

"Yes." She bowed her head as if she were being introduced. "And unleashed a hellstorm of flashing green lightning. I recall it so vividly. It was wonderful. One of her best performances. It was a shame I was her only audience. But it became a famous story. I told everyone. I've told it hundreds of times."

"Why did Gabriela want me to talk to you?"

Ada folded her hands together, amethyst and pearl, blue veins and bone, and rested them on the aluminum walker. "First of all," she said, seeming to relish what was before her, "Gabriela has told me everything that's happened. She's called me twice, after the two of you talked last night, and then only minutes ago to tell me you were on your way over here. She told me about the photographs you've been receiving." She opened her eyes wide at him. "You didn't happen to bring them, did you?" she asked hopefully.

Haydon shook his head.

"Too bad! My God, I would have loved to see them. Especially Amaranta naked. She was magnificent! I've seen that one before, you know. Amaranta loved it. Your father had a marvelous eye with a camera."

"*He* took that picture?"

"Oh, yes." Ada closed her eyes, nodded, and then opened them. "He took it. Yes. And others. But he would have been furious had he known she showed them. He had this formal Saxon sense of propriety, you know. On the other hand . . . well, Amaranta was attracted to the visceral. There was a facet of his psyche that he hid from everyone but her. Only her. It was a curious relationship."

Ada held her head back and let her eyes close in a gesture

of weariness, then she opened them and smiled at Haydon. At least that is the way he interpreted her expression, though he couldn't be sure. Time indeed had not been kind to Ada. The flesh of her face was so furrowed, so awkwardly and thinly stretched over the frame of her skull, that it was sometimes difficult to discern whether a smile was kindly, or whether it was really a smirk, or even a grimace.

"I have no idea what the arrival of the pictures can mean," Ada said. "Gabriela told me about each of them. They seem harmless enough to me, as she described them. But she is frightened by them. I don't know why. It's the Indian in her, that sixth sense they have. I don't know; I think I would take her fear seriously."

"Who would have access to those photographs?"

"Good Lord, who knows."

"Wouldn't they be Amaranta's possessions?"

"I'm sure they were, at one time. But now?" Ada shrugged.

"She *is* still living?"

"Oh, most definitely."

"When did you last see her?"

"Years ago. Eight or nine years ago, I guess."

"Do you correspond with her?"

"Never."

"I got the impression from Gabriela that you were rather a good friend of hers."

"That was in another country."

Haydon looked at Ada's rings, at her silver necklace. "How did you happen to come to Houston?"

Ada provided the lazy-eyed smile again, the display of teeth and gums. "Well, you see, twenty-four years ago I finally managed to marry. The man was not extraordinary, but he was good. An importer in Mexico City, his business eventually brought him here. We had seventeen years together before he choked to death at dinner one evening. He was eating whitewing dove he had killed on a hunting trip to the Valley. He left me everything."

"Why didn't you return to Mexico?"

"I hadn't lost anything down there," she said in a tone of asperity. "Nothing I wanted to recover, anyway."

"Mrs. Venecia," Haydon said cautiously, "do you have any

idea why anyone might hold a grudge against my father from those days in Mexico?"

She shook her head, lowering it and swaying a little so that her silver necklace clacked against the aluminum walker.

"No. But then I'm not the person to ask," she added. "I didn't know him that well. Only through Amaranta. I know nothing of his business associates, nothing of his life away from her. I was her friend, and I saw him only at her parties, and occasionally during the days at her studio."

Haydon nodded. "How did Gabriela know you were living here?"

Ada crooked the wrist of her amethyst-ringed hand and pointed to herself. "Because of my own curiosity, fifteen years ago. When I moved to Houston with my husband—that would have been 1972—I was here only a few months before my curiosity got the best of me. I knew your father lived here, and I knew that Gabriela had been with him since he left Mexico. One day I called her up. I was going to ply her for gossip, but she wouldn't have it. I persisted for a while, trying for a few months to befriend her, but nothing ever came of it. She saw right through me, and besides, her loyalty was absolute. However, as the years passed I stayed in touch with some of the old group in Mexico and once or twice every year or so I would call her and tell her weddings-and-funerals gossip, always hoping I could pump her for some news of your father, which I knew would be relished back in Mexico. She always listened politely, but I never got anything out of her. Anyway, she knew where I was."

Ada paused, her lips slightly pursed around her prominent teeth. "And you know, she came to my husband's funeral. I had been so distracted I hadn't even thought to let her know. We weren't really friends, after all. But she was there. Came to the cemetery, too."

Haydon watched as Ada Venecia grew pensive and turned her eyes toward the great mouth of the fireplace. After a few moments her studied expression slowly changed to one of gentle amusement, some long-forgotten thought passing before the waning light of her memory like thin clouds drifting across a pale moon.

"Mrs. Venecia," Haydon said, interrupting her thoughts. "Are you aware of anyone else living in Houston, other than yourself and Gabriela, who was part of your group in Mexico during those days?"

"No one."

"Anyone related to that group, however remotely?"

She shook her head.

Haydon wondered how she could be so sure. He wondered, but for some reason he accepted her word. It seemed that if anyone knew, it would be Ada.

"Why did you laugh when I asked you if Amaranta has possession of these pictures?" Haydon asked.

Ada turned her eyes to him. "In her old age, I understand, Amaranta has become 'eccentric.'" She stopped and made a face. "What a joke," she said. "She was always eccentric! But . . . she has gone beyond that now. I heard she gave away one of her houses! That must have given her children a jolt. She has, or had, several houses. In these last years she seems to have been trying to get rid of everything from her past. She's burned letters, some canvases . . . photographs. She had hundreds of photographs. When her children realized what was going on, they naturally made an effort to stop her. Several years ago, her daughter moved in with her in her main house in San Ángel. Isabel now looks after her mother there."

"And what about her son?"

"Well, he certainly isn't going to live with the old woman," Ada huffed. "Saturnino! That boy was always a problem. Surly, moody. Ah! Nino never gave them anything but trouble. I guess there was too much of Amaranta in him. His father, Sarmiento, kicked the boy out of the family when he was a young man. Frankly, people thought old Sarmiento was always too hard on the boy, but in the end nothing could be done about it. The old man has been dead for years now, but Saturnino has continued to live on the edges of the family. There's a trust fund for him, I understand, but he's never used a dime of it. I think he refuses it to spite Amaranta. It doesn't make much sense . . . but they are completely confused people, all of them, and what makes sense to everyone else has no meaning to them whatsoever. And the other way around, too."

"Did Amaranta get along with him?"

"Listen," Ada said. "Realistically, no one could get along with either of them, so you certainly couldn't expect them to get along with each other." She shook her head and frowned. "Amaranta, actually, had a soft spot for the boy all the time Sarmiento was alive. Emotionally she gave him more than she ever gave anyone else. But he made it impossible. He was a hard one to love, even for his mother."

Haydon took his pen out of his shirt pocket and turned over one of the cards he kept tucked in the slot behind his shield.

"Would you mind telling me how I could get in touch with Amaranta?"

Ada reached into her dress pocket, apparently pressing a remote pager. Immediately the maid came into the room. "Sally, would you get my address book, please?" When the maid had disappeared again Ada fastened her eyes on Haydon and once more made the face he believed to be a smile.

"How do you feel about all this?" she asked gently. "About this secret of your father's?"

Haydon made a couple of marks on the blank card and shook his head, then looked up at her. "I don't know," he said. "I'm surprised, of course, but then he's surprised me before. Though not quite like this."

"You were very close to him."

"Very." Haydon was surprised to hear himself admit this so readily to a stranger. It must have shown, for Ada nodded with a knowing show of her teeth.

"Yes. You're so very much like him."

Haydon said nothing.

Ada leaned her head back, then looked at him with clear eyes. There was no trace of the smile. "Let me give you some advice," she said. "And contrary to popular lore, this advice is valuable. I know, because I have lived long enough to know. Do not judge him harshly, no matter what you might discover. In the end, compassion is the only thing that redeems us. And we all are in need of redemption."

Haydon was caught off guard at the sentiment, and the unmistakable tone of kindness in the old woman's voice. He thought she was going to add something else, but the maid appeared at the door, carrying a small and age-worn black book.

HAYDON SAT IN THE CAR STARING AT THE ADDRESS ADA HAD GIVEN HIM: No. 6, Plaza de los Arcángelos, Colonial San Ángel, 01060

Mexico, D.F., Mexico. He looked up and saw the wavering lawns and the rippling, tree-lined street through the windshield and remembered that it was nearing the end of the rainy season in Mexico City. He wondered about the rose-tinted colonial house in San Ángel, about its studio with ceiling-high windows and the women who looked out of them when it rained. He thought of the young man who had watched those windows from the cobblestone streets at dusk, and of the young maid concealed in the shadows peering down at him from the darkened studio filled with canvases, and the odors of turpentine and oils. He thought about the young Amaranta, about the old woman she had become, about her emerald eyes, and how they might have fared with the years.

From last night to this morning Haydon had been hit with a lot of new information, all of which he was having a difficult time assimilating. He was surprised, first of all, by the incredible fact of the missing years. He knew events could be hidden or exorcised from family histories, even significant events, but the obliteration of two entire years was extraordinary. Had his father done this with or without his mother's knowledge? Surely she had to have known about it. And if so, had she consented or had he done it on his own? Had this been a point of contention between them that he had never detected? He was incredulous, still overwhelmed by the existence of so great a secret kept for so long a time.

And then there were the allusive references to his father that seemed to hint that Webster had been even more of an enigma than Haydon had already believed. Both Gabriela and Ada Venecia had referred to his father's reserve, his *gravedad*, or as Ada had put it, his "Saxon sense of propriety." These were descriptions consistent with Haydon's own remembrance of his father. But then both women had used other phrases too, which had lodged themselves in his imagination. Gabriela had spoken of the privacy of Webster's relationship with Amaranta, that "whatever they talked about, whatever they did when they were alone," it was that which created the "fierce bond" between them. And even more intriguing, more to the point of Haydon's perplexity, was Ada's remark that "there was a facet of his psyche that he hid from everyone but her. Only her. It was a curious relationship."

These last words had burned in Haydon's mind when she

had spoken them, and they burned in his mind still. How much of this should he give credence to, coming from the memories of old women? How much should he attribute to the romance of remembering, and how much should he accept as accurate testimony? And even if he accepted what they had said at face value, how much of it could he assign to the energies of any young man in love for the first time, and how much of it could he consider the early, subtle limnings of a more curious side of his father's personality which would one day cause him to feel it necessary to erase two complete years of his life from the memory of others, if not himself?

Haydon had no answers, only questions, unsettling questions that he was compelled to pursue with a complex sensitivity that combined feelings of urgency and trepidation. From this point on, he knew he was entering a world of people and places and ideas that his father had not wanted him to know, and had even gone to great lengths to conceal.

He turned his thoughts to the present and reached into his coat pocket for his key ring. He put the key into the ignition and started the car, looking one last time at the dun-colored Spanish home of Ada Venecia. When he pulled away from the house, the rain was coming down in torrents. He made his way slowly back to Kirby Drive and headed home through streets that in some places were swollen to the curbs with swirling brown water, the fresh deluge having flooded the storm sewers and pushed up their iron manhole covers to spew like lowland geysers. The long-suffering traffic churned through the shallow waters and was occasionally stymied by wrecker trucks wrestling stalled cars from flooded intersections. Haydon's mind was elsewhere, and he moved through the laggard traffic with a detached preoccupation, arriving at the long boulevard of overspreading oaks without realizing how close he was to home—until he saw the mail truck, its delivery lights blinking, stopped between the stone pillars of the iron gates.

The mailman was hurrying back to his truck as Haydon drove up and stopped in front of the gates. They waved at each other as the mail truck pulled away. Leaving the motor running, Haydon put the Jaguar in park and got out in the rain.

He opened the mailbox from the outside, pulled out the manila envelope along with the other letters, circulars, and magazines, and ran back to the car. Dripping from the brief exposure, he sat behind the steering wheel, facing the iron gates through which he saw the curving brick drive leading to the front of the house. He laid the mail in the passenger seat, pulled out his handkerchief, dried his hands, wiped the water off the steering wheel, and quickly blotted the cuffs of his coat. Then he reached over and picked up the manila envelope.

With grim fascination he examined the envelope. He could not detect even the slightest deviation from the others. The precise, identical appearance of each envelope was beginning to have a disquieting effect on him. Not having his letter opener, he inserted the end of his fountain pen in the end opposite the brass clasp and tore the envelope as cleanly as possible. There was one tissue-wrapped photograph. Impatiently, he unwrapped the thin paper which had been taped at the back of the picture, slipped it off, and turned over the print.

What he saw hit him like a physical blow to his stomach, and he almost gasped, a convulsive wave of nausea rising from deep within him, his face flushing hot and clammy in the same instant. It was a photograph of himself, a radical and shocking departure from the others. He stood in his raincoat, one hand in his pocket, the other holding his trilby as he stared back at himself from the glossy surface of the paper, his eyes preoccupied, vacant, and unseeing as he looked directly at the photographer through the plate-glass walls of Mitch's Car Center.

But there was more.

With a black felt-tipped pen, a smoothly arcing, dotted line had been drawn depicting the trajectory of a bullet crossing from the left side of the picture entering Haydon's head through his right eye. A red felt-tipped pen had then been used to draw the resulting blast. But the explosion was not just a quickly tossed-off jumble of scribblings, rather it was a curiously stylized effluence of curlicues, tiny starbursts, spirals, and sparks, wedges of bone and tufts of hair flying from his skull in moist and graceful patterns. It was at once fanciful and macabre, and as he studied the picture he had the distinct feeling—or even more than that, a sure, intuitive knowledge—that the artist had immensely enjoyed depicting these grisly embellishments to his creative rendering of Haydon's death.

Instinctively he knew he was looking at the last photograph.

Chapter 11

IN THE CLOSE QUARTERS OF THE JAGUAR, THE DAMP MANILA ENVELOPE
filled the air with its distinctive, earthy odor, its peculiar smell
permeating every breath Haydon took and becoming, in his
mind, the scent of death, like the clayey must of graves
redolent with dread. After a few moments he overcame the
nausea, the feeling of claustrophobia subsiding as he forced
himself to slip the photograph back into the envelope, out of
sight. He laid the envelope on the car seat and stared out
through the rain hitting the windshield, through the opened
gates to the green oval of lawn encircled by the brick drive.
The old limestone house was slightly out of focus, as if it were
the setting in a hazy scene from a romantic European film.
Haydon wiped a hand over his face, unable to distinguish
between the rain and the perspiration.

It was not as though he had never received a death threat.
It happened sometimes, but they rarely were taken seriously,
being made as they often were by men who had come to the
end of their freedom. Haydon had never known a homicide
detective killed in connection with a death threat, but that was
little comfort when the threats came from the right kind of
people under the right circumstances. The faces of some men
were never forgotten, nor were the crimes they had committed. The details of what they had done never dimmed in
memory as did birthdays and anniversaries, or even the
fervent vows that were intended to last a lifetime. The
viciousness of these crimes imbued them with a vivid immor-
tality, and in the minds of the unfortunate men who investi-
gated them they often outlasted the memories of happier
events and kinder times.

But there was nothing of that here. This was a confrontation
altogether different from anything Haydon had ever encoun-

tered. It seemed to be motivated by remote events that occurred before Haydon was born, and yet because it involved his father it was at the same time deeply personal, even intimate. And as for the sincerity of the threat, Haydon harbored no illusions. He was faced with a series of decisions, and he had to make them quickly.

He put the Jaguar in gear, punched the remote control for the gates, and then realized they were already open. He looked at the gaping entrance, nothing between him and the house but the rain. He would have to do better than that, he thought, a hell of a lot better than that.

When he stopped under the porte cochere he turned off the engine and gathered the mail that was scattered on the passenger seat. He had no idea what else was in the pile of envelopes and packets, and he didn't care. He was already preoccupied, his thoughts disassociated from his actions, when he got out of the car and let himself into the front door, forgetting to remove his dripping coat and hat in the entrance hall. Tossing the mail on the small hall table, he carried the manila envelope into the library and walked directly to one of a pair of tall rosewood cabinets containing rows of small drawers. He reached up to the bookshelf beside the cabinet, took down a volume of Luis Borges stories, and let it fall open to a key. Unlocking the fourth drawer from the top, he placed the envelope inside and then relocked it, catching the smell of tung oil from the hand-rubbed wood as he did so. The key went back into the book, and the book onto the shelf.

This photograph he would not share with Gabriela or Nina. As far as he was concerned, it had changed everything. The tenebrous secret at which the photographs had seemed to hint from the beginning had become darker and more intriguing as a result of his conversation with the wizened Ada Venecia. And now, with the arrival of this last photograph, the dread was justified. Though this threat was easily the most bizarre he had ever received, he sensed that it was also the most resolute. Haydon's intuition told him this, but it was bolstered by two preeminent pieces of evidence: the intimate knowledge of Haydon's family history that had been demonstrated by the unknown correspondent, and the convicted intelligence that seemed to lie behind the elaborate scaffolding of the photographs' presentation. Considerable thought had been given to

Haydon's impending demise, and whoever was making the threat seemed to know him well enough to heighten his fear by manipulating a quality of his personality that was not only a great strength, but also a potential vulnerability: his curiosity.

"You are dripping all over the floor," Gabriela said. She was standing in the library door, hands on her hips, her tone of voice without accusation, almost gentle, as if she were trying simply to bring him back to the present.

Haydon looked down at the scattering of puddles on the marble around him, wondered what Gabriela would do if he showed her the photograph he had just put away, and proceeded to take off his trilby. He hung it on a large Mayan stone figure that stood near the French doors and then pulled off his raincoat, which he draped over a bronze hook on a nearby wall.

"I talked to Ada Venecia," he said, running the ends of his fingers over his temples.

"Did you call the lieutenant?" Gabriela intervened.

"Dystal?"

"Yes." She nodded at the yellow slips of paper on his desk. "He has called you twise in the las' hour."

Haydon frowned and walked around to the front of the desk and picked up the slips of paper. "What did he want?" he asked, looking at the notes.

Gabriela shrugged. "I do not know, but he said for me to tell you myself as soon as you came home."

"Thank you," Haydon said, and he watched Gabriela turn and walk away. The number was Dystal's office, but when Haydon called in the division operator told him Dystal was out and that he wanted Haydon to call him on the radio. Haydon picked up the handset, which he had left on the side of his desk, and called Dystal's number. After a few moments of static he heard the lieutenant's baritone.

"Twenty-one sixteen."

"This is Haydon."

"Yeah, good, Stu. Listen, huh, need you to come to 501 Stratford. It's north of Westheimer a couple of blocks, dead end to Baldwin."

"Okay, I know it," Haydon said, jotting down the address. "What's going on?"

"Little house here's a guy's office. He turned up dead on Brays Bayou late yesterday afternoon."

"Okay, I'm on my way."

Haydon didn't ask why he was being called in on his day off. If Dystal was on the scene, getting personally involved in the investigation, there was a good reason.

Stratford was a short street in the old Avondale section in the southwestern edges of downtown, close enough in for the sheer faces of the downtown skyscrapers to be an ever-present landmark over the treetops. It was a street of small wood-frame houses built in the thirties and forties, most of them now rental property, some of them derelict, a few of them being reclaimed by optimistic young couples with a missonary commitment to move back into the inner city and restore old neighborhoods. Not many blocks to the north was one of the city's largest and rankest slums; a few blocks to the south was an exclusive boulevard of grand old homes with manicured lawns and broad-canopied trees older than Houston itself. Avondale was neither here nor there, a neighborhood in limbo, its past forgotten, its future uncertain, its present without clear definition.

There was nothing remarkable about 501 Stratford. Haydon pulled to the curb across the street and looked over at the house. He recognized two unmarked department cars parked in front along with one blue-and-white. The front door of the house was open, and he could see men standing around inside, a patrolman leaning in the doorway looking out to the rain. Haydon tugged at his trilby and got out of the car. Dodging the puddles in the pitted asphalt, he hurried across to the buckling sidewalk that led up to the house. The patrolman spoke to him and stepped out onto the stoop to let him through the doorway.

Detective Alan Chesney stood inside the front room, which appeared to have served as a receptionist area, scribbling something in a pocket notebook.

"Hey," Chesney said, looking up at Haydon, who held his hat away from him in the doorway, letting his brim drip as he surveyed the sparsely furnished room. There was an old wooden office desk near the door, a couple of vinyl-upholstered armchairs against the opposite wall, and several filing cabinets on either side of a window framing the dirty plastic grille of an air conditioner. The wooden floors were gritty and blotchy with gray stains. The place smelled faintly of cats.

"What kind of business?" Haydon asked.

Chesney jabbed his ballpoint at a yellowing certificate on the wall above the old wooden desk. "Private detection," he said.

"What was his name?"

"Ira G.—Galin—Swain," Chesney answered, pretending to refer to his notebook, the thinning patch of hair at the back of his head tilted at Haydon. "Ira G.," he repeated idly, looking up and raising his eyebrows. Then he returned to his notebook. Haydon thought he seemed a little reserved. Chesney was normally a chatty sort, always ready to set aside the work at hand to exchange pleasantries and maybe smoke a cigarette.

Dystal's low, deep voice drifted through a door to Haydon's right. Haydon noted Chesney's diligent note-taking once again, then turned and entered a short hallway, which he followed to what would have been a back bedroom if it hadn't been Ira G.'s office.

Gus Cirano, Chesney's partner, stood beside another wooden desk, behind which Dystal had stationed himself in a tatty high-backed executive's chair. He was poring over a stack of files that must have come from the opened drawers of the army-green filing cabinets nearby. There was a dim light bulb in the ceiling fixture, but the center of the desk was bright from a tiny goose-necked Tensor lamp sitting to one side.

Cirano nodded at Haydon as Dystal closed the file folder he had been reading and handed it to Cirano, who turned and refiled it in the opened cabinet drawer. Dystal groaned and leaned back in the chair, which had a tuft of stuffing coming out of a hole in the vinyl behind Dystal's head.

"Guy was a private investigator," Dystal explained to Haydon, pulling a white pack of generic cigarettes out of his pocket and shaking one out. "Ira Swain," he said, lighting the cigarette. "You ever hear of him?" Cirano stepped past Haydon and left the room.

Haydon shook his head.

"Kind of an Irish-lookin' fat guy, built kind of toady. I met him once or twice. They found him on one of those residential streets off North Braeswood, one of those close down on the bayou. Kitchen knife sticking clear through his jowls, one side to the other," Dystal said, poking the left side of his own neck with a thick middle finger. "'Cording to the lady who called him in, Swain's car was parked in front of the house next door to hers yesterday morning when she left for work. She didn't think anything about it particularly. The house had been vacant for a couple of weeks. When she came home and the car was still there she got to wondering about it a little bit, looked out at it once or twice between TV shows, and then before she went to bed she decided to report it. Patrolmen got out there and found Swain slumped over in the seat, half off on the floor. Reed and Lopez caught it last night, passed it on to Cirano and Chesney this morning. They came over and started going through Swain's files."

Dystal paused and pulled on the cigarette. "Couple of hours ago they came across this." He took a closed file from under his elbow, opened it, turned it around on the desk, and shoved it over to Haydon.

He was astonished.

From where he stood he saw the exact photograph of himself he had pulled out of the damp manila envelope less than an hour earlier. For an irrational instant he thought Dystal knew about everything, the anonymous pictures, his father's affair, the death threat, and felt a flush of anger at the breach of privacy. Then he recovered and concentrated on the file. It was a thick one. He approached the desk and bent down and turned over the photograph, half expecting to see a portrait of his father, or the reposing, naked Amaranta. Instead it was another photograph of himself. In fact there were eight, all apparently taken with a telephoto lens like the first one: him talking to the groundskeeper in the apartment complex off Memorial Drive; standing at the doorway of the condominium on Westheimer talking to the elderly cousin of the sister of the convenience-store-shooting victim; a different shot of him at Mitch's Car Center; him sitting in the window booth at the seafood franchise; him walking across the street somewhere on Westheimer. He couldn't believe his eyes.

The thick stack of papers under the photographs tugged at him like magnets. Standing in his dripping raincoat, he began turning through the file page by page, amazed that this man Swain had managed to talk to so many people who affected his daily routines. It was as if someone had jerked a fist out of his stomach when he came upon the photographs of Nina, the house, even Gabriela and Ramona leaving the drive in their station wagon. Absorbed, he forgot about Dystal as he read photocopies of reports Swain had written to a Señor Barcena in Mexico City. He wasn't many pages into the file before he received his second shock. A letter to Swain from Barcena, signed *Nino* Barcena. *Nino* Barcena. Ada Venecia's disdainful words came back to him with cold clarity: "Saturnino! That boy was always a problem. Surly, moody. Ah! Nino never gave them anything but trouble."

Haydon's thoughts scattered and he felt a little light-headed, but he continued, mesmerized by this obscene intrusion into his life, as if the voyeuristic Swain had seen him naked and shared every detail of his anatomy with Barcena. He quickly passed over the newspaper clippings to Swain's reports of Haydon's reputation, hearing about his family, his father's business, his own inheritance, his interests, his penchant for privacy, even trivial details of his visits to art galleries and his preferences for Conté drawings and etchings.

By the time he came to the end of the file, which had been arranged back to front in chronological order, he had reined in his emotions, the kaleidoscope of feelings that ran from shock and fear to indignation and anger, and then the sudden horror that this might be only a fraction of what Nino-Saturnino/Barcena-Sarmiento really knew about him. When he closed the folder he did so with resolve, knowing now that he could not afford to hold anything in reserve. There was really only one way to deal with it.

"Know anything about this stuff?" Dystal asked. He had had time to smoke the entire cigarette and was mashing the butt in a glass ashtray.

Haydon stepped back and sat in a chair against the wall in front of the desk. He shook his head. "Swain was good, wasn't he." He could feel his heart rocking inside his chest.

Dystal nodded. "Yeah, he was." There was a pause as he measured Haydon's reaction. "The last entry was about three months ago. Don't know about those photographs. They recent?"

Haydon shook his head. "I'm not sure." He wanted to say no, but he knew better than that. They would be checked.

"You know this guy . . . Barcena," Dystal asked, leaning forward and reaching out to turn around the file again.

Haydon shook his head once more. "Never heard of him." He had the presence of mind to know that he had to be careful. He did not want to provide Dystal with any more information than he could garner from the present facts: that the recently murdered private investigator Ira Swain had compiled a file on homicide detective Stuart Haydon for a client named Nino Barcena of Mexico City. Until Dystal was privy to more facts than these, there was little he could surmise beyond these few details. Haydon did not want to be the subject of a death-threat investigation. If he allowed that to happen he would be opening his entire family history to outsiders. Not knowing himself why Barcena wanted to kill him, he sure as hell didn't want to share the investigation with the police department. It was personal and he wanted to keep it that way. But the only way to assure that was to conceal events of the past week, keep the threat itself a secret, and let the Swain investigation play itself out.

"Ever run across Swain?"

"I knew the name." Haydon was watching his fingers feel their way around the brim of his hat, and wondering if Dystal was already suspicious. "I was aware he was in the business."

Dystal nodded, letting his eyes rest on the blank front of the file as he pensively tapped it with a thick thumb.

"This looks like pretty sincere stuff," he said, looking up at Haydon. "Got any thoughts about it?"

"I'd like to know where this guy's been since that last entry nearly three months ago." It was a benign response, but the sudden appearance of the dossier and its familiar correspondent was a jolt, and Haydon wasn't sure he trusted himself to know how to act. He couldn't put the anonymous photographs and the conversations with Gabriela and Ada Venecia out of his mind, and he wasn't sure how he would have reacted to the discovery of the dossier if none of the rest of it had ever happened, if he had never heard the name Saturnino.

"Maybe the guy lost interest," Dystal said. "Maybe he's dead. On the other hand, maybe he doesn't live in Mexico City anymore. Generally I'd say it's a good thing, the file being stale. But with something like this . . . I don't know. There's lots of possibilities here."

"I'd rather that file wasn't kept with the rest of Swain's material at the office," Haydon said.

"I'll take care of it." Dystal slipped the folder back under his elbow. "You'd better take some time to look into this one," he added, getting back to the point.

Haydon nodded. He would have to go through the motions. "I'll put Barcena's name through NCIC." He knew it would yield nothing. "Interpol." Same results. "Then try the Mexican police. See what they can give me." That would take forever, if anything came of it at all.

Dystal was looking at Haydon with an emotionless expression that Haydon had seen often before. He was analyzing Haydon's reaction, and Haydon was thinking his performance was not convincing.

"Whatever you want to do about it," Dystal said slowly, his eyes on Haydon. "But if I was you, I wouldn't shrug off this one till I gave it a good going over." Then abruptly he shook his head and snorted as he took another folder off the pile at his elbow. "God knows how many people in all this crap had a reason to cut this guy. This one could take a while."

"I'd like to get copies of my file," Haydon asked, standing. "To know what he knows."

"Sure." Dystal tossed his head, wearily opened the folder, and leaned his elbows on the desk. Before he started reading he gave one last look at Haydon. "Check him out, Stu. Take it seriously."

Haydon turned and walked out of the office, leaving Dystal to his labors.

WHEN HAYDON GOT HOME, HE CLOSED THE DOOR TO THE LIBRARY AND sat down at his desk with the telephone book. It didn't matter that the last entry in the file was nearly three months old, though the lapse of time was curious. The fact was, Swain's interest in Haydon had been revived within the last week, whether on his client's behalf or on his own. Haydon remembered that the first photograph, the first portrait of his father, had appeared in his mailbox without a postmark. That was the single irregularity among all the photographs. It was obvious that the first envelope had to have been put in the mailbox by someone other than the mailman. Haydon was beginning to believe that "obvious" was the key word.

Remembering the clothes he had worn, the places he had gone, Haydon knew that the photographs of himself at the beginning of Swain's file had been taken on Wednesday—and that night Swain was killed. It could be that Swain had been killed for some reason totally removed from his recently revived interest in Haydon, but Haydon didn't think so. If he found what he was going to be looking for, he would know.

In reading the file in Swain's office, he noticed that whenever Swain had taken his investigation of Haydon in a new direction it was usually preceded by a brief letter from Mexico City requesting such information. Haydon hardly knew how to frame his thoughts about Nino Barcena, being convinced that he was in fact Saturnino Sarmiento, but not being convinced that such a conclusion was not precipitate. There was no such letter ending the three-month hiatus preceding the recent appearance of the photographs. Had Swain taken it upon himself to obtain the photographs? Haydon doubted it. Why would he? It was entirely possible that Swain's client was now in Houston and personally had revived the investigation. And it did not seem outrageous to believe that this same client also had been involved in the detective's death. In fact, Haydon was taking it for granted.

Haydon opened the telephone book to hotels, and began calling, putting a check mark beside the names as he called. It was a monotonous procedure and a long shot, but it had to be done, if for no other reason than to narrow down the possibilities. He always canvassed hotels by trying to put himself into the situation of the person he wanted to find. What was his economic status? What were his personal tastes within those financial limits—was he stingy or a spendthrift? Where in the city would he be conducting business? Would he be trying to hide, or was he unaware that he was being sought? Was he alone or with another person of the same sex or a different sex? How would he be traveling?

It was difficult to say whether any of this made any difference. Except for broad, commonsense guidelines (you didn't call the high-dollar hotels when you were looking for a skid-row suspect), most detectives felt that going from A to Z was just as good, or choosing the numbers randomly. In any case, Haydon's technique was of little help to him since he knew nothing concrete about Barcena.

He had called about three-quarters of the hotels and motels listed in the telephone book, checking the most prominent high-dollar ones first as he made repeated passes through the listings, gradually working his way down the economic scale, when he was startled to hear a phlegmy voice say,

"Not 'nymore. He's done gone."

Haydon stiffened. "He was? He was there?"

"'At's right. Was." The voice could have been a man's or a woman's, raspy and lifeless. "Ya missed 'im."

"When did he check out?" Haydon was leaning forward, the nail of his left index finger digging into the page under the address of the Rio Courts. He was gripping the telephone with his right hand as if it were a lifeline.

"Yesterday afternoon, twelve o'clock. Stayed to the last damn minute, too. Got 'is money's worth."

"Have you cleaned his room?"

"What? Cleaned it?" The voice smacked, eating something. "What, you want it?"

"Have you cleaned it?"

"Hey, who is zis?"

"My name is Stuart Haydon, with the Houston Police Department," Haydon said, frustrated at having to explain. "We've been trying to locate Mr. Barcena. It would be helpful to us if you have not cleaned his room. Has it been cleaned?"

"Police?" There was a pause; the voice was thinking, trying to put it all together. "Fact of the matter is . . . we have a policy, you know, to clean 'em right up. We call 'em 'bungalows.' But this's not exactly the busy season for us, an', well, I been a little under the weather emotion-wise, which, God knows, it's easy enough to do with this goddamn rain—not that I clean 'em myself, but I got to see it gets done . . ."

"You *haven't* cleaned his rooms yet?" Haydon could feel his neck tightening, pulling at his shoulders. Couldn't he get an answer to this one question?

"No."

Haydon closed his eyes. Christ. "Who am I speaking to?" he asked evenly.

"I'm the owner," the voice said defensively. "This's my place."

"What is your name, sir?"

"Lloyd E. Waycott." He spelled his last name and then repeated it.

"Mr. Waycott, don't touch Mr. Barcena's room. Do not go in it. I am going to drive over there. It's important that I see the room just the way Mr. Barcena left it."

"What's the deal? What'd this guy do, anyway?"

"I can't discuss that with you right now, Mr. Waycott."

"How'm I gonna . . . then I'll have to see your identification," Waycott said with a sudden sternness. "I cain't just let anybody in there, you know."

"Of course," Haydon said. "That won't be a problem."

"Then when're you coming?"

"Right now."

While Haydon had been on the telephone the weather had grown worse. A blustery wind had picked up and was throwing sheets of rain across South Main as Haydon spotted the Rio Courts with its jittery neon sign and two rangy palms leaning inward toward each other on either side of the sign. He pulled the Jaguar off the street and onto the crumbling asphalt drive in front of the flat-roofed stucco building that was the motel's office. Through the office's rain-spattered plate-glass window Haydon could see the owlish face of an older man peering out at him from over a local boxing-match poster taped to the inside of the glass. As Haydon reached for the door handle to get out of the car the man moved away from the window and retreated behind the sales counter.

The wind and rain slammed into the glass door as Haydon forced it closed behind him and stood inside the motel office looking across the counter at a seemingly belligerent Lloyd Waycott and his wife, a woman of uncertain will who stood slightly behind her husband with an expression of general anxiety.

Haydon reached into his coat pocket and produced his shield as he introduced himself. Waycott examined the shield and worked his mouth in judgmental configurations as his wife stayed back and looked at Haydon over her husband's shoulder.

"You gonna tell me what the guy did?" Waycott asked with a gruffness he seemed to hope would get results. His rubicund face was lumpy in a lopsided kind of way, as if he had an uneven distribution of welts from bee stings. The sweet smell of bourbon hung in the air with Waycott's breath.

"I'm sorry," Haydon said, taking back his shield. "I'm not allowed to talk about it."

For a moment Waycott regarded Haydon with a scowl and then said, "I can unnerstan' 'at. There's gotta be rules." He turned and took a key from a pegboard on the wall behind the counter. "Come on," he said with a swaggering attitude, as if he had just been deputized. "Let's go take a look at that bungalow."

Haydon followed Waycott past his shrinking wife, through the back room of the office where there was an ancient Coke machine and a variety of mops and buckets and other janitorial supplies, and out the back door, which the wind slammed shut behind them. Tilting his head sideways against the rain, Waycott stomped past a barbecue pit made of an old oil drum and crossed the asphalt drive, brashly splashing through puddles he easily could have avoided, to apartment number five, directly behind the motel office. Rain ran off the flat roof of the bungalow and splashed muddy water on the pea-green pants leg of Waycott's jumpsuit as he wrestled the key into the deadbolt of the door. Finally he shoved the door open and the two men entered Barcena's ground-level bungalow.

"This is it. Just like he left it," Waycott said proudly.

The small apartment was dingy and stale-smelling. The bed had been slept in, but the covers had been thrown over the pillows in a reflexive gesture of neatness. Newspapers on a small telephone table near the glass-louvered windows had obviously been read, but had been refolded and assembled in a neat stack. Half a dozen small roaches moved in and out among a few dirty dishes on the tile cabinets, and the sink faucet dripped into a coffee cup overflowing with discolored water. Haydon stood still, his eyes moving over the details of the bungalow with deliberation, as if he were trying to recall the physical presence of Barcena. The heavy odor of old tobacco made his eyes seek out an ashtray and confirm his guess that Barcena had smoked filterless cigarettes. With his hands in his raincoat pockets, he walked over to the edge of the cabinet and bent down to the ashtray. Pall Malls. He straightened up and looked at Waycott.

"I guess he didn't say where he was going after he checked out," Haydon said.

"Yeah. 'Smatter of fact, he did. Goin' home, he said. Back to old Mexico. But he didn't look like a Mexican much, not like an illegal or anything."

"He didn't say where in Mexico?"

Waycott shook his head.

"Did he fill out a registration card when he checked in?"

"Yeah."

"Is his address on there?"

"Yeah. I remember somethin'."

"I'll need to get that from you when I leave."

"Sure," Waycott said. "Yeah, that'd be a good way to track 'im down."

"Thank you," Haydon said. "You don't have to stay."

"Hey, I don't mind," Waycott said. "You might . . ."

"It would be best if I did this alone," Haydon interrupted.

"Oh, yeah. Sure. Well, then I'll be gettin' that registration card for ya."

"I'll be over there when I'm through," Haydon assured him, his eyes already scanning the rooms again. As Waycott opened the door and closed it behind him, the wind whipped cigarette ashes out of the ashtray onto the chipped tile cabinet.

Alone, Haydon moved away from the doorway to the cabinet. He took a pair of latex surgical gloves from his rain-coat pocket and pulled them on. He examined the dirty dishes. He picked up a glass in the sink beside the coffee cup and held it up to the leaden light that came through the closed glass louvers. There were vague lip smears around the top of the glass, but that was all. He turned and walked around the corner between the unmade bed and the flimsy desk and stopped, his attention arrested by the odd sight of a stained cloth draped over the face of a mirror that hung above the desk, the top edge of the cloth tucked between the mirror frame and the wall. He leaned closer to the cloth, saw that it was a pillowcase, lifted one corner of it, and looked underneath at the speckled mirror. Then he saw the cheap glass vase with a couple of wilted marigolds in murky water, and the scratched surface of the desk littered with shriveled, butter-colored petals. He looked on the floor and there were more petals, a pile of them, many more than could have fallen from the wispy pair of flowers in the vase. Suddenly, without any clear correlation, these two incongruous discoveries gave Haydon a feeling, a sense, of the irrational.

This gut feeling of eeriness was intensified when he moved away from the desk and went into the bathroom. A threadbare towel hung over the medicine-cabinet mirror above the sink. When Haydon opened the cabinet door the towel fell into the rust-stained basin. The condition of this mirror was even worse than the one around the corner. The cabinet was empty. He turned and bent down to the trash can, where he found a few tissues, a used razor blade, the paper wrapper off a bar of soap, and a cellophane wrapping with its red "open here" tab. He couldn't determine what had been packaged in the cellophane. Pulling aside the shower curtain, he looked in the shower, saw a washrag hanging over the shower nozzle, and took it down. Holding it by its corners, he unfolded it and let it hang open as he turned it around and examined both sides. He cautiously smelled both sides, then refolded it and returned it to the shower nozzle.

The bed would be the next place. He went straight to the nearest side and bent down and smelled the pillow and the sheets near the head, then rounded the bed and did the same to the opposite side. Standing up, he looked around the rooms. He could think of no other place. He was satisfied that Barcena had not been with a woman. In fact, he saw no evidence of two people having been there at all.

Returning to the tiny kitchen, he looked through the cabinets, noticing that the bungalow was furnished with serving and cooking plates and utensils. Except for the few dishes in the sink, Barcena seemed to have been a fairly neat occupant. Haydon looked through the small refrigerator. Barcena had not eaten a wide variety of food. From the empty carton of a dozen eggs in the trash and a second carton in the refrigerator with only two eggs left, Haydon surmised that Barcena had fallen back on the easily prepared omelette as a staple diet during his stay. Omelettes and beer. The empty egg carton in the trash was wedged in among a thick jumble of Tecate bottles. He turned to the drawers in the cabinet where the cooking and eating utensils were kept and went through them carefully. He made a mental note and closed them.

Moving across to the small table beside the bed and

windows, Haydon picked up the folded newspapers and spent
the next few minutes spreading them out on the bed and going
through them one page at a time. Nothing was missing,
nothing was marked, nothing was there. He put the papers
back on the table, made a mental note of the telephone
number, then noticed a small foil pellet on the cement tile
window ledge. Carefully he unfolded the tight ball, saw that it
was the top paper-and-foil covering of a new package of
cigarettes, and rewadded it and put it back on the window
ledge. Looking at the ledge more closely, he found a few
shreds of tobacco and some scattered ashes. There was a
puzzle-pattern of interlocking circular water marks where
someone had repeatedly set down a sweating glass, or a bottle
of Tecate. Apparently Barcena had spent some time here,
perhaps with the louvers open, looking out at the rain. It was
hard to pass time in a strange city.

Haydon looked under the bed, but found nothing; went
through the empty drawers of a chest, but found nothing.
There had to be more, something else. Barcena would not
have relied on anything so risky as Haydon having to ask the
right questions of the manager of the Rio Courts. So far
Barcena had depended upon Haydon having a modicum of
investigative skills, but only a modicum. He had not been
subtle to the point of endangering the continuity of the leads,
and Haydon had no reason to believe he would suddenly
refine his technique at this point. There was still something in
the bungalow.

Shedding his raincoat and opening the glass louvers for air,
Haydon proceeded to spend nearly half an hour checking the
obvious (between the mattresses, inside the pillowcases, behind pictures, in the commode tank, inside lampshades, inside
the freezer of the refrigerator, the bottoms of drawers, chairs,
and sinks) and the obscure (in the cracks along the kickboards,
behind the covers of the electrical outlets, the cracks between
the cinder-block walls and the steel window frames, under the
yellowed shelf paper of the cabinets), without success. Baffled,
then angry, he stood in the middle of the bungalow and made
one last visual survey, 360 degrees, and decided Barcena had
not followed through. There should have been something, one
more enticement, one more seductive curl of the finger to

keep him coming. But there wasn't. The only things of interest had been the covered mirrors and the profusion of marigold petals on the floor beneath the desk. They didn't tell him much of anything.

He took his coat and hat off the bed and put them on, cranked the louvered windows closed, and walked outside. The blustering wind had died again, and he followed the asphalt drive around to the front of the office in a light rain. When he stepped into the office once again, Waycott immediately reached under the counter and laid a white card on the scarred Masonite surface.

"Took ya a while, huh?" His face seemed freshly stung and his eyelids a little heavier. There was a stronger smell of bourbon hanging in the air. "This's his registration card. His address is on there all right."

Haydon took out his pen, but before he looked at the card he said, "Do you keep track of the amount of plates and cooking and serving utensils you provide in the kitchenettes?"

Waycott looked at him. It didn't seem like a detective-type question. "Well, yeah," he said. "Damn right we do."

"The same amount for all of them?"

Waycott gave a snappy nod. "That's how we keep track," he said. "Three of everything. Of the plates an' cups an' forks an' spoons an' stuff, I mean—they're double-occupancy. That's one extra. We come up missing we bill the sons-abitches."

"What about knives? Do you furnish carving knives?"

"Carving knives?" Waycott seemed unsure of the term. "Each bungalow gets one butcher knife. They can 'carve' with that." He grinned lopsidedly.

Haydon nodded. Waycott was going to have a hell of a surprise when he found out what had been carved with the butcher knife that was now missing from bungalow number five.

"I'm going to be sending our lab technicians over here to go through the bungalow—this afternoon or tomorrow. I want you to leave it as it is. Don't go inside. Okay?"

Waycott nodded briskly, a deep frown demonstrating he was aware of the gravity of the situation.

Without saying anything more, Haydon looked down at the

registration card. Sr. Saturnino Barcena, No. 43 Avenida Sarmiento, Mexico, D.F. 01060, Mexico.

He stared at the card. Then he slowly screwed the cap back on his ink pen and put it in his shirt pocket. It wasn't an address he was likely to forget.

Chapter 12

THOUGH IT WAS MIDAFTERNOON, THE SKY HAD GROWN GLOOMY AND heavy, the lowering clouds glowing from within with a hint of a sickly green aura that changed to stone gray as the rain began to fall again. Haydon stared past the clean sweep of his windshield wipers and watched the drops of water on the glass turn cherry then white as they picked up the taillights of breaking traffic in front of him and then the headlights of the cars from the approaching lane.

With the limpid understanding of hindsight, he was reviewing what now had become the obvious. Saturnino Sarmiento had been a formidable player, and Haydon had felt the full force of his cunning. So completely had Haydon responded to his manipulations that it was almost as if Sarmiento had crawled inside Haydon's body and acted his part for him. It had been a virtuoso performance.

His first move had been to let Haydon know straight out that they were actors in a play, the tempo of which was dictated by the measured arrival of the photographs. It was a bold tactic, not a stealthy one as it had seemed from the outset. Sarmiento was declaring and not declaring. While everything had not yet been revealed, there was no doubt that a revelation was taking place in the form of a modern mystery play, a drama in which the allegorical images in the photographs were locked in a struggle for Webster Haydon's memory. And yet, at the same time, Haydon had been mistaken to have believed that the photographs were the play itself. They were only the opening flourish, a leitmotif that would double back upon itself again and again as Haydon was coaxed to learn of a hidden episode in his father's life.

The very first indication that Sarmiento had planned his strategy far ahead of the events had been the absence of the

postmark on the first manila envelope. Haydon had recognized
it as an anomaly from the beginning, but it became a crucial
clue, a small tension-heightening touch, only after he had
received the last photograph with its life-threatening message.
That small detail then became a warning that danger was close
at hand, had been, in fact, at his very doorstep. It was the same
kind of perverse inspiration that caused Sarmiento to mail the
photographs without any kind of traceable identification,
knowing that he could rely on Haydon's curiosity and investigative instincts, and on his close relationship with Gabriela,
who would eventually provide the background Haydon
needed.

Perhaps Ira Swain's role had been the biggest gamble, but
even there Sarmiento had hedged his bet by selecting the
right man for the job. Most private investigators would have
tipped the police to anyone wanting to compile a dossier of this
intimacy and scope on one of their detectives. Not Swain. He
had kept his mouth shut, either because the pay was too good
to turn down, or maybe because he was hoping eventually to
parlay the information into something with even greater
rewards. It was more likely the latter possibility that earned
Swain the knife in the neck. Sarmiento didn't seem to be the
type to sit still for blackmail.

On the other hand, there was the matter of Haydon's dossier
in Swain's file. How could Sarmiento have overlooked it? Why
hadn't he ransacked Swain's office looking for it? Surely he
must have known a man like Swain would have kept a
duplicate file. Haydon could only believe that Sarmiento had
wanted it to come to light to serve, perhaps, as yet another
goad to Haydon. It had been a big risk, but so far Sarmiento
hadn't flinched at taking risks.

Finally, everything had been brought out in the open when
Sarmiento used his real name as the address of Nino Barcena.
It was as if he had stepped forward in the wings, just out of
sight of the audience, but in full view to Haydon, who was still
on the stage. At last he had revealed himself, and with a
taunting gesture had challenged Haydon to take the drama
into one last, and as yet unwritten, act. If Haydon wanted to
discover the answers to all the questions that had been laid
before him during the last five days, if he truly wanted to know
the why of it all, he would have to stay on stage to the end,

alone, and let Sarmiento direct him from the darkening wings.

Alone. That was a key ingredient, and Haydon felt it as surely as he felt the real danger he would be facing if he took up the dare that Sarmiento was clearly offering. Here again, Haydon wondered if Sarmiento had engineered the circumstances. Because this entire series of events revolved around Haydon's father, Sarmiento—understanding Haydon's near obsession with privacy—could be assured that Haydon would do everything in his power to keep it out of the way of an official investigation. He could be assured that Haydon would approach the events that would eventually result in a confrontation between the two men in a manner that would attract as little attention as possible. As badly as Haydon hated to admit it, Saturnino Sarmiento had anticipated every move Haydon had made, each of which had lent itself to the ultimate intent of Sarmiento's design. It was almost as if Haydon could not choose an independent course, one that Sarmiento had not already predicted. It was as if Sarmiento had been at every turn before him, had foreseen the only possible choice Haydon could make, and then had planned his next move accordingly.

The oppressive thought crossed Haydon's mind that his role in the coming events was predetermined. It was a thought that left him feeling at once queasy and defiant. From this point on he would have to play his role with an even greater indebtedness to Sarmiento's plotting, for it would be on his schedule and on his stage that the rest of the drama would be performed. The most Haydon could hope for would be that his own inner instincts for innovation would not desert him once he had entered Sarmiento's world.

At no particular point during his drive back from the Rio Courts did Haydon consciously decide to go to Mexico City. It did not seem to have been a decision at all, but simply came about as the next phase in a course of events that he accepted unquestioningly. Aside from the personality of Saturnino Sarmiento, aside from the web of hidden answers he had spun around himself in the hopes that Haydon would become inextricably entangled, there was the even greater lodestone of Amaranta's presence. Now that Haydon knew of her existence and of the central role she had played in his father's life, there was nothing that could stop him from going to see her. It was an attraction that had little to do with reason, logic having been dislodged by emotion and curiosity. In the back of Haydon's mind there still rested the small kernel of adolescent yearning, the longing to resolve the mystery of his father's stoic gaze when their eyes met in that silent and misunderstood communication across the hot distance of summer light so many years ago. Despite their closeness, or maybe even because of it, there always had been a measure of emptiness between them, a void that Haydon believed his father had created and sustained to prevent a true intimacy between them. Now Amaranta had emerged like an exotic flower from the dark soil of his father's past, and it seemed to Haydon, however irrationally, that one riddle might well enlighten another.

Once he was back home, Haydon wasted no time. Remembering to leave his hat and raincoat in the entrance hall, he walked straight to the library and over to his desk. He sat down and took a yellow pencil from a small clay jar, one of a variety of similar containers of undetermined age that his father had collected from all over central and southern Mexico, that sat toward the back of the desk with Adelson's *The Pathology of Homicide* and the OED. He quickly jotted down the mental notes he had made driving back through the rain, the telephone calls he needed to make and the order in which he needed to make them. The first call was to confirm Sarmiento/Barcena's departure for Mexico City. He hit with the second call. Saturnino Sarmiento—he had already switched personas, confidently assuming, Haydon guessed, that by now Haydon would know whom he was looking for—had flown out on Aeromexico's flight 690 for Mexico City at one-forty in the afternoon on the previous day.

The second call was to Jack Crowell at Southwestern Bell's central metropolitan exchange. Crowell was one of those rare and valuable contacts that only existed because an old friend just happened to have worked his way into a position crucial to Haydon's profession. Men in such logistically advantageous positions could not be cultivated for their usefulness, they simply were there or they weren't. In addition, Crowell knew the true meaning of "unofficial." Haydon asked favors of him sparingly, and when information Crowell had given him led to evidence that had to go on the record, Haydon always backtracked and filed formal requests to cover for Crowell's out-of-channels assistance. Now Haydon gave Crowell the number from the telephone in Sarmiento's bungalow and asked if he could get the out calls from Monday through Thursday. Crowell said he would get back to him and Haydon hung up.

While he waited, he pondered the best way to pass the information on to Dystal. Technically he was already dangerously close to obstructing justice by withholding information that would directly implicate Sarmiento in Swain's death. However, he had to consider the realities of making this a legitimate homicide investigation. The evidence of Sarmiento's role in Swain's death soon would be incontrovertible: Sarmiento's client relationship with Swain would be discovered; Sarmiento's fingerprints in his bungalow would be matched with those on the butcher knife taken from the bungalow and later found in Swain's neck; and almost certainly additional corroborative evidence would come to light as this accumulation of facts gave the investigation leverage. Even though Sarmiento would be indicted, it was only a remote possibility that Haydon would be allowed to pursue him into Mexico. And even if he was, he would not be permitted to go alone. Beyond that, there would be no way they could avoid having to work with the Mexican police, a Byzantine experience by anyone's standards, and it was a sure bet that from the moment he entered Mexico City Haydon would be tailed. It would be an impossible arrangement, doomed from the beginning. Nothing would be resolved, no practical purpose would be served.

And none of this even took into consideration the fact that Haydon's family history would come into it as a matter of public record. Even if Haydon could tolerate all the other frustrations, this he could not allow.

When the telephone rang he picked it up and listened as Crowell read off the calls Sarmiento had made from his bungalow. There were only four: two to Swain's office, and two to Aeromexico. The man had stayed in that dismal little bungalow at least five days, maybe longer, and had made only four calls, two of them to book his flight out. Haydon tried to imagine Saturnino's solitary figure sitting by the opened glass louvers, looking out at the rain, smoking. Thinking.

Haydon picked up the telephone again and called his travel

agent. He booked a flight to Mexico City late the next morning and reserved a room on the seventeenth floor of the María Isabel-Sheraton downtown on the Paseo de la Reforma. Next he called Wes Tate, who he knew had Sundays and Mondays off, and then Hink Mills, who was off on Tuesday and Wednesday. After some negotiations, both men agreed to trade days off with Haydon in the coming week.

With Bob Dystal, however, Haydon had more trouble. Even over the telephone Haydon could hear the edge of wariness in the lieutenant's barrel-chested baritone. Haydon didn't create a complete fabrication—it would have been too easy for Dystal to check it out—but he did find it to his great advantage that on the one hand neither Nina nor Gabriela knew about the file in Swain's office and on the other hand Dystal didn't know about the anonymously posted photographs. And none of them knew about the pictorial death threat. Haydon told Dystal that he was simply acting on Dystal's admonition of that morning to take the existence of the file seriously. He said he knew some people in Mexico City who might help him learn something about Barcena without his having to get formally involved with the Federal District police, and he wanted to give it a shot. He knew Dystal would understand the efficacy of this kind of discretion, and he knew that by and large Dystal would trust him not to do something foolish. As far as the police department was concerned, Haydon was off duty.

"There's just one other thing," Dystal said.

Haydon hadn't forgotten. "They're posting the lieutenant's position on Monday and I'll be gone," he said.

"That's right, and you're not going to be back until Thursday. That gives you four days after you get back to give them an answer."

"I've thought of that," Haydon said.

There was a long pause, and Haydon knew what Dystal was thinking, that he wanted to ask Haydon if he had talked it over with Nina. The silence between them seemed to last a long time, and then to Haydon's relief Dystal finally said, "Okay, Stu." His voice had the flat tone of resignation. "Keep your head down, and check in with me on Thursday."

When Haydon hung up the telephone, he had nearly five full days to try to do something about Saturnino Sarmiento.

* * *

A SMOKY EVENING LIGHT HAD SETTLED OVER THE CITY, A SWARTHY stillness hovering near darkness. There had been no real dusk for weeks now, the murky rainy weather having completely eliminated the gradations of dying light so that night came suddenly and unannounced out of the prolonged gloom of gray days.

For once, Haydon was too preoccupied to notice. Sitting at the refectory table in the glow of the green-shaded lamps, he was finishing writing in the small leather pocket book in which he kept addresses and notations about people and places in Mexico City. The notebook, periodically updated, included the names of persons Haydon had known all his life, men and women his parents had known when they had lived there just after they were married and with whom his family had kept in touch over the years, visiting them regularly during vacations as long as Haydon could remember. Even after Haydon married, he and Nina often joined his parents on their trips to Mexico to see their old friends. But in the six years since their deaths Haydon had not kept up the close contacts. With some there was still the ritual exchange of Christmas cards, the occasional note regarding the illness or death or change in fortune of people whose lives had touched his only through his parents, and yet they wrote him, Cordelia and Webster's son, a part of them still through ghosts and memories.

Now he had added Amaranta's home in the *colonia* of San Ángel to the address book, and was making sure that the information regarding U.S. contacts—the law enforcement liaison at the American embassy, the DEA office, an artist who lived in the Colonia Roma, the ex-HPD homicide detective who had moved there several years ago after marrying a woman from Cuernavaca—was current. The list was varied and several years old, and Haydon did his best to bring it up to date by entering changes he had known about but never recorded and by using directories and making a few telephone calls.

When he finished, he turned and laid the address book on the corner of his desk and picked up the five envelopes with their photographs that were still sitting on the refectory table, where he had stacked them in chronological order. He methodically removed each photograph and on a single sheet of blank paper wrote a description of the photograph and the date on which he had received it and put the sheet of paper into the envelope. After he had done this for each of the five photographs, he got up, took the key from the Luis Borges book, and removed the last photograph from its drawer in the rosewood cabinet. He followed the same procedure as with the others and then put all six envelopes into the cabinet drawer and locked it, returning the key to the Argentine. He put all six photographs in an acid-free archival envelope that was heavy enough to travel well and closed the flap with a quick wrap of its nylon string.

Taking the envelope and notebook, he walked out of the library and into the hallway, glancing through the dining room and catching a glimpse of the brightly lighted kitchen doorway from which issued the faraway voices of Gabriela and Ramona, preparing dinner. He continued on to the curved stairway, which he climbed distractedly, his thoughts already gravitating to the smoggy streets of Mexico City.

Tossing the photographs and address book in an armchair in front of the bedroom windows, he went to one of the closets and took out his old leather suitcase and opened it on the bed. Standing beside the bed, he reached around and unclasped the Beretta from the waist of his pants at the small of his back. The drug wars in Mexico had put a lot of strain on the informal twenty-year agreement between Mexico and the United States allowing U.S. federal agents to take their firearms into Mexico. Several times within the past two years it had looked as if the agreement would be suspended because of tension between the two governments. But regardless of that, metropolitan detectives had never been allowed that privilege even in the best of times. It was an offense of considerable seriousness to be caught on the other side of the border with an unauthorized firearm, and Haydon had taken his with him on only two or three occasions, each time without the department's knowledge and always at his personal risk, knowing he could not expect help from the department if he was caught. This time, however, he didn't feel he had a choice.

Using a coin from his pocket, he unsnapped a catch designed to look like a rivet on the wide side of the suitcase's hinged bottom. He opened the compartment with its "pocket" designed for the Beretta and ejected the clip from the handgun before he laid it into the depression. He put the clip in its fitted slot across the top of the gun's barrel, and snapped the cover closed. Years ago he had had this compartment made just for this purpose. It was not the sort of deception that would have survived a professional search, but it sufficed for its purpose, to get through the cursory inspections that luggage received going into Mexico from the United States. Returning to the States was another matter, however, and Haydon usually brought the gun back in air freight.

Suddenly the bedroom door opened and Nina walked in. She stopped a couple of steps inside, a roll of drawings in one hand and the smile on her face already fading as she looked from Haydon to the suitcase on the bed, and then back at Haydon.

"Going somewhere?" The flippant question was meant to cover the anger reflected in the now stiffened smile. Haydon knew she had already guessed what was happening.

"Mexico City."

"Tonight?"

He shook his head. "Tomorrow morning." He moved around the end of the bed and gestured toward the sofa. "Come on, let's sit down. I'll tell you what's happened."

There was a lot to tell, and Haydon himself was amazed at all he had learned during the last eighteen hours. He told Nina of waking during the previous night and finding Gabriela in the library and of their subsequent long conversation with all its revelations. He told her of his follow-up conversation with Gabriela that morning after she had gone to the office and then of his visit to Ada Venecia and all that she had related. With deliberate attention to every detail, even his own ambivalent feelings as he listened to these two old women uncover layer after layer of his father's curious past, he told Nina everything. He did not want her to think he was leaving anything out, nothing to rouse her suspicion that he was hiding something. His only desire was to make her believe that the only reason he was going to Mexico City was that he had an irrepressible desire to learn as much as he could of these new revelations of his father's past. Which was true, up to a point. He stopped with his visit to Ada Venecia, as if that were all he had to say.

When Haydon had started talking Nina had sat across from

him with one leg characteristically folded under her on the sofa, as she toyed with a single hairpin she had taken from her chignon without bothering to take down her hair. She gave him all her attention with an attitude of forbearance, as if she would listen to his story but knew beforehand its culmination would be the dropping of the other shoe, the sound of something she would not like. But as Haydon spoke her posture relaxed and her face softened as she let down her defenses and then became absorbed, her cynical expression replaced by genuine attentiveness and fascination. By the time he stopped she was mesmerized.

There was a brief silence before she said, "That is an absolutely astonishing story." She let her hands drop to her lap. "Can you imagine something like this having been kept quiet all these years? And Gabriela! What an incredible secret for her to have kept."

"I don't find her role in this particularly puzzling," Haydon said. He was leaning forward in his armchair, forearms resting on his knees, idly moving his blank signet ring around on his finger. "To her it was all over with. The past best left to the past. Daddy was dead. Mother was dead. So what did it matter? Why would she ever need to bring it up? Also there was the fact that apparently Daddy didn't want me to know about it. This business of his condensing the two different times he had lived in Mexico when he talked to me, it's pretty obvious now what he had been doing. And I'm sure Gabriela was well aware of it at the time. If that's the way he wanted it, then that's the way Gabriela was going to keep it. I understand her perfectly in that respect."

"And I guess your mother knew what he was doing?"

"She must've."

"What an extraordinary collaboration," Nina said softly, thinking of it.

"Yes," Haydon said. "That bothers me a little, I'll have to admit."

"Bothers you?"

"Yes. It's not that they had a secret and kept it. It's the collaboration, among the three of them. You know, thinking back, I'll bet a lot of those stories he used to tell me actually took place during the time of his first residence in Mexico, Amaranta's time. I wonder how that made Mother feel when he did that? You'd think it would have made her uncomfortable. But I don't remember ever sensing any tension regarding those stories. None at all."

"It's . . . well, it's hard to believe," Nina said, frowning at him.

Haydon nodded. "It is, but I believe every word of it." He paused. "As far as it goes."

Nina looked at him. "That's what this is all about, then?" she asked, tilting her head toward the suitcase on the bed. "You're going to try to find out . . . what?"

"As much as I can. Everything. I want to talk to Amaranta. There are hundreds of questions. I want to see her studio in San Ángel. I want to see her paintings, or what's left of them. There are bound to be letters between them. She couldn't have destroyed everything."

"What makes you think she'll even consent to see you? Shouldn't you write her first, request an appointment?"

"I don't want to give her the opportunity to turn me down," he said, shaking his head. "That'll be a lot more difficult to do if I'm standing at her front door."

Nina didn't respond to this last statement. She had grown quiet, her eyes having settled on the spangled panes of the windows that faceted the darkness outside. Haydon looked at her, saw that she had grown pensive, that something had changed. He hardly had time to anticipate her before she said,

"That's not all there is to it, is it?"

He tried to deflect her suspicion.

"No. I doubt it." He paused. "I think when I finally get to the bottom of this I'm going to discover a very strange story. I guess I'm a little taken aback. I'm more than a little apprehensive at the prospect of uncovering something about him that promises to be . . . maybe shocking. Beyond that . . . I don't see anything beyond that."

This last statement, at least, was straightforward. Beyond the vague feeling that a scandal lay at the bottom of all this his imagination failed him.

"I don't mean that," she said. She turned her eyes to him. "I mean this sudden departure. What we've talked about so far, it's not that urgent." She stopped. "What about the photographs. Did you get another one today?"

Haydon met her eyes, watching her watch him, assessing

his reaction to her question. Cynically he felt he had nothing to fear from such an assessment. He had too much experience; lying was part of his expertise. And working in his favor also was the cruelest advantage of all: he knew she didn't want to believe he would deceive her.

"No, nothing," he lied. He could feel the pull on his eyes coming from the heavy, archival envelope on the other armchair across from them. "And that's something else," he said, digging in deeper. "I don't think there will be any more photographs. It's a hunch. I can't explain it, but I'll be surprised if anything else turns up." He hesitated. "And even if something does, it won't matter. I don't know what kind of foolishness lies behind those photographs, but I do know that I've got to meet Amaranta. Regardless of any of the rest of it."

This much was not deception. Amaranta had hardly been out of his thoughts since he first heard Gabriela speak her name the night before. Even when he was lying, he wasn't lying. The things that drew him to Mexico were potent attractions, compelling and addictive seductions: curiosity and fear. Even when he lied, he wasn't lying.

Nina had not taken her eyes off him. "You've talked to Bob Dystal about this?"

"Of course. I had to get permission for the extra time off. Actually," he said, trying to cover every angle, "I didn't want to go into it with him. I just told him I had some personal business to look after." She still seemed to have something on her mind. "I'll be back in plenty of time to make a decision about the lieutenant's position," he added.

But her concern was more immediate. "I'll tell you something, Stuart," she said evenly. "If you don't call me every night, if I haven't heard from you by the morning of every single day, I'm going to go straight to Bob Dystal. I'm going to tell him everything that's happened. I'm going to tell him I think you've lied to me about what you're doing down there, and that I think you're in danger." She paused. "I'll do it in an instant and I won't give it a second thought. No hesitation whatsoever."

Haydon heard the rain, listened to it pelting the Belgian slate roof outside the windows. She simply had told him what he could expect. Instead of accusing him of misrepresenting his intentions, of duplicity, she had decided to act alone as if they were acting together. If he wasn't lying then he shouldn't object if she acted accordingly. It was her right to worry. All she was asking him to do was reassure her. It was an ordinary request.

"Fair enough," he heard himself say.

Chapter 13

THE FIRST OILY TENDRILS OF OCHER SMOG THAT CONSTANTLY enveloped Mexico City could be seen creeping toward the foothills as soon as the descending plane approached the upper reaches of the Valley of Mexico. The city that lay in the womb of the valley, in the dry bed of Lake Texcoco at 7,350 feet above sea level, was a true monster of the twentieth century. It was a metropolis that could be described best with superlatives: with a population of over twenty million, it was the fastest-growing metropolis on the face of the earth and demographers had already predicted it would become the world's largest city before the turn of the century, its population swelling past thirty-two million; it was the world's most polluted city; it ranked first in the world in the amount of acreage given over to slums; it was the oldest constantly occupied city in the Americas; it boasted the world's cheapest (and arguably one of the most efficient) subways; and it operated (or tried to operate) a telephone system that was a top contender for the world's worst.

Haydon had a lifelong knowledge of this sprawling, out-of-control megalopolis and an alternating affection and abhorrence for all that it represented. When he had first visited there in the late 1940s, the city was situated quite comfortably in the old lake bed although its population had already reached two million. The urban area extended only a few blocks past the Merced Market on the east, stopped at Chapultepec Park on the west, had not yet encompassed the village of San Ángel to the south, and did not extend beyond the Avenida Río Consulado on the north. You could still look toward the pine forests that surrounded the city and see beyond them the majestic snowcapped volcanoes Iztaccíhuatl and Popocatépetl riding high in the lapis-lazuli sky. In those days you still breathed crisp, clean mountain air and the afternoon siesta was an accepted necessity.

Today, however, Mexico City spread out like a gargantuan, teeming ant bed and covered a land area of more than six hundred square miles. The marshy lake bed had been drained long ago in the interest of progress and expansion, and the resulting imbalance in the ecological system had turned parts of the valley into a desolate, alien landscape. Because it was surrounded by mountains—some peaks nearing eighteen thousand feet—the city was constantly smothered by thermal inversions which trapped an unbelievable quantity of pollution generated by the exhausts of more than three million vehicles. Every day a staggering daily production of nearly twelve thousand tons of metals, chemicals, bacteria, and dust poured into the thin atmosphere of the urban basin from more than 130,000 industries. The result for the population was a plague of respiratory ailments, and for many, a chronic condition of burning eyes, sore throats, and skin ulcers.

Adding to the pollution were the *tolvaneras*, annual dust storms that whipped across the Valley of Mexico from the east and northeast in the early months of each year, their gritty, suffocating clouds often permeated with dried excrement and bacteria from the open sewers of the slums which occupied vast, barren stretches on the eastern margins of the city. In the city's seven major—and colossal—open-air dumps and in its thousands of smaller ones, spontaneous methane fires often smoldered for weeks at a time, sometimes making it necessary to temporarily evacuate nearby slums, while in some areas much of the eight thousand tons of garbage produced daily was simply tossed into the streets, where it accumulated in rotting piles, its choking stench attracting swarms of rats. More than a third of the city's residents lived in poverty, and more than half earned less than the minimum wage of three dollars a day and had no running water in their homes.

Mexico City had become a grotesquerie.

And yet, as if still clinging to the dualism that pervaded the ancient Aztec theology that had flourished in the once-beautiful Valley of Mexico six hundred years earlier, the city had another face. In 1803 the famous German naturalist and traveler Alexander von Humboldt wrote, "Without a doubt, Mexico must be one of the most beautiful of the cities founded

by the Europeans in either hemisphere." Despite the horrors
brought on by modern urbanity, it was still the "City of
Palaces," an appellation it had earned by the late nineteenth
century because of its rich architectural heritage. Though the
city enjoyed a kind of wild architectural eclecticism from Aztec
to High Tech, it was most strikingly marked by its colonial
past, a city intoxicated with its vivid history. Broad avenues
alive with the color of the flowers and semitropical trees that
flourished in the temperate climate crisscrossed the urban
valley, and practically every neighborhood, or *colonia*, had a
quiet plaza of its own where families and children and lovers
could find brief refuge from the city's harsher realities. And in
the western and southern portions of the city the slums of the
east side were little more than slightly disturbing dreams,
easily forgotten. Here, in the pine-covered foothills overlooking the steep ravines where tall eucalyptus trees swayed in the
variant breezes coming off the mountains, the wealthy lived in
unabashed splendor on winding tree-lined avenues in districts
with the lyrical names of Lomas de Chapultepec, Lomas Altas,
Palmas, Bosques de las Lomas, and Jardines del Pedregal.

The plane pushed through the smog to Benito Juárez
International Airport, and Haydon was jolted back to the
present as the tires hit the tarmac and the roar of reversing
engines filled the cabin. He waited until the plane had
emptied and then followed the others through the corridors to
the customs booths, where he surrendered a carbon copy of
his visa to the uniformed agent and then followed the crowd to
the baggage claim, where he grabbed the old leather suitcase
off the conveyor belt. In the main concourse of the congested
airport he stopped at an exchange booth and picked up a
couple of hundred dollars in pesos, and oblivious to the
crowds, made his way to the nearest exit.

Outside the temperature was easily fifteen degrees cooler
than it had been in Houston and the humidity eighty points
drier. He stopped at the ticket window that brokered fares for
the thirty or forty cab drivers waiting for their numbers to be
called as they hung around an assortment of large, small,
clean, dirty, new, and battered cabs of various makes, their
only common attribute being that they were painted yellow
and had some kind of driver. Haydon bought a ticket to the
María Isabel-Sheraton in the heart of downtown.

Over the years he had made many trips in taxis to and from the Juárez International Airport, and he knew when the driver hustled out of the crowd and grabbed his ticket and suitcase and led him out of the shade and into the jaundiced afternoon haze to a small but clean Volkswagen beetle that they would be taking a ride through the city's heart. It seemed a general rule that the larger cars, a Mexican-made Ford or Chevrolet or Chrysler, would take advantage of a longer but quicker route like the Circuito Interior expressway, while the smaller cars, the majority of which were Volkswagen beetles with the front passenger seat removed to facilitate easy access to the three-passenger rear seat—a tiny step-in limousine—would take the labyrinth of interior city streets which provided an endless variety of routes through some of the city's oldest and poorest *colonias*.

His driver, a rail-thin man with coarse hair, an Indian face, and Virgen de Guadalupe tattoos on both forearms, crossed himself and kissed his thumbnail before starting the car. Three plastic statues shared their mobile altar space on the dashboard with the photographs of young girls and a small plastic plaque that read: "Holy Virgin preserve my life on these streets for the sake of my daughters." The driver turned on his radio, and with a reckless nonchalance entered the melee of Mexico City traffic. Haydon settled back, his suitcase on the seat beside him, having learned from experience to let fate take care of the backseat driving, and squinted into the greasy air, laden with the stench of diesel fuel, that whipped in through the front passenger window. He resigned himself to it. As long as he was in Mexico City he would draw very few breaths that were not saturated with that smell.

The city's layout owed more to romance, emotion, and caprice than it did to logic. Overall it was divided into *delegaciones*, which were like wards and served as boundaries of areas of local government. Within each *delegación* there were neighborhoods, or *colonias*, with no specific boundaries or official purpose. But over the decades the city had grown to such gargantuan dimensions that it seemed to have outstripped the city officials' abilities to think up new names for the increasing numbers of *colonias*, and so now there were many of the same name: six called Las Aguilas, seven El Rosarios, nine named after former president Benito Juárez, eleven named after the revolutionary hero Emiliano Zapata. And often these *colonias* of the same name were also in the same *delegaciones*. To make matters even worse, most of the streets in the city had more than one name (usually many names), often changing names as they passed through different *colonias* and sometimes changing names within only a few blocks. And as with the names of the *colonias*, there were many streets by the same name, as well: there were forty-four Guerrero streets and 115 Vicente Guerrero streets (many of which would be called simply Guerrero by the residents of its *colonia*). Knowing which of the 159 Guerreros you were talking about at any given time depended on where you were standing and the context of your conversation. For nonresidents of the city, and for many of its natives too, it was necessary when inquiring about a street to know which *colonia* and which *delegación* you were asking about as well as which street. It was a nightmare system for anyone not familiar with the city (and even for most who were), a system that raised the metaphor of the city as labyrinth to a higher level of meaning. Sometimes it bordered on the abstract.

As he looked out the grimy Volkswagen windows at the moil of Mexico City street life, Haydon thought of this and how it was going to complicate his efforts to locate Saturnino Sarmiento. The driver cut through the narrow streets of Tepito, the oldest and one of the poorest and roughest *colonias* in the city, where black market smuggling was the major enterprise and a common adversity united the people with fierce loyalties that produced an insular distrust of outsiders. At the intersection of the famous Paseo de la Reforma the driver turned south and headed down the grand avenue. Despite the ever-present overcast of smog that made so many Mexico City days seem as if it were under a solar eclipse, Haydon thought the Paseo was one of the most elegant boulevards in the world.

The María Isabel was still undergoing the last of its repairs and remodeling made necessary by the damage it had sustained in the earthquake of 1985. Most of the work was being done on its north side where Río Danubio separated the hotel from the adjacent U.S. Embassy, an inconspicuous, blocky white building with a facade of gray iron bars along the shrub-crowded sidewalk that fronted the Reforma. Haydon rode the elevator to the sixteenth floor, where the concierge for the Towers section of the hotel held his reservation.

Within minutes he was opening the curtains in his room, looking down to the Paseo de la Reforma, a view he never tired of seeing. Considered the city's main street, the Reforma was a beautiful twelve-lane boulevard running generally north and south, its esplanades crowded with rangy palms and camphor trees and grassy plots with park benches. The long, straight course of the boulevard was interrupted occasionally by *glorietas*, or traffic circles, which circulated around a variety of fountains, statues, and monuments of significant personalities and events of Mexican history. The most famous of these monuments was just outside Haydon's window towering high above the traffic, the golden angel of the Monument of Independence.

Loosening his tie with one hand, Haydon looked at his watch. He had had to take a late flight out of Houston, and it was now a little after six o'clock in the afternoon. Mexico City was on approximately the same latitude as Bombay, but its high altitude provided a year-round temperate climate. Between late May and early October it rained practically every day, but only in the late afternoon and early evening, a natural cleansing that made for refreshing nights. As Haydon stood at the window, he watched one of these rainstorms push through the gray haze and move northeastward across the grimy city, darkening the sky in a bruised light. Now and then he could catch glimpses of the blue foothills below the peak of the Cerro de Tlaloc. As the rain moved in a backward slant across the skyline, the streetlamps came on and the headlights of the cars on the Reforma made yellow streaks on the wet pavement.

He pulled a chair up to the window and sat down, his forearms resting on the railing below the window as he stared down to the street. Now, looking at the city, he was less sure of himself. He felt a vague uneasiness, the feathered edges of doubt. Maybe it was because of the gloom that was settling over the city in the rainy dusk, and the fact that he was still disconcerted by what he had come there to do. It had been only hours since he first learned of the strange Amaranta and the part she had played in his father's past. Maybe it was only that, an uncomfortable peace with a new knowledge, a feeling that he had never really known his father at all. Or maybe it was the valid tremor of his sixth sense, a feeling that in this city things could easily get out of control, that the surreal was in fact reality.

HAYDON TURNED AWAY FROM THE WINDOW AND WENT TO THE telephone near the bed. He took his address book from his pocket and found the number he called every time he came to Mexico City. He listened to the circuits connecting, then silence, then the dial tone again. He redialed. This time he heard the telephone ringing at the other end of the line, and then a woman answered. Haydon asked if this was the Arreola law firm and the woman said no, was that who he wanted, the Arreolas? He said he was trying to reach the Arreola law firm. She asked if that was Renaldo Arreola, she didn't know he was in law, the one with the blond wife? If he wanted that Arreola she could give him the number of her sister-in-law's sister who used to let Renaldo and his wife use her telephone because they lived in the same apartment building. She probably could tell him how to find Renaldo. Haydon remembered the old joke that in Mexico City the best way to meet a stranger was to call a friend.

The telephone system was itself a joke. Always a poor and antiquated service, after the earthquake of 1985 it suffered a disruption from which it may take decades to recover. There were only three million numbers available to serve twenty million people, and hookups were so difficult to obtain that when a private line was finally installed in a residence it was usually considered a permanent part of the property. When the house was sold, one of its major selling points would be its private line, an amenity which could demand a healthy premium. Because of this, the infrequently printed city directory was woefully out of date, and *chilangos*, as Mexico City residents were called, tended to know something about the previous owners of their line, because those persons continued to receive calls there for months and even years afterward. The convenience of the telephone was something the city's residents did not take for granted.

Finally Haydon said no, he was looking for another Arreola, apologized for disturbing her, and hung up. On the third try he reached the firm, gave his name to the receptionist, and asked for Gaston Arreola. The response was immediate.

"Stuart, *mi hijo*! You are in Mexico?" Arreola's voice was raspy, an old man's voice, but with his familiar enthusiasm.

"I just got in," Haydon said.

"Not at the María Isabel?"

"Yes."

"Of course! My God, why do you do that, boy? Always I ask you to stay with us. Two old people and a house of empty rooms. Luisa is going to kill you . . . Is Nina with you?"

"Not this time. This trip is not for pleasure."

"Ahhhh," Arreola growled. "Is it something that you need my help?"

"Not professionally. But I'd like to talk to you."

"Of course, of course. Can you come to the house for dinner? I'll call Luisa."

"Thank you, Gaston, but I think not. This isn't a good time. Can you join me at the Champs Élysées?"

Arreola gave a gruff chuckle. "Like your father, a man of habit. The Champs Élysées. Okay, what time?"

"Eight o'clock?"

"I will be there."

After hanging up, Haydon picked up the telephone again and called the restaurant and made reservations. With that done, he turned to his suitcase, unsnapped the latches, and opened it. He unpacked his suits and shirts and hung them in the closet and put his shaving kit and toilet articles on the bathroom counter. Everything else he left in the suitcase, except the Beretta. There was a problem about the Beretta. Technically, he had brought the gun into the country illegally and was subject to arrest if he was found wearing it. A serious offense. Still, Haydon didn't want to leave it in his room to be discovered by the maid, who would surely report it, or by anyone else who might enter the room less legitimately. It might have been a mistake to bring it, but now that he had, it would surely be a mistake not to carry it with him. He took it out of the suitcase and laid it on the bed with a box of ammunition.

He hung his suit coat over the back of a chair, rolled up his sleeves, and went into the bathroom. He washed his face and forearms with soap, rinsed with cold water, and dried with a towel. He avoided looking at himself in the mirror. He hung up the towel and walked back into the room, going once again to the window. The rain had slackened, the storm having moved north toward the center of the old city, toward the broad stone field of the Zócalo and the National Palace.

Now that he was here he had to determine how worried he should be about being blindsided by Saturnino. How would Saturnino know when Haydon had arrived and where he was staying? Would he simply watch Amaranta's home, knowing Haydon would eventually show up there? Or might he have arranged something more elaborate than that? Was he aware of Haydon's habit of staying at the María Isabel? Of dining at the same restaurants? Haydon doubted it. Saturnino might know such details regarding Houston because of Swain's research, but surely he had done no such background investigating regarding Haydon's occasional trips to Mexico City. But once Haydon showed up at Amaranta's, he would have to start looking over his shoulder.

In the gray-green light he watched the traffic on the Reforma come to a stop at a signal light. While the signal held the cars, flower vendors who had been huddling on the esplanades rushed out into the lanes of traffic hawking roses and yellow chrysanthemums to the captive drivers. Half a dozen ragged little boys raced to the nearest cars, mounted the bumpers, and began wiping windows with their hands, the smallest boys climbing onto the wet hoods, lying prone on their stomachs as their small dirty hands smeared the windshields. Having perfected their timing, just before the signal changed they hopped off the cars to run around to the driver's window, extending their opened palms to receive tips for their unsolicited services. As the traffic began to move into the circle around the *glorieta*, they scrambled between the bumpers to the esplanades, where they counted their booty and waited for the next red light.

Haydon watched this ritual for nearly half an hour before he grabbed his coat off the back of the chair and left. Outside on the sidewalk he waved off the taxi drivers who lingered like buzzards around the entrance of the hotel. These men, driving American cars, often charged twice as much as the drivers of the little yellow Volkswagens you could hail fifty feet away on the boulevard. He crossed the street that went in front of the hotel to the first esplanade and followed the diagonal sidewalk through the trees. The night air was crisp, newly washed by the rain and as fresh as it would ever be. It felt good on his face.

When the traffic light stopped the cars, he crossed the six center lanes of traffic separated by a hedge, weaving in between the bumpers of the cars to the second esplanade. The rush-hour traffic had not entirely subsided, and commuters were still scattered along the curbs of the esplanades trying to hail taxis or *peseros*. The *pesero* was a Mexico City phenomenon, a Volkswagen van which served as a multipassenger taxi. *Peseros* had regular routes into the city's various *colonias*. Always crowded, these jitneys breezed along the city's avenues loading and unloading passengers. The driver, ever eager to get the most passengers for their money, drove along with one hand raised out the window, holding up the number of fingers he determined he had space for in the van. His estimates frequently were ambitious, resulting in a sardine-can density inside. Haydon again angled through the trees to the other side of the Reforma. Here, under the camphor trees at the corner of Amberes and Reforma, was the forest-green canopy of the Champs Élysées.

He had started on his second glass of a white Chambertin when he heard Arreola's voice on the stairwell. He stood as the stocky old man was ushered across the dining room to his table. Without speaking he gave Haydon an enthusiastic *abrazo*, slapping him on the back.

"You are looking good, Stuart," Arreola said, grinning and sitting down. He had the thick hair of a young man, though it was completely white now, and his voice was phlegmy, as if he had to clear his throat. He had gained a little weight. He caught Haydon looking at him, and his face fell in mock seriousness. "You think I am too heavy. The old man is going to pot, huh?"

"Not at all," Haydon said. "In fact, I was thinking you seemed to need a little nourishment."

Arreola laughed. "My God, yes." He reached out and grabbed the waiter's arm as if he were going to get away. "Give me one of those," he said, pointing to Haydon's wine. "What is it you have," he asked Haydon.

"Chambertin."

"Yes, the same, a Chambertin," he said to the waiter, patting his arm. "Good boy." He settled himself in his chair, pulling on the sides of his shiny polished silk suit to get comfortable. "Before you get started on your business, tell me, how is Nina?"

They spent a few minutes catching up on family news, discussing Arreola's two sons, who were practicing law with him and on whom he lavished all his love and for whom he had pulled many strings. In the Mexican way, his affection for them was unrestrained.

"But I am an old horse now," he rasped, leaning back in his chair and taking a sip of wine. "My desk at the office is my pasture. It's the biggest desk—the best view—but I do the least work. Actually, I spend most of my time with my facsimile collections of the codices—which is getting expensive. But at the office, the boys, they take care of everything. That is as it should be, though, huh?" He looked at Haydon and was silent for a minute. "So. What business do you have in Mexico?"

Haydon told him everything, or almost everything. He related the sequence of events in chronological order exactly as they had occurred right up until Friday afternoon when he received the death threat. He didn't tell Arreola of the file discovered at the private detective's office and his subsequent discovery of Saturnino Barcena's "address" on "Sarmiento" Street. Early in the story Arreola's face assumed its lawyerly firmness. It betrayed no emotion, no surprise, no sadness, no judgment. He was hearing the facts.

When Haydon finished, Arreola drained the last of his wine, which he had sipped steadily throughout the narration, and started shaking his head slowly. Only then did his face soften to that of Gaston the friend instead of Arreola the lawyer.

"Ahhhh, Stuart. This is bad business," he said, tugging on the lobe of his left ear, a familiar gesture when there was heavy thinking to be done. "You know, the past is never forgotten. Like our shadow, it belongs to us, the silhouette of what we are." His voice dropped and grew huskier. "And where does this past go when we die? It stays behind, as you have seen. This world is littered with the pasts of dead men, and those of us who are still living must carry them around on our backs like loads of lead."

Haydon waited. Arreola had always been a great talker, but in his old age he had grown garrulous in the extreme. Still,

Haydon knew that whatever the old lawyer said was worth listening to, though it might require a good deal of patience to hear it.

Arreola shook his head heavily. "You don't want to go see that old woman, *hijo*."

"Why?"

"Why?" Arreola frowned, looking at his empty glass. "You know, when your father and I worked together as young lawyers back in those days with Royal Dutch Shell, I was also taking courses in anthropology at the university—it was not out in ritzy Pedregal in those days. No. Here, downtown. Anyway, on quite a few occasions your father took trips with me down into the Yucatán to the ruins." He smiled. "We had some good times. Well. This was the beginning of my preoccupation with the codices—the painted books of the Maya, the Aztecs, the Mixtecs, Tarascans, Otomis. I have lived with the gods in these books all my life now, and we have become old friends. I respect them, maybe I even fear them a little as my ancestors did. The Indian was not such a fool, you know. His gods reflected his own soul, his fears, his hopes, his dreams, even his speculations. They were the means by which he tried to understand the complexities, the incongruities, of this life."

The waiter reappeared with the Chambertin, and Arreola allowed him to refill his glass. Haydon shook his head.

"No more?" Arreola raised his eyebrows at Haydon. "Well, I am a few more pounds. I can absorb it better." He smiled and sipped from his glass, savoring the aftertaste with his tongue. "So, what did the Indians learn about life, about themselves? At the very core of the later Mesoamerican religions is the concept of duality . . . the unity of basically opposed principles. Life and death, light and darkness, good and evil, up and down, yes and no. Each god was more than one god; sometimes he was many, depending upon the circumstances. Nothing was simple, nothing straightforward."

Warming to his subject, Arreola pushed aside his wineglass and put his opened hands together as if praying. "Take for example the extraordinary Tlazolteotl," he said, moving his hands apart, creating a distance between them. "Considered as a deity, the moon was Tlazolteotl. She was the goddess of fertility, the mother goddess, and therefore one who perpetuated life. She was also the one to whom confessions were made of sexual transgressions. Only she could pardon such sins. On the other hand, Tlazolteotl was always depicted in the codices as being bare-breasted and was frequently associated with the coral snake, the symbol of lust. It was she who had the power to stir up sexual passions, and it was she who was the patroness of prostitutes and adulterers. The most licentious phallic rites were performed in the temples in her name and honor. And yet—" Arreola raised a hand as if to stop Haydon's thoughts. "And yet she was known as the 'filth eater.' That is, when one confessed one's sexual transgressions to her, unburdened oneself of all the guilt attached to illicit sex with its disruptive, and sometimes even fatal, consequences, this Tlazolteotl—which literally means 'filth goddess'—ate the sin, the 'filth.' It existed no more, and you were forgiven."

Arreola brought his hands back together, looking at Haydon. Slowly he reached for his wine and pulled it over in front of him again. Haydon waited. The old man wasn't through. Arreola sipped the wine.

"You see? Is the goddess good or bad? What is man, good or bad? The goddess inspired him to sin, the goddess saved him. There are no answers here, only an acknowledgment of the two hearts within us, and more questions." Arreola gestured toward Haydon with the two fingers of his right hand extended in the manner of a priest making the sign of the cross, blessing a confessor. "What you will find with that old woman, Amaranta, are not answers. Only questions. What are you going to accomplish by talking to this old woman? Nothing. You will peer into a deep well and you will see two kinds of darkness. Or, if not two kinds of darkness, you will see a mirror. And that could be even worse."

Chapter 14

HAYDON TOOK HIS EYES OFF GASTON ARREOLA, WHO WAS LOOKING AT him with the expression of a man who has delivered sad news. Down on the Reforma, under the green haze of the lighted trees, only a few flower vendors remained. The bustle of rush-hour traffic had slackened and the signal lights at the Ángel *glorieta* now caught only a dozen or so cars each time they changed. The little boys were gone. On the sidewalk beside the Champs Élysées, two policemen were earning substantial tips by standing guard over several double-parked cars. Their uniforms were smartly cut and the highly polished visors on their caps glistened in the light of the streetlamp as they chatted with two women who had walked down Amberes from the Zona Rosa.

Arreola's circuitous response to Haydon's question had been an artful demonstration of Mexican dissimulation, a national attribute that Haydon found alternately maddening and beguiling. It was the Mexican way to avoid directness. To be too definite was to run great risk; one might offend, or one might commit oneself to an irrevocable path that one might later regret. It was best to be oblique, to leave room for other options, for an unforeseen change of heart or mind. Better to couch one's ideas in flowery language, in ambiguities which later could be interpreted in a variety of ways. Better to be cautious.

Haydon didn't blame the old man for skirting the question. If Arreola knew that scandal lay at the heart of the matter—and Haydon was sure that he did—then his was an understandable reluctance. Arreola did not want to be the one to reveal such an embarrassment to the well-loved son of an old friend. It was a painful exercise the old man would prefer to avoid.

But Haydon persisted. "You knew her well?" He was still

looking out on the Reforma, to the esplanades where an old Indian woman wrapped in her *huipil* was crossing the boulevard with an infant in her arms and a small child tagging along behind her.

"I knew her," Arreola said noncommittally.

"Did you like her?"

"Like her? My God, I was in love with her."

Haydon looked at him.

"Every young man worthy of his nuts was mad about her," Arreola said. He was speaking conceptually again. His professed love had not been a confession after all.

"But did you know her well?"

"No one knew her well, I think, except your father. And he never revealed anything personal about her. Not to me, anyway."

"Have you seen her in recent years?"

"I used to have business with her husband, Everardo Sarmiento, from time to time. I saw her at social functions."

"He's dead, I understand."

"Yes, nearly ten years ago now. He died in Cuernavaca on a weekend with his mistress."

"Was that a well-known relationship?"

"Oh, yes. Everardo was an insatiable womanizer, unfaithful to a degree extraordinary even for a Mexican." Arreola laughed.

"And how did Amaranta regard his infidelities?"

"I do not believe she gave a damn," Arreola said, his smile gradually fading. "Their marriage was not a normal one in any respect, even from the beginning. You know, Amaranta was such a free spirit, no one could settle her down. Everyone said that if Webster could not control her then no one could. When he went to England and came back with your beloved mother—God bless her—everyone held his breath to see what Amaranta would do. Well, she continued to live the life of a wild bird, and everyone said she would come to no good because the one man who seemed to understand her had given up on her. About a year after Webster moved to Houston, she surprised everyone by marrying Everardo.

"You see, everyone was so surprised," Arreola continued, seeming still to find it an inexplicable marriage. "First of all because she married without any hint . . . no one had ever seen her anywhere with Everardo. And secondly, because she married *him*, of all people. He was handsome, yes, but he was not her type. He was superficial in every way, a shameless social climber. As it turned out, he was a fairly good business-man, considering that he had married a fortune."

Haydon motioned to the waiter, who came over and replen-ished their Chambertin.

"You said their marriage was not a normal one from the beginning," Haydon reminded. "What do you mean by that?"

Arreola reached into the inside pocket of his suit and pulled out two cigars. "How about one of these?" he said, grinning slyly. Haydon declined. "Well, I am going to have one. I cannot smoke them at home—doctor's orders—and I cannot smoke them at the office because the boys tattle to Luisa, who gives me hell when I get home. Sometimes I stop off for drinks at the Citadel on the way home and smoke them, and if Luisa smells them on me I tell her it was the men at the club." He lighted the cigar, puffed energetically to get it started.

"Not a normal marriage," he said, cuing himself and smack-ing his lips slightly, enjoying the taste of cigar and wine. "Well, they had this boy right off. No one would have guessed that. Myself, I predicted a stormy six months and then divorce. But wham! Goddam, a baby boy; that poor, unfortunate Saturnino. Almost a year of silence when nothing happened at all. And then there were rumors of Everardo with this woman, then with that one. Rumors of Everardo at the best bordellos. Rumors of Everardo setting up a *casita*. Of course, none of it was rumor. It was all true. And what did Amaranta do? Nothing. She painted. She made no scenes, she threw no tantrums. She ignored him as though he were of no conse-quence to her. And to tell you the truth, I think this was exactly the case. I believe he knew this and it infuriated him and drove him to greater infidelities. Her family was aghast. They pleaded with her to divorce him. Amaranta was silent. She painted. A couple of years went by. Everardo's infidelities continued. And then Amaranta is pregnant again! It was Isabel, beautiful Chabela. People thought: my God, have they patched it up? But within a year Everardo was at it again. It continued until he died."

"What was Amaranta doing all this time?" Haydon asked.

The cigar smelled good, and he was sorry he hadn't accepted Arreola's offer. "Was she a recluse?"

Arreola laughed. "Ah, that woman! She was and she was not. Most of her time was spent in her studio in San Ángel. It was on the top floor of a rose-pink colonial house, the place where she now lives, in fact. When she was painting she was indeed a recluse. No one saw her for months on end. She kept the children with her, and she established an Indian family in the house too—a husband and wife and the wife's two sisters. These people became her inner circle. They protected her privacy, raised her children, ran the house. She and the children loved this Indian family very much. The few people I knew who had visited her there said she dressed in simple cotton smocks. She let her hair grow wild. It was rumored that in the heat of the summer she painted only in a thin cotton skirt, nothing else, bare-breasted. Sarmiento led a separate life. Their paths crossed, but they did not meet. Not until later anyway, when Saturnino got older, and then with disastrous results."

Arreola grinned through a cloud of blue smoke. "But once every year or two Amaranta came out of seclusion, usually at one of the prominent social events. Even though she had, in effect, turned her back on society, the grandes dames of society did not turn their backs on her. No. She received invitations to every social event of any consequence in the city—and she still does—because every hostess knew that if of all the parties held that year Amaranta happened to come to hers, the event would be immortalized.

"Only one example. This occurred, I suppose, in the sixties. It was a time when Mexican artists were being heavily influenced by international trends. Many Mexicans studied in Europe and many Europeans came here. There was a very healthy exchange of ideas. Some of the members of the art establishment decided to honor the foreign artists who were then living in Mexico. I do not know the exact details of how this came about, but I do remember that 'everyone' was there. It was held in the ballroom of the National Palace, and for a few weeks beforehand everyone was frantically trying to wrangle an invitation because it promised to be the biggest event of several years. The walls of the ballroom had been lined with the paintings of these honored artists, and of course there was

a reception line, politicians and senior members of the Acad
emy or something. It had been arranged so that everyone
entered the palace through the central porch, with limousines
circling the Zócalo to the entrance and doormen ushering the
guests into the palace.

"There were tuxedos and ball gowns, everyone taking
himself very seriously, the ogling crowds in the plaza held back
by barricades and hundreds of lackey policemen. Amaranta
Sarmiento de la Sierra arrived at the most conspicuous moment in a very long, very old Rolls-Royce. When the footmen
stepped forward to open her door, Amaranta emerged from
the darkened interior with her two escorts—both of them
dwarfs. Very tiny dwarfs. The two young men were dressed
impeccably, of course, and Amaranta herself wore a long black
gown that clung to her like a second skin. The back of it was cut
so low it exposed the dimples above her hips, and the front was
made of something—I do not know what—so thin that the first
stunning impression was that she was bare to her navel. I
remember her necklace, the largest emeralds I have ever seen
outside a museum, and her eyes burned above them like green
fire. She had had her long, wild hair cut straight across her
neck, straight bangs. It was a dramatic style, calculated I think
to make her seem somehow even more naked."

Arreola drew on his cigar, his eyes looking across the table
but, Haydon was convinced, seeing images nearly thirty years
in the past. When the old man continued, he spoke slowly,
savoring the memory.

"The three of them ascended the grand staircase beneath
that glorious mural of Diego Rivera, Amaranta standing erect
and tall like a queen, each hand holding one of the hands of her
tiny escorts as if she were holding the hands of small children.
It was a slow progress, because the little men were actually
climbing. People stopped and stared at them. The reception
line was long, President Díaz Ordaz, Interior Minister
Echeverria . . . When Amaranta entered with her escorts,
the attention in the ballroom was unsubtly directed to the
receiving line. It was there that Amaranta's calculating genius
for spectacle was consummated. She and her two escorts
carried themselves with great dignity, while managing to make
the pompous officials appear utterly ridiculous. Each flustered
personage—man and woman alike—looked like a hobby horse.

each bending down, one at a time, to meet the first dwarf, standing up to encounter Amaranta's majestic breasts and blazing green eyes, down again to meet the second dwarf, and up again to meet the next guest, who, poor soul, had probably never felt more insignificant in his entire life, because each man who took his hand did not look at him. No, he had swiveled his head around to take in Amaranta's long bare spine."

Arreola's laugh scrabbled hoarsely in his throat and his eyes sparkled in delight at the memory. He very clearly appreciated Amaranta's eccentric penchant for the absurd. He coughed a couple of times, and continued, "After this queer revue of the long, bobbing receiving line, she and the dwarfs toured the ballroom in an unhurried promenade, stopping in front of each painting as if giving it due respect before moving to the next. She made one circle, spoke to no one even when she was spoken to, and then left with as much grace and self-presence as she had entered, like Empress Carlota at Chapultepec Castle. That was all."

Arreola drained his glass, his face slightly colored from laughing, and added, "She is known for more outrageous behavior, of course, but this performance I witnessed myself, and I liked it. It is indicative of the woman. God only knows what purpose she saw in such things. She never really yearned for the limelight, it wasn't that. Who knows."

Haydon looked at Arreola, a little puzzled by the story, or at least by the tone of relish with which it was told. Then the old man sat back in his chair and let his eyes wander out the windows to the Reforma. Haydon followed his gaze. It was raining again, lightly, and umbrellas had sprung up like dark mushrooms along the esplanades. The golden angel raised her garland and spread her gilded wings toward the lowering night sky.

Haydon looked back to Arreola and was surprised to see a sudden change. He had grown quickly and curiously quiet, even melancholy, as his thoughts had wandered into more solemn memories, making his eyes water with the ease of the elderly who discover as they grow older that sometimes remembering can catch them off guard, that sometimes it can be an all too vivid experience, more akin to the gift of conjuring.

*   *   *

TO DISPEL THE SOMBER MOOD THAT HAD SETTLED OVER THEIR
conversation, Haydon motioned to the waiter to bring menus.
He knew from past experience that Arreola enjoyed the
French dishes of the Champs Élysées, where Haydon ate
many of his meals when he stayed at the María Isabel across
the Reforma. They took their time discussing the menu,
Arreola gradually becoming interested in the dishes, discussing the merits of each entree with the waiter until he had
narrowed his choices to the duckling and the filet bordelaise.
Finally deciding it was too late for beef, he took the duckling,
and Haydon ordered the Dover sole. As the waiter turned to
go, Haydon asked him to bring the rest of the bottle of
Chambertin and leave it on the table.

Haydon changed the subject altogether and asked Arreola
about his latest acquisitions to his facsimile collection of
pre-Columbian codices. The old man readily picked up the
subject, spinning a long tale of his many and arduous negotiations. After a while the waiter brought their dinner, which
Arreola ate with obvious pleasure, hardly breaking his stride as
he continued to relate his quest for the replica of the Borgia
codices.

Haydon ate his sole and listened to Arreola, his mind
divided between the old friend's impassioned preoccupations
with his beloved painted books and his own preoccupation
with his father's past. It seemed that everyone he had spoken
to so far was willing to reminisce about Amaranta or about his
father, but not about the two of them together. Had their
relationship really been so closely guarded, so private that no
one knew the nature of it? Or was there something about it
that no one wanted to discuss? Haydon was curious that
Arreola had not shown more interest in the death threat,
seeming to be more fearful of Haydon talking to Amaranta.
Perhaps the old man didn't take the threat seriously. Maybe he
knew a reason not to; or maybe he saw it as something else, as
a sign not of danger, but of old pains resurrected for no good
cause.

His straying thoughts came back to silence. Arreola had
stopped talking and was looking at him, his elbows on the
table, his hands clasped above his plate. The noises of the

restaurant returned as he stared back at Arreola's eyes, which seemed to be assessing him with a quiet sobriety, as if the old man had realized in the last few moments the extent of Haydon's absorption in the questions of Amaranta.

"I'm sorry, Gaston," Haydon said, putting down his fork and wiping his mouth self-consciously. "I guess I'm tired. I can't keep my mind on what I'm doing."

Arreola waved away the apology, his rough voice mellowed by compassion. "No, it is my fault, Stuart. These old man's ramblings . . . I should have seen . . . I should have been more aware of your concern. It was foolish of me to think I could divert you."

Haydon reached for his wineglass, not knowing what to say.

"Tell me," Arreola said, pushing away his nearly empty plate, "have you ever heard of Juan Lockhart?"

"Lockhart?"

Arreola nodded.

"I don't think so."

"I am not surprised." Arreola shook his head pensively, seeming to marvel at something he was remembering. "You know, your father, I loved him very much, Stuart, but he really was a very unusual individual." He shrugged philosophically. "Well, anyway, this Lockhart, he is a man you must speak to." Taking his napkin off his lap and putting it on the table, he said, "If you will wait a moment, I will be right back." He pushed his chair away from the table and got up.

Outside the rain had stopped and a fine mist hung over the palms, made haloes around the streetlamps, and kept the boulevard as shiny as glass. Haydon couldn't keep his mind off Amaranta and was beginning to wonder if he shouldn't forget about trying to learn more about her from his father's old friends before meeting her. Maybe he should go on to San Ángel the next morning. He wondered if he was playing games with himself, unconsciously creating diversions to postpone the moment when he would see her face to face.

Arreola lumbered around the corner from the telephone and came toward the table pulling firmly at the sides of his suit, flexing his arms out in front of him to loosen the shoulders of his coat. He sat down in his chair with a slight grunt.

"Okay, I talked to him," he said, turning and motioning to

the waiter. "He would like to see you." The waiter approached, and Arreola ordered coffee for both of them.

"Who is he?" Haydon asked.

"Juan Lockhart was probably the closest friend your father ever had in Mexico."

Haydon looked at Arreola. He couldn't believe it. It didn't make any sense at all. In one brief moment the thought occurred to him that the father he had known was slipping away from him; with each new discovery Haydon lost a little more of the context of old memories. It was never going to be the same again.

The old man nodded, as if he understood. "It's true. Lockhart's father, Erskine, was the chief executive for Royal Dutch Shell in Mexico in those days. He had lived in Mexico for many years and was married to a Mexican woman. They had two boys: Juan and his older brother, Simón, who was killed when he was thrown from his horse while riding in Chapultepec Park. It was Erskine who hired Webster during a trip to Boston in 1934. He knew your grandfather and they arranged it. Juan also worked for his father. No concern about nepotism back then." Arreola snorted. "Anyway, Webster and Juan were about the same age, and became the very best of friends."

"I've never heard of him," Haydon said, frowning skeptically at Arreola.

Arreola moved his hands off the table as the waiter set down their coffee. He was silent while the waiter served them. When he left, Arreola continued.

"It was only natural that they became such close friends," he said, spooning sugar into his coffee. "There was the Anglo relationship, and Erskine took an even closer interest in Webster after Simón was killed, and in a way, Juan did also. Your father very quickly filled the empty space that Simón left in that family. As far as becoming a part of Mexican life, he was actually more inclined to that than was Juan, even though Juan had lived here all his life and his mother was Mexican. In his heart Juan was Anglo, and, I think, he has always felt a foreigner here. None of his Mexican friendships were close. It was Juan who drew Webster to him, not the other way around."

"What happened?" Haydon asked. "Why didn't I ever hear of him?"

Arreola shook his head, taking a testing sip of coffee. "I don't know for sure. All the trips your father made down here over the years . . . I do not believe he ever saw Juan. There was some kind of falling-out."

"When would that have been? When did it start?"

"It was after your parents were married."

"How long after they were married?"

Arreola lifted his shoulders; he didn't know. "I asked Webster about it once, but he said only that it was just one of those things. Nothing more."

"Did you ever ask Lockhart about it?"

"Well, first of all I did not—and do not—have a close friendship with Juan, as I did with your father," Arreola said. "But we've stayed in touch over the years. He is a lawyer, too, and we live in the same district. But, as with your father, I brought up the subject with him one time. Juan was not so easygoing about it. He simply stared at me coldly, as if I had asked him about his most private secrets. I think he was offended that I should even have thought about it. It never came up again."

"But surely you have some idea."

"Yes, it was something to do with Amaranta," Arreola said in a tone of resignation. "It caused a complete breach between the two men. But, I will tell you, I never heard either of them say anything derogatory about the other. It was not their way."

"What did you say to Lockhart when you spoke to him just now?" Haydon asked.

"I told him that you were here in Mexico," the old man said, glancing out the window to the night street past Haydon's shoulders. "That you were looking for some answers about your father's past, and that he should talk to you. I told him you would explain everything."

"And how did he take that?"

"Quietly," Arreola said, shifting his eyes to Haydon again. "He takes everything quietly. It will be a cold day in hell when you catch Juan Lockhart off his guard. I have often wondered how one does that, to be always anticipating in every exchange with another human being. When you think about it, it is almost too much to believe. It seems to me that it does not bode well for happiness . . . never to be surprised, always to fear it, always to be on guard. Juan Lockhart is not a joyous man."

"When can I see him?"

"He wants to see you tonight."

"Tonight?"

Arreola looked at his watch. "He said to give him half an hour, so I guess it is time. We should go."

"Isn't this a little unusual?"

"I think so." Arreola nodded.

"What do you make of it?" Haydon asked, taking out his credit card and motioning to the ever-watchful waiter.

Arreola smiled. "I do not 'make' anything of what Juan does. He has his own reasons for everything, and he does not explain them."

Chapter 15

SATURNINO SAT IN HIS CAR PARKED AT THE CURB ON AMBERES watching the Champs Élysées through the rearview mirror. Every half hour or so one of the policemen from the sidewalk outside the Champs Élysées would saunter down the street to look in on him, touching the shiny plastic brim of his cap as he ducked down and peered into the car window as if he were inquiring as to whether he needed any assistance. He never did, but in appreciation for the officer's concern he would slip him a couple of thousand-peso notes and the policeman would hitch up his leather belt and holster, look up and down the street to check the status of law and order, and then saunter back to the Champs Élysées, leaving Sarmiento double-parked under the camphor trees.

They were in the heart of the Zona Rosa, the triangular section of downtown bordered by the Paseo de la Reforma, Insurgentes Avenue, and Chapultepec Avenue, and which reached, on its longest side, from Chapultepec Park to the *glorieta* of the Monument of Cuauhtémoc. Within this triangular wedge in the center of Colonia Juárez, some of the city's toniest shops, restaurants, art galleries, and sidewalk cafés were clustered among luxury hotels. In the twenties these streets had been exclusively residential, but in subsequent decades they had fallen into dereliction before being revived by shrewd developers. Now they were the nighttime playground of wealthy Mexicans, and tourists from all over the world.

On the left, just in front of the car, Saturnino saw the myrtle-green awning of Ralph Lauren's Polo Shop; Cartier was on the right. At the corner of Hamburgo and Amberes he could see the Gucci store, and to its right was Ariès. Pelletier de Paris was a little farther down. A couple of blocks away, on the corner of Londres, he could see Napo coming out of the Denny's—an American import that enjoyed a lively popularity among Mexico's trendy young set—carrying a Styrofoam cup of coffee. He crossed to the east side of Amberes, the side where the rental car was parked, and disappeared into the unlighted sidewalk scaffolding of a construction project. After a few moments he reemerged into the light, then inexplicably crossed to the west side again before continuing. He stopped at the Gucci store windows and peered inside, ignoring an old Indian woman huddled on the sidewalk beside his leg. Wrapped in a soiled but colorful *huipil*, she held a ratty-haired infant in her arms while a small boy pumped away on a rickety accordion twice his size with half its keys missing. The little boy turned to the young man, playing to him as Napo continued to gaze into the Gucci window, lusting after the leather bags, the navy blazer, the natty shoes. When he finally turned and started toward the car, the tiny musician followed him a short distance, pumping ever harder on the accordion, before finally giving up and returning to his station beside the old woman.

Napo had to cross the street once more to get to the car, where he stopped in the street beside Saturnino's door and handed him the white cup through the window.

"Haven't gone nowhere yet, huh?" he asked, bending down and resting both hands on his knees as he looked in at Saturnino, who hated the young man's excessive application of cologne. "Hey, you shoulda seen this muff I saw down at Denny's. Ohh-wheeee, baby! I coulda used some of that."

Saturnino knew the crowd that gathered at Denny's late at night. Young, wealthy kids with plenty of time and money on their hands; the traveling rich from the hotels in the area stopping in for pie and coffee before going back to their rooms for the night.

"So what's happenin'?" Napo asked.

"I had to give another couple of thousand pesos to the policeman."

"Shit, man," Napo said disdainfully.

Napo—Saturnino didn't even know his last name—was one of *los juniors*, the pampered kids from the southern suburbs like Pedregal who often hung around the clubs in the Zona Rosa at night (currently the Carousel at Niza and Hamburgo was the hot spot), dressed in the latest fashions, and honing their natural skills as con men. They smoked marijuana as if they were Winstons, did a little coke and dealt a little coke, impregnated girls, and during the day attended (about half the time) one or two classes at the National University. That was where he had spotted Napo, recognized him for the little shit that he was, and arranged for him to help him out. Napo had realized early on that what they were doing was something a little shady and sucked right into it. He had let the kid arrange everything (after telling him how to do it): the bribe of a night clerk at the hotel to let them know when Haydon checked in, and the bribes of waiters (who could sneak looks at the reservation lists) at the two or three restaurants near the María Isabel where Haydon always ate when he was there.

Saturnino sighed wearily. He took a tissue from the box on the dash and wiped around the rim of the Styrofoam cup. He dried the inside of the plastic lid and placed it on the seat beside him with two other lids. This had been Napo's third trip to Denny's. He thought of the kid as a dog, a trained German shepherd that had just a little more brain than other dogs and therefore sometimes made the mistake of trying to think for itself. It never worked out, of course, so he had to put up with a lot of silly behavior. Still, he needed the dog, and when it followed commands it performed very well indeed.

"Okay, Napo, that's going to be it for tonight."

"What?" Napo whined, putting his arms on the top of the car where his heavy gold bracelet clanked on the roof as he jutted his head down between his arms. "Come on, man. I thought you was goin' to let me tail these bastards with you, man."

The use of the words "tail" and "bastards" gave the kid away. He thought he was into something seriously clandestine. Aside from his little duties Sarmiento hadn't given him the faintest idea of what they were doing, but the kid had created a cinematic scenario of intrigue.

"Tomorrow. I'll get in touch with you tomorrow," Saturnino lied. "There's more to do. You've got to be patient."

"Shit!" The kid jerked away from the car, but calmed down immediately. "Okay," he said. "Call me. You got my number." Another line from a movie.

Saturnino gave him a thumbs-up, hating the goddam gesture but knowing the kid would like it, and Napo turned and started down Amberes headed for Hamburgo as he reached in his pocket, going for a joint.

It was a little after ten o'clock and the sidewalks on Amberes were bare except for an occasional couple passing under the camphor trees to the busier streets farther into the Zona Rosa. By nine o'clock when the shops on Amberes closed, most of the action had moved toward the clubs and cafés in Hamburgo and Londres, to Genova Street, which had been permanently closed to traffic, making it a broad outdoor mall, and to Copenhague, with its crowded sidewalk cafés. A couple of kids carrying red and yellow plastic buckets, a squeegee, and some rags approached him and asked if he wanted his car washed. They had washed two of the three cars outside the Champs Élysées, and Sarmiento guessed the policeman had sent them his way. He declined, gave the kids a few pesos, and watched them lug the buckets around the corner to Hamburgo, where the action wasn't so slow.

Saturnino had been parked there for nearly two hours now, and he wondered for the fourth time if there was a rear entrance; why any meal would take this long if Haydon was eating alone; if he himself had been spotted; if the cop he was giving the pesos to had also informed Haydon of his presence.

The ramifications of this last possibility had begun to mushroom in his imagination when two men came out of the restaurant and stood momentarily on the sidewalk. One of them, an older gentleman, walked around to the front of a Mercedes parked at the curb and talked to the two policemen while the second paused in a splash of light from the street-lamp and then moved into the dappled shadows next to the Mercedes. In that brief moment he recognized Haydon.

Saturnino's heart raced, and he turned around, wanting to get a better look than he had gotten through the mirror. He watched as the old man chatted with the two policemen and then he felt a hot rush of fear, thinking that at any moment the old man was going to turn and look toward him, that the policeman was going to betray him. But it didn't happen. The old man chatted with the two obsequious policemen, who had made sure no one had leaned on his car while he was in the restaurant. It was a time-honored ritual. The old man exchanged a few words with "the boys," who smiled from beneath their thin mustaches like undernourished neighborhood dogs who developed instant loyalties to anyone who tossed them scraps. He slipped something to each man, and one of them followed him around and opened his door, wishing him a good night, a safe trip. They were helpful in directing the old man out of his parking place, and as he pulled away they saluted with the casual elegance of a quasi-official gesture born of respect for the man with the money.

Saturnino turned around quickly and fixed his eyes on the mirror. He watched as the Mercedes came toward him, squeezing past him in the narrow street, so close that he could have reached out and touched the old man, whom he did not get a good look at because at the last· moment he turned his face away. Then suddenly he remembered, snatched a ball-point pen from his shirt pocket, and jotted down the license number from the rear of the Mercedes as it swung onto Hamburgo and headed toward the palm-studded Florencia Boulevard. He pulled away from the curb and nosed his car around the corner. When he saw the Mercedes enter Florencia, he gunned the car onto Hamburgo, flew the two blocks to the next corner, and made it onto Florencia just in front of a string of oncoming headlights. By the time the Mercedes circled the Ángel *glorieta* and started toward Chapultepec on the broad avenue of the Paseo de la Reforma, he was comfortably situated in the flow of traffic three cars behind.

At the monument of Diana Cazadora much of the traffic bled off onto the western segment of the interior circuit expressway, and Saturnino dropped back a few cars as they entered Chapultepec Park but not far enough behind the Mercedes to be cut off by the occasional traffic signal. He turned on the wipers to clear the fine mist stippling the windshield. The traffic hissed along the wet streets gliding under the forest of towering *ahuehuetes*, cypresslike trees that already had achieved their full majesty long before Spaniards spotted the Mexican coastline from their caravels. To their left the lights of Chapultepec Castle glittered occasionally through the breaks in the trees. They passed the sign that marked the entrance to the Museum of Anthropology on their right and then Chivatito Boulevard, which led deeper into the thousand-acre park to President de la Madrid's residence of Los Pinos. Saturnino was surprised. He was doing a better job than he had expected. Following them wasn't that difficult after all.

But when they passed the Winston Churchill monument and approached the Petroleum Fountain at the Periférico—the outer-loop expressway—the problem of tailing became considerably more difficult. Once again they lost a great deal of traffic—this time to the Periférico—and only a few cars stayed on the Reforma as it continued into the Lomas de Chapultepec district.

Saturnino dropped back even farther. It made him nervous, but he couldn't afford to be spotted. He watched the Mercedes's taillights recede, the car itself growing less and less distinct as it passed in and out of the pools of pale light from the streetlamps on the winding boulevard.

Without any warning he was conscious of his arms trembling on the steering wheel. He thought of Haydon sitting up there in front of him, and suddenly he was hungry. Hungry? Was that a metaphor? A sentient metaphor? For what? In what way? People thirsted for truth, but hunger? That had sexual connotations. He was revolted. It was not the kind of imagery he wanted to enter his mind. Not at all. Then he smelled them, the strong gamy fetor of the iguanas. He had been so preoccupied he had forgotten about them. They made no noise but he knew they were still there, piled on top of each other, blinking stupidly in the darkness of the backseat.

AS THEY EMERGED FROM THE NORTHWESTERN EDGE OF THE PARK, they circled the Periférico interchange around the lighted Petroleum Fountain, an enormous monument commemorating President Cárdenas's expropriation of Mexico's petroleum industry from foreign proprietors in 1938, and then Arreola took the Mercedes up into the newer section of the Reforma in the western foothills. During the city's first great expansion in the forties and fifties, Mexico's wealthy elite had built large rambling homes on these slopes overlooking the city. In the district of Lomas de Chapultepec, the Reforma and the quiet tree-lined streets that branched off from it ascended in serpentine turns higher into the hills, the extravagance of the homes becoming more conspicuous as the streets climbed. Haydon recognized the route and kept his eyes on the headlights as they panned around the curves, lighting secluded drives and an occasional glimpse of luxurious homes.

The Reforma broadened into a spacious parkway and then

narrowed again and grew steeper as it ascended into the district known as Bosque de las Lomas, one of the most exclusive in the city. It had come into being during the economic boom of the late seventies when it had seemed to nearly everyone in Mexico that the enormous oil reserves would catapult the country into the upper echelons of the world's financial giants. There was enormous prosperity during those few short years before the bust, and the immoderate appetites of those who benefited the most from the rise of the petropesos were a major impetus for a period of unprecedented exuberance for opulent architecture. As Arreola took a sharp curve that doubled back along one of the ridges, Haydon saw that the hills and slopes and ravines that formed the ever steeper ascent to the extinct volcano Ajusco were bejeweled with the topaz sparks of homes nestled in the pine and eucalyptus woods of the mountains.

Since they had gotten in the car Arreola had shown no inclination to talk, seeming to be wholly attentive to the task of negotiating the city's night traffic, and then the twisting streets of the western hills. But Haydon believed those weren't the only things occupying the old man's thoughts. He guessed that in his own journey into his father's past he had picked up a fellow traveler, and that before it was over Arreola would not be the only voyager to join him.

Haydon had been lost for quite some time when Arreola slowed the Mercedes and eased off the main street into a private drive that took a series of steep turns, each doubling back on the other until the headlights left the forest and picked up a high stone wall on the mountain side of the drive. To the left, the land fell away into a charcoal mist. They passed under several stone arches spanning the drive and then turned one last time up onto the crest of a ridge.

Lockhart's home stood alone, its white marble exterior illuminated by soft lights that made the slightly Moorish structure seem to levitate in the damp night haze. There was one last arch, and a gatehouse. Two guards, both with machine pistols strapped over their shoulders, were waiting for them. One guard stepped into the beam of the headlights, blocking the entrance, while the other quickly approached the driver's side window. Arreola identified himself with a document in his wallet, and they were allowed to pass.

They entered a cobblestone courtyard in the center of which a decorative tile fountain sprayed sparkling streams of water from the stamen of its floral centerpiece. Arreola pulled around the fountain to the portico and parked beside another Mercedes and a steel-gray Rolls-Royce. The front of the house was set back under a colonnade, and as Haydon looked up he could see that the second and third floors receded, one behind the other.

Arreola cut the car's engine. As he unbuckled his seat belt he said, "Juan is not the sort of man this home might lead you to believe." Without further comment he opened the car door and got out.

The two men walked onto a marble pavement that led to the colonnade, where the exterior lighting was softened even more by the warmth of the stone. Arreola proceeded directly to the front door and rang the bell as Haydon looked both ways along the rows of columns. There was an occasional white clay urn planted with fan palms, but otherwise the colonnade was bare.

The front door opened and a tall, thin man with fine features and cloudy blue eyes stood before them, his sandy hair shot through with gray that created a brindled effect. He wore casual, dun-colored linen trousers and a lightweight V-necked cotton sweater with a wheat-pattern weave. His white shirt was open at the neck.

"Gaston," he said in a mellow voice, and extended his hand to Arreola without a smile.

"Juan, it is good to see you." The two men shook hands, and Arreola turned and put his hand on Haydon's shoulder. "This is Stuart Haydon."

Lockhart fixed his eyes on Haydon as they shook hands. There was a momentary silence and then Lockhart said, "Yes, I can see." There was still no change of expression in his ruddy Scottish features. "I'm glad you look like him." His voice had no trace of a Spanish accent. He stepped back. "Please, come in."

The entrance to the house was its highest level on the ground floor, and they immediately stepped down into a large octagonal anteroom, its white walls covered with what Haydon took to be family portraits from eighteenth- and nineteenth-century Scotland, etchings of manor houses and castles, framed bits of fabric, and yellowing documents with red wax seals over faded ribbons. There were a few heavy pieces of furniture and beside the wide portal to the next room a table vitrine with an assortment of personal items, a sporran, rings, jewelry, medals, and a porcelain coat of arms and the accouterments from a writer's desk, wire-framed eyeglasses, an old fountain pen, inkwell, blotter, letterheads, and seals.

The next room was a huge expanse of white marble situated a couple of steps below the anteroom and located slightly to the right of it. It was constructed in the shape of a fan, an occasional marble column supporting the broad span of the high ceiling. The wall of the crescent side of the room was entirely glass, presenting an Olympian view of Mexico City, which lay in the valley below in shimmering iridescence, its farthest suburbs in all directions melting into the mist that shrouded the basin. As they crossed the marble floor to an arrangement of sofas and heavy armchairs near the windows, it was clear that the home was built on a ridge that fell away into the barrancas on either side, the neighboring slopes dotted with lights.

With a perfunctory gesture Lockhart offered Haydon and Arreola their choice of seats and then sat across from them, his back to the expensive view for which the entire home had been designed. He made no pretense to the preliminary small talk adhered to so rigorously in Mexican society prior to any discussion of serious business, nor did he bother offering them drinks. His manner was not abrupt or discourteous, however. He simply appeared to be uninterested in the conventions of such niceties.

"Gaston tells me you are here trying to satisfy certain matters of curiosity you have regarding your father's past," Lockhart said somewhat formally, crossing his long legs and settling his blue eyes on Haydon. "Would you mind telling me a little about yourself, and the circumstances that brought you here?"

Haydon understood the request perfectly, and spent the next twenty minutes giving Lockhart the kind of information he would need to put Haydon's position into perspective. Once again he related the sequence and description of the photographs, what he had learned from Gabriela and of his conversation with Ada Venecia. And once again he omitted the information about Sarmiento. He watched Lockhart closely to see if he portrayed even a subtle reaction to any particular aspect of the story. Lockhart listened patiently, his eyes never leaving Haydon. At one point he crossed his arms and lightly stroked his chin with the backs of the fingers of one hand; otherwise, his expression and posture never betrayed anything other than attentiveness.

When Haydon finished, Lockhart nodded slightly, as if he were thinking that everything had been as he had suspected. He didn't glance at Arreola as Haydon was expecting, but kept his gaze on Haydon.

"How do you feel about discovering, so late, this 'other' aspect of your father?"

Haydon stiffened inwardly at the pointedly personal question, but immediately resigned himself to this kind of inquiry. There was going to be no way to avoid a certain degree of personal vulnerability in this.

"After the initial shock . . . I was enormously curious. I wanted to answer all the unanswered questions. I felt, perhaps, betrayed," Haydon said, surprising himself a little with this confession. "I didn't—don't—see the need for him to have played out such a lengthy lie."

"Lie?"

The riposte caught Haydon off guard. "Pretending that it had never happened," he explained.

"Secret. I think he must have looked on it as a secret," Lockhart said. "Perhaps you think of it as a lie because you feel it wasn't something he should have kept from you. I would wager you were very close to him."

Haydon did not respond, but as he looked at Lockhart he had no doubt that the older man was interpreting his silence as a sign of affirmation. Why did Haydon feel that way? There was something about Lockhart that Haydon understood, something about his demeanor, his attitude, that seemed strangely familiar, even comforting. Perhaps it was the occasional Scottish inflection that surfaced in the full vowels of his smooth voice. His manner of speech was intriguing, an amalgamation of Spanish cadences with American and Scots diction.

"Do you believe talking with Amaranta is going to help you understand your father?"

"Yes." At this, Haydon thought he detected in Lockhart's eyes a flicker of sarcastic amusement at Haydon's naiveté.

"What do you expect to hear from her?"

"I have no idea," Haydon said. "But I'm sure you can understand my wanting to see her."

Lockhart nodded slightly again. "Yes, I think you should." For the first time he took his blue eyes off Haydon and looked at Arreola. "He ought to meet her, Gaston."

"I advised against it," Arreola said. "It will save him some grief."

"How can you be so sure of that?" Lockhart asked.

"I am sure of it, Juan," Arreola said sullenly. He turned to Haydon. "She is cursed with bad luck. It is no fault of hers, I know that. But there it is. What can she do?"

Lockhart looked back at Haydon. "Do they know you're in Mexico?"

"No."

"Do you plan to call before you go out there?"

"No. I'm afraid if I do she'll refuse to see me."

Lockhart shook his head. "She would see you, but you might have a hard time getting by the daughter. Isabel is protective. She believes her mother has been through enough, and her only intention is to prevent her from being hurt any more. But she would try to stop you." He paused, not taking his eyes off Haydon. "I'll talk to her for you and get her consent."

"Thank you, but there's no need to do that."

"I know. I should like to do it anyway."

"I can't guarantee I won't upset her."

Lockhart waved off the remark with a long, thin hand. "That's not necessary. Amaranta . . . will not be upset."

There was a pause in the conversation as Lockhart's pale eyes drifted away and Arreola stared at the high polish on his shoes, refusing to become involved in the conversation any further. Haydon felt as if both men had cut themselves loose from the present, willfully setting themselves adrift on the receding waters of the past. Haydon looked at the great space of the white room. Light fell in pools from the ceiling, leaving patches of shadow among the columns. There were a number of nude bronzes on pedestals; a grand piano; a wall of lighted cabinets displaying pre-Columbian terra-cotta; a collection of black Oaxacan pottery standing together in a curious configuration near one of the marble columns like an arrangement of votive altar vessels. Haydon was trying to understand the disposition of the pottery when he felt Lockhart's eyes on him. He turned back and found the elder man studying him with an intensity that was startling.

"There's something more I should tell both of you," Haydon said suddenly. It seemed the right moment to inform them of Sarmiento's role. He hadn't been sure he should do so until now. Lockhart's expression did not change, though Haydon was sure he saw a shift in the tint of his pale eyes. Arreola, however, was more obviously interested, raising his gaze to Haydon with a look of expectant trepidation.

"There was one other picture in the series, the last one," he continued. "It was a photograph of myself that had been taken with a telephoto without my knowledge only a few days before I received it. It had been disfigured, depicting my assassination. Thursday night the body of a private investigator was discovered in a car near one of Houston's bayous. The butcher knife which had been used to kill him was still in his neck. A police search of the files in the investigator's office revealed a dossier he had been compiling on me for a client here in Mexico City named Saturnino Barcena. I discovered that Barcena had been in Houston for several days beginning on the day before I received the first photograph and departing on the day I received the last one. He had been renting a small, furnished kitchenette apartment at a cheap motel. After searching the rooms and checking with the motel manager, I determined that the kitchenette's butcher knife was missing. I checked Barcena's registration card at the motel office, and found that he had given as his address here a number on 'Sarmiento' Street. I've already checked the city maps and no such street exists."

There was no reaction from Lockhart. Arreola was appalled, the muscles in his jowls working furiously. "Goddam," he said.

"I didn't inform my superior officer of my suspicions," Haydon added. "However, I left a message for the investigating detectives to check out the motel. It will be only a matter of time before they connect Sarmiento's fingerprints to the butcher knife."

"Goddam," Arreola repeated, and looked at Lockhart, who remained motionless, his expression stony and impenetrable.

Chapter 16

SATURNINO LOST THEM IN THE EARLY STREETS OF THE BOSQUE DE LAS Lomas district, where he had to drop back so far to avoid being spotted that he was only guessing at the turns they had made around the corners out of sight. But by this time he already had grown suspicious; he knew this part of the city, and he knew who lived here. All he needed to do was to confirm his intuition.

He quickly steered the car higher into the foothills, taking care to note the occasional sign to keep his bearings, for it had been a few years since he had been here. Finally he came to a familiar bend and an obscure narrow lane leading off on a still steeper grade into the pines. He turned in, attentive to the shoulder on the downside of the mountain as the drive doubled back on itself in several sharp turns, passing under a series of stone arches that extended like flying buttresses from the mountainside to the low side of the road. Suddenly he turned a corner and the headlights slammed into a gatehouse. Out of nowhere an armed guard stepped in front of the car while another appeared at Saturnino's side, his face in the opened window.

"Can I be of service, *señor*?" he asked, the smell of garlic hanging in the air from his breath.

"I certainly hope so," Saturnino said in a tone of frustration. "I was following some friends to a house I've never been to, and I lost them on the winding streets. They were driving a black Mercedes sedan and we were going to the home of Juan Lockhart Chavero-Casas. Can you tell me if I'm at the right place? Have they just come through here?"

The guard frowned, unsure of himself. "I will have to call up to the house," he said, pushing back from the window.

"Wait," Saturnino said quickly, and caught the man's attention with the pale green side of a ten-thousand-peso note held out of the view of the other guard. It was more than the man's daily salary.

The guard glanced at his partner in the bright headlights at the front of the car, and then bent down again and dangled his wrists over the sill of the open window. "*Sí, señor,*" he said.

"I just want to know if the car came in here," Saturnino said in a low voice.

The guard looked at the note and nodded. Saturnino pulled the note out of reach, raising his eyebrows to indicate he needed better verification than the guard's word.

"Two men," the guard said, unperturbed. "An old one was driving. The other was younger, sitting at the other door."

Saturnino slipped the note into the fork of the guard's scissored fingers.

"*Muchas gracias,*" Saturnino said, and backed away in a turnaround in front of the gatehouse, heading the car downhill. He looked back and saw the guard shrug to his partner, explaining, no doubt, the confusion of the wrong address. The ten thousand pesos would already be out of sight and his partner would never know the difference.

Saturnino's heart hammered in his chest. So the dogs were pissing on each other's legs. How quickly Haydon had found his way to the source. He began a contemptuous smile but didn't finish it. The damned little capuchin on the seat beside him had gotten its hands on something and was toying with it, sitting there like a hirsute child, keening with curiosity, its tail brought around to its side and poised above it like a question mark. Saturnino's excitement at his new discovery turned to nervousness as his eyes darted from the winding downhill drive to the monkey's tiny, probing fingers. What *was* he fooling with? He began to be aware of the perspiration under his arms, and an unsettling, mounting anxiety. When he got to the bottom of the drive he stopped the car and turned to the capuchin. The little creature was frustrated now, and stood up in the seat, chattering, the flat silver object flipping over and over so fast in its dexterous black paws that it was impossible for Saturnino to get a look at it in the dim light of the car. He reached down and picked up the flashlight and flicked it on just as the capuchin managed to succeed in prying open the seamed edges of the object. The instant the beam of light hit the exposed mirror the capuchin shrieked and snapped its face around to Saturnino, its sharp teeth bared, its round eyes and flat nostrils flared, its tongue wagging hysterically out of its mouth as if it were a separate living thing trying to escape the gaping throat behind it.

THIS TIME IT WAS HAYDON WHO STUDIED LOCKHART. THE OLDER MAN had been sitting in his armchair with the relaxed assurance of someone accustomed to authority. It never occurred to him to demonstrate a false modesty in the way he dressed or spoke or carried himself. His privileged social and financial standing did not affect him at all, having always been a part of his life as much as the color of his hair or his height. The things that affected the thoughts and values of Juan Lockhart came from within, not from the computer printout of his portfolio or the real estate value of his home.

There was something else that struck Haydon about the man who sat opposite him. He recalled from Arreola's conversation earlier in the evening that Lockhart and Haydon's father had been roughly the same age. If Webster Haydon were living now he would be seventy-seven. Lockhart easily looked ten years younger than that, and it seemed to Haydon that his father had appeared older than this man even at the time of his death six years earlier. Lockhart was totally lacking in the body language and mannerisms of the elderly. No one would mistake him for a young man, but he did not fit the stereotype of an old man either.

But now, after hearing Haydon's recitation of the events involving Sarmiento, Lockhart looked at him with the preoccupied concentration of a man who suddenly had a lot to think about. He could feel Arreola looking at him, so he glanced at him to acknowledge the other man's concern, and then looked back to Haydon.

"You're very astute," he said. He hesitated only slightly before he asked, "The name Sarmiento appeared nowhere in the investigator's file?"

"I went through it rather quickly, but I didn't see it."

"You're sure there had been a butcher knife in his motel rooms?"

"The manager said one was furnished."

"He could have worn gloves."

Haydon nodded. He didn't necessarily like the tack of this last observation. He wasn't interested in developing a defense for Sarmiento.

"It's obvious that by informing me in the way he did of my father's past, he was deliberately luring me here," Haydon said. "It's a more conducive environment for what he wants to do. He's shrewd enough. He knew I would understand that, but he also knew that I would come anyway. He's studied me pretty well." Haydon looked alternately at both men. "I don't have any doubt about whether the man is capable of fulfilling his threat, but I do have one question for the two of you. Why is he doing this?"

Neither man answered immediately. Arreola shifted impatiently on the sofa and tugged at the lapels of his dark suit. Lockhart, though he was looking at Haydon, seemed to be pursuing thoughts elsewhere.

"You must understand," Lockhart replied at last, the mellow burr in his voice seeming to lend authority to his judgment, "that Saturnino is not an easy man to anticipate. His relationship with his family has, for long years, been one of alienation. He has been an outcast. However—and this is important—it was his choice. Up until the point that he made that decision, he had no self-confidence, no inner strength, no conviction . . . no guts. All of that had been exorcised from him by his father when he was a boy. When he decided to cut himself off from his family, his father was still living and Nino was in his second year at the university. At that point he changed radically. It was a complete personality reversal. Very disturbing for everyone, including himself. He is a man of contradictions; he is intelligent and can be entirely charming, but he has an erratic personality. He's wholly unpredictable. You should fear him for his mercurial nature, not because of his wickedness." Lockhart paused. "On the other hand, maybe he should be feared all the more for that. One at least can understand malice."

"Then you have no doubt that he'll try it?"

Lockhart's cool eyes rested on Haydon. "Of course not." It was said matter-of-factly. Then he added, "From my perspective, however, to say he will 'try' is to put the wrong emphasis on it. Unless you leave Mexico City, I would say he can pick the time and place for it. He probably already has."

Lockhart added this last without emotion, in the cold, flat tone of a man calculating the odds on a horse race at the Hipodromo. There was nothing in his voice that indicated he was talking about something as momentous as Haydon's assassination. Haydon found it a strange thing to hear, as if he had somehow lost his own identity and was participating in a conversation about his death by disinterested parties. It was oddly like hearing his funeral discussed by strangers who had only a casual interest in it. Plainly, the peculiarity of this dialogue did not occur to Lockhart.

"Why would he do it?" Lockhart continued, positing the initial question without being prompted. He slowly massaged the wrist of one hand with the long fingers of the other. "There may not be a reason that any of us would understand. I mean, I doubt that Saturnino looks at life in anything like the way we do."

Haydon wondered at the "we." Did Lockhart believe that the three of them shared a common worldview? If so, it seemed presumptive, at least as far as Haydon was concerned. What did Lockhart know about Haydon's opinions? Or why did he believe he did?

"From Saturnino's infancy to the time he was of school age," Lockhart began, "he lived an idyllic life with his mother and her beloved Indian housekeepers in San Ángel. He was not around his father. I do not know why Amaranta arranged things this way, but she did not afford Everardo much of an opportunity to be close to the boy. Saturnino knew only the housekeepers, and of course his mother, for whom he developed a profound attachment. She has always been an exotic woman, Amaranta, and he adored her and all her uncommon ways. The housekeepers indulged him, Amaranta indulged him. I suspect that his childhood fantasies were far more vivid—and immediate—than those of most children who can more easily put such extravagant inventiveness in perspective as they grow older because they constantly have to compare it to reality. But for Saturnino, reality was an ever-shifting experience. It did not have the constancy by which most of us recognize it. *His* reality was quite fantastic in itself. His was a strange, perhaps, but innocent childhood.

"All that changed when Amaranta suddenly decided it was time for Everardo to be 'father,'" Lockhart said, shaking his head at Amaranta's capriciousness. "When Nino was two Amaranta gave birth to Isabel, but that did not change her monastic separation from Sarmiento. That continued for another eight years. Then she abruptly announced she was moving in from San Ángel, and came like a gypsy to the home she owned in the Polanco district, where Everardo had been living all this time."

Quietly, their bare feet moving silently over the marble floors, two Indian servants—a man and a woman—appeared from behind Haydon and Arreola, each carrying a tray. Lockhart stood and moved a low table from a few feet away and placed it between his chair and the sofa, motioning for the servants to put down the coffee server. He thanked them with a nodding, almost Oriental, bow of his head and they left.

Without asking either Haydon or Arreola if they wanted coffee, he began pouring into the three cups already sitting in saucers. When each was filled he took his and sat back in his chair, crossed his long legs, and resumed talking as he held his coffee in his lap.

"This new move of Amaranta's was a disaster," he said, watching Arreola heave himself up to the edge of the sofa and begin doctoring his coffee with cream and sugar. Haydon followed suit, taking only cream. "Everardo's bachelor existence was turned upside down. Until now his mistresses actually lived in the Polanco house about half the time, convenience winning out over convention. He never had to worry about whom he brought home or when. Suddenly all of that freedom was ended. Now he had a wife, two children—an eight-year-old daughter and a ten-year-old son—and servants, where before he had none. He had not been consulted in either instance. True, the man was a bastard, but even a bastard can be treated badly. It would have been ludicrous had it not been for the children."

Lockhart stopped to sip his coffee, as they all did. It was strong, but Haydon found it delicious. Though he had not seen Lockhart request it, he was grateful for its arrival.

"Under the best of circumstances, it would have been unlikely that Everardo would have any rapport with Saturnino," Lockhart continued. "The boy was entirely like his mother, and I think Everardo looked upon him as some kind of freak. But under these conditions the relationship never had a chance. At first Everardo simply ignored him. It was complete alienation. Children can survive that, I suppose. They will find something else to love, and imagine they are being loved in return. And he had his mother, though admittedly this kind of tension did not bode well for a healthy relationship. But being ignored by one's father is not the worst of things." Lockhart stopped. "The worst of things came next."

Behind Lockhart's back the lights of the city far below the mountain caught Haydon's attention as they suddenly began to twinkle and glitter. Focusing his eyes on them, Haydon realized that it had begun to rain again. It was a silent rain, no sound of it penetrating Lockhart's stone-and-marble fortress— only the Brownian movement of the flickering city lights.

Lockhart's voice brought Haydon's attention back from the space beyond the sweeping crescent of glass. "As Saturnino grew older, Everardo developed what seemed to be a true loathing for the boy's very existence. Alienation evolved into a sinister antagonism. Everardo was vicious. Saturnino was physically and mentally molested. The least he could expect from his father was ridicule. It was torment. It was a living hell for him, all through his adolescence."

"What was Amaranta doing during all this?" Haydon interrupted. "Couldn't she stop it?"

"Oh, of course she tried," Lockhart said. "There were pitched battles. Horrible scenes, an endless war of wills. To you, to me, it is a mystery why a woman tolerates this sort of madness. But you're a policeman. You've seen this kind of thing before. God knows why it happens."

"But Amaranta, as she's been described to me, doesn't seem to fit the personality profile of a woman who puts up with an abusive husband," Haydon said. "She's too independent, too strong. It's not consistent."

Lockhart didn't respond immediately, and Haydon looked at Arreola. The old man's face was drawn, his eyes gazing far away into the rainy Valley of Mexico. Just as Haydon was sensing that he had hit upon a significant point that neither man wanted to address, Lockhart spoke up.

"You must always remember that it is a major miscalculation to apply that word 'consistent' to Amaranta," he said. "I know what you mean, Stuart." The use of Haydon's first name caught him by surprise, though it did not seem particularly out of place from the lips of Juan Lockhart. "But rules, personality profiles, psychological diagnoses—none of these work in her case. She simply defies that sort of logical assessment."

He leaned forward and set his empty cup on the edge of the table. "Amaranta loved the boy unreservedly, in her odd, exotic way. She never demonstrated a mother's stability in the way we would think was ideal. She wasn't capable. But he never had to doubt she loved him, never. Still, the sublimity on the one hand and the agony on the other were too great for the boy. By the time he was in his late teens he had developed into an absolutely fragmented personality. If Amaranta was erratic, Saturnino was bizarre. He didn't react to anything in a normal way. Amaranta and Everardo had created a one-of-a-kind creature."

With this remark Arreola also put his cup on the table.

"They have had sad lives, Stuart," he put in. "Nothing good can come from digging into it. If this thing, this threat, is from Saturnino . . ." Arreola left the sentence hanging, seeming suddenly to find himself at a loss for words. He shook his head and sat back on the sofa with a tremendous sigh.

"When I spoke to Ada Venecia in Houston," Haydon said, looking from Arreola to Lockhart, "she told me that Sarmiento 'kicked Saturnino out of the family when he was a young man.' She said that Saturnino was 'a hard one to love, even for his mother.'"

"Jesus Christ!" Arreola spat suddenly, jarred from his brooding, his eyes glaring at Haydon. "That old woman! Ada was a crone even when she was still young enough to have her tits above her waist. She was never a friend to Amaranta, even when they were friends! Shit!" He cut his eyes at Lockhart and shook his head as he returned to his former silence.

Lockhart nodded pensively, but Haydon could not tell if he was agreeing with Venecia or Arreola.

"It's true that Everardo tried to disinherit Saturnino," he said. "During Saturnino's last year at the university, Everardo did bar him from the house in Polanco, but it was a weak and petty gesture, since Saturnino had already withdrawn from them. I don't know how Everardo managed to gain Amaranta's consent—after all, it was her fortune—but he manipulated the boy's inheritance papers, introducing strictures that delayed his full endowment. This legal battle was prolonged over

several years, during which time Saturnino—in his mid-
twenties by now—turned against Amaranta with a fury. She
moved back to San Ángel. Saturnino became active in the
student rebellions of the sixties, got in trouble with the police.
Serious trouble for a while. But finally he received his
doctorate in anthropology in France, at the prestigious Centre
National du Recherche Scientifique. He studied under
Jacques Soustelle, a world-renowned authority in Mesoamerican culture." Lockhart let that hang in the air a moment. "You
see, he's no fool. Mad perhaps, but no fool."

Lockhart glanced at Arreola, who had once again retreated
into a sullen privacy, and then he looked at Haydon. "They
were, and are, a wild family indeed," he said. "Such a great
amount of strangeness shared among them."

"Do either of you know where he lives?"

Arreola shook his head sharply as he cast a quick glance at
Lockhart.

"I can't help you there," Lockhart said. "What are you going
to do? Mexico has no extradition treaty with the United
States."

"I'm aware of that," Haydon said. "What about the daughter,
Isabel? How has she been affected by all this?"

Arreola looked up, his eyes fixed on Lockhart.

"Chabela," Juan Lockhart said, using the endearing form of
her name, "is a saint."

Arreola's face relaxed, and Haydon thought he saw the old
man's eyes glisten as they moved from Lockhart to him.

"She was the only chance any of them ever had for achieving
redemption," Arreola added. He shook his head slowly. "But it
was not to be."

"What is she like?" Haydon asked.

"Chabela will speak for herself," Lockhart said. "When you
go see them." He was clearly not going to elaborate.

"I have one other question," Haydon said. He was looking at
Lockhart, but out of the corner of his eye he saw Arreola's
posture stiffen. "I know you were my father's closest friend
here. Shortly after he married there was a split between you.
I would like to know what happened."

Arreola hung his head, a gesture of invisibility. Had he
possessed the power he would have disappeared. Lockhart's
reaction was a glacial gaze of his pale eyes. Haydon had the

impression that Lockhart did not know from one second to the next how he was going to answer him, that he was deciding, that he was tempted, but that a lifetime of restraint had predetermined his response.

"I can understand why you think you have the right to ask that," he said. "Under the circumstances."

It was said in a tone that implied that Lockhart was going to forgive Haydon his rashness in having asked, and though there was an edge of the imperious in his voice there was also an unmistakable melancholy. That was all. He stood. Their conversation had come to an end.

Lockhart saw them to the front door, he and Arreola walking together, talking softly as Haydon went a little ways ahead, letting them have the privacy of those few moments.

At the front door Lockhart shook Haydon's hand.

"Regarding Saturnino," he said, "I would advise you to return to Houston as soon as you can. There is nothing Gaston or I can do for you, and you know how the police are here. Besides, the man is out of control, surely you must see that. In such situations there is little anyone can do, even under the best of circumstances. If you remain in Mexico City you will be running a very foolish risk."

HAYDON HAD INSISTED THAT GASTON LET HIM TAKE A TAXI BACK INTO the city, since they were already in the same district where Arreola himself lived, but the old man wouldn't hear of it. He would make the drive in and back out. What else did he have to do? Haydon assumed he wanted to talk, but most of the drive down out of the mountains was made in silence, Arreola negotiating the winding streets and boulevards with a relaxation that came of a familiarity with the route, his mind elsewhere.

Haydon was preoccupied too, and for the first time he was conscious of the Beretta resting in its clip in the small of his back. Juan Lockhart had given him a lot to think about. Lockhart himself would be puzzle enough, his face and body seeming to have cheated the decades like the picture of Dorian Gray, his self-possession, his perceptive observations about the personalities of Amaranta and Saturnino for whom he seemed to display a sincere, if restrained, empathy . . . there were a hundred things. But what Haydon found most imme-

209

diately curious was the fact that though Lockhart had no doubt whatsoever that Saturnino intended to kill Haydon—indeed, would kill him if Haydon remained in Mexico City—he demonstrated no real anxiety on Haydon's behalf, expressed no concern that Haydon should act cautiously or quickly, offered no advice, offered no suggestions as to how he might be able to help. There was no indication at all from him that he found the situation shocking or even cause for alarm. Either he actually did not believe what he had told Haydon, or he was a man capable of extraordinary detachment. Or . . . or he was feigning.

They were already in the darkness of the vast Chapultepec Park, the streetlamps casting pools of pale light under the mighty *ahuehuetes*, when Arreola broke the silence.

"So what did you think, huh? Juan is not an easy man to understand."

"No," Haydon said, "he isn't."

They rode in silence a little farther, past the fountain, *glorieta*, before Haydon asked, "What about his family? Does Lockhart have children?"

Arreola shook his head of thick white hair. "No. He married late in life, maybe he was thirty-five. His wife was a Brazilian woman, a lot of black blood in her. *Muy exótica!* She was barren. I do not know which of them had the problem, but they never had children. And he had bad luck with her. She was not entirely faithful to him, I understand. It was talked around quite a bit for a few years. Juan did the Anglo thing, endured it stoically, wore the horns for several years pretending it wasn't happening. And then she got sick, cancer. A very great shock, this beautiful, promiscuous woman. When it got bad, toward the end, he took off from his firm and nursed her personally. For months and months, more than a year, he was a recluse up there with her while she was shriveling to nothing but eyes and bones. She had these big eyes. Anyway, she died. And Juan went back to his law practice."

The angel of independence stood lighted in the night sky above her *glorieta*, the mist making her sparkle as if she were the only clean and hopeful thing in the city. Arreola swung his Mercedes around the traffic circle and pulled over to the curb.

As Haydon thanked him and put his hand on the door handle, Arreola reached across and touched Haydon's arm.

"Stuart, I would be more than happy to take you to San Ángel tomorrow. You know that."

Haydon nodded. "I know, but I think I should go alone."

"Of course," Arreola said.

Haydon got out and closed the door, waved at the old man, and started across the narrow neck of the esplanade to the front of the hotel.

Half an hour later he stood at the window of his room, bathed and dressed in his pajamas, looking down at the empty Paseo de la Reforma. Someone had used the broad avenue to paint a slogan on the pavement in front of the U.S. Embassy next door: *Paz en Nicaragua! Paz en El Salvador!* A dove carried an olive branch. A few couples strolled across the esplanades from the Zona Rosa, and a young girl sat in a glass kiosk on the near esplanade waiting for a taxi to come in sight so she could step out and wave it down. It was late, and Haydon was already feeling an uneasiness in his stomach about the next day.

He turned away from the window and walked over to the bed. He sat down and picked up the telephone to call Nina.

Chapter 17

HAYDON HAD NOT ASKED FOR A WAKE-UP CALL BEFORE GOING TO BED, knowing he would not sleep well. He had tossed restlessly, hearing sirens on the Reforma below and hearing Lockhart's Scottish burr repeating phrases of their conversation, going over and over some of them until they became unintelligible and he was left with the muddled sound of Lockhart's voice droning on and on into his dreams. Sometime during the early morning hours he was shocked awake by an obscenely violent nightmare, an arabesque narrative in which a naked but faceless Saturnino pursued him through a maze of black mirrors, through a world of vague and deceptive reflections where Haydon himself existed only as a reflection, stalked by an aroused and satyrlike Saturnino who chased Haydon's shimmering image down endless obsidian corridors. Suddenly awake, he found his heart beating wildly. He sat up in bed until it calmed, until he had forced his thoughts away from the nightmare to something trivial and far away. After a while he lay down again, and eventually slept.

He woke late the next morning. Sunday. By the time he had showered and shaved and arrived in the lobby downstairs it was nearly ten o'clock. He picked up a copy of the *News*, the city's largest English-language newspaper, and went outside on the Reforma. Though the feel of the midmorning air was light and crisp because of the altitude, a thick layer of smog had already settled over the highland basin and the daylight was being filtered through a light sepia haze. Because it was Sunday and the downtown traffic was sparse, the smog in the immediate area was not as bad as it would have been on a weekday. Even so, by the time Haydon had crossed the boulevard, which was practically deserted, his eyes had already begun to sting.

Walking under the camphor trees past the closed shops in the Zona Rosa, he proceeded along the narrow Amberes to Hamburgo and turned right, forgoing the popular Denny's on the corner and continuing another block or so to the Salon de Te Auseba near Florencia. He moved down the long glass case of fresh pastries, chose a couple of glazed *tortas*, and ordered a cup of Viennese coffee. With a newspaper under his arm, he carried the pastries and coffee down into the small dining area that was a couple of steps below the sidewalk level. He chose a round black-topped table near the street and sat down.

He ate the pastries while glancing through the newspaper, then lost interest and sat back to drink the coffee. All along Hamburgo, shop and café owners were outside washing down the sidewalks or cleaning windows or taking in produce from trucks parked along the curbs. Occasionally a taxi or delivery van drove by slowly, making the interlocking pavers on the street rattle like a sack of wooden blocks, a comfortable sound that seemed to Haydon to belong more properly in a village than in the heart of a city of twenty million people.

He sipped the dark-roast coffee, and his thoughts turned to San Ángel. How many times had he been to San Ángel over the years, never knowing they were there, unable to imagine the woman with green eyes whom his father had loved? How could his father have come to Mexico City year after year without seeing her? After having loved so strongly, how could he have acted as though she never had existed? Had he not, if only once, had an irresistible desire to see her again? Arreola had said that Webster was the only person who had ever understood Amaranta. Surely that implied an extraordinary relationship; could it have been so completely severed as everyone believed? And yet, from Haydon's own experience, from his own knowledge about his father, that seemed indeed to have been the case. But then, as he had been discovering during the last few days, what did he know, really?

One of the women behind the pastry counter used her white apron to wipe the flour from her hands and came down with the coffeepot to refill the cups of the few scattered customers. Haydon thanked her and added cream to his second cup. There was time. On a Sunday morning it would take a taxi only twenty minutes to get to San Ángel, and lunch wouldn't be served until around two o'clock. He sipped the cup of fresh coffee and watched two elderly Indian women and three small children make their way along the sidewalk. One of the women carried an infant tucked into her *huipil*. Stooped, beaten down by circumstances and the calendar, they probably had slept in a doorway during the night. The children were not theirs, the old women were well past the age, but they probably belonged to daughters or granddaughters. Because the Zona Rosa was frequented by wealthy Mexicans and tourists, the police allowed only the most colorful Indians to beg there, those with the brightest *huipiles*, with their thick jet hair braided in traditional Indian knots, those most recently in from the mountains and whose colorful blankets had not yet worn out to be replaced with the filthy rags that normally covered the backs of the millions of denizens in the *ciudades perdidas*, the "lost cities," like the sprawling slums of Neza-hualcoyotl. He watched the women pass.

He finished his coffee, left the newspaper on the table, and walked out onto the street, turning toward Florencia at the end of the block. At the corner he looked to his left at the receding column of tall palms that lined the median of the avenue all the way to Insurgentes. Looking in the other direction, one block away, he saw the Ángel *glorieta*. It was on that circle, under the last palm on Florencia, that Amaranta had stood in sunlight and smiled at an unknown photographer, her skirt caught and lifted by the gentle breezes of the valley. Haydon wanted to walk down there where she had stood, where the photographer had stood in front of her. He was sure he could put his feet in the exact spot. All these years he had stayed in the Hotel María Isabel and he could have looked out his window and seen it, had done so in fact, without ever knowing what he was looking at.

A car honked and he looked across the avenue on the other side of the palms. One of the city's thousands of sharp-eyed taxi drivers had pulled to the curb and was looking at him, his head cocked back questioningly. Haydon nodded and started across the street.

The driver went to Insurgentes and turned right, following this longest street in the city straight into the southern *delegaciones*. Insurgentes was one of the major shopping thoroughfares in the capital. Its middle-class stores included an abundance of U.S. chains, though the street gave way to a more continental atmosphere once it passed the Plaza México, the largest bullring in the world. From the Felix Cuevas intersection all the way out to San Ángel, Insurgentes became a beautiful tree-lined boulevard with exclusive boutiques, and some of the city's best clubs and international restaurants.

The *colonia* of San Ángel lay on the western side of Insurgentes just north of the enormous campus of the National University. The community dated all the way back to the Aztecs and until the late 1930s had been a country village. Gradually, however, it had been incorporated into the larger environs of Mexico City, though, like its sister *colonia*, Coyoacán, it retained a village charm with narrow winding cobblestoned streets, shady plazas, sixteenth-century churches, and elegant mansions hidden behind high stone walls. It always had been a popular haven for artists and writers.

The driver dropped Haydon at the Sanborn's restaurant across from the Parque de la Bombilla. He did not want to be taken directly to Amaranta's address. Starting south, he went to the end of the long block and turned into the narrow, high-walled crook of Monasterio that climbed sharply and crookedly until he saw the sky-blue cupola of the convent of El Carmen. The church walls rose to his left, and he followed them until the narrow lane opened onto the busy intersection of Avenida de la Revolución and La Paz. He crossed to Plaza del Carmen, ignoring the modern bustle of the crowded intersection, and headed up the steep curve of Madero to Plaza San Jacinto, the old center of the *colonia*. Within a few blocks the streets grew less crowded, then nearly empty, almost pastoral in their serenity, with only an occasional sandaled Indian moving along the cobblestones, keeping his own counsel.

By the time Haydon reached the Plaza San Jacinto, all was quiet, the traditional art bazaar that dominated the plaza every Saturday having come and gone for another week, leaving the topiary hedges along the walkways to the villagers. Even the electric buses that stopped in the plaza moved silently except for the crackling of their trolley-type guides connecting with the overhead wires above the streets.

He wondered if it would be here that Saturnino would wait for him, in the darkened doorway of one of the old colonial buildings, behind a privet hedge on the other side of the plaza. But why here? This was the most obvious route, it was true, but there were others as well. He thought Saturnino might try to narrow it down, wait closer to Amaranta's, in order to reduce his chances of staking out the wrong route.

It was late morning as he made his way up the gentle rise of Frontera and turned into the first of its two side streets leading higher up in the village. The high mountain air was cool, with a thin mist, almost a fog, hanging in the narrow lane, making the cobblestones shiny, and deepening the pink and cerise blossoms of the bougainvilleas that draped over the walls and doorways that opened off the street. He had passed only a few doorways when the lane opened into the tiny Plaza de los Arcángelos, which was, in essence, a private courtyard for the colonial homes whose walls fronted its circular drive. The drive itself was paved with small blocks of the dark volcanic stone indigenous to this southern region of the city; a fine green moss grew in the joints of the stones. The plaza, roughly a hundred meters square, had an old stone fountain at its center, and the tall trunks of the pines and *ahuehuetes* and eucalyptus trees were profusely entwined with bougainvilleas, whose blossoms draped from high up like waterfalls of red spume. The homes that surrounded the plaza were muted shades of pumpkin and parchment and the reddish-brown hues of the common volcanic stone known as *tezontle*.

Hearing a girl's soft laughter, Haydon glanced around at one of the high-backed stone seats that constituted the diminutive plaza's corners, and saw two students preoccupied with each other, ignoring the books that lay unopened on the stone seat beside them. There was no one else. He turned away toward the only drive off the circle that led down a walled private driveway. At the end of the driveway a high double-arched entrance gate made of stone stood across the drive like the ancient remains of an old aqueduct. The arches served as an entry from the walled street, and at either side tall cast-iron streetlamps stood like lean sentries. Beyond the arches the tops of *ahuehuetes* and eucalyptus hinted at the grounds of Amaranta's rose-colored house.

Walking under the old stone arches, Haydon entered a large walled courtyard about fifty meters square which served as a turnaround and parking space in front of the house. Immedi-

ately to the left were two iron gates, which were the entry and
exit of a circular drive to the side of the house, the upper floor
of which he could see over the high wall across its front. He
was surprised that it appeared exactly as he had imagined it.
The wall in front of the house contained a third gate, a narrow
one which introduced the front of the house and which was
hinged on both sides so that it opened from its center, each
half folding back against the thick wall. As Haydon approached
this gate he noticed to its right a recessed niche in the wall
covered by a hinged wrought-iron grille, a replica of the gate
itself. Inside the shrine was a white marble crucifix of unusually good quality, and beneath it a terra-cotta bowl of fresh
marigolds.

He pushed the button beside the latch, and looked up to the
tall windows on the second floor, and thought of his father,
standing where he stood now, looking up to the empty
windows. And he thought of Saturnino again, too, perhaps in
the underbrush of the grounds that surrounded the walled
courtyard, watching him. But there was nothing he could do
about it. Having been incautious to this point, it seemed
absurd to become suddenly conscientious.

Haydon flinched at the sound of the electric latch snapping
open, and was surprised to see the gate swing out a few inches.
Why didn't someone come out to inquire? Surely they had
looked out and seen a stranger. He pushed open the gate and
entered, closing it until it clicked shut behind him. Wondering
how quickly he could get to his Beretta in the small of his back,
he walked across the courtyard to the front door, which was
flanked by two brass lamps mounted on the stucco walls on
either side of the portico. There was another bell on the front
of the door, and he rang it, looking at the walkway that went
around the corner of the house.

When the door opened, Haydon turned, and his knees
almost buckled. Standing under the flat arch of the entrance
was Amaranta, only a few years older than she had appeared in
her photographs taken fifty years earlier, her green, her
emerald eyes as breathtaking as everyone had said they were,
her skin as remarkable as Gabriela had described it, even to
the detail of the small blue vein at the corner of her mouth,
which, he observed, was more sensuous than even the photographs had portrayed. Her thick cinnamon hair was full, to the

shoulders, but pulled back loosely and clipped at the nape of
her long neck, the wiry strands of gray spreading out from her
forehead like the rippling path of a summer moon. Haydon
was momentarily disoriented, unable to grasp the obvious, too
startled to know the truth of what he was seeing, too beguiled
to care that what he was thinking made no sense. He saw the
first slight quiver at the corner of her lips, his eyes fixed on it
disbelievingly as he held his breath, realizing that finally,
inexplicably, he was going to hear her speak, hear the same
voice his father had heard, the voice of the odalisque, silent for
so long, animated after half a century.

But the smile he was anticipating never materialized. It died
near the blue vein where it had begun.

"I am Isabel," she said. "I was expecting you."

There was a moment's silence. "Isabel," he said blankly.
She nodded.

He recovered, came in a dizzying rush to the surface like a
drowning swimmer freed from a strong deep current, back
through time, back to the present and the rational.

"Excuse me," he heard himself say. He could see in her eyes
that she knew what had happened.

"Please, come in," she said, stepping back. He saw the toes
of her sandaled feet slip from under the hem of her skirt as she
moved back. It had an instantly erotic effect on him, as if she
had raised her skirt all the way to the inside of her thigh. He
didn't move.

"You know who I am, that I was coming?"

"Yes. Juan . . . Lockhart called."

Of course. Of course he would have let them know. Again
Haydon had missed the obvious. He hadn't even thought of it,
but it was obvious. Lockhart wouldn't have let him surprise
them.

"I should have called," he said.

"No, it's all right, really," she insisted. "I understand."

And immediately Haydon believed her. He knew she did
understand, and he was grateful for it, relieved. He believed
her completely.

She stepped back a little farther, and he entered the rose house.

THEY SAT IN THE MAIN *SALA* AS THE SUN BEGAN TO BREAK THROUGH
the cloud cover outside, scattering bars of unsteady light

through the tall bare windows. The rising and dying rays caused Haydon sometimes to see her as if through a sheer rippling veil, a phenomenon that created moments when she seemed to float before him in the mote-laden ribbons of sunlight.

She faced him from the center of a wine velvet divan, straight-backed and observant with her sandaled feet close together and flat on the floor. Her blouse was short-sleeved, with a deep scooped neck which she wore without artifice. She looked at him calmly, her hands resting in her lap, waiting for him to speak.

"I didn't want to give you the chance to turn me away over the telephone," he explained. "I know that showing up like this is impertinent, but it would have been even more difficult to come here after a refusal. And I would have had to do it."

"There is no need to go into this," she said. "Juan told me everything. I know why you're here, and I can imagine how difficult it must be for you." Then she added, "I wouldn't have objected." She seemed always to be on the verge of smiling without actually doing so. Her English was excellent, with a graceful lilt of an accent.

Haydon wondered if Lockhart really had told her everything.

"Have you spoken to your mother about me?"

"No," she said, without elaboration.

Haydon couldn't take his eyes off her. Quite apart from her extraordinary beauty, her uncanny resemblance to her mother was actually distracting. "I hadn't thought you would look so much like her," he said.

She didn't react. "Which pictures of her have you seen?"

"There were three," he said, paying more attention to what he was seeing than to what he was saying. "In the first she was sitting at an easel in her studio, painting. It was too dark to see any significant details. I could see only her profile. In the second one she was standing under a palm on Florencia, at the Ángel *glorieta*. In the third, she was lying on a narrow bed, actually a *lit en bateau* . . . also in her studio, I think."

At this Isabel smiled and gave a brief throaty laugh at his discretion. "Well, those are good pictures," she conceded. "But she was a lot younger than I am when those were taken."

Haydon had already calculated her age. She was forty-one.

Then her smile faded quickly, and she looked at him more seriously. "Juan told me you had received these photographs and two prints of your father's portraits. Which ones were they?"

He described them, and she nodded, seeming to recognize them.

"They were mailed anonymously? In Houston?"

"That's right."

"And you haven't any idea who mailed them, or why?"

So Lockhart hadn't told her everything after all, having wisely left the rest of it up to Haydon. But he hesitated, suddenly unable to respond in a way that seemed appropriate.

"You understand that in a very real sense I have a right to know," she insisted. "Those photographs belong to my mother. No one else has access to them."

"Someone must. Unless you sent them yourself."

She didn't even respond to his last remark, appearing to take it as rhetorical.

"Whoever sent them seems to have a grudge against me," Haydon said.

"How do you know this?"

"There was a message with the last photograph that indicated that this person held me responsible for something. It wasn't clear what it was."

"With the nude photograph? There was a note with that?"

"No. The last photograph was a picture of myself, taken on the streets of Houston."

Isabel looked at him, studying him with a frankness that had the unlikely effect of putting him at ease.

"Doesn't your brother have access to the photographs?" he asked.

Her face changed to an icy rigidity. "Oh, I see," she said. "This has gone much farther than I realized. I suppose Juan has talked to you about Saturnino?"

Haydon nodded. "Yes, some."

"Fine. He knows him as well as anyone, I suppose. Maybe better than anyone."

"Why is that?"

"The last time I saw Saturnino was nearly two years ago," she said, not hearing his question, or ignoring it. "We talked for nearly an hour, here. He sat . . . exactly where you're sitting, as a matter of fact. Before then it had been a little more than two years since I had seen him." Her eyes had settled to the chair, but then she brought them up quickly. "Sometimes he calls, but rarely." Then she looked away again, toward a tall, dark wood cabinet with glass doors that was filled with pre-Columbian ceramic vessels and clay figures.

Haydon looked at her profile, her straight back, and the lines of her breasts. He imagined her in the long black evening dress, her back exposed all the way down to the dimples above her hips, imagined her breasts, dusky behind the veil of material.

"Is that his collection in the case?"

"Oh, no. They're mine." She looked at him. "We have the same degree, did you know that? Anthropology. Mesoamerican specialists, though God knows that's not anything unusual in Mexico. But he became a professional, went into the university to teach. I chose to stay here," she said, tossing her head to indicate the old house. "But every year I spend a month in the jungles, along the Usumacinta, the Lacanja, sometimes in the Yucatán. It's grueling and refreshing all at once."

"Do you go with the expeditions from the university?"

"No, with a friend, just the two of us, except for a couple of guides. Though we've been many times it's easy to get lost. You've got to have someone get you in and out."

Haydon kept wanting to ask her questions about his father. What had he been like in those days; what did she think about him; what had they talked about; what had they seen in each other that so quickly created a bond of such intensity? And why didn't it last? That she should not be able to answer these questions made him restless, as if he had awakened from having dreamed of her and was left with nothing but a vague longing.

"How much do you know about their relationship?" he asked suddenly.

She looked at him with an expression of undissembling compassion. He could tell in an instant that she knew what he meant, and that she understood how important it was to him.

"Quite a lot," she said. "Perhaps as much as another person can possibly know."

He didn't stop to think what she might have meant by this

cryptic remark; he should have, but he didn't. Instead he asked, "May I speak with her?"

"I wouldn't deny you that," she said. "But—this is difficult— I don't really know you. . . . In these later years, well, we've grown quite close, in our way. It wasn't always so. She is an enigmatic woman and I didn't really begin to understand her until . . . relatively recently."

She kept her green eyes on him, speaking without trepidation, hesitating only to choose the precise words.

"After moving here, at a certain point, I became entranced with her. I went about rediscovering her as if I had not been her daughter, but a stranger writing her biography. This house, in which I had not lived since my early years in college, was my library. I found old letters and read them. I pored over photographs. I found old clothes, old paintings, mementos of stories I hadn't known. I talked with those who knew her best, collected anecdotes and gossip as greedily as if they were about myself . . . after a while they seemed to be. And now, for some time, I have come to identify with her. She doesn't seem quite so inexplicable to me, perhaps because I am older now, not so self-centered. I see more of myself in her, in what she was, than ever I had imagined."

She stopped, and appeared to make a decision not to elaborate. "I am eager that you do not misunderstand her," she said. "With the exception of your father, I think she has too often been a victim of that. I would like to suggest something. You cannot meet her just now, anyway. Celerina and Paulo have taken her to mass with friends in Jardines del Pedregal. She never used to go to mass, but now she wants to go regularly. They will eat afterward, and not return here until quite late in the afternoon. Let me take you through the house, show you the studio. There are photographs you should see." She looked at him pointedly. "We can talk. It will help you to understand . . . when you meet her."

Chapter 18

SATURNINO SAT UNDER THE JACARANDA IN A MILD STUPOR, BARE-footed and shirtless, and stared without interest at the pair of iguanas mating under the broad leaves of the plantain near the rear wall of his patio. The two beasts had been at it at least twenty minutes, he knew, since before he heard his telephone ring and went to talk to an excited Napo.

"He's here, man," Napo had said breathily. "Chiquis and I were sitting on the bench, the one on the high side of the little plaza like you said. It was *easy*, man. We just made out the whole time and then here he comes up Frontera, circles the plaza, lookin' around, you know, and then he heads up the street to number six."

"Where are you calling from?" Saturnino had asked.

"From down in Plaza San Jacinto, you know, the public telephone."

"You left the drive unwatched?"

"No, man. Chiquis is still up there."

"Okay. You stay with him. When he leaves, follow him until you know where he's going and then call me."

"You got it."

Saturnino decided that would be too much for the little shit, but if he actually succeeded then so much the better. So he went out to the patio again and resumed his observations, smoking a Pall Mall. He noticed movement in the front leg of one of the iguanas. It was very slight. Otherwise they were as still as copulating statuary, destined to everlasting coitus.

"Hey. What's the deal with your mirrors in this place?"

Isolda Bodet stood in the doorway that opened out to the patio. She was stark naked, a cigarette in one hand and a cup of coffee in the other, her black pubic hair punctuating her pelvis in a vertical rectangle—rather than nature's imprecise

triangle. This linear alignment of her pubes was her idea of
being sexually *au courant,* she having seen her first copy of
Penthouse some months earlier. Isolda was the only girl he
brought here who walked around stark naked. The others
would lounge around afterward in one of his shirts like the
models they saw in the magazines, or at least they would wear
a pair of panties. But not Isolda. At first he thought maybe it
had something to do with her being a nursing student, but now
after all this time he thought not. She simply liked being
naked.

She walked out to him and lay one of her heavy breasts
against his neck. "What at are you looking, Nino?" She blew a
stream of smoke out into the patio.

"The lizards," he said.

"Whaaat?" Her voice rose and curved in the form of a
question mark. Silence. "Lizards? I don't see them. Show me."

He nodded toward the plantains. "Over there."

Silence.

"Did you do some acid or something?" she asked. She pulled
back and stepped over to another bamboo chair and sat down,
crossing one leg over the other and immediately beginning to
swing it. Her pubes peeped up behind her thighs. "What's the
deal with the mirrors?" she asked again. Isolda was a practical
girl. She didn't see any lizards, so she wasn't going to worry
about them.

"I covered them," Saturnino said, keeping his eyes on the
iguanas. He had a vague feeling that they were going to do
something remarkable.

"I *know* that," Isolda whined. "Why'd you . . ." She decided to draw on her cigarette. She did that sometimes,
interrupted herself to smoke or sip her drink or finish reading
something in the paper. ". . . cover them?"

"Had to. Precautions." His eyes on the iguanas. He thought
he saw one of them—the one on top—enjoy it a little.

Isolda dropped her mouth at him, nonplussed. "*Vete a la
chingada!* You're getting weirder and weirder, Nino." She was
silent a while and then he heard her saying, whispering,
"Ni-*no* . . . Ni-*no* . . . Ni-*no* . . ." as if she were the voice
of a vast crowd calling for him.

Saturnino looked around. She had set her coffee on the
stones and was opening and closing her legs to the rhythm of

her words. "Ni-*no* . . . Ni-*no* . . ." Holding a breast in each hand, she was pointing their ample dark areolas at him, offering them, smiling seductively. She was a bleached blonde, white between her ears and black between her legs, as she liked to say. She was very good in bed, very creative, but sometimes—he looked at her flapping herself at him— sometimes she had very bad taste. He returned his attention to the iguanas.

Isolda stopped, not particularly offended by his indifference. She took her cigarette from where she had wedged it into a crack of the bamboo chair and dragged on it.

"Nino, you're getting old," she said.

He heard church bells, the large ones at San Juan Bautista and the smaller ones from Santa Catarina. They echoed over the tops of the trees and down the cobblestone street, settling over the *colonia* like music from a lost world. Isolda got up from her chair and walked back into the kitchen. He could hear her puttering, making something to eat.

After he had followed Haydon to Lockhart's, he had driven back to the Periférico expressway and returned to Coyoacán. He was excited. He had arrived. Just the way he'd imagined he would, just as he had planned. Such a wild plan, such an outrageous plot, that every time it succeeded a step further he was amazed. Amazed and ghoulishly nourished. He had such a pent-up store of excitement that he stopped by San Xavier Hospital and picked up Isolda Bodet as she got off her shift and took her home with him. He had unleased all of his excitement with her, had taken her time and again during the night; Isolda who never said no to anything; whose body, like that of a fertility goddess, had been created for this very act; whose heart beat only to accommodate.

And then he had gone to sleep. He dreamed the mirror dream, the one he feared and hated, the one he watched in his mind's eye with a mixture of fascination and horror, wanting to turn away but never able to, having to watch it to the very end, the worst, the part he lived in dread of, never happening. But it might. Each time he dreamed the mirror dream he thought: This is it. It was a simple enough dream, and though it had its variant plots the denouement was always the same. He confronts his reflection in a mirror. His reflection speaks to him, telling him something vital, something crucial. But he can't hear what his reflection is saying! He can hear everything in the dreams until the very moment his reflection opens its mouth. Then: silence. He is petrified. The lips of his reflection move, they form vowels and consonants and syllables and words, but he can't hear them. The lips of his reflection purse and grimace and stretch, form sibilants and plosives and fricatives, but he hears nothing. There is only silence; and the horrifying foreknowledge that the time would come in some future dream when finally he would hear the mirror speak.

In the corner of the courtyard opposite the plantains, a thick stand of Aztec lilies grew in the bend of the buff-colored wall. The massive scarlet flowers had been planted there several years before by—who was it?—Loreta Modesta, a chemistry major who had moved in with him for a period of time and whom he had moved out again when she began to demonstrate incipient domestic instincts. He had asked her to plant the lilies there, and she had obliged. Any woman who stayed with him any length of time was asked to plant flowers, which he loved. Alicia Flores had planted the *floripondios*—that had been especially symbolic. Teresa Cifuentes had planted the amaryllis by the windows; Leticia Monteforte had spawned the morning glories against the opposite wall, which received the most sun; Lenor . . . he had forgotten her last name, but not her extraordinary buttocks . . . had seeded the marigolds, which were everywhere. The women and the flowers—he was never sated with either, could not get enough, could never, never get enough.

The Aztec lilies flourished; their profusion was probably the result of their having been planted on either side of a leaky faucet sticking out of the courtyard wall. It was here, in the muddy earth under this dripping faucet, that he saw the second pair of mating iguanas. They faced him from the boggy soil like stacked sphinxes, their impenetrable stares telling him nothing of the myths behind their glassy eyes. The iguana on the bottom had settled stolidly into the mud with little hope—and perhaps little desire—of extricating itself while being mounted by its scaly partner. The two of them gazed imperturbably from under the faucet, which dripped steadily onto the head of the top iguana, the water running in glistening trickles onto the other, staining the slaty hides of both with streaks of a darker gray. All around them the firebursts of the Aztec lilies bloomed in gaudy floral splendor, their monstrous stamens rising out of their splotchy yellow pistils as if from braziers of molten lava.

He had checked it out. In the heart of Mexico City, in the Federal District alone, there were nearly three thousand homicides annually. That was twice the number in all of New York City. Mexico City was so vast, its rate of growth so out of control, that there was no way of accounting for such statistics in the greater metropolitan area. The police were so inept and corrupt that only a fraction of these killings were ever solved, and probably in half of those cases they arrested the wrong person. It was going to be so easy.

But then, he really didn't care. The way he was going to do it there would be plenty of witnesses anyway, and for him it wasn't a matter of avoiding prosecution. Still, it had been the right thing to bring him here. He had *had* to bring him here. It was the only way it could be done correctly, because of the old simian.

Turning around, he looked through the opened doors to the kitchen. Isolda was standing at the bar spreading honey on her toast. He couldn't see that, but he knew her habit. It occurred to him that he had made the coffee and then come outside to smoke and had never gotten a cup.

"Isolda," he said, his voice still husky from sleep.

She leaned back in the doorway and looked around at him: strawy blond hair, two dark eyes and a nipple, the soft curve of stomach and a comma of black pubes, a tensed buttock.

"Could you bring me a cup of coffee, and a piece of toast?"

"You got it." She smiled, instantly cheerful, obviously glad he was communicating again.

"You got it." That was what Napo had said. "You got it."

He lighted another cigarette and glanced up to the pieces of opal sky showing between the leaves of the jacaranda.

Chapter 19

THE HOUSE WAS A TWO-STORIED STRUCTURE COMPLETED IN 1789 for the sister of the viceroy of New Spain, Teresa Núñez de Haro y Peralta. It was built in a U shape with a tall garden wall sealing the inner courtyard at its open end. Its walls were four feet thick, which made deep sills of the tall windows that reached nearly as high as the vaulted ceilings. It was quiet as they moved through the rooms, Isabel telling him the story of its furnishings, of how Amaranta had purchased them impulsively, which accounted for the apparent discontinuity in style. The rooms were large and uncluttered yet filled with objects that Amaranta had fancied, relics of a mind that acknowledged no boundaries and searched for inspiration in the far borders of esoterica.

An abundance of art hung on the stucco walls throughout the house, and even Haydon recognized that it represented an expensive, if incongruous, private collection: a bleak and strained Dauringhausen portrait in disturbing clashes of deep colors; a voluptuous Art Deco nude by Tamara de Lempicka (he remembered the portrait in Ada Venecia's house), who had lived not many miles away in Cuernavaca; a Francis Bacon portrait *in extremis*, a silent, sepia scream; a massive gilt frame containing the original number of twenty-two *attuti*, or tarot cards, in which all the characters were cadavers including the horses in the Chariot and the wide-pelvised Popess; a stiffly formal portrait of a dead child in funeral clothes by the obscure Mexican painter Hermenegildo Bustos, who was rediscovered by the young artists of the 1930s; a series of harsh nudes in red Conté chalk resembling the raw and bony women of Egon Schiele; and an untitled portrait by an artist whose work Haydon greatly admired, the tragic and long-neglected Romaine Brooks.

He watched Isabel's bare ankles as he followed her up the stone stairs that took them to the east wing of the top floor. At the head of the landing they walked immediately through an opened door and entered the long, cavernous studio.

"Nothing has changed here," Isabel said. "As far back as I can remember, this is the way it has always been."

Haydon stood quietly, remembering the stories, taking in the long boards of the wooden floor, the high windows flanking both sides of the room with canvases stacked against the walls in between. The windows that looked onto the inner courtyard were actually tall French doors that were thrown open to a loggia that went around the entire second floor. Tall, frondy Guadalupe palms growing in the courtyard provided a screen from the opposite wing on the other side. The resinous odors of oils and turpentine and gesso and varnishes permeated the lumber and the stucco walls, the aromas of a past that seemed not so long ago among the work tables cluttered with cans and jars of old brushes, with twisted tubes of hardened paints, coils of wire, and bits of aged canvas. Halfway down the length of the room stood a random scattering of empty easels, large ones, stained with oils and drippings of pigments. At the far end where the windows continued around the wall to meet the French doors was the *lit en bateau,* alone, evoking neither regret nor longing for the past, but simply a part of it.

Haydon began walking toward it, the sound of his footsteps on the dark wooden floor accompanying him as he passed in and out of the shafts of sunlight that fell through the enormous windows. Stopping in front of the low narrow bed, which he now saw was a rich mahogany, he was pleased to see that it was not excessively ornate, having only the finely carved sphinxes with uplifted wings that formed the graceful sweep of the bed's head and foot, and a thin polished brass ormolu of wheat sheaves tracing its length from one end to the other. The covering on the bedding was a simple spread of unbleached muslin.

"They made love there," Isabel said. She had followed him and stood a little to one side, her arms crossed, her green eyes studying him with interest.

They made love there. He had known that, instinctively, the moment he saw the photograph. How could they not have done so?

"This was their atelier, not hers, but theirs, during those

years," Isabel continued. "It was here that he sat for most of the portraits, not all of them, but most. And he photographed her as she worked."

"He photographed her," Haydon said pensively, still staring at the bed. "I was told he had done that." He turned to her. "You said you had photographs. Do you have any of those?"

Isabel nodded tentatively. "This was his camera," she said, turning her shoulders to guide his eyes, but keeping hers fixed on him. A chill crossed Haydon's neck as he turned slightly to see the extended brass legs of an old tripod holding a Hasselblad at its apex. It looked like a museum piece, as if a velvet rope should have been stretched in front of it to keep the meandering crowds away. He approached it as if it were the first tangible proof that a long-held fable actually had been based on fact. The first thing he noticed was that the nickel plating had been worn from the brass fittings. So it had not been a toy; his father had used it in earnest. It had been more to him than a mere amusement. He wondered when it last had been touched, and by whom. Had one of his father's fingerprints remained there, its oil having etched its pattern on a neglected nickel surface? How unlikely was it? How unlikely had he believed any of this to be only a few days ago?

"He left this here?" Haydon asked.

Isabel nodded. "One day he didn't come back. He never asked for it."

It was the kind of unannounced resolve that Haydon remembered in the older man, a characteristic Haydon himself always had attributed more to age than to personality. He wondered how much more he had misunderstood about his father.

"It seems to have been well used," he said.

"Come look." Isabel took his arm and tilted her head toward a wooden cabinet a few feet away. She went to it and opened its doors to reveal a series of deep drawers. The top drawer was labeled "Negatives"; the remaining four were simply numbered. She pulled out the first numbered drawer and stood back, almost smiling, watching him.

The photographs were all eight-by-tens, thickly packed into the drawer and filed on their edges like sheets of paper in a filing cabinet. Amaranta. All of them. Amaranta at the easel; mixing paints; stretching canvas; laughing at the camera as she sketched a mustache on her upper lip with a piece of charcoal; a detail of her in profile as she bent close to a canvas, absorbed in the details of a larger work; painting in the center of the large studio wearing a long Tehuana skirt, but nude from the waist up; reading on the *lit en bateau*, the leaves from the trees outside dappling the windowpanes behind her; going through canvases stacked against the studio wall, her bare back narrowing to the waist of the long skirt; a portrait with her hair up against a light background; a portrait with her hair down; a portrait with her hair braided; a portrait in profile against the blurred square frames of the windows; a portrait of her on the balcony; a nude bust against a self-portrait in oils; a nude on the narrow bed; a nude on the burnished floors of the empty studio. Amaranta flirted with the camera, pouted for it, laughed at it, wooed it, ignored it, made love to it, allowed it candid access to her daily routines, spoke to it, undressed for it. The lens were insatiable, preoccupied with her to the point of enchantment.

Row after row of photographs.

Four drawers, tightly packed.

An incredible obsession with a single subject, a woman whose green eyes could not even be understood by the black-and-white film of the 1930s.

He didn't ask permission to go through each drawer or apologize for the time it took him to do so, but he couldn't stop and didn't stop until he had seen every photograph. Some of them proved to be experimental—with mixed success—and not a few of them were erotic.

When he finally pushed closed the last drawer and swung the cabinet doors shut, his mind roiled with images of Amaranta, but more than that he was left with an astonishing insight into the young man behind the camera. He would not have believed that his father, even in his youth, could have been capable of such obvious pleasure in pure sensuality.

"What are you thinking?" Isabel asked.

Haydon looked around. She was sitting in an ebonied cross-framed armchair looking at him with eyes softened in concern. Her hands were toying with a sable paintbrush she had taken from a jar on the work table next to her.

"Christ," he said, shaking his head. Her eyes didn't move from him as he went over and sat down on a bench near her.

"You can't imagine. My first impulse was to write this whole thing off to . . . youthful impetuosity." He continued to shake his head. "But that's not it. There's more to it."

"Does this upset you?"

"No, 'upset' isn't the right word." He paused. "I don't know the right word."

"Of course, much of it must have been youthful impetuosity," Isabel said. "On the other hand, he seemed never to have been frivolous with any of those," she said, nodding toward the cabinet. "He only allowed himself to show that kind of . . . freedom when they were alone. She saw him as no one else saw him, because she was the only one to whom he gave everything."

"I think . . . what surprises me," Haydon said, leaning forward, "is that I have the impression from looking at those photographs that he was significantly different then. Though, as the photographer, he was passive, I sense in those photographs that he was capable of . . . abandonment with her."

He quickly looked back at Isabel, who he realized was watching him with open curiosity.

"You're very perceptive." She smiled.

He was glad she smiled, glad that she was there.

"Had she arranged the photographs like that herself?" he asked, changing the direction of their conversation. "I noticed there were occasional dividers."

"God, no. I collected them," Isabel said. "When I told you that the studio was exactly as it's always been, I mean in its essentials. There were scores of cardboard cartons and wooden crates of things she had accumulated over the years. They were piled along the walls, stacked on top of each other. A mess. Amaranta was a collector, but she was not an organized woman. Everything was here, but scattered. Over a period of months I cleaned it up. Some of the photographs had dates, some didn't."

"He never showed an interest in photography," Haydon said. "But a lot of those were very good. Much of the time he left the edges of the negatives, framing with the viewfinder. Really very good."

The windows of the studio were thrown open, and Haydon could feel the light mountain air moving through the room.

"We have different problems, you and I," Isabel mused, idly

dusting the sable bristles against her cheek. "You knew your father so well you thought you understood everything about him; I understand so little about my mother that I feel as if I never knew her at all."

"That's hard for me to believe," Haydon said. "You seem to be able to read people rather well."

"Is that how I 'seem'?"

"To me, yes." He found it difficult to look at her without staring at her. There was a difference and he could feel it. He remembered what Gabriela had said about Amaranta, that she had been "created to look at."

"What happened?" he asked. "What came between them?"

Isabel distractedly ran the fingers of one hand across the top of her breasts, catching at a loose strand of her long hair that had come loose. She looked at her hand, pulled the invisible hair away, and let it fall on the floor. She smiled ironically.

"He grew up," she said. "It was never more complicated than that. She was like the wind . . . after a while he had to question the wisdom of what he was doing. 'What profit hath he that hath labored for the wind?'"

She reached over and slipped the brush back into a jar crowded with them and then picked up an old twisted tube of carmine paint. Lifting it to her nose, she smelled it, and idly began straightening it out.

"You see, he was wise after all," she said. "He loved her, but he knew it was hopeless. He walked away from it. It was difficult for them, because he was the only man for whom she had ever had any ambivalence. Before him she always had been able to take them or leave them, both of which she did with a raging independence. But he was the only one for whom she cared enough for it to cause a conflict, here, inside. What she felt for him was not compatible with her fierce independence, she couldn't reconcile the two. It wasn't in her. She simply didn't know how."

"So when he left she burned the portraits she had painted of him."

"Nearly twenty of them, counting the Conté drawings and sketches. She carried them out to the veranda and tossed them into the courtyard," Isabel said. "Then she went down, poured turpentine on them, and set them on fire."

"But you do have the two remaining ones."

"Of course," she said, getting up. "I'm sorry. I should have shown them to you the first thing." She walked across the room to the wall where the French doors opened onto the loggia. Six or eight canvases rested against the wall. She leaned them forward, pulled out the two portraits of Haydon's father, and handed them to him. He turned them face out and placed them against the remainder of the wall.

They stood back and looked at them. The colors were more vivid than he had imagined them to be, and with their added dimension he saw greater detail. To his surprise his father seemed even younger; the cigar in his hand in the formal portrait seemed even to be a little pretentious, though it had become almost a trademark in later years. Haydon noticed also that the vague cambered background of the painting was in fact one of the arches on the loggia outside. And where had the more casual portrait been painted? Cuernavaca, Isabel told him. The wall on which his father sat was on the terrace of Amaranta's home there, and the breeze that ruffled his father's hair was fresh off the long slopes of the purple mountains in the background.

Seeing the portraits in color had the effect of authenticating the affair in the same way that seeing the well-worn camera had done. His father had indeed been here, had spent languorous afternoons and cool breezy nights in this broad fragrant studio with the most beautiful woman he had ever seen, had come to a final, dreadful realization that he could never have a life with her, and had walked away from her, leaving behind a part of himself, more than a camera, more than photographs and portraits.

"She's very good," Haydon said. "I've seen that expression in photographs when he was young."

"Young, yes," Isabel said. She stood with her hip cocked on one side, one hand holding the wrist of the other as it rested on her waist. "They were too young, weren't they, for what they were going through."

"How old do you have to be for that kind of thing?" Haydon asked.

"I don't know," she responded, thinking. "But you ought to be older than that."

She was standing close beside him looking at the portraits, preoccupied with them, so that he truly believed she was unaware that her hip had touched him, gently, intimately. He believed too that had it been any other woman he wouldn't have noticed it himself. So why was he aware of it now? He took a deep breath, pulling in the smell of oils and canvas. He didn't know what to think anymore.

"I believe this was the last one," she said. "There was no date on it."

"Doesn't she remember?" Haydon asked, looking at her.

Isabel shook her head, and before he could ask anything else she flashed her eyes at him, turned, and walked out the French doors to the loggia.

WHILE THEY HAD BEEN INSIDE, THE SUN HAD BURNED OFF THE morning mists, and the loggia was providing the shade for which it had been designed. The low tile wall around the loggia overlooking the courtyard was lined with terra-cotta urns of geraniums, their blooms bent slightly toward the well of the courtyard seeking sunlight. Isabel stepped out and sat on the low wall, leaning her back against one of the pastel pillars. She frowned a little as she looked across the courtyard where the sun, though not shining directly from above, was reflecting a muted light off the surrounding pale walls. With the first hint of the warming day the mourning doves had begun their soft, indolent calls from the *zapote* and eucalyptus trees in the grounds on the other side of the walls.

Haydon leaned his forearms on the wall and looked down into the courtyard beneath the palms. There was a fountain, a patch of green lawn, and a scattering of fan palms. In one corner of the high wall a fiery bougainvillea climbed from the ground all the way to the top of the wall, while in the other corner a drapery of *floripondio* vines did the same, their white rococo blossoms turned toward the sky.

"Saturnino sent the photographs, didn't he?" she said, reaching toward a geranium and snapping off a vermilion flower. "And there's more to it, isn't there?"

He no longer wanted to deceive her.

"Yes," he said. "You're right. He did and there's more to it. Did you know he was out of the country this past week?"

"He called me," she said. "I could tell it was long-distance, but that's all I knew."

"Weren't you surprised to hear from him?"

"Yes, of course. I've already told you how rarely we communicate."

"What did he want?"

"Money. He was overdrawn and wanted me to deposit some to cover him for a month or so."

"Is that unusual?"

"It has happened before, but it's rare."

"Did you do it?"

"Yes."

"He was in Houston," Haydon said. "During the past year he has employed a private detective to gather a file on me." Isabel grew still, holding the geranium bloom in her lap. "He apparently mailed the photographs to me while he stayed in a motel there. He . . . I'm quite certain . . . he killed the detective three days ago." Isabel's head dropped slightly as she kept her eyes fixed on him. "The last photograph he mailed me was a death threat."

"Oh, God," she said. "No. He can't be doing this." She looked at him in disbelief, but he knew she had no doubt. She put one hand over her stomach, leaned her head back against the pillar, and closed her eyes. She stayed that way a moment, and he watched her breasts rising and falling, watched her bring herself under control.

When she opened her eyes he could see she was unsteady. Quickly he took her arm, put his arm around her waist, and helped her stand. She pulled away, gently but firmly, and began walking along the loggia, her head down, her hands fidgeting with the flower. Reaching the end, she turned into the open French doors at the far end of the studio and began walking back the other way, her footsteps echoing on the floor as his had, only lighter, more remote. When she reached the portraits lined against the wall she stopped and faced them. Haydon was a few steps away. Suddenly she turned.

"That's what you came for, then. To take him back." It wasn't a question. Her eyes were oily with tears.

"No," he said. "I can't do that. There's no extradition treaty; I have no jurisdiction. It would take a long time to arrange something like that."

"Then what do you want?"

He stood looking at her. It was a fair question. If he had stopped to think about it he would have realized that he was introducing himself into a family that was very likely approaching its extinction, the beginning of the declining years of a long and tortuous history, an aging matriarch and her two children nearing middle age, unmarried and childless and burdened with memories.

"Answers," he said. "I want some answers. Unfortunately for you they all seem to be here."

"God," she said, turning away and folding her arms as if she were hugging herself.

"Last Monday, nearly a week ago, I received a photograph of this portrait," he said, pointing to the formal portrait of his father. "Painted here, in this studio. I hadn't the faintest idea that anything like this had ever existed, or still existed. In only six days I've learned enough about my father to alter my understanding of all that I had ever known about him before. But I haven't learned enough. I know that as surely as I'm standing here. I may never penetrate these questions as much as I would like, but I intend to learn a hell of a lot more than I know now."

Isabel was still turned aside from him, but he saw a hand go to her eyes and wipe them, and then she began rubbing her hands together, drying the tears in her palms. She moved away, her arms hugging herself again as she strolled past a set of French doors, head down, thinking, her sandaled footsteps sounding small and lost in the high-ceilinged studio. She stopped and turned to him again.

"I am not completely insensitive," she said. "I understand how it is, for both of us. I can appreciate your curiosity, even if it is a little reckless, but I think you are a fool for coming here in light of Saturnino's message. You see, even from the very outset you misunderstand him. It was not a death 'threat' he sent you, it was an 'announcement.' Believe me, he knows very well the difference."

"What does he think I've done?" Haydon asked. "What is motivating him?"

"You may never understand that, even if he tells you."

"You have no idea?"

"None." She shook her head in frustration. "It's so complicated. You can imagine how Byzantine his mind is from what you must've learned from Juan. There's simply no way to know 'why,' and really, even if you knew it wouldn't make any difference, would it?"

Haydon didn't answer.

"I am not entirely surprised by this," she said. "Surprised that you are involved, yes, but not by what is happening. This was inevitable, not this precisely, but in some way, somewhere, for some reason, he was destined to destroy himself. His loathing for Amaranta is so intense that after I came to live with her I hired a man to stay here for security. He was with us for nearly six months. I began to feel as though I had overreacted and let him go."

"Why did you decide to move here?"

"About nine years ago it was apparent she needed closer supervision. Though she had servants here, she intimidated them. She wouldn't let them clean the house properly; sometimes she wouldn't let them open the curtains. The house was growing cluttered, ill-kempt. It was becoming an eerie retreat for an eccentric old woman. So I came back."

"What were you doing?"

"I was a curator at the National Museum of Anthropology."

"You've always gotten along with your mother?"

"Rarely," she said, wiping at the corner of an eye again. "But I am not intimidated by her. Even Juan tends to accede to her in many ways."

"Does he have occasion to see her often?"

"He meets with us at least once a month."

"Meets with you?"

"I insisted on the regular meetings. With the Mexican economy the way it is I thought we should review our investments more frequently."

"Lockhart handles your investments?"

"As our family lawyer he handles everything."

Haydon nodded. How had that fact managed to go unmentioned the previous evening?

"How long has he represented the family?"

"Well, actually, his father's firm represented my grandfather and then everything simply moved forward with the next generations. Both Amaranta and Juan simply continued with a long-standing arrangement."

"Does he communicate with Saturnino?"

"Certainly more than we do, but I think it's infrequent. I don't know really."

"Would Lockhart know how to get in touch with him?"

"I'm sure he does." She glanced away uncomfortably and then looked at him again. "Saturnino has been refusing his inheritance, you know."

"Lockhart mentioned it."

"It's idiotic. He doesn't make much at the university; he could use the money. Juan puts his share in a trust and invests it. I suppose he'll take it when Amaranta dies—I don't know what he has in mind. But sometimes, rarely, as I said, he needs a short-term loan. He always calls me, never Juan. I take care of it, and some time later he sends me a check for it. It's absurd. He has all this money in the bank. Refusing it means nothing to anyone but him."

"What does your mother think about it?"

Isabel shook her head. "She's never said anything to me about it."

"Where does Saturnino live?"

"In Coyoacán, Colonia El Carmen."

"What is his address?"

She ignored the question. "What did Juan think about this?"

"He said Saturnino was fully capable of killing me, and probably would."

Isabel looked shocked. "And?"

"That was it."

"He's not going to intervene?" Her voice was raised, incredulous. "Juan has influence. He could have Saturnino arrested or committed—something."

"I need Saturnino's address," Haydon said again.

Isabel simply looked at him, stupefied. He could see that her mind was racing, that she was trying to fit the pieces together. He could also see that she was beginning to realize that some of the pieces were missing. He knew that too, but he didn't know which ones they were. Isabel did.

"No," she said. "I can't give it to you. It would be irresponsible of me."

"What do you expect me to do?"

"Return to Houston. This is a sordid story here. You would do well to walk away from it."

"I can't do that," he said.

She started toward him. "Is your curiosity that strong? You have no vital reason to be here. Let the authorities in Houston handle the death threat. Surely there is something that can be done. My God, he's killed a man. Some kind of legal action will have to be taken against him, even if it has to go through the wretched political channels. Make the necessary bribes, you know how it works. You could have him arrested in twenty-four hours." She stopped in front of him.

Haydon looked at her. He felt like a fool. She was shaken, fighting tears again, he could tell, and all he could do was look at her as if he had never before seen such a beautiful woman. He felt hopelessly transparent before her, knew it was no longer possible to disguise what his eyes were doing, knew that she understood their movement across her face and breasts as surely as if they had been his fingers. He felt the palm of her hand flat against his chest before he actually understood that she had reached out.

"Listen to me," she said. Her voice was calm, somehow telegraphing her understanding but not giving in, not even consenting to what was happening. Her hand was touching him to communicate a bond, but nothing more. It was an honest gesture, more honest than his eyes. "I won't, can't, give you his address, but I will go with you. I will take you there." She pressed her hand against his chest, then lifted it slowly and took it away.

"Do this for me," she said. "It's getting late. I would prefer that you didn't meet Amaranta today. She doesn't know you're here. Give me time to talk to her, to prepare her. This is all so sudden, everything. I need some time to think too, time to collect my own thoughts. Come back tomorrow and I will drive you to El Carmen. And you can meet Amaranta."

Chapter 20

SATURNINO HAD SHOVED THE IGUANAS OUT OF THE WAY AND KNELT IN the mud among the Aztec lilies to wash off the blood. He had it all over him, so he washed his hands first. It didn't come off easily and seemed to get into the tiniest creases of his fingers, even into the whorls of his fingerprints, as if they were tiny vortices sucking it, absorbing it. He rubbed mud into his hands, on the palms and into the backs, rubbed the grit under his fingernails to get it out. When he was clean enough, he washed his face, and the sensation of his fingers moving over the slopes and planes of his features presented him with an unexpected fascination. Kneeling in the mud, he became engrossed in the contemplation of his own face, going over it with his fingers, lightly, with the balls of his fingers, with the ends of his fingers, over the bridge of his nose, around his eyes where the cheekbones fell away to make sockets, over his lips, the dip above his chin, the line of his jaw, the breadth of his forehead, like a blind man searching for the mental image of a stranger. Never before had he experienced this. One moment it was as if his hands were the appendages of another being and he was that other being touching himself from elsewhere, and then the next moment he was in his face, immobile, unprotesting as the fingers lightly probed and dusted over his lidded eyes, circumscribed the orifice of each nostril, paused at the slightly raised curiosity of a mole.

This was not his authentic face. No. His authentic face had not existed for many years, perhaps ever, and only now was it coming into being. What did the *tlamatini* say? Only with an authentic face and heart can each man escape the dream of this earth. And they devoted their lives to helping men find a face with which to survive the dream. Saturnino had not been privileged to have access to a wiseman, no *tlamatini* had guided him with the red and black ink of wisdom. The mystery of his own life and suffering had remained a secret, and he had been bound in the dream of the world. But the Mocking God who presided over life's reversals, who toyed with men as if they were tiny round pebbles he rolled around in the palm of his hand for his own amusement, had spun his dangling obsidian disk, and in the whirling face of the Smoking Mirror, Saturnino had seen his own, the old face, for the last time.

With his face still dripping, with his knees burying deeper into the mud, with the phallic stamens of the scarlet lilies all around him, peering over his shoulder, he held the gristly heart under the trickling faucet and washed its openings and channels, its mottled and venous surface. He was pleased, even thrilled—it proved that the time had come—that everything had fallen into place. He hadn't known, it hadn't even occurred to him, that Isolda was the *ixiptla* of the filth-eating goddess Tlazolteotl, the person chosen as the goddess's earthly representative, who became the goddess incarnate, dressed like the goddess, acted like the goddess, was revered as the goddess, and then was sacrificed to the goddess. He hadn't realized until she had gone upstairs to the bathroom and later returned, still naked, wearing a bright serpent bracelet. It was the coral snake, the Aztec symbol of lust. Of course! Even after all that Tezcatlipoca had done for him he was still blinded, unable to see fully what was put before him. If anyone was meant to be sacrificed to the goddess of adultery and sexual passion, to be Tlazolteotl's incarnation, it was Isolda Bodet with her love of nakedness, her frenetic libido, her ample waggling breasts and eager pudendum.

But it was not, correctly speaking, something for which he should have made an offering of propitiation. It had not been his sexual sin, but the old woman's, that needed to be devoured and destroyed by Tlazolteotl in the Aztec way. It had been she who had given birth to him as to misery, making him the issue of a lie.

Lady, our lady . . . it is not known how this newborn has arrived, how he is arrayed, the nature of that given him in the beginning, the nature of that which he comes bearing, the attributes with which he comes wrapped, with which he comes bound. But behold, perhaps he

cometh laden with evil; who knoweth the manner in
which he cometh laden with the evil burdens of his
mother, of his father? With what blotch, what filth, what
evil of the mother, of the father doth the baby come
laden?

IT WAS SHE WHO HAD MADE HIM BOTH CAIN AND ESAU, THE FIRSTBORN
but the misbegotten and the deprived, the cheated and
defrauded, the rejected man whose mother turned her face
away from him in favor of his brother and who, because of this,
had no face of his own.

Until now. Until now even Tezcatlipoca had favored the
younger brother, had blessed him instead of the firstborn.
However, everything was changing, and the god of Cain and
Esau would be chastised. Though Cain had revenged himself
against Abel for his supplanted sacrifice, he still was cast out by
the god; and though Esau truly had been wronged and
defrauded by Jacob and his mother, Rebekah, he weakened
and forgave them the wrong. But now comes Saturnino of the
cold and surly disposition who will neither forgive nor be cast
out any longer. Time had turned upon itself, the black god
once again had indulged his caprice and set in motion the
cosmic reversal of fortunes, now the one brother would suffer
and the other ascend and no one could stop it, no one could
defeat the will of the Smoking Mirror.

He had read that in a single year the average human heart
contracted forty-two million times, and pumped 700,000 gallons of blood.

The water around his knees was grimy with mud and dark
venous blood. The iguanas wanted in it and gathered around
him, peered at him from under the leaves of the lilies, their
saurian eyes seeming never to look directly at him but, like the
eyes of portraits, followed him everywhere. He turned off the
water and carefully stood, holding the heart away from him,
letting it drain. The damn thing still ran red, dripped red in
the brew around his feet. Isolda watched him from her
bamboo chair under the jacaranda, the astonished expression
still on her face but her eyes as indecipherable as the iguanas'.
She sprawled ungracefully. He wouldn't correct that; the
natural sprawl of the *ixiptla* seemed to be something he

shouldn't interfere with, it being a detail of what was required, the spoor of the raging climax of her role.

He stepped away from the puddle under the faucet and heard the iguanas scuttle into the mud behind him. He walked over to the wicker table under the jacaranda, reached up and pulled a handful of leaves from a low-hanging branch, and made a nest of the wispy pieces. He laid Isolda's heart on the nest and wiped his hands on his pants. Turning to the flower bed next to the house, he pulled half a dozen marigolds—known as *cempoalxochitl* to the Aztecs, their sacred flower of death—and walked over to the *ixiptla* and began plucking the marigold petals and scattering them over her. He covered her face first, thought for a moment that he shouldn't put them in her mouth, then went ahead, careful to sprinkle them all around her eyes but not to cover the pupils, sprinkled them in the stiff wire of her bleached-to-death hair, sprinkled them over her shoulders and in the wide cavern between her breasts where the stick held her open and made her breasts hang absurdly to her sides. This wound consumed the rest of his marigold petals, and he had to return to the flower bed and pick some more. Back again, he continued covering her with the butter-colored slivers the texture of taffeta, past her navel, past her loins, chrome-and-black, down her thighs, and then because of the slant of her legs they would not stay on but where there was splashed blood he stuck them to it, which gave a nice effect. The handful of remaining marigold petals he tossed into the air above her and let them flutter down onto her; he thought about Zeus and Danae and the golden rain and how it was consistent with all that Isolda represented and then he was through with her.

He went over to where the hatchet lay on the ground beneath the coral hibiscus and picked it up and walked back to the faucet, where he kicked at the iguanas and scattered them out of the muddy sink and into the lilies in a rattling rout of splashing and rustling. He washed the hatchet under the faucet, ankle-deep in bloody mud, and returned it to the side of the house, where he leaned it against the wall next to the pile of kindling. He looked around. Everything was back in order.

When he had first struck Isolda with the hatchet, she had been lounging there as if sunning, her arms and legs open to the air, to the sensual tickle of the least little breeze on the tender parts of her body, which were usually bound in constraining underclothes. He had approached her from behind and swung the hatchet with both hands over her head, striking her chest with the thud-splitting sound of cutting open a ripe melon. She had leaped up, knocking over a small table beside her chair, breaking her coffee cup and saucer and a plate of honey toast. She had stood with her back to him a moment, her arms held out from her sides as if she were dripping wet, and stared at the hatchet handle trembling in front of her face, and then her legs began slowly to warp and bend and she seemed to hang in the air as if supported by the tiny invisible hands of angels. Suddenly she crumpled from the waist down, kind of sat down on her rubberized legs, sitting on her feet, her buttocks hanging over the backs of her twisted heels. She didn't fall sideways, but squatted crookedly, canting impossibly. He helped her back onto the bamboo chair, noticing the wonderment in her face, leaned her back the way she was, arms spread, legs spread, and, with some effort, extracted the hatchet. Then he swung it again, this time splitting her open the rest of the way.

So there had been quite a mess with the broken pottery and he had had to clean it up.

Now he stood at the back door and slipped off his pants and boxer shorts, and because he was already barefooted and without a shirt he was now completely naked. He thought at first that he would just throw away the pants and then he remembered that Felicia was buying a new kind of detergent and maybe it would get the blood out, so he stepped inside to the washroom and threw them into the clothes hamper. Then he went outside again and picked up the heart along with its nest of jacaranda leaves and took it into the kitchen. He put the heart on the end of the cabinet and cleaned up the mess Isolda had left after breakfast. He put away the toaster, wiped off the honey jar, and put it in the pantry along with the bread. He rinsed out the dishes and put them into the dishwasher, and wiped off the table and countertops. Lastly, he rinsed out the washrag and folded it once and draped it over the faucet to dry.

Before he went upstairs he wanted to replenish the vases. He went through the living room and removed the dead or wilting flowers from their various receptacles of glass and clay and brass, and took them outside and threw them away. He picked fresh ones from the vines and plants in the courtyard and took them inside, where he took great care in arranging them, deliberating on the aesthetics of texture and shape, and especially the balance of colors. When he was satisfied, he picked up the heart again and a cluster of Aztec lilies and went upstairs to his bedroom.

He stood in the doorway just inside his room and looked through the short corridor into the next room, the room of the wisteria-blue light. He wouldn't go in there, not now, not until he was in possession of everything, not until the end, when he would bring all the reliquiae together, those that he already had and those he soon would acquire. A single drop of something fell on the top of his bare foot, and he looked down. A bit of discolored water had worked its way through the mat of jacaranda leaves. His naked feet reminded him of the naked Isolda, and he was suddenly heavy with weariness. He needed to sleep. He walked over to his bed and sat down, and held the heart and the flowers while he looked at the pornographic painting that covered one wall. He leaned over and put the bloodless organ, now looking waxen and flaccid, on the pillow on the opposite side of the bed with its nest of leaves and then lay down beside it. As he held the flowers, his arms and legs felt as heavy as lead, his eyes sagged. He went to sleep.

Amaranta, the old Amaranta, was walking through the Chapultepec forest in a nun's habit. Her face was gaunt and ashen, her eyes glowed eerily like dying green embers, and the hump of a full-term pregnancy pushed upward grotesquely under the black cloth. Other elderly nuns, also pregnant, moved along the footpaths under the great, centuries-old *ahuehuetes*, gliding along through the pale rays of light that broke through the towering branches high above them, gliding smoothly as if they were not touching the earth. He stepped out of the woods behind Amaranta as she passed by him with a companion, a thin man dressed in a Jesuit's cassock and so tall he had to stoop his shoulders toward her as they moved along. On Amaranta's own shoulders rode the hairy little capuchin, perched beside her wimple like one of Goya's pointy-eared hallucinations, whispering in Amaranta's ear while the old Jesuit murmured in the other. Occasionally the Jesuit would glance back at Saturnino, though it was clear the old priest had

not informed Amaranta that he was there. Everyone knew, all
the other nuns who floated through the forest twilight, that
Amaranta's womb was filled not with a child, but with a huge
black stone, a globule of polished obsidian. The capuchin
continued to whisper, his tail hanging down behind him,
twisting lazily like a satisfied cat's, a cunning cat, his narrow
little shoulders hunched and hirsute, hiding his face. Saturnino drew near, hoping to overhear their conversation, but
to no avail. They passed a group of nuns huddled beside the
path, talking, their eyes following the strange quartet, their
white hands lying lightly on their swollen black habits. Then
they overtook another group that paused to let them pass,
whispering, their eyes following them. Soon another cluster
was doing the same, then three more here and several more
there, until Saturnino, looking around him, saw that all the
nuns in the forest had paused to look at them. Then with a
sense of increasing dread he realized that they were not
looking at "them" but at him, and at that very moment
Amaranta and the Jesuit whirled around to confront him and
he saw with a cold rush of horror that the Jesuit was Lockhart,
the capuchin bore the likeness of Haydon, and Amaranta's face
had become the visage of her youth. Both the Jesuit and the
capuchin leaned close to Amaranta, their eyes fixed on Saturnino as they whispered silent counsel to her. As Saturnino
watched, her eyes filled with sparkling tears that rolled down
her cheeks in oily emerald beads, though her face remained
unmoved and she gazed at him with the passive features of a
gravestone seraph.

When he opened his eyes he found that he had rolled to the
center of the bed and the heart had tumbled off its nest of
jacaranda leaves and rested against his forehead, the flowers
crumpled beneath his chin. He lay there a moment, feeling
flesh against flesh, swimming in the cloying scent of the scarlet
lilies, then he took the heart and put it back on the leaves and
got off the bed. He walked into the bathroom and showered
and then shaved, feeling his way over his face as he progressed, a technique to which he had grown accustomed. Still
naked, he went outside again and clipped a wad of Isolda's hair
for the arrangement of her clothes under the pornographic
painting with the lilies.

Then he dressed. By the time he tied his shoelaces, which

was always the last thing he did, he had grown restive. It was time to finish it. Isolda had been the beginning, and not many hours should pass before he brought it to an end. He wouldn't be coming back here—tomorrow, shortly after noon, Felicia would come in to clean and find Isolda and then he would be set adrift, unable to return. From then on he would have to work fast. But he was prepared. By now he had taken almost everything to his rooms in Licenciado Verdad, only a few yards from the historical center of Mexico City, the Metropolitan Cathedral, adjacent to the excavations of the Great Temple of the Aztecs.

Chapter 21

ISABEL HAD CLOSED THE FRONT DOOR BEHIND HIM, AND HE WALKED to the front gate feeling completely disordered. He stepped out of the gate in the wall that surrounded the rose house and latched it behind him. The late-afternoon sun had fallen behind the high poplar and eucalyptus trees of the district, throwing the narrow lanes and the courtyards that lay behind the high walls into the long hours of blue light that preceded evening. Haydon glanced once at the tortured Christ in his grated shrine in the wall and turned toward the two stone archways with their crests of bougainvillea.

To get off the ankle-wrenching cobblestones he stepped onto an ancient sidewalk made of sandstone blocks that hugged a vine-covered wall around the shallow curve to the tiny Plaza de los Arcángelos. When he got to the circular lane that enclosed the plaza, he crossed over to the red tile walk that went around the island of trees and tropical plants. So preoccupied were his thoughts with Isabel and all that he had just seen and heard in the rose house that he almost failed to observe the two young people who were still sitting on the same enormous curved stone seat. But reflex took over; they were noted, and he continued around the white wall of a house with a blue tile plaque at its wrought-iron gate that cryptically stated that it was "The Cell of the Archangels' Plaza."

As he turned down Frontera he got a glimpse of the distant sky between the courtyard walls of another falling street, dark clouds moving across the valley, beginning to obscure the volcano Ajusco. A quick breeze stirred the trees and the manicured hedges in the almost deserted Plaza San Jacinto as he entered and gratefully spotted the five or six orange-and-white cabs waiting in front of the dove-gray awnings of the Fonda San Ángel. An alert young driver fiddling with a plastic transistor radio on the top of his Chevrolet saw him first and tossed his head at Haydon, who nodded and stopped beside a closed news kiosk. In the few seconds he waited his mind darted back to Isabel, the weight of her hand on his chest, the timbre of her voice, and then the cab pulled up in front of him and the rear door flew open. The rain started just as he ducked his head inside the car and started rolling up the window, which had been down. The taxi started moving, and in a split second, through the blurred glass, he saw the young couple from the Archangels' Plaza running with newspapers over their heads toward the five remaining taxis.

He was glad the driver didn't cut across to the Periférico expressway. It was an ugly route downtown and there were no people to watch. But he didn't take Insurgentes either, but rather the equally direct though less elegant Avenida Constitución that ran an almost straight shot into the eastern edge of Chapultepec Park.

After the driver readjusted his dashboard radio and established his position in the dense traffic, Haydon settled back to watch the crowds along the sidewalks, letting his thoughts flit from Isabel to Saturnino to the photographs of Amaranta to his father. Never would he have imagined that he would one day discover such an elaborate world hidden within his father's past. It was astonishing and sometimes unreal, as if he had shrunk like Alice and fallen into the animated world of Hieronymus Bosch.

The driving rain had temporarily emptied the streets of their teeming crowds. *Chilangos* were used to having to duck into any convenient shop or café doorway or under any nearby awning to escape the sudden showers of the rainy season. But the downpours rarely lasted long, and it was a good excuse to take time out for a leisurely cup of coffee and conversation. The sky had grown dark, and the streets were dreary under a burdened sky. Haydon had let his eyes lose focus against the rain-spattered window in the stalled traffic when suddenly a flash lighted the car, and then another. Haydon whirled around in time to see a long tongue of flame die in the mouth of one of the city's renowned fire-eaters, young men, often peasant boys, who stood in the boulevard medians and practiced the deadly art of spewing mouthfuls of gasoline into the air which they simultaneously lighted with a burning rag tied to a long stick, creating enormous, rolling fireballs. When the traffic stopped, they went from window to window collecting tips for their performance.

The cab driver laughed at Haydon's reaction and shook his head as he looked out his window at the filthy boy whose smoke-matted hair and grimy face betrayed his occupation.

"Little fucker," the driver said. "Even driving this damn cab is better than that, huh?" He tilted his head back and looked at Haydon in his rearview mirror. "A doctor told me, he said those guys die after about a year of that, you know, of blowing that shit. It's the lead in the gasoline. Gives them brain damage, or they get throat cancer, stomach cancer, you know, because they swallow a little bit of that shit every time."

He shook his head at the hopelessness of it and reached in his pocket and took out a couple of bills. When the traffic started moving again he leaned out the window and waved at the boy, who ran over and snatched the money, thanking him with a greasy smile. "Little fucker," the driver said grimly, still shaking his head.

As the traffic began to move, Haydon turned to watch the next display of pyrotechnics. The traffic surged and stopped, surged again, cars changed positions in the different lanes, some pulled ahead, some dropped back, and suddenly as Haydon was twisting around his mind registered a fleeting image of something familiar. And the hair on the back of his neck prickled a warning. Which window in which car? Orange and . . . Another taxi. But which one? They were all over the place. He spun around in the other direction, scanning the windows of the orange taxis, then two lanes over he saw the back of her head, now obscured, dropping back, getting in his lane again, two cars between them. He leaned back in the blind spot and watched the taxi switch lanes again, this time to his left, but moving up. It was too dusky outside to see the license plate, the numbers on the doors weren't large enough, but it was a large car too, a sedan. The girl was on the wrong side now, her face turned away again, but he saw the boy. He got a good look at the boy from the Archangels' Plaza.

He leaned forward. "How far are we from the bullring?"

The driver turned his head sideways. "Plaza México? Let me see—ten or twelve blocks."

"It's on the right?"

"Yes."

"Fine. Get over there and turn on that street that goes on its north side."

"Avenida San Antonio?"

"Whatever." He couldn't remember the name of the street, but he could picture its configuration in his mind. He sat back again, his head pressed against the side of the car. It took him a second to find the right taxi again, and when he did it was switching back across traffic, too. Still two cars between them. Then quickly Haydon's driver turned right.

"Okay, now turn north on Insurgentes," Haydon said, never taking his eyes off the corner they had just turned even as his driver began to switch back across traffic for the coming left-hand turn. By now everyone was using headlights and the streetlamps had come on even though it wasn't completely dark, and all the lights reflecting off the wet streets were going to make it more difficult for him to track them. But it would work to their disadvantage as well. Then the headlights of the second taxi panned around the corner going fast, not switching lanes, speeding up, then switching abruptly as they crossed Avenida Patriotismo, now only one car between them as they careened onto Insurgentes.

"Do you know Plaza Río de Janeiro?" Haydon asked.

"Yes . . . well, do you mean that one in Roma Norte, on Durango?"

"Yes, that's it."

The driver nodded and raised a thumb, but Haydon didn't see it; his eyes had never left the pair of headlights flickering through the streaks of rain. They were not that good, it had been a clumsy tail, but he was grateful for it. He had been so distracted a professional might have followed him all night. Soon they were in the hospital district west of the Medical Center—fifteen or twenty hospitals within a twenty-block radius—and then they slowed for the Durango intersection and turned right.

Two blocks ahead a green dusk was settling over the plaza, a quiet neighborhood square with an abundance of poplar and eucalyptus trees. The plaza's focal point was a large shallow fountain with an eighteen-foot replica of Michelangelo's *David* in its center, a gift from Italy sometime in the sixties. Durango Street terminated on the west side of the plaza and picked up again on its east side, while Orizaba did the same from south to north.

"There's an art gallery on the northeast corner, at Durango," Haydon said. "You can pull over to the curb there."

"*Bueno.*"

As they circled the plaza Haydon watched the headlights of the second taxi ease down Durango and stop just at the edge of the plaza. The rain was slackening as Haydon's driver approached the front of the four-story stone building, constructed during the reign of Porfirio Díaz.

Haydon leaned over the front seat again. "Can you wait for me?" he asked, handing the driver enough pesos to have made the trip three times.

"Of course, of course, no problem."

"I may be twenty minutes."

"No problem, definitely. I will be here."

Haydon got out and hurried into the entrance set into the corner of the building at an angle. Immediately inside the front door two short flights of marble stairs curved upward and met at the top at the gallery entrance, forming an archway over another opening that led down below street level to a series of workshops for artists. Haydon ducked into the lower passage and ran down a long corridor past an occasional lighted doorway until he came to a streetside exit that opened onto Orizaba. He continued across the street and circled the plaza, sticking close to the buildings, until he spotted the double-parked cab, its parking lights glowing orange as it waited at the other side of Orizaba, its two youthful passengers watching his own cab sitting in front of the gallery.

He quickly realized the boy was on the sidewalk side of the cab, which was perfect, and as he eased around in the shadows he could see that he was smoking. If the rear doors were locked, he had a problem. He moved up until he stood in a darkened doorway directly across the sidewalk from the cab. The few streetlamps scattered around the plaza provided enough backlight that he could see that all three of them had their heads turned in the opposite direction. Haydon pulled his Beretta, stepped out of the shadows and slid between the parked cars at the curb, jerked open the rear door of the cab, and shoved the boy over onto the girl, pinning them next to the opposite door.

"Don't move," he snapped, jabbing the barrel of the Beretta into the side of the boy's neck below his jawbone, his eyes meeting the cab driver's. "No one moves," he repeated with deliberation. "Put your hands on the wheel so I can see them." The driver slapped the steering wheel and gripped it tightly. He was not going to be a problem.

The boy's eyes were rolling sideways at him, sparkling, and he wasn't breathing, while the girl seemed to have frozen in the middle of a silent scream, her mouth open, her teeth bared as if someone had stopped the film a millisecond before the gunshot. Haydon had his fist twisted into the collar of the boy's black silk shirt, which he had yanked up out of his oversized Italian sports coat, using the material as a garrote, his knuckles buried in the boy's carotid artery. He was calm.

"Who are you?" He was inches away from the boy's face, a little to the side so the kid couldn't get a good look at him. The kid was clean-cut and swimming in cologne. The moist glaze glistening under his nostrils and the glint in his eyes told of cocaine.

When there was no response he tightened the twisted collar and raised the barrel of the Beretta until its forward sight bit into the underside of the kid's jawbone.

"Napoleon Cuevano." His voice was tight.

"They call you Napo?" Haydon would have bet a hundred dollars on it. The kid nodded.

"How old are you?"

"Twenty."

Haydon looked at the girl. "What is your name?"

It took her a moment to gather enough saliva to make her mouth work. "Chiquis. Bejar. Eighteen." She was a quick study. She wore a casual shirtwaist dress, but even in the dim light of the car Haydon was close enough to tell that the dress was not inexpensive.

Back to the boy. "Why are you following me, Napo?"

"No." Napo shook his finely barbered head. "We aren't following you. We're waiting for a friend. We are supposed to meet a friend here."

The girl nodded tentatively.

"Were you waiting for him in the Plaza of the Archangels, too? All afternoon?"

"We . . . we go there a lot. Her father, he doesn't want us to see each other."

"Did you just happen to see me there, also?"

The girl nodded again, but the boy didn't see her. He shook his head.

"You'd better help me out on this, Napo."

The kid set his lips, his jaw muscles hardened. Big man. He probably could have played it a lot smarter, but the brainful of coke was shoring up a stubborn machismo. He wasn't going to give in so easily, not in front of his girl.

"Chiquis," Haydon said. "Get the rest of the coke and toss it out the window." The girl might have been a quick study, but she wasn't used to the street. She went straight for the bulky side pockets of Napo's natty sports coat and took out a shiny silver ampule. She held it up to Haydon. "Out the window," he repeated.

· Napo tried to arch his back in protest, but Haydon dug his knuckles deeper into the kid's carotid as the girl quickly lowered the window and tossed it, then raised the window again.

Looking at the kid's chin quiver in anger, Haydon was not so sure this Napo would not try something stupid. He needed to prevent that, and decided to take him down a notch in the process.

"Take off your pants," Haydon said.

The kid was perfectly still, trying to anticipate where this was leading. Haydon gave the Beretta a nudge. If the barrel went any deeper it was going to cut him. Napo started unbuckling his belt. He unzipped his pants and hesitated.

"You're making a big mistake," he said. He had watched his share of television.

"How is that?"

Napo didn't answer.

"Chiquis," Haydon said. "Help him get them off."

Napo got busy, pulled them down—pleated linen trousers, expensive—raised his hips off the car seat and slipped them down to his ankles.

"Stop there," Haydon said, and pulled Napo back up by his collar. "Chiquis, get the belt out of his pants."

The girl looked at Haydon, then at Napo, then back at Haydon, who nodded for her to go ahead. She squirmed out from between the door and the boy and bent down and got the belt.

"Napo, put your forearms and wrists together." The kid held them out in front of him, an expensive dress watch on the left, a heavy gold bracelet dangling on the right. "Now, Chiquis, wrap the belt around them until you are able to buckle it tightly."

When she had done this Haydon pushed Napo forward and worked the silk shirt and baggy sports coat down around his upper arms until they were pinned tightly to his side.

"Good," he said, moving back a little, easing the Beretta away from the boy's jaw. He reached across and slapped down the door lock next to the girl, then sat back, keeping the nose of the Beretta in the boy's ribs. "I need to know what's behind this."

"Napo . . . " the girl said.

"Shut up!" the kid snapped.

Haydon looked at Chiquis. "Pull his underwear down."

Napo's head jerked around at Haydon, his eyes narrowed. "You son of a bitch," he said.

"Hey, Napo . . ." Chiquis pleaded, but the boy didn't even look at her, his eyes were boring into Haydon.

"Pull them off," Haydon said.

"Tell him, Napo."

"You son of a bitch." The boy's face was rigid.

"Pull them *off*," Haydon snapped, guessing that the girl could be intimidated, that she was probably thinking that she was in way over her head and just wanted to avoid getting hurt, wanted it to be over. She turned around quickly to face her boyfriend, her knees on the car seat, and grabbed the thin sides of his skimpy nylon briefs. With a few sharp jerks she had them down, pulling them past his knees, down to his ankles.

Napo's humiliation was obvious. He wouldn't look at the girl, his macho belligerence condensed into the small dark orbs of his eyes, which were boring into Haydon as much from hate as from a need to look anywhere but at the girl. It was suddenly clear to Haydon that this had been a mistake, that it had galvanized the kid's resolve and now nothing short of a beating would make him talk. The girl was the vulnerable one; he should have started with her.

"Okay, Chiquis, you're next."

"What!" She gaped at him.

"Take off your clothes."

The boy spat suddenly, but Haydon had been anticipating it and it missed, hitting the window behind his head. His hand shot out and he grabbed Napo's hair and pinned his head back against the seat. He waved the barrel of the Beretta at the girl. "Go ahead," he said.

The cab driver, who until now had been staring straight out the windshield, not moving a muscle, could not resist cutting his eyes up to the rearview mirror.

"Wait, wait a minute, No. Napo . . . listen." The girl's eyes darted back and forth from Haydon to the boy, finally stopping on Haydon. "I'm not sure of his name . . . he's a professor at the university . . . uh, in archaeology, no, anthropology, yeah, anthropology. I don't know him . . . Sarmiento, I think . . . I don't know him, but his name's Sarmiento."

"Does Napo know him well?" Haydon was ignoring the boy now, as if he didn't exist.

"No, they just met, you know, in one of the cafés around the university . . . I don't know how. He wanted Napo to watch the house in San Ángel and let him know when you arrived. And we did that, then he said for Napo to follow you when you left and let him know where you went. . . . That was it, that's all. Honest. I just, you know, came along . . ."

"For the excitement," Haydon said.

The girl nodded.

"Have you ever met him?"

She shook her head.

"How long has Napo known him?"

"I don't know."

"A year? More than a year, less?"

"Months maybe, six or something."

Napo was staring straight ahead.

"How did you know how to recognize me?"

"We have a picture."

"Where?"

The girl bent down again and got a purse from the floor of the car. She snapped it open and took out a five-by-seven photograph and handed it to him. Haydon tilted it toward the window to catch the glow from a streetlamp. He remembered the picture from the files he had seen in Swain's office, an old newspaper photograph. He put it in his coat pocket.

"What were you supposed to do after you called him to tell him where I was?"

The girl threw a puzzled look at Napo. "Nothing," she said looking at Haydon again. "Just call him and tell him where you were."

"Do you have the telephone number?"

She bent down to the floor again, this time frantically pawing through Napo's linen trousers until she came up with a piece of paper with a telephone number on it. Haydon put this in his pocket as well.

"Do you know who lives in the house I went to this afternoon?"

The girl shook her head.

"I suggest you learn a little more about what you get involved in," Haydon said to her. "This is something you don't want any part of."

The girl shook her head again, vigorously, agreeing.

"Where do you live?"

"Lomas Virreyes," she said.

Haydon nodded. He had been going to pay the cab driver to take them home, but if they lived in a posh district like that the kids could foot the bill themselves.

"When I get out of the car I want you to turn right on Orizaba and keep driving until I can't see you anymore," Haydon said to the driver, who tentatively raised one hand off the steering wheel to acknowledge the instructions. "Okay, start the car."

As the driver turned the ignition, Haydon reached behind him and opened the car door. He backed out of the car, slammed the door, and stood watching as the taxi lurched forward and then roared around the corner. The driver did as he was told, straight down Orizaba.

The rain had stopped completely. Haydon started across the plaza in the early-evening air filled with the scent of damp plants. A small group of schoolgirls in their navy-blue skirts and white blouses crossed in front of him, circling the *David* statue and talking furiously among themselves as they hurried toward Orizaba. He heard running footsteps, a child's, and a small boy ran past him carrying a box of Ritz crackers, stopping abruptly to pick up a stick and throw it into the fountain, then hurrying on. His driver was waiting inside the car with the windows rolled down, his left arm reaching out the window to balance the transistor on the roof of his car. He held one side of a broken set of earphones to his right ear. Haydon tapped him on the arm and crawled into the backseat. "María Isabel," he said.

EVEN AFTER HE HAD SHOWERED AND MADE A DRINK, AND WAS SITTING in front of the windows in his robe, Haydon felt tired. The Reforma was bathed in the golden-green light from its street-lamps, and the old part of the city stretched before him as far as he could see, its night lights seeming sharp and bright after the rains. This day, at this hour—just before the dinner hour on Sunday evening—was as quiet as the city would ever be.

He tried to keep his mind off Isabel. The encounter he had just had with the two pampered youths flirting with intrigue was of far more urgency to him. It seemed a sloppy involve-ment on Saturnino's part, even if he had told them nothing of why he wanted Haydon followed. Unless, of course, Haydon was still underestimating the man. It could be that Saturnino knew the kids would be inept, that the chances were good that they would be spotted, that if they were it would serve to make Haydon nervous and if they weren't he could learn something about Haydon's movements. Either way, Saturnino wasn't going to lose any ground, even if—as it proved to be—Haydon caught them and they told him who had put them up to it. It would be no revelation.

By now Haydon should understand that in following Sat-urnino to Mexico City he had agreed to play Saturnino's game, a game in which the tacit agreement was that the professor would make up the rules as they went along.

By now, too, Haydon was realizing that the manner of his killing as depicted on the photograph was only a metaphor, not an actual portrayal. He would not be shot down unawares on a crowded Mexico City street by a sniper who gave no warning. No, Saturnino had had ample opportunity for that. What he had in mind for Haydon was something more imaginative, something that would take a little more negotiating, a kind of maneuvering at which, up to now, Saturnino had proved himself a past master.

But it seemed curious to him that both Juan Lockhart and Isabel had dismissed so quickly Saturnino's motive for wanting to kill him as something inexplicable. Who knows why, they had said, it was obviously something he had twisted in his mind, something, they implied, that had no basis in reality. Haydon doubted that, though he himself had no basis in reality for doubting it. It was only an intuition, but he had never been one to ignore the potential of intuition.

He rose from his chair and stepped to the window. He once had heard Gaston Arreola say, perhaps only half in jest, that every Mexican had something to hide. It was a reference to the difficulty of surviving in the strained and complex world that was modern Mexico, a reference to the fact that almost everyone had to compromise something, to resort to the devious, to be as wise as a serpent, to pit his own ingenuity against the events of everyday circumstances that seemed predisposed to defeat him. Arreola had been speaking of the everyday practicalities of a society that gave rise to the cynical phrase *La ley se obedece, pero no se cumple,* "The law is obeyed, but then it is disregarded," a society that every day must come to grips anew with the ambiguities inherent in its national custom of distinguishing between the law as it is written and the law as it is practiced

It seemed to Haydon that that same dichotomy operated within the person of Saturnino. To his colleagues at the university he appeared no different from the rest of them, lecturing to his classes, dealing with students, meeting the daily routines of his profession, but to those who knew him more intimately, he appeared no less than psychotic. And yet, how did one define psychosis in a world where reality itself was so nebulously defined? Haydon was wary. He would reserve his judgments about Saturnino.

Calmed by the drink and the time to reflect, he dressed and went out to get something to eat. He stood under the hotel's portico looking across the broad Reforma to the streets leading into the Zona Rosa. He didn't want to bother with a big dinner, was in no mood to be catered to and hovered over. Instead he turned right and walked around the corner to the Sanborn's on the corner of Río Tiber next door to the hotel on the Ángel *glorieta*. He walked through the department store, stopped in the book section to buy a *New York Times*, and then walked into the restaurant and got a booth by a window. He paged through the newspaper until his meal came, and then laid it aside and ate as he watched the people who stopped by and hung around the magazine and newspaper kiosk outside on the street corner.

By ten o'clock he was back in his room. Before he undressed he sat down at the round table near the windows and called Nina. She picked up the telephone on the first ring, and he could tell from her voice that she was relieved to hear from him. They chatted in generalities for a moment. The night before he had told her briefly about meeting Lockhart, and she asked if Haydon had spoken to him again. He said he hadn't.

"Gabriela's been as nervous as a cat," Nina said. "She asked me if you had been to see Amaranta yet."

"I went out to San Ángel today," he said. "But I didn't get to see her. Apparently she goes to Pedregal every Sunday to visit friends. I spoke to her daughter, Isabel. I'm supposed to be able to talk to Amaranta tomorrow."

"Then you're returning to San Ángel?"

"Yes."

"Did you learn anything from her daughter?"

"Quite a lot . . . and not nearly enough. It's extraordinary. He had a whole other life here. I never would have been able to imagine it. It's unreal." He couldn't bring himself to elaborate, wouldn't know where to begin.

"What's she like?" Nina asked.

He hesitated only a second, but it was long enough. "Who, the daughter?" He didn't know why he had said that; it was a stupid and unnecessary pretension. "She's nice," he said tersely, and for some incredible reason he felt as if he had just lied to her, or deceived her in some way.

There was a pause on Nina's end before she asked, "Are you doing all right?" It was a straightforward question, the kind he instinctively tried to second-guess. But it was a mistake to do that with Nina.

"I'm fine," he said. He wanted to say more, but it was no good, not over the telephone, not now.

They chatted for another couple of minutes and then hung up, and he remained in the chair, looking out to the boulevard.

It hadn't been a good call. Nothing was wrong, but then nothing was particularly right, either. He knew he had left Nina with the impression that he was holding back. But there was nothing he could do about it. The luminous green haze along the Reforma reminded him of Isabel.

Chapter 22

MONDAY MORNING THE FRENETIC TRAFFIC SCRAMBLE THAT NORMALLY characterized the Mexico City streets was in its full vigor, and by nine-thirty when Haydon walked out of the Auseba pastry shop on Hamburgo it was obvious that a thermal inversion lay over the city and the smog was going to be deadly. The sky was obscured by a taupe, acid haze so laden with contaminants that Haydon could actually taste it. It was easy to see why more than a hundred thousand *chilangos* died of pollution-related diseases every year. With his eyes burning, Haydon once again turned toward Florencia, where he quickly picked up a cab the moment he approached the intersection.

He had called Isabel from the Auseba at nine o'clock as they had agreed, and was surprised to find that she did not sound at all tense or even reserved. He didn't know what effect the unpleasant information about Saturnino might have on her after she had had time to think about it. She said that Paulo had gone to fill her car for her and that by the time he got there she would be ready to go. He was relieved that she did not seem to be depressed, though he himself was uneasy about what they were about to do. It was unprofessional of him to use her in this way, to allow her to walk into something that he had every reason to believe could be dangerous, but it wasn't the only thing he had done in this affair that could be considered poor judgment.

This time he allowed the taxi to take him up into San Ángel, exiting Insurgentes on La Paz, going up Madero to Plaza San Jacinto, and then climbing even higher on Frontera to the tiny Archangels' Plaza. He got out on the mossy cobblestones and paid the driver, who made a tight turn around the fountain and disappeared slowly down the narrow street. San Ángel was far enough from the central city that the air was considerably lighter here, and the cool morning dampness still lingered among the suburb's profusion of trees and flowers. It would not burn off until noon.

Haydon turned down the narrow walled lane and passed under the two stone arches to the wrought-iron gate. He let himself in, approached the front door, and rang the bell. The harsh shriek of a cockatoo broke the still air from a nearby courtyard, and Isabel opened the door. She wore a white petal-sleeve dress of light silk, and her long hair was pulled back loosely at the temples and clasped in the back. He had not remembered her eyes being so brilliant the day before.

She smiled. "Good morning," she said, bending to pick up a handbag from a table inside the door. "Paulo is coming around with the car." She closed the door behind her, and by the time they stepped to the gate a deep blue Mercedes was emerging from the driveway at the end of the wall. It pulled up in front of them and stopped, and a Mexican man in his forties got out and held the door open for Isabel.

"Mr. Haydon," she said over the top of the car, "this is Paulo. We are fortunate to have had him with us a long time."

They spoke and then Haydon and Isabel got into the car and within moments were rounding the fountain in the plaza and heading down the narrow streets toward Insurgentes.

"I should tell you," she said, having to stop at the first traffic light on Revolución, "that yesterday after you left I called Juan. I asked him why he hadn't done something immediately about Saturnino, why he hadn't sent someone to pick him up. He said that actually he had. After you left his home the night before last he sent for Saturnino, but he was not home. Juan has continued to try to get in touch with him, but can't find him anywhere. I suppose when we get to Coyoacán we are going to be out of luck."

"Did he say why he had lied to me?"

Isabel shot a quick look at Haydon, then the light changed and she returned her attention to the traffic. "You mean about not knowing how you could get in touch with Saturnino?"

"That's right."

"He told me about that. He said he needed the time to reach Saturnino first, to try to talk to him. Surely you don't expect any of us to simply stand by and watch this madness play itself out."

"He might have told me he was going to do that."

"I don't know, I suppose he thought it was best not to."

"I suppose he did."

"I don't think he meant to deceive you maliciously," Isabel said, detecting the note of sarcasm in Haydon's voice. "You have to understand that Juan has spent quite a few years getting Nino out of various kinds of trouble. If this is true about the private investigator, Juan has to know."

Haydon nodded.

"I don't know what we can expect to accomplish by going to Coyoacán if Nino is gone," she said, changing the subject.

"When was the last time you were there?" he asked.

"Years ago. I don't know, maybe it's five or six years."

"Does he live alone?"

"He has girlfriends, or he used to, different ones who come and go. Most of them are his students at the university."

"No maid?"

"I'm sure he has someone who comes in, but I doubt if she lives there. His house is not that large."

They were on Avenida Sosa now, approaching the gardens of the Plaza Hidalgo and the parish church of San Juan Bautista, one of the first churches to be built in New Spain. Isabel followed the edge of the plaza and then turned into the *colonia* of El Carmen. She made one wrong turn, but quickly realized her mistake and then within moments entered a *cerrada*, a small dead-end street in which all of the residences are behind walls that are flush to the curb, forming a private enclosed compound.

She parked beside a dark wooden door set in the wall. Beside the door buzzer was a black glazed tile embedded in the wall with a white number 8 on it. "Yes, this is it," she said, bending down and looking out Haydon's window.

They got out of the car, and Isabel went up to the door. There was a grille at eye level and she peered through as she pressed the ivory button below the number. Haydon cringed. It was a good place to have your face blown off. She pressed it several times more, then opened her purse and produced a key. She was about to put it in the keyhole when Haydon reached out.

"Do you mind if I do that?" he asked, taking the key from her. He inserted it into the lock and turned it. The deadbolt chunked solidly, and the wooden door gave way to the pressure of his hand.

Behind the door was a small courtyard about six meters square with a short tiled sidewalk going to the front door, which appeared to be the same color and same kind of wood as the wall gate. Flanking either side of the sidewalk was a thick border of lavender poppies, and beyond them the courtyard was filled with the deep green of lush plantains. Haydon immediately saw another grille in the house door. He felt the same discomfort at approaching these as he did about approaching a screen door in the Houston barrios in the summer when the houses are thrown open to the heat and the inhabitants in the darkened interiors can watch you coming all the way from the street. There was nothing you could do about it.

"How did you get a key?" he asked as they approached the door, which was set into the house within a double-row framework of glass blocks.

"I have made it my business to keep one," she said unhelpfully.

"What if he's changed the lock?"

"It's the same as the wall door."

Haydon inserted the key. "What did Lockhart think about our doing this?"

There was a slight hesitation before she said, "I didn't tell him."

The response was unexpected, and Haydon was both relieved and encouraged. It was the first indication he had had that she trusted him.

Inside the front door there was a shallow landing and then two steps down to the living room, which lay before them in the limpid light that came in from the glass blocks. The living room was of a comfortable size, with its longest wall, to their left, dominated by rows of glass shelves laden with pre-Columbian treasures. Scattered throughout the room were numerous vases, amphoras, urns, and ewers filled with a large variety of freshly cut flowers. But there was a predominating color; every vessel glowed with the same saffron petals that Haydon recognized as marigolds such as he had seen in the shabby little kitchenette in the Rio Courts.

A double door at the opposite end of the living room seemed

to lead into a dining room and kitchen, and a courtyard in back. To their right rose a flight of stone-and-stucco stairs.

"That goes to his bedroom and a study," Isabel said, following Haydon's eyes to the stairs. She stepped down into the living room and approached the wall of glass shelves, moved to one side, and flipped a switch that turned on a series of subdued overhead lights that illuminated the wall. She stood back again and looked at the collection.

"This is a selective, very fine collection," she said, surveying the wall. "Nino always looks for the extraordinary pieces, things seldom recovered in the digs, one-of-a-kind objects." She moved to the shelves and pointed to a clay figure about the size of a large teapot and shaped roughly like a gourd with its smaller, upper part in the image of a wizened old man. "That is an effigy whistling jar, a water or pulque container. It has two connecting chambers, and when you pour the water through the spout, air is forced through a whistle in the old man's mouth." She looked at it and smiled. "If I remember correctly its provenance was unsure." She lifted her head, gesturing at the collection. "He has something from every major period here: Olmec, Maya, Toltec, Aztec," she said, pointing at an object from each period. "Carved jade figures; a hunchback dwarf clay figure from Colima; a 'pretty lady' type, from the Guanajuato region I would guess; cylinder stamps from Tlatilco; a pitcher of Thin Orange ware . . . my God," she said admiringly. "He is a brilliant collector. Much more discerning than I, much more capable."

Haydon watched her move along the shelves, looking at the objects of jade and obsidian and simple clay, sometimes stopping to examine a piece more closely, then moving on until she reached the far end. There above a low shelf of large books was a long ebony frame encasing a series of colored illustrations, images of elaborately costumed figures.

"The Aztec gods," Isabel said. "Very well executed. The colors and the symbolism are accurate." She moved closer to them. "They're done on *huun* paper, made from fig trees. That's what the codices were painted on."

"These are old, then?" Haydon asked.

Isabel shook her head. "He's had these commissioned. There are people who have learned the ancient methods of making *huun* paper. Anthropologists are great experimenters and are forever tracking down Indians who can duplicate certain old methods for them. I imagine he had them use as many of the original pigments as he could find, cinnabar and maybe cochineal. He was fanatical about that sort of thing—I mean the authenticity."

"He's done similar projects?"

"Many times when we were growing up. You know, he very much wanted to be an artist when we were young, until everything fell apart."

She turned and looked at him, a little sadly he thought, and then she started toward the stairs. Haydon followed her up the steps that rose steeply and made a turn over the door they had just entered to a small balcony overlooking the living room. Demonstrating a real curiosity now, no longer simply accompanying Haydon, Isabel entered the room first, stopping a few feet inside the door.

The bedroom had one large window that overlooked the *cerrada* and the small courtyard in the front.

"He was always orderly," Isabel said, looking at the made bed and the opened closet door that revealed his clothes arranged by type of garment and color. His shoes were polished and rested on a wooden shoe rack sitting on the closet floor. Then her attention moved to the low dressing table between the glass wall and the bed, and her eyes stopped on the mirror above it, covered with a woman's silk slip. She considered this a moment and turned to their right, where a small settee sat against the wall on the other side of the bed. On the floor in front of the settee was a single pair of high-heels, the toes pointing toward the wall. On the settee itself a woman's clothes were neatly folded and laid out: a lavender dress of something light and thin like rayon challis; a bra with its cups folded inside each other and made of material so sheer it seemed to be cellophane; panties that were little more than a G-string; stockings arranged so that the darker tips of the toes appeared on top; and, inexplicably, a single unused tampon partially covered over with cuttings of short black hair. Sprinkled here and there among these items were scarlet fragments of an unidentified flower, like bright splashes of blood.

Isabel's eyes were riveted on the settee, and Haydon was fascinated to see her approach it and study this unusual arrangement with genuine intellectual interest rather than mere curiosity, as if she were the detective rather than he. He already had noticed the picture above the settee and was awaiting her reaction when she looked up and saw the pornographic etching so large it covered most of the wall. But this she also examined with clinical interest, then she turned, caught his eye, and walked to the closet. She opened the door wider and began looking at Saturnino's clothes.

While she was doing this, Haydon stepped over to the bathroom. The exterior wall was made of glass bricks beginning at a height of about four feet all the way up to the ceiling. Immediately in front of the door was the sink and medicine cabinet, which, Haydon was not surprised to see, had its mirror covered with a towel that was held in place with heavy tape. Haydon opened the medicine cabinet to confirm his suspicions: Saturnino's razor and shaving cream were missing, as were his toothbrush and toothpaste, deodorant and aftershave. He opened the shower door, looked around, and closed it, then checked the linen cabinets.

When he came out Isabel was standing in the middle of the room, looking at the settee.

"Was the mirror in the bathroom covered too?" she asked.
"Yes."

"You said that you went to the motel where he was staying in Houston," she said. "Were they covered there as well?"
"Yes."

Isabel continued standing with her back to him.
"What have the mirrors got to do with it?"

"I am not sure, really," she said, shaking her head as she turned around. "We have to finish here. His study is through there." She nodded to a doorway leading out of the bedroom. "Or it used to be."

AGAIN SHE PRECEDED HIM, NOT HESITATING, ENTERING INTO THE beryl-blue light that he could see even as they approached the doorway, and then inside, an eerie glaucous aura bathing the room from the wall of glass bricks, backlighting a standing figure poised against the pale glow. Haydon flinched, knowing in an instant his reflexes were too late, then realizing by Isabel's attitude that there was nothing to fear, then realizing again that she was dumbstruck by what she saw as they both stood stock-still and looked at the life-sized figure frozen in the water light that rippled through the bricks. In the moments his eyes adjusted, he made out what appeared to be a mannequin strangely balanced, dressed in the most exotic attire Haydon had ever seen.

"My God," Isabel said, standing amazed in the center of the room. "Tezcatlipoca."

The figure stood sideways to them, its knees flexed in a slight crouch—though it stood only on one foot, its other seeming to have been severed—its arms outstretched in a scissoring fashion in front of it. The body and limbs of the figure, which Haydon could now see was a terra-cotta statue, were painted black and covered with faint circles that resembled smallpox scars, and its face was painted gold, with three black horizontal stripes crossing the brow, the nose, and the chin. The legs were decorated with ankle cuffs of what appeared to be leopard or jaguar skin, and a huge backpiece of elaborately arranged feathers was strapped to its shoulders. Two long and graceful white feathers were braided into its hair. There were two distinguishing pieces of ornamentation: a reflective disk was attached to the statue's head with a strip of leather, and another mirror dangled from the stump of the severed foot.

"What is this?" Haydon asked, turning to Isabel, who was staring at the terra-cotta figure with visible discomfort. Haydon was vaguely aware of a musty odor, like the soil of a deep cave.

"Tezcatlipoca," she said, seeming to be disturbed not so much by its appearance as by the fact of its presence. "An Aztec deity, the supreme god in a very elaborate and confusing pantheon." She stepped closer to the figure, which they now saw was slightly raised on a base of stone. "It is extremely well done. The terra-cotta statue alone is extraordinary. I've never seen another like it." She bent forward and touched the ankle bands. "That is actual jaguar skin. It's illegal to have it. The feathers are real, too. Heron feathers."

"Have you ever seen it before?"

"Never."

"Why do you think he has it?"

"This . . . Tezcatlipoca, the god, was the subject of Saturnino's dissertation," she said. "I've forgotten the exact

orientation, something to do with the god's numinous quali-
ties, something arcane, like all dissertation subjects." She
shook her head as if she were marveling at the eccentricity of
it.

So preoccupied were they by the sight of the statue that it
was several moments before something else caught Haydon's
peripheral vision. He turned. The stucco walls were painted a
rubiginous brown, and hanging from them in alternating
sequence were black reflective disks of various sizes and small
bodies dangling from ropes by their necks.

Beside him Isabel gasped once as if someone had hit her in
the stomach, then again, clutching at Haydon's arm with one
hand and covering her mouth with the other. They turned
slowly and took in the grotesque drapery that circled the
entire room. Outside the morning haze was burning off, and
the light coming through the beryl-blue glass surged and faded
as the clouds drifted across the face of the sun, giving Haydon
spectral glimpses of clarity. He moved toward the wall he was
facing, without Isabel, who remained rooted near the center of
the room, and was within three feet of the nearest small figure
before he realized it had a long, rigid tail, and that he was
looking at a monkey. All of them were monkeys, small
dehydrated creatures with hunched shoulders and petrified
rictuses and sightless eyes, their mummified bodies being the
source of the musty breath that hung in the room.

"Unbelievable." Isabel was moving toward another wall, her
attention focused not on the strangled primates but on the
disks. She looked at one, then another, and another, careful
not to touch the monkeys, but too fascinated by the disks to
stay away from them. Even in the stillness of the room the
slight movement of their bodies created subtle eddies that
turned the suspended disks and made them glitter.

"What in the hell is all this?" Haydon was repelled by the
magical ambience conjured by the hanging objects.

"Madness," Isabel said. "A very special kind."

The tone of her voice was like the chime of a tocsin to him,
an inflection, a nuance that had more to do with awe than
horror. He was instantly chilled and infuriated to think that
she could have had any other response than repulsion.

"Special?" He checked his temper; he didn't want to misinterpret her remark.

She did not respond immediately and he waited, waited as he looked at her profile and wrestled with his anger, which had begun to dissipate almost from the moment he began to study her. The forehead that had inclined before the easel in the half-lighted studio fifty years earlier now tilted in concentration before a wall of inexplicable images; the thighs he had seen beneath the curl of the lifted skirt on Florencia he now saw backlighted by the moving, aqueous light that came into them past a stalking terra-cotta god. The anger that had flared so suddenly only moments before dissipated to a kind of disheartened bitterness, and he realized that however she might "explain" herself, whatever views she might express or beliefs she might profess, he would never be able to condemn her. There was more magic in the room than that of Saturnino's god.

"Special in its particulars," she said. "Only one kind of myth could have created this, could allow it to exist."

Haydon found the room and its spirit of violence too familiar, unsettling to the point of anxiety. "The only thing special about this is its depravity," he said. "And I've seen too much of that to think it special any longer."

"You have learned everything there is to know about such things?" she asked with a hint of sarcasm in her voice. She was touching one of the glistening disks. "That must be very comforting. I should think you are a member of a very small minority, a handful of privileged men."

"'Privileged men,'" he said, feeling the spleen returning, trying to control it. "Yes, perhaps you are right in a way. My 'privilege' is to be a seer, a reader of signs. And what signs have I seen? A prophecy of my own death and a promise of shocking revelations; a dead man and shrouded mirrors; pornographic etchings and the ritual cuttings of pubic hair; old gods and new fears; whistling jars and hanged monkeys. I've never seen these specific signs before, but I've seen signs like them, and I know the kinds of things they portend." He stopped. "The only thing comforting about what is going to happen here is that sooner or later it will be over."

He could tell by her posture, by the angle of her head, that what he had said had given her pause. She reached out and touched another of the disks, moving her fingers in a circular motion toward the concave center of its surface.

"Some of these are hematite, some magnetite," she said. "And these are obsidian mosaics, all exquisitely polished dark stones. All mirrors. He was the Lord of the Smoking Mirror, and through the mirror he wielded his power. Tezcatlipoca spoke to the Aztecs through his mirror, which had the property of continually bringing faces to its dark surface, faces which seemed to be peering out through rolling smoke. When the god looked into his mirror he could see into the hearts of men and uncover their secret intentions so that he always knew their sins. When men looked into the mirror it became an instrument of the god's deception, for in its concave surface, or its surface of mosaics, man's image appeared distorted and broken and he perceived himself as horrible. Man was at the mercy of the god who controlled the mirror and therefore controlled man's fate. This clairvoyance was unique to him—in all the Aztec pantheon none of the other gods were capable of such penetrating power."

Haydon noticed that the ripples of emerging sunlight that had periodically brightened the beryl-blue glow from the glass bricks had gradually ceased, and outside he heard the first smothered mumblings of thunder.

"He was *el mayor de los mayores de sus dioses*, the great god of all the great gods, and had many manifestations," Isabel continued, unaware of the changing light, seeming to be talking to herself, recalling. "He was the Lord of the Near Vicinity, ever present, close at hand; he was the Mocking God, who deliberately deluded men, the author of life's sudden reversals, the cruel god who toyed with man's fate; he was the Enemy on Both Sides, the god who favored neither good nor bad, or capriciously favored both alternately. His rule was discord. He was Night Ax, the god of ill omen who in the form of a headless man roamed the streets at night with a horrible gaping chest wound which continuously opened and slammed shut with a deep resounding boom; Lord of the Night, the god who at the end of the present age of the fifth sun will steal the sun away and plunge all things into eternal night."

She stopped and turned her head, and for a long while stood looking toward the deepening blue wall of thick glass. Haydon waited, wondering if she was looking at the dying light or the eerie posturing terra-cotta god; he waited, hating the darkening room with its musty stench and its hanging madness and all the misery it presaged.

"It's going to rain," she said suddenly. "Is there anything else here you want to see?"

"Nothing."

As she turned and walked past him with her head bent he heard her whisper, a brief supplication to a god Haydon did not recognize.

This time when they passed through the bedroom Isabel had no brave encounter with the strange things they had seen before, but kept her head turned aside until they were safely on the balcony. She kept her silence as they descended the stairs, placing a flat hand against the white stucco wall to steady herself, something she had not had to do when they had gone up.

"There's nothing else to see," she said when they reached the living room. "Only the kitchen, and the patio." The house was quite gloomy now except for the muted lights above the glass shelves of artifacts. The thunder was more prominent. "Are you ready to go?"

"Yes," he said, stepping to the shelves to examine some of the human figures one last time. A few of them were quite exotic, with lovely features that were unexpectedly finely sculpted for what were normally considered "primitive" works. He turned to ask Isabel a question and saw that she had wandered back to the kitchen. Just as he was about to speak she looked out toward the patio and stopped abruptly.

"There's someone out there," she said, opening the door, and before he could stop her she had stepped out into the courtyard.

Haydon ran across the living room, his eyes locked on her through the panes of the doors as she approached a lawn chair, craning her head and speaking with obvious curiosity to a woman whose naked legs and blond hair were all that was visible above the back of a bamboo chair. In the instant he burst through the doors Isabel recoiled convulsively with a piercing, stuttering wail, flinging up her hands and flailing the air, pushing it away from her as she lurched backward with a riveted stare, retreating, stumbling toward a drapery of bougainvillea. As Haydon reached the center of the courtyard the rain fell on them like a curtain, a hard-driving deluge, and he

spun around between Isabel and the bamboo chair and saw
the naked woman spread before him, sprawling obscenely,
her thighs splayed out, and above them the great,
yawning laceration that opened her from throat to navel, like
a slaughterhouse carcass. Her rib cage was propped open with
a crooked stick. She was yellow with shreds of flower petals,
which, in the pounding rain, were quickly washing away in
rusty rivulets that plastered her strawy hair and revealed the
glassy gaze of a doll's eyes. Staggered by what he saw, Haydon
gaped at the awful pocket of the enormous wound where the
churning rain beat a frothy soup of viscera and yellow petals.
Immobile, he couldn't close his ears to the roar of the
downpour, or shut out the hysterical crying behind him, of
Isabel tangled in the wet vines and amethyst stars of bougainvilleas.

Chapter 23

BY THE TIME HE GOT HER BACK INTO THE HOUSE BOTH OF THEM WERE soaked by the torrent of cold highland rain, and for a moment they stood inside the door and he held her as she cried. Outside, the blurred white limbs of the naked woman, sprawling in unreal and disjointed angles, were almost obscured by the roaring downpour.

Isabel let him guide her as he turned and took her out of the kitchen and started through the living room to the front door. His heart was pounding, his mind racing. As he held her he replayed their movements through the house, remembering that he had touched the medicine-cabinet mirror, the shower door, perhaps the frame of the bedroom door. Isabel had touched several of the disks, the back door . . . had she touched a cabinet, one of the glass shelves that held the artifacts? He remembered her hand on the stucco wall of the stairway. How thorough would the Mexican police be? Did any of it matter?

"Isabel," he said. He took her shoulders in his hands, her wet dress clinging to her, and tried to get her to look at him. "Isabel, I've got to go back upstairs." She kept her head down, holding her wet hair away from her face with her hands. He felt sorry for her. He should have known, he should have anticipated something . . . not that, he couldn't have anticipated that, but something. He looked at the translucent silk clinging to the tops of her breasts. Jesus Christ. "Sit here," he said, taking her to one of the living-room chairs. "Sit here and don't move."

She nodded, and he left her there. Pulling his handkerchief out of his pocket, he ran up the stairs. He went into the bedroom and hurriedly wiped every surface he could remember touching, every surface he remembered her touching, even returning to the eerie room of the smoking mirrors and

wiping the disks—he thought he remembered which ones—
and then he returned to the stairs and wiped at the stucco wall
as he descended, guessing at the height of her hand. In the
kitchen he wiped off the edges of the tile cabinets just in case
she had leaned on them or touched them, and then he wiped
the back-door handle, keeping his eyes on the task at hand, not
letting them look outside where they strained to go like metal
to the grotesque and powerful magnet of the soggy corpse. By
the time he got back to the living room she had stopped crying
and was staring vacantly at the glass shelves, which reminded
him of the light switch. He wiped it off and turned off the
lights.

"Come on," he said, taking her again and going up the two
steps with her. He fumbled at the door, wiping the inside knob
as they went out, then pausing outside to do the same as he
inserted the key and turned the latch on the deadbolt. They
ran across the shiny tile walk between the rows of lavender
poppies and plantains to the door in the front wall. Haydon let
them out and quickly helped Isabel into the car on the
passenger side. He returned to the dark door and repeated the
same key-and-handkerchief motions as he had at the house,
then ran around to the driver's side of the Mercedes and
crawled in.

The rain thundered on the roof of the car. He looked at
Isabel, who had taken a handkerchief out of her purse and was
drying her face. Her wet dress clung to her thighs all the way
to her groin.

"Are you all right?" he asked, twisting behind the steering
wheel as he removed his suit coat. She nodded, but didn't
speak. He threw his coat over into the backseat, wiped his face
with his hands, and started the car. He made a U-turn in the
cerrada and drove out to the intersecting street, made a left
turn, and started toward Plaza Hidalgo with the rain pounding
the car. Neither of them said anything until Haydon slowed to
turn the corner at the church of San Juan Bautista and entered
Avenida Sosa.

"I'll have to stop somewhere and call the police," Haydon
said. "I don't want to call from your home."

Isabel was wiping her nose, staring out her window to the
rain. She said nothing.

"We can't leave her there, in the rain," he said.

"Of course." She turned to him quickly, a look of pain on her face. "It's not that, no. Poor creature. God." She started crying again, but swallowed hard, bringing it under control. Then she gave up and buried her face in her hands and leaned against the door, sobbing.

Near the Parque de la Bombilla he spotted a telephone under a covered walkway between a beauty shop and a bakery. He pulled to the curb and got out and ran to the telephone. He had to make three different calls before he finally got the *delegación* of Coyoacán police. Not wanting to give away his North American accent, he slowly repeated a very simple phrase twice: "Listen carefully. There is a murdered woman at . . ." He gave Saturnino's address. In a few moments he was back in the car.

It took him a little while to get through the intersections at Insurgentes and Revolución, the rain causing the traffic to balk and move sluggishly. Isabel had stopped crying again. She was leaning against her door in exhausted silence. He could smell their wet clothes, and he thought of the woman in the bamboo chair. He felt sorry for Isabel. The impact of something like that was difficult to deal with even when you were prepared for it, expecting it. But when it was the farthest thing from your mind and you stumbled upon it innocently as she had done, the intensity of the shock, the pure horror of it, was impossible to absorb. Haydon knew that the sight of that yawning wound and the woman's blank, blood-splattered stare had seared themselves into Isabel's psyche. She didn't know it yet, but they would come back to haunt her at unexpected moments and against her will for the rest of her life. It was not the sort of thing everyone could deal with successfully.

The rain had slackened by the time the Mercedes climbed the cobbled streets to the Plaza de los Arcángelos and drove under the stone arches to the front of the pink house.

"There is a covered entry through the gates," Isabel said, and Haydon turned into the entrance gate, which had been left open, pulled in under the portico, and stopped.

"I'm sorry I can't offer you any fresh clothes," she said. "But I'll have Paulo make a fire in the *sala* and we can dry off that way. I've got a chill anyway."

Haydon simply would have gone back to his hotel if the circumstances had been different, but he felt responsible for her having been exposed to the scene at Saturnino's. He didn't want to leave her alone for a while, and besides that they had a lot of things to discuss, not the least of which was the danger he felt that Saturnino posed for everyone in the household. He didn't know if Isabel had thought that far yet, if she realized the immediate implications of what they had just seen.

Haydon reached over and got his coat from the backseat. They got out of the car and entered the house. As they were walking down the tiled corridor to the *sala*, Celerina came out of the kitchen and smiled in her surprise to see them, and then immediately her face fell as she saw Isabel's red eyes and rain-soaked dress. Without even asking what had happened, she quickly put her arm around Isabel as they walked and urged her to go upstairs and undress while she drew a warm bath. But Isabel waved off her entreaties and asked only if she would make coffee for them and bring it into the *sala*, and have Paulo come in and lay a fire. She forced a smile at the frowning servant, who reluctantly left them to do as she was asked, and they continued toward the other end of the hall, where they turned into the smaller vaulted parlor just off the living room.

"Here," Isabel said, laying her purse on a French console and turning to take Haydon's coat. "Let me put this over a chair near the fireplace. Paulo will be here in a minute."

Haydon gave the coat to her and undid his tie as he stepped over to the windows and watched the rain come down beyond the colonnade in the courtyard between the two wings of the house. Amaranta's studio was directly above them. Paulo appeared with an armload of kindling, followed closely by Celerina with a bundle of towels for them. Isabel thanked her and talked with her quietly for a few minutes near the door. As Paulo got the fire going, Haydon turned around to thank him and caught the servant's eyes in a sidelong glance at the Beretta in the small of his back. Paulo nodded a shy *de nada*, and showed Haydon where the bin of extra wood was to one side of the fireplace. After asking if Haydon or Isabel would need anything else, and being assured that everything was fine, and thanked again for their services, Paulo and Celerina left the room.

"Why don't you go ahead and change into something dry," Haydon said. "There's no reason for you to be wet, too. I'll be fine."

Isabel shook her head. She took a couple of towels from the table where Celerina had left them and walked over to him.

"Here," she said, handing one to him. "I'll be fine, too. Really. You'd better dry off as much as you can. Let me have the tie."

He slipped it off, and she took it and placed it over another chair near the fireplace.

"And your shoes. Come, take them off and put them in front of the fire also."

He untied them and brought them over and put them on the tile, as she bent over and blotted her hair with her own towel, ruffled it with her hands and then blotted it some more. Haydon watched her, the movement of her hips, her bare feet. Suddenly she straightened up, flinging her hair back, her green eyes locking directly on him, catching him motionless, watching her.

For a few seconds they simply looked at each other, neither of them making any move to cover up their candid appraisal of each other, neither of them uncomfortable with what they saw or felt.

Finally Haydon said, "We've got to decide how we're going to handle this."

Isabel nodded, and slowly blotted the towel around her throat, into the opened front of her dress.

"If you want someone over there, if you don't trust the police with the artifacts, you had better call Lockhart," Haydon said. "You tell him you received an anonymous call that something had happened at Saturnino's. He will learn later that that corresponds with how the police heard of it." He paused. "I don't know. Maybe that's not something you would think of initially, in light of what has happened, but later you might wish you had. That is, if the collection is as valuable as you say."

"No," she said, as if she had just heard him. "You're right." But she didn't move to do anything.

"You've got to call him now," Haydon said. He could tell she didn't want to. "I can't do it," he added.

She nodded again, leaned her head back, and took a deep breath as she looked at the ceiling. "This is so hard," she said. Then she seemed to set her resolve and walked over to the telephone, which sat on a lemonwood secretary. She turned her back to him and dialed, got a wrong number, and dialed again. Apparently a servant answered, because she had to ask for Lockhart, give her name, and wait. After a moment she began talking to him. She told him about the telephone call, that she didn't have any idea what it was about, had *he* learned anything of Saturnino . . . no . . . no . . . yes, he's here now . . . no. Fine, she said, thank you, and she hung up.

"Okay," she said, turning around.

"He asked about me?"

"Yes. And had you met Amaranta. He will know what to do about the artifacts; he's aware of them."

He waited a moment. "I take it then that you agree we should keep our trip to El Carmen to ourselves. If we weren't seen by neighbors we should be all right."

She nodded. "I agree, but I am not sure why."

"The police aren't going to appreciate my presence here. They could cause me a lot of trouble, have someone follow me. I wouldn't want that."

He came over and stood by the fire, looking down into it. It felt good. The rain had been cold.

"What are you going to do now?" she asked. She was standing beside him, holding her skirt out toward the fire.

"You're in danger," he said. "All of you here."

"Yes," she said. "I think so."

"How much do Paulo and Celerina know about Saturnino?"

"They understand everything. They grew up here. Their parents were Amaranta's servants."

"They know all about him?"

"Everything. They are intelligent people, and they care very much."

"Does anyone else work here?"

"Agripina, a girl from Tlacopac, comes in every day to help Celerina, but she goes home every night. And an old man named Justino is the gardener. He comes in every day also."

"You need to inform Celerina and Paulo of the situation. They mustn't let Saturnino into the house, even onto the grounds, for any reason whatsoever. You should have Paulo hire a man to watch the entrance to the outer courtyard," Haydon said, unbuttoning his sleeves and turning his back to the fire. "Day and night, around the clock. Keep the gates locked at all times, and don't open them for Saturnino or anyone else you don't know. I've seen the two streetlamps on either side of the arches. Do they work?"

"One is burned out."

"Have Paulo replace it, or see that it's replaced. There is a wall all around the property?"

Isabel nodded.

"What's on the other side?"

"The private properties of other homes, similar to this."

"Ask Paulo if he can hire watchdogs, turn them loose out there."

Celerina came into the room, placed the coffee server on a sofa table, and left again.

"How do you like your coffee?" Haydon asked, draping his towel on the chair and walking around to the server.

"Only cream."

He poured a cup for each of them, put cream in both, and brought the cups around to the fireplace. He handed Isabel's to her and stood by her as he took a tentative sip. It tasted strong and rich, just right.

THEY BOTH WERE SILENT FOR A WHILE, WARMING THEMSELVES WITH the coffee, grateful to have something to do with their hands. Haydon wondered what she was thinking, but didn't look at her, not wanting to intrude at a time when he himself would have preferred to be left alone. He was uncomfortable in a role he would have given anything not to have to play.

"It's very much like a dream, isn't it?" she said unexpectedly. "One of those common nightmares of impeded flight . . . no, worse, one at which even your unconscious rebels, like incest or unspeakable acts by, or to, or with someone you love; the worst kind of thing, but something one normally can escape by waking. But this . . . my God, the unspeakable thing comes with you, riding the bony back of the nightmare right out of its dream and into reality."

She stopped, not waiting for him to respond, but thinking. "Once that happens, once something like that has crossed that border, nothing is ever again the same. There is no way to go back, is there?"

"I need to ask you some questions about that," he said, avoiding a response. He didn't think she really would want to hear his answer. She raised her eyes to him, but she did not seem apprehensive, though she must have known what was coming. "I would like to know what you thought about it, if you sensed any kind of meaning behind what you saw."

She continued looking at him, her green eyes losing their focus as she began to recall the house in Coyoacán. "I'm not a psychologist," she said, slowly shaking her head. "I didn't understand anything I saw there."

Haydon looked at her. "I don't think that's true," he said. "I think you understand a great deal about what you saw."

"No," she persisted, "I didn't *understand* anything. But I know what you mean. I know what you want." She sipped her coffee again, thinking. "It seems apparent that he has some . . . preoccupation with that god. Tezcatlipoca. But . . . obviously he's completely lost his mind. I can't even imagine . . ."

"But he is operating within a certain kind of logic," Haydon said. "It's not the logic of reasonable minds—in fact, it's probably no one's logic but his own. It only makes sense in his world."

"That pitiful arrangement of clothes in his bedroom," Isabel said. "The hair."

"Yes, that and all the rest of it. We need to try to determine what fits and what doesn't."

"And the things that don't fit are the important ones."

"Often, yes."

She turned and set her coffee on the carved stone mantel and folded her arms.

"I told you a little about Tezcatlipoca when we were there," she said. "All of the paraphernalia was consistent, of course. Physically, that terra-cotta statue was accurate to the most minute detail. The smoking mirrors—polished stone disks and polished obsidian mosaics—I have already told you about them."

"What about the covered mirrors?"

"I am not sure if that has anything at all to do with Tezcatlipoca or any of the concepts around the idea of the smoking mirror. I've thought about them, and I just don't think they do. But who can know, the way his mind is."

"What would he know about mirrors? I mean, what kind of myths deal with mirrors? What might he be confusing? I remember a mirror in Spenser's *The Faerie Queene* which

Merlin gave to a king. It informed him of treason, secret plots, and projected invasions. And there was one in *The Canterbury Tales* that warned another king of the approach of ill fortune and told him if his love for a woman was returned."

She thought a moment, then nodded. "Yes, folklore and myth, superstitions. Lao's mirror reflected the mind and its thoughts. Vulcan's mirror showed the past, depicted the present, and revealed the future. A variety of primitive people believed their reflections, like their shadows, were projections of their souls. That was why it was considered dangerous to look into water—your reflection might be stolen away by crocodiles or water spirits. There was the widespread custom of covering mirrors in a house after someone died lest your reflection, or soul, be carried off by the spirit of the deceased, which lingered about the house for a few days before departing. It was the same way with sick people—mirrors should be turned to the wall in their rooms to prevent their soul's departure in their weakened state. Sometimes the mirror was considered a symbol of twins—our self and our other self. I don't know. Beliefs like this are innumerable, and certainly among the Indians there are many and varied local superstitions that he could have learned about and that might possibly be playing a part in what he is doing." She stopped and looked at him and shrugged.

"And the monkeys?"

Isabel shook her head. "No. They played a role in Mesoamerican culture, but only incidentally and mostly in the southern regions where they were prevalent."

"And the woman outside. She was 'sacrificed'?"

Isabel closed her eyes and nodded and ran her fingers through her drying hair, which was becoming curly and full, the gray showing even more strikingly.

"And the yellow flower petals?" He was having to pull everything out of her. She seemed to find the consideration of every new idea an ordeal.

"Marigolds," she said, inhaling deeply and turning around again. "The Aztec's sacred flower of death. They still are considered a symbol of death to many Mexicans. In many places they cover entire graves with marigold petals on the second of November, the Day of the Dead. You noticed they were planted everywhere there, those and other flowers. All flowers were sacred to the Aztecs. When the priests and wise men referred to poetry it was called 'flower and song,' and the holy wars they conducted in order to obtain sacrificial victims to keep the sun alive were called the 'flowery wars.' But aside from all that, this love for flowers has been a lifelong preoccupation of his. You saw them—they were everywhere."

Haydon looked at her, regretting that this was the way he had met her, in the distorting atmosphere of death and old secrets. From the first moment they met there had been tension between them, restrained and beneath the surface perhaps, but both of them were constantly aware of it. He supposed that it would always be there because of who they were and what they were, an unpleasant reality like sadness and disappointment. He decided to turn the conversation to more concrete questions. He remembered Lockhart's point about Amaranta, and Saturnino as well; their minds were not subject to the strictures of logical analysis.

"You realize that as far as Saturnino is concerned, he's entered into the last days," he said. "He's probably keyed up, frantic, maybe desperate. Certainly he's a fugitive now—he can't go back home and he knows it. Does he have a second residence? An apartment somewhere, anything?"

Isabel shook her head. "I have no idea. I just . . . haven't been close enough to him to know." She turned toward him a little and looked into the fire, remembering. The thin silk of her dress was drying and becoming opaque again, and he was no longer able to see the tint of her skin through it as he had when it was wet and clinging. "It has been forever since I was close to him. Since childhood. But he was a wonderful boy. Amaranta spoiled him. She actually spoiled both of us, but with a girl and her mother it is different. I think even as a child I understood her better than Nino. I mean, on an intuitive level. He adored her, you see. To me she was very marvelous, creative, mercurial, funny, a joy. But I knew also that she was only a woman, my mother, a person who could be petty, and at times even unjust. But to Nino she was all of the good things and none of the bad. To him she was nothing less than a goddess.

"You know, as he got older he must have had to go through incredible psychological contortions to maintain that kind of ideal," she said, and then raised her eyes to him. "Then of course, when he turned against her he did so with the fervor of a zealot. She became the great Whore of Babylon."

"How did she react to that?" Haydon asked.

Isabel looked toward the windows. Though the sky was still dark the rain had almost stopped and water was dripping off the entablature of the colonnade.

"I don't really know how it affected her," she said. "By that time—this was in 1967 or 1968—it was Nino's last year at the university, and my first. An exciting time for me, but also because of the unpleasant tensions at home I was spending as much time as I could with my friends at the university. It must have been in 1968, because I remember that Saturnino had been with the students at the time of the shooting, when the government troops fired on the demonstrators in the Plaza de las Tres Culturas in the Tlatelolco housing projects, just before the Olympics. He was mixed up in all of that business, which only added fuel to Everardo's fury against him. He wanted to take Nino's inheritance from him."

Haydon had noticed that Isabel never referred to Amaranta as "Mother," but consistently used her first name. Now she had done the same thing when speaking of her father. It did not seem to be so much a sign of formality as it was an indication of the remoteness of their relationship. He wondered how it must have been for Isabel the child, surrounded by so much eccentricity.

"Anyway—how did she react?" she said, restating Haydon's question. "She went into seclusion and painted endlessly. Really, I saw her very little. Amaranta was an anomaly, always out of step. She was much more like the career woman of today, in many ways. You see, she was thirty-three when Nino was born, so by this time she must have been, what, around fifty-seven. Not only were Nino and I entering new phases in our lives, so was she. We all had been growing farther and farther apart for some time. My father was only an infrequent guest, it seemed. He 'lived' with us in Polanco, but he was never there. I am not even certain he kept clothes there. It was a strange life. I had gone through high school pretty much on my own. I don't know. Our ties to each other were tenuous; we weren't a family, we were a bloodline."

Isabel's attention had been fixed on a clay bowl with three stubby legs and decorated with a meander pattern in a faded brownish red. But she wasn't seeing the bowl; her green eyes were deep in a lost world. "The little boy I knew is as extinct as the people who made that bowl," she said. "I will tell you something. When I saw . . . that poor woman, in that moment when I realized what I was seeing, I felt such an overwhelming wave of compassion for him, such an aching and hurting for him, for the child in that faraway memory who loved his mother so completely and so innocently, that I felt that I would die too, that I was falling slowly, slowly through the immeasurable empty spaces of a great sadness." She stopped, and shook her head slowly. "Then instantly—like that magician's paper that flashes brilliantly and disappears—it was gone. My feelings for him no longer existed, not even their ashes."

The thick walls of the old house encompassed them in a silence disturbed only by the small, nibbling sounds of the fire, which had died to a few wavering tongues of saffron flame.

"I'm sorry," Haydon said. He would have liked to hold her again, as he had in those brief hectic moments she had just recalled, but he didn't move. He wondered if he would ever hold her again, and what the circumstances might be that would make that possible. "What about you?" he asked. He thought he should move, do something, so he stepped around to the coffee server and poured another cup. "What happened to you after the university?"

She looked at him, and for a moment Haydon thought she wasn't going to answer, that she was going to tell him it was none of his business. But she surprised him.

"I finished my first degree and was two years into my doctoral program when I met an Argentine scriptwriter who wrote for Televisa. I fell in love, and married. It was a glamorous life, and I had the opportunity to meet many actors and actresses, famous jet-setters. I traveled all over Europe and the States with my husband. Had a good time. It lasted eight years. So what happened? In Portofino I found him in bed with two actresses. But I must admit it wasn't that much of a shock. I think I had been refusing to accept the realities of his philandering for a long time. But when that happened, I left him. Divorced him, which was a very long and involved process, since I am Catholic. I returned to the university and resumed my doctoral studies as if the intervening eight years had been only a blink of the eyes."

She lifted her head at him. "How are your clothes doing?"

"Fine. Almost completely dry."

She regarded him a moment, her emerald eyes seeming to take his measure, her thoughts obscured by her beauty so that he was more inclined to undress her with his imagination than to read her mind. She moved away from the fireplace and walked to the window that looked out to the colonnade. Haydon's eyes followed her as she stopped and watched the rain that had begun again without his noticing, a still, slow rain. When she turned around the leaden light from the window was just strong enough to penetrate the silk and show him the dusky lines of the insides of her thighs.

"It is almost two o'clock," she said, glancing at the long wooden case of a wall clock. "I think it would be good if we both had an opportunity to bathe and rest a short while. Paulo will be here in a moment to take you to a guest room. There will be something there for a light lunch, and everything you might need to freshen up. If you will undress and put your clothes on a chair in the hall outside your door they will be cleaned and pressed and returned to you within an hour. I will come by for you at three-thirty, if that is not too early, and we will go around to the studio . . . to meet Amaranta.

"Is this all right with you?" she asked.

"Yes, of course," he said. "Thank you. One thing," he added, sitting down on a sofa in front of the fireplace and putting on his shoes. "Will you have Paulo start on those things I mentioned earlier?" He finished tying his shoes and stood, taking his coat off the chair. "It's important," he said.

Chapter 24

HAYDON FOLLOWED PAULO'S STOCKY FRAME THROUGH THE LARGE rooms, through the three-foot-thick doorways and vaulted corridors. The house was much larger than it appeared from the outside, and Haydon noticed now what he had not noticed before when all his attention was concentrated on its furnishings, that it had been very well maintained. It did not evoke the feeling of melancholy that had often oppressed him in many of the old homes in Mexico which were furnished in a dark and heavy colonial style. As always, Amaranta had followed her own muse in this, and aside from the Mexican architecture of the actual structure, the house could not be identified as being done in any "style" at all.

After climbing the stairs that took them to the western wing of the house, Haydon patiently followed the unhurried Paulo along the terra-cotta tiles of the white hallway, the servant's leather sandals creating muted echoes as they struck the clay floor. There were rooms on both sides of the hallway, those on the left having windows that overlooked the wooded grounds, and the ones on the right opening out to a loggia overlooking the enclosed courtyard and facing the opposite wing of the U-shaped house.

It was in front of one of these rooms on the right that Paulo stopped and opened the dark wooden door recessed into the three-foot-thick walls under a flattened arch. He did not go into the room but backed away from the door and asked Haydon if he would need anything. Haydon resisted the temptation to ask him into the room and talk to him about Saturnino's situation and about the security measures he had discussed with Isabel, but he knew that was out of the question, even in light of its urgency. A servant with a lifetime of service to a family was not going to appreciate that kind of intimate approach from a stranger. He simply had to trust that Isabel would do as he had asked. Still, before he left he would check with her again.

He thanked Paulo, said everything was fine, and watched as the Indian turned and padded down the hall the way they had come. The room was clean and spacious, and a platter of fresh fruit and cheeses and bread sat on a table near the bed. Haydon went over to the French doors, which were covered with a light muslin, and opened them, looking past the pots of geraniums to the dripping fronds of the Guadalupe palms which screened his view of the studio across the way. He took a deep breath of the light highland air and then stepped inside again and closed the doors.

Finding a fresh cotton robe on a chair in the dressing area of the bath, he removed his clothes and put on the robe and then removed the things from his pockets before setting the wrinkled and still slightly damp suit and shirt out into the hall on a chair as Isabel had directed. He took the Beretta into the bathroom with him and laid it on the marble dressing counter while he took a long, hot shower.

After toweling dry and putting the robe back on, he combed his hair and tried a splash of the cologne he found there, curious to see what Isabel had chosen, since he was sure that she had been responsible for its being there. He returned to the bedroom and walked over to the French doors. He opened them to the afternoon rain, which was clacking softly against the palm fronds just a few yards away from the loggia. Leaving the doors open, he turned to the room, pulled a chair over to the table, and sat down facing the courtyard. He picked up a paring knife from the platter of fruit and sliced an apple into half a dozen wedges, poured a glass of wine from the small decanter, and began eating.

Maybe, at last, he was going to get some answers. He had been in Mexico City almost forty-eight hours and was only just now getting the opportunity to speak to Amaranta. Lockhart had known what he was talking about when he said that Isabel was protective of her mother. Even though Lockhart himself had called on his behalf, and even though he had spent a large part of two days in the same house with the old woman, he was only now being allowed to see her, under Isabel's careful orchestration. She was indeed closely protected, and he wondered how it was that such a forceful woman was letting herself be so thoroughly cared for. But Isabel herself had said that Amaranta had become so eccentric she couldn't really care for things properly. Perhaps, like many older people, she gladly had given up the responsibility of having to tend to the day-to-day decisions of life. And there was always the possibility that Isabel didn't have it so easy, that her mother simply no longer had the mental capacity to take care of herself and Isabel had had to step in with, or without, her mother's consent. Whatever the circumstances, Isabel was now clearly the mistress of the house.

He finished a slice of the apple, which turned out to be unusually sweet, and sipped the wine. It was probably from a Mexican vintner, but it was dry and he liked it. Outside there was a momentary roar as a hard downpour drummed against the palm fronds. It lasted maybe two minutes before it subsided again to a slow, light drizzle. He slumped in the armchair and held the glass of wine in his lap as he stared outside.

He couldn't help it, the image of the poor woman in Saturnino's courtyard came back to him along with the entire bizarre furnishings of the house in Coyoacán. He should have known early on what he was getting into, that he was dealing with someone who had created his own world complete with its own theology and rules of behavior, with its own constructs of good and evil. And he also should have realized that as time went on the situation could only grow more distorted, more extreme, until it was completely out of control, as it now had become. Why hadn't he snapped to that more quickly? Why had he tended to relegate Saturnino's lethal presence to a secondary role? He thought there were several answers. The most obvious one was that the manner in which it all had come about was in itself a separate intrigue, one that had completely captured his interest by the time his own death threat had come along. He was so preoccupied with unraveling his father's past that he could not see the seriousness of the more immediate threat. In a sense that was true even now.

He did not really believe that he would learn from Amaranta anything that would help him deal with Saturnino. The more urgent question now was not why, but how. The man had to be found and stopped, and the only thing that was going to do that was methodical attention to detail, not a voyage into his father's past or into Saturnino's harried psyche. His self-preservation was going to depend on his ability to focus upon the immediate threat of Saturnino himself: when and where and how. Knowing how his father's past was interwoven with this, was even an integral part of it, might not be something that would actually help him defend himself from Saturnino. The "reason" could well be an absolute fantasy that existed only in Saturnino's disintegrating mind.

BY THE TIME HAYDON HAD FINISHED THE APPLE AND HAD PEELED AND eaten a mango, he realized that he had poured the last of the wine, which reminded him of the time. He hadn't yet put on his watch. He reached across the plate and got it, strapped it on, and saw that it had been almost an hour since he had gotten out of the shower. He got up and walked to the hall door and opened it to find his clothes hanging neatly on the back of the chair, still warm from the pressing. He brought the chair and the clothes inside and began to dress.

He was putting in his last cufflink when there was a knock at the door. Again he glanced at his watch. It was ten after three. He took the Beretta off the table, clipped it on the waist of his pants in the small of his back, and went to the door.

"Excuse me, I know I am early," Isabel said. She stood away from the door a little formally, seeming slightly uncomfortable, with her arms folded over each other in a manner that he was beginning to recognize as natural for her. She was beautiful; her jet hair, shot through with gray in front, was hanging long and full over the scooped neck of a coral cotton dress that reached almost to her white heels and was cinched at the waist with a wide white leather belt with an ornate gold buckle. Her eyes, like her face and hair, seemed to have taken on a new brilliance and freshness.

"It's all right," he said. "Come in, I'm nearly ready."

"I would like to talk to you," she said. Her manner made it plain to him that she had something to tell him, something she found it extremely uncomfortable to talk about. "Before we go see Amaranta."

He opened the door wider, stepping back. "Of course, come in." As she stepped past him he said, "It was very kind of

Celerina to press these. They're done very well. Tell her I
appreciate it."

"Actually it was Agripina, the girl I told you about," she said,
turning to him in front of the French doors. "I will tell her you
were pleased."

Haydon wanted to put her at ease, but could feel his own
heart beginning to pound. He walked over and got his tie and
slipped it under his collar, which he then buttoned. He
stepped to a mirror, made a few quick loops and tucks with the
tie, tightened the knot, then turned to face Isabel. She was
looking at him with an expression that surprised him, one of
nostalgia or perhaps a sad memory of the domestic routine of
watching a man tie his tie.

"Has something happened?" he asked.

"I know quite a lot about you," she said. "Much more than
you realize." She paused, still unsure of herself.

"You've seen Saturnino's file, then?"

"No," she responded quickly. "I haven't. I don't know
anything about that. I learned about you in a much more
intimate way, from a person who described you so well that I
felt as if I knew you from the moment I opened the door two
days ago and saw you standing there. I knew your father very
well," she said.

Haydon was dumbfounded. He couldn't and didn't respond.
He looked at her, watched her eyes search his face for some
reaction, for some indication that would tell her how she
should proceed. But there was nothing he could do except
stare at her as if her words were visible like the Mayan glyphs
depicting speech, not readily understood. He waited and
watched her watch him.

"Once a year, sometimes twice or more, but at least once a
year, every year, he came to see her," she proceeded, her
words soft with consideration for him, one hand of her folded
arms rubbing the upper part of her other arm. "I did not learn
of this until halfway through my marriage. It was a shock to me
too, despite the fact that by then I should have been used to
anything she did, or might have done. I think it was the
consistency of their relationship that caught me off guard at
first, the years she had devoted to this solitary, annual liaison,
a greater demonstration of constancy than I had ever imagined
possible for her. And then the more I learned about it and

them, about their strange, abiding fidelity, the more intrigued I became."

"How did you discover this?" Haydon was staggered. Christ. His father had been a stranger. He had no idea who the man had been. No idea.

"It was in 1976," she answered. "I was supposed to have been going to Mallorca with my husband, who was working on a script that was being filmed there at the time. At the last minute I backed out, I don't remember the reason, and in the afternoon I drove over here—my husband and I lived in Lomas Chapultepec—to visit. It was a low time for me, and I had nothing to do. When I drove up and went into the house I met Celerina inside the entry looking flustered and slightly panicked. She was surprised to see me, she said, so surprised to see me. I told her what had happened and said I was going up to talk to Amaranta. Celerina said she thought Amaranta was asleep, and I said I would go up and check, and she said oh no, please, let her do it. Well, it was immediately obvious to me that something was odd, so I asked her what was the matter and she said nothing, obviously lying, fluttering around like a mother quail, so I simply walked past her and started up the stairs. At that moment Amaranta appeared at the head of the landing and told Celerina that it was all right. Then she said to me, 'Come on up. I want you to meet someone,' and that was it."

Haydon felt as if his feet were barely touching the stone floor. He watched her speak as if she were an oracle, the source of wondrous revelations.

"That was in 1976?"

Isabel nodded.

"What happened?"

"I went upstairs and she introduced me. He had been sitting in one of those cross-framed chairs she has scattered around up there, smoking a cigar and watching her paint. It was all very sedate and proper. He was sixty-six and she was sixty-five. It was several years before he died in the plane crash with your mother. They acted quite natural about his being there. Amaranta continued painting while your father pulled over another chair for me. He was so gracious and elegant in his ivory suit—it was July—with his longish hair graying and swept back at the temples and his slender hands. He seemed genuinely pleased and eager to talk to me. I don't know why, but I had the impression that it was his idea to have me join them. Very subtly, very expertly, he proceeded to interview me, though it was some time before I realized what he was doing. Here he was, the mystery man whose possible discovery by me had nearly caused poor Celerina to have heart failure, revealing nothing of himself and learning everything about me.

"Amaranta seemed unusually quiet as your father and I talked, and several times I thought I caught an amused expression on his face at my obvious curiosity, at my wondering glances toward the now uncharacteristically silent Amaranta, who was painting furiously. I stayed a long time, too long, I realized later, but I had a wonderful time talking with him. He was the only man I have ever known whom I considered 'charming,' without the cloying connotations that often accompany that word. He revealed nothing of their relationship that afternoon, only that they had been friends for years and that he had been in the city and had stopped by to visit. He knew that explanation did not satisfy me, but he made no effort to elaborate. I suppose that part of his amused expression was because he was imagining the conversation Amaranta and I would surely have after he had gone."

Isabel shrugged, a mild smile on her face.

"Well, I should try to get to the point of your question. I left them after several hours and did not go back to see Amaranta until the next day, though I was dying of curiosity. For some reason I caught her in a thoughtful mood. Perhaps it was the picture she was painting, or his visit, or in retrospect, I wondered if she didn't have a premonition of what was about to happen to her, but anyway, she told me everything. All of it, their early years together with all their fire and fury; your father's abrupt move to London and subsequent marriage; his return to Mexico City and absolute refusal to see her for over four years; his ultimate move to Houston and then return here for two months to tie up some loose ends with his practice; her learning of his return and pleading with him to meet with her, to help her with a disaster that had befallen her; and the beginning of a lifetime of stolen afternoons.

"In the ensuing year before his next return I learned all I could about him, from Amaranta, from a trunkful of old letters which, unfortunately, she burned shortly afterward. When he came again in 1977 I asked Amaranta if she would arrange for me to meet with him before he left the city. She did and we spent an entire afternoon together, talking. He knew she had told me everything, or at least quite a lot, and he very graciously—and circumspectly—agreed to talk about it as well. I must tell you I was obsessed with their story. He was everything my father had not been, and I was mesmerized by the thought of my mother maintaining the slender thread of her sanity for the sake of these one or two days every year when she gave herself absolutely to the only man she had ever really loved. I had not believed her capable of that kind of romantic idealism. It was . . . unbelievable. Every year for thirty-seven years. I didn't know what to think of it. I still regard it as one of the most remarkable relationships I have ever known."

When she stopped, Haydon was captivated by the silence, as if his aural sense had suddenly become his only means of gathering information. He heard the hollow sound of the light rain on the stiff fronds of the palms; the timid and intermittent soughing of a mourning dove, far away and faint in an afternoon of rain; his own heartbeat pulsing in his ears. He stared unseeing, meeting Isabel's emerald gaze.

"And he continued coming to see her," she added softly. "Even when there was no longer a reason for him to do so."

Haydon was so numbed by this revelation that he completely missed the point of the last remark.

"Jesus Christ," he said.

"I don't know," Isabel said hesitatingly. "I think you must feel . . . cheated, perhaps, that I, a stranger, know this intimate thing about your father. I feel very much like an interloper with you, but I felt, now, you should know. I never dreamed that I would meet you, that this would be something my conscience would compel me to reveal. But under the circumstances it would have been cruel, even unjust, to keep it from you."

Haydon didn't say anything. He simply shook his head in disbelief and moved past her to the French doors. He stood in the opening and looked out to the palms, whose pointed, sagging fronds were dribbling tiny streams of water as if they were fed from an inner spring. He felt as he had at those times when, as a boy, he had stumbled onto one of the harsher facts of reality which brutally unseated something he always had accepted as a fundamental truth. Now, as then, he realized that everything he believed must be reexamined in light of this new discovery, that nothing could be assumed to be as it appeared to be. Once more the comfort of a naive misconception had been jerked away forever. At forty-three he was still having to relearn what it felt like to have the wind knocked out of him.

"I can only imagine how you must feel," Isabel said behind him. She had turned and was speaking to his back, both of them facing the gray rain, the deep-sea-green palms. "But I hope you do not . . . condemn them too quickly. I believe they could no more stop themselves from loving each other than they could stop themselves from growing old. It is important to understand that it was more than a sexual relationship. There had been that too, of course, especially in their earlier years—a kind of fierceness that it seemed neither of them really understood. But their passion for each other was beyond that; it was an attraction of psyches in which the physical was simply swept along in the wake of something larger, more encompassing, more complex. I think . . . it would be an injustice to pass judgment on them because you believe you understand."

Haydon shook his head. "I'm not going to understand this for a long time." He looked at the geraniums in the terra-cotta pots lined up along the top of the balustrade, wrapping around to the other side of the loggia until they disappeared behind the palms, their red-orange blooms as bright as receding dollops of oil in a van Gogh. How many pots? How many blossoms? How many years? "Thirty-seven," he said. "All of my life, until he died." He paused. "Do you know if my mother knew this?"

"I don't think so," Isabel said. "He never told me and I did not ask, though I wondered. I think she didn't."

"Did anyone else? Lockhart?"

"No. Only the servants here, Celerina and Paulo, and their parents before they died."

"Not Saturnino?"

"No."

"And she burned the letters?" He was still standing with his back to her.

"Yes."

Christ. Whatever it was Saturnino had against him, it wasn't this; the poor bastard didn't even know about it. And yet if it hadn't been for him, Haydon probably would never have learned of it himself.

"Do you still want to meet her?" Isabel asked.

"Yes, of course I do," he said, turning around. "I was just . . . I don't know, trying to stay up with this."

"We ought to go," she said gently. "We can talk more later, if you wish."

Haydon took his coat off the back of the chair, and they left his room and walked without speaking down the long hall of the west wing to the center section of the house, where they turned left and proceeded through the upstairs vestibule that opened onto the center loggia. They entered the studio on its southern end and saw the old woman sitting in a wheelchair toward the center of the long room, near the portraits of Haydon's father which still looked out at him from against the wall. Celerina stood nearby like a lady-in-waiting, and perched on the right arm of Amaranta's chair was a glossy-haired and beautifully groomed capuchin monkey, the gray-and-black hair on its head a perfect example of the characteristic monk's-cowl markings that gave the breed its name.

Amaranta and the capuchin watched them come across the wooden floor, and the old woman's regal bearing that had been immediately apparent even from a distance was reinforced by the expression on her face as they approached. Her dress, of unbleached linen, reached all the way to her sandaled feet; it had a fitted waist—which Haydon could see was small—long sleeves, and a high collar of handmade Mexican lace. On a coarse gold chain that reached to the middle of her chest she wore a single emerald cabochon of almost the exact color and size of her eyes, which regarded him with an even gaze impossible for him to interpret. Sitting straight-backed and square-shouldered, she was more elegant than he had imagined, and it was not difficult still to see the girl of the black-and-white photographs in the face of the older woman, who, almost magically it seemed, had retained the same clear skin he had heard described so often. Her hair was largely gray, though there were still streaks of jet, and she had it pulled back softly and knotted at the nape of her neck.

The little capuchin keened softly at her side, wringing its tiny hands, its dark eyes darting rapidly all over Haydon, appraising him from head to foot, searching his face and seeming to see there cause for concern as it swiftly moved onto Amaranta's shoulder and put its wizened, worried face close to hers and held her throat with its delicate, nigrescent fingers. Keeping her eyes on Haydon, Amaranta reached up and stroked the simian coat, arranged her lips in a soft pucker, and made suckling noises to comfort the alarmed creature. As the two of them stared at him in silence, face by face, a sense of misgiving slowly formed at the back of his mind and worked its way forward until suddenly, with a piercing ache of recognition, he realized that it was only the capuchin's eyes that communicated with him, that expressed apprehension and curiosity and affection. Amaranta's eyes were dead, as cold as the raw stone she wore around her neck; she was completely mindless.

"It began quickly after that first summer I met your father," Isabel explained softly, sensing his discovery. "By the time I realized what was happening, and how quickly it was happening, it was almost too late."

Haydon's muscles shivered as if they were being drained of their tensity, their ability to hold him up. He was afraid he was going to have to sit down, but his amazement kept him there, standing in front of Amaranta's dead green eyes, which indeed might as well have been emeralds for all that they could know or disclose.

"I got in touch with your father, and he came immediately," Isabel continued. "She knew him only intermittently; the comprehension went out of her eyes like flickering lights, sometimes bright, sometimes dim and fading. It was agonizing, because she knew what was happening. They sat up here together for the biggest part of two days, saying goodbye to each other in a process of communication that was heartrending. It must have been like trying to compose lyric poetry with dots and dashes. We left them alone as much as possible, and on several occasions I would pass on the loggia and glance in through the opened doors and see them sitting here. They held hands and your father spoke quietly to her for hours.

Occasionally she spoke to him, and it was one of those times that I saw him kneeling in front of her, their hands clasped together in her lap, and he was crying. It was very hard on him, very sad."

Haydon moved a few steps closer to Amaranta, causing the capuchin's eyes to flare open in amazed fear as he tightened his left arm around his mistress's neck and stroked the side of her face with the palm of his right hand, his eyes riveted on Haydon. As Haydon looked at Amaranta he remembered all the images of her he had gathered from the photographs and from the stories of Ada Venecia, Gabriela, Gaston Arreola, Juan Lockhart, Isabel. She had lived in his mind larger than life, vibrant and complex and wild. Why had he never imagined her any other way? Why had he taken it for granted that when he finally confronted the woman his father had loved in so strange a fashion, he would find her as she had been described, unchanged from the memories that had created her myth? Why had he believed, like a child convinced of enchanted princesses, that he also would be allowed to know the incomparable Amaranta?

He felt Isabel move up beside him, close, touching him, her arm sliding inside his.

"He returned every year, as always. He came up here to the studio and sat with her, holding her hands, talking, sometimes simply sitting and remembering, both of them in silence. It was during those times, after he had spent his afternoons with Amaranta, that I would visit with him at length, often over dinner and afterward. I came to know him rather well, I think, and to love him, too. But of course, we didn't know he had only a few summers left."

"And that was when he told you about me?"

"Yes, all about you," she said softly.

Jesus Christ! Haydon felt as if he could scream. How *could* he have been robbed of talking to this woman? She could have answered his questions; she could have enlightened him; she could have told him so many things that a son should know about his father that a father couldn't tell. She could have revealed to him that part of his father's heart that had felt such a profound need for thirty-seven years of secret afternoons. What had Haydon missed of him? What piece of him had

Haydon never understood, never even imagined? And would it have made any difference between them if he had?

He almost knelt before her himself. He almost believed that if he spoke to her, was able to make their eyes meet with any gravity at all, she would speak. But the capuchin would not have allowed it; it perched there on her shoulder like the revenant of her consciousness, satisfied to be apart from the body that once had retained it with such disquietude. It was over. He bent down and touched Amaranta's hand, which lay in her lap, let his hand rest a moment on hers while she looked at him with her green eyes and the hollow gaze of unknowing.

When he stood he turned away from her toward the loggia, not looking at his father's eyes following him from their canvas past. He went out until he could smell the damp vermilion geraniums, until he could see the green fronds of the Guadalupe palms bobble and swim in the rain.

Chapter 25

LICENCIADO VERDAD WAS A SHORT STREET WITH A LONG HISTORY. IN the early sixteenth century when Hernán Cortés with his Spanish soldiers and Catholic priests crossed the long causeway and entered the Aztec capital of Tenochtitlán, the grand city of canals in Lake Texcoco, the stretch of cobblestones that was now Licenciado Verdad was in the heart of the sacred *teocalli*, the religious ceremonial center of that ancient city. The street was not a street then, but a span of paving stones that ran from the Temple of Tezcatlipoca on its south end to the Great Pyramid with its twin temples to Tlaloc and Huitzilopochtli on its north. Situated on its west side were the colonnaded courtyards of the public meeting places, and on its east side were the city's beautiful sprawling gardens and the *calmécac*, the school where the young men of the day were taught how to acquire "an authentic face" by Aztec wisemen.

After the Spaniards conquered the Aztec empire in 1521, they razed the ancient city, methodically tearing down the elaborate palaces of the Aztec dignitaries and the towering temples dedicated to the Náhuatl gods, and, using the same stones on the same sites, began building their own government buildings, palaces, and monuments to the Spanish king and their own churches and cathedrals for the worship of the Christian God. Eventually the governing center of the Aztec empire was completely covered over by the buildings of the governing center of the newly created empire of New Spain. As the centuries passed, colonial Mexico replaced New Spain and then modern Mexico replaced the colony, but the geographic center of each of these empires remained the same, the heart of Mexico City. The narrow, alleylike street of Licenciado Verdad had seen it all.

The building at No. 1 Licenciado Verdad had once been the

site of the Temple of Tezcatlipoca, and after its razing it became the Archbishop's Palace in the mid-sixteenth century. In the eighteenth century the church remodeled the building and it took on its present appearance. In 1861 an anticlerical government "secularized" the building, as it did many of the holdings of the Catholic Church, and it was partitioned and sold to private citizens. It was now greatly reduced from its former glories and was almost derelict. It was one of the many old buildings still standing in the crowded colonial center of the city that were known somewhat derisively as *casas con cinco patios*, houses with five patios, because they were five stories high and were composed of rooms or apartments of various sizes that opened onto a galleried central courtyard. The courtyard, surrounded by rising tiers of iron railings and switchback stairwells, was approached through a long murky corridor that opened onto the cobblestones of Licenciado Verdad.

But Saturnino was not there in the late afternoon when the rain stopped for almost half an hour, while the smog and clouds cleared in a thin ribbon over the mountains toward Toluca and a ragged seam of molten sunset flooded the rooftops of the monstrous city in golden light. Instead, he was several blocks away, crossing the Plaza Loreto to the church of Nuestra Señora de Loreto on San Ildefonso. There was no particular reason for meeting Napo near this church—the Colonia Centro was full of them, sixty or more, as if the colonial fathers had tried, in a baroque example of edificial excess, to crush the memory of the Aztec gods beneath the proliferating rocks of St. Peter, convents and chapels and monasteries and temples and cathedrals. Even before he emerged from the aromatic paths of rain-dampened poplars and pines, Saturnino saw the enormous dome of the church breaking through the upper stories of the trees, washed in the rays of falling western light.

He paused at the edge of the park and looked across at the impressive facade of the church with its elaborate carvings of stone and marble. The rich light of sunset changed rapidly on the slopes of its dome, for once the sun reached the crest of the mountains it sensed its death and plummeted quickly to end it.

Crossing San Ildefonso to the front of the towering church, where its massive wooden doors were thrown open to evening, he could hear the vesper voices, few and untrained but devout, insisting on faith, insisting on something better than what life itself was proving to be. Five hundred years earlier he would have been hearing different kinds of voices, a different kind of singing, different rhythms, for here near this church were the Aztec priests' quarters, not far from the island city's northern gates and the causeway to Tepeyacac. From the flat temple tops the low rumble of drums and the shrill cry of the conch-shell horns would be blowing the last of the four times of day and the priests would be offering up incense to the departing sun and to the approaching lords of the shadows.

"HE JUST WENT BACK TO HIS HOTEL," NAPO SAID. "THAT'S ALL."

They were sitting at a tiny round table in the sallow light of a narrow step-down tavern a short distance from the church. Outside on the sidewalk the rain beat down steadily, seeming to entertain the bored and wraithlike Indian woman who sat on a stool behind a grill of smoking *carnitas*. On a cement ledge that supported one side of the grill were four bottles of different-colored pastel fruit drinks, which she sold warm from a tub on the floor. Beside her on the thick cement wall with peeling blue paint the prices of the diced pork and the warm soft drinks were written on a chipped blackboard advertising a brand of fruit drink she did not keep in her tub. There were only five or six tables, four of them occupied with unshaven old men, or out-of-work laborers.

"Why didn't you tell me where he was?" Saturnino asked coldly. "Why did you think you were following him?"

"Hey, man." Napo was belligerent. "I called you. Nobody at home, huh?" He cocked his head sideways at Saturnino and pulled down the sides of his mouth as he raised his eyebrows in mock surprise. "Nobody at hooome . . ." He toked on a stained joint, the sweet, oily aroma of its smoke mixing with the tangy scent of grilled pork.

Saturnino watched two old men playing checkers at a table near the glistening sidewalk. The checkerboard was painted on the surface of the wooden table itself and the checkers were represented by bottlecaps dipped in green or yellow paint. One of the men drank a bottle of beer and the other sipped a fruit drink. Saturnino lighted a Pall Mall—the last of the packs he had brought back from Houston—with a Mexican waxed-paper match and listened to the cars splash past on the cobblestoned street. People were passing on the sidewalks carrying umbrellas. A lottery-ticket vendor paused outside and peered into the opened front of the tavern, holding up reams of tickets he had draped over his arms and shoulders like bandoliers and which he protected with a clear plastic umbrella with lavender flowers. No one paid any attention to him and he moved on.

"We have to find him again," Saturnino said. "It's time to talk to him."

Napo was suddenly interested. Yes, he would like to talk to the man again, too. He studied Saturnino with sullen dark eyes, his dove-gray silk shirt hanging open at the neck revealing the requisite gold chain and religious medal, the limp thin material sagging to one side, weighted down by a pack of cigarettes.

"What does this guy do, anyway?" he asked.

"Does it make any difference?"

"If I'm going to follow him for you," Napo argued, "I think I have a right to know something about him."

Saturnino shrugged.

"Hey, you *do* know the guy, huh?"

"Not really."

Letting his eyes drift away, Napo seemed to give this some earnest thought, though Saturnino couldn't be certain. Perhaps he was just jigging along on the cocaine.

"I don't know him," Saturnino said.

Napo shot his eyes at him without moving his head.

"And yet, I do."

"Shit, man," Napo whined.

"We are *fratres animi*."

Napo looked at him, his eyebrows arched in an effort to keep his eyes open, an elbow on the table holding the last centimeter of the joint, a heavy gold bracelet slipped down, caught around the cuff of his silk shirt.

"And *fratres vivi*."

"Shit, man." Napo suddenly squinted, exasperated. "Do you know the guy or what?"

"Yes."

"Okay."

"But I've never met him. Now it's time to do that."

Napo regarded him with darting eyes, his mouth slack,

wheezing through nostrils racked by cocaine. It was indeed time to do that.

"I want to pick him up as soon as we can," Saturnino said.

"Pick him up?"

"Yes. I do not think he is going to want to come along with us of his own free will. In fact, I think he will resist."

Napo seemed to be remembering something, something unpleasant. "We have to plan it . . . very carefully. This man is not easy to deal with."

Saturnino turned to him. "Oh? How do you know this?"

"I could tell by watching him; I could tell."

"Very good, Napo. You are right. He is not going to be easy to persuade." •

"He carries a gun," Napo said abruptly.

"How do you know that?"

"I saw it, in San Ángel. When he got into the taxi in Plaza San Jacinto I saw it under his sports coat. Just a flash of it, but it was there."

"It is not going to be easy," Saturnino repeated, watching Napo. Was this little shit going to back out on him now? He couldn't let that happen; there needed to be two of them. "That doesn't scare you, does it, Napo? If you don't want to take the risk, then I can get somebody else. I can't have you chicken out on me at the last minute."

"Hey," Napo said stiffly, his top lip curling defiantly. "Nobody's going to chicken out, okay? But I don't like not even knowing what the hell it is I'm supposed to be doing. I mean, I'm not that goddam stupid. The guy's got a gun and you want me to make him do something he doesn't want to do? What does that mean, huh? I could get my balls shot off. I mean, Christ!"

Napo had raised his voice and was gesturing, making wide sweeps of his arm and then tapping himself on his chest with his middle finger, scattering the remaining ashes of his marijuana joint onto the next table. The wraith-woman turned around and glared at them, and the two men at the adjoining table decided it was time to go back out into the rain.

"Okay, okay," Saturnino said, his voice smooth and conciliatory. "You have a point; you're right." Out of the corner of his eye he glanced at the two old checker players, who had suspended stratagems in order to watch them with undisguised frankness as being temporarily more interesting than what they were doing. A traffic altercation in the street would have been an equally amusing diversion and would have been observed with the same detachment. "Okay," he said soothingly, and as the hair on Napo's neck settled down the old men returned to their bottlecaps.

"You know what I mean?" Napo said, one last thrust to his point, now that he had gotten Saturnino's attention.

"Yes, I do, of course," Saturnino replied, trying to decide how to present it, how best to play to Napo's self-image. With Napo the money was not a big thing. He was from a wealthy family, and the money Saturnino was paying him would be a drop in the bucket for his cocaine habit. No, for Napo it was the game he was playing; for him everything was like the movies, and he wanted to feel the way he imagined the men in the movies felt; for him the movies were reality.

"Listen," Saturnino said, leaning his forearms on the table and bending slightly forward confidentially. "The matter is very personal, Napo, so I cannot give you all the details"—secrecy—"but I can tell you that it is a matter of a point of honor that goes back many, many years"—machismo. "I have to have someone I can trust explicitly"—intrigue—"someone not afraid to use force if they have to"—machismo. "That is why I have used you for this"—a special breed of cat. "I felt I could trust you"—camaraderie—"rely on your judgment to handle a sticky situation correctly"—a man of the world.

Napo listened to him. He took a cigarette out of his shirt pocket and lighted it. He crossed his legs, rearranging the sports coat draped over his lap, and listened with gratification, a serious look of collaboration coming over his face.

"First of all," Saturnino continued. "Do not call my home anymore. I have moved away from there. Do not call there. They are watching the place."

"They?"

"Think of it as a conspiracy, Napo. Others are involved, but I cannot tell you about them just yet . . . I will, but not just yet. You will see why later. You have to have discipline in this. Be patient. I want you to go to San Ángel once again. Watch the house you watched before and let me know if that man comes or goes. If you see him, call me at this number." He took out a pen and wrote a telephone number on the back of a lottery ticket he got off one of the dirty tables. "If there is a recording, leave a message. Give the time." He wrote this down too. "Tell if he is alone or if anyone is with him, and if people are with him describe them. Tell me if you have been able to follow them or not." He shoved the ticket to Napo. "All right? Any problems with that?"

Napo nodded, reading Saturnino's notations on the lottery ticket. "No problem, but what if he doesn't return there? How long do you want me to wait?"

"If you have any doubts, call me, leave a message and a telephone number, and I will call you back."

Napo thought this over. "If I see him, just follow him?"

"That's all, then let me know where he goes."

Napo wondered nervously if he should inform Saturnino that the man was aware that Saturnino had hired people to follow him. He couldn't imagine how that would matter, and because of the humiliation he had suffered he didn't want to go into it. Saturnino would want to know every detail, and Napo didn't trust himself to fabricate a story Saturnino would buy. The professor was very perceptive. Napo was eager to tail the man again. His mistake the last time had been taking Chiquis with him, and using a taxi. This time he would be alone and he would use his own car; and before it was over he would make sure he had the chance to take his own revenge. He wouldn't let Saturnino deny him that. This man had gone out of his way to humiliate him in front of Chiquis, and even now it made Napo's face burn to think of it.

HE WALKED IN THE LIGHT RAIN ALONG THE NARROW STREET OF SAN Ildefonso, past Carmen Street, past the massive stone College of San Ildefonso faced in red *tezontle* stone, until he came to the Templo de Santa Catalina de Sena, where he turned left on Seminario. A yellow Volkswagen puttered by on the muddy cobblestones, the driver bending down, looking through his rain-spattered window to see if Saturnino was a possible fare. Saturnino simply ignored him and kept walking.

As he crossed Justo Sierra, walking across the street from the archaeological excavations of the Aztec Templo Mayor, a dog emerged from the damp shadows and started following him. At first the mongrel trotted at his side, but when Saturnino refused to acknowledge its presence it dropped back a few feet, where it ambled contentedly, willing to postpone his acceptance of the friendly gesture for another block or so.

The sound of dripping rain was everywhere, from the trees, the tile roofs, the stone walls all around him, the lampposts, the gutters, the signs. It seemed as if he heard every individual drop, dripping filled his head. He continued past the Casa de las Ajaracas and came up beside the towering Metropolitan Cathedral on the Zócalo, the thirteen-acre main plaza of the city. Because of the rain the plaza was sparsely populated. The lights mounted along the top of the colonial façade of the National Palace and among the spires of the cathedral reflected off the lowering night clouds and washed the vast expanse of the stone-paved plaza in a pale coppery glow. Volkswagen taxis moved about the plaza like night beetles, and occasional groups of people moved along the edges of the colonial buildings surrounding the plaza trying to use the tall stone structures to fend off the rain. A few vendors had pushed their carts to nearby doorways for shelter, or had pulled down canvas flaps as awnings to cover their wares. They huddled patiently under the awnings, legs exposed. The rain would stop. Eventually.

Without going into the plaza, Saturnino turned into Calle Moneda and walked a little distance before he remembered the mongrel and looked back. The dog had stopped at the entrance to the narrow street and was watching him, lifting his muzzle in the mist to catch some scent that would help him divine his next action. Then he suddenly dropped his head and headed in the other direction, across the plaza in front of the cathedral. Saturnino turned and continued between the sheer high walls of the old Archbishop's Palace on his left and the National Palace which towered above him on his right, the floodlights on its roof creating a reflected cupreous haze through which a copper rain drifted down to gilded cobblestones. He kept his shoulders hunched reflexively against the weather, trying to avoid the gathering scattered puddles.

Stopping under a vendor's awning on the corner of Licenciado Verdad, he bought a few lottery tickets from the rows hanging under the canvas. As he was waiting for his change he noticed a couple standing under an umbrella at a telephone box on the opposite corner. The girl was talking on the telephone as the young man held the umbrella and stared up

the street toward the Academy of San Carlos and with his free
hand rubbed the girl's stomach. Saturnino watched. He noticed the way the young man, by the manner of his casual
caress, seemed to take the girl for granted. He could handle
her; he could leave her alone; he could take off her clothes; he
could do obscene things to her. Then he noticed also the way
the girl was letting herself be handled. She let his hand drop
lower than her stomach. She let his hand move up to her
breasts. She let his fingers slip inside her blouse, then his
hand. She ignored him and continued talking, and Saturnino
found her nonchalance wonderfully erotic. The copper rain fell
around them like dull fire. Saturnino pocketed his change and
turned away.

The alleylike Licenciado Verdad was almost empty. Only a
couple of doorways allowed their dim glimmer onto the
cobblestones. The first doorway on the left was the corridor to
his *vecindad*. He turned into the dark passageway, immediately slowing, knowing he would have to negotiate between
the knees of the people squatting against the damp corridor
walls waiting for the rain to stop, possibly spending the night.
He smelled unwashed bodies and urine, damp wool garments
and something sour. He came into the courtyard, open to the
sky five floors up, surrounded by galleries and wrought-iron
railings. Here in the dark confines of the courtyard were
different odors: marijuana and hot tortillas. Fried onions.
Turning the stairwell, he started up the stone steps, his right
hand pulling on the ornate railing.

The landing of each turn was a surprise. Some were clean;
some crowded with the kind of flowers that would grow
anywhere, like begonias and petunias and geraniums; some
were cluttered with pieces of bicycles or other scavenged junk;
some with tired people in broken chairs, smoking and drinking
and staring silently out to the other galleries across the way.

When he got to the fifth floor he paused at his own
wrought-iron railing and looked out over the shabby tile roofs
of the old colonial inner city. From the galleried courtyard a
child's voice began singing a jerky little song about a yellow
sparrow, the words coming up through the well of balconies in
wavering phrases, the soft words drowned out by other sounds
that echoed in the well: a hacking tubercular cough; a high-
pitched woman's voice scolding, complaining about wasting

good pesos on lottery tickets; someone whacking on a railing with a stick; a man's voice growling like a tiger.

This derelict building in which Saturnino had his rooms had been built in 1545, the headquarters of the archbishop of Mexico. Like many of the holdings of the Catholic Church, it was "secularized" in 1861, partitioned, and sold to private citizens. Now a tenement, it was nonetheless a building of wonderful history and still occupied a historically important location: across the street from the National Palace, across another street from the great Metropolitan Cathedral, across another street from the site of the first printing press in all the Americas, adjacent to the original site of the National University of Mexico, and—the reason Saturnino had long ago sought out rooms here—it was sitting on the exact plot of ground where five centuries earlier the blue temple of Tezcatlipoca rose out of the island city's sacred district of temples, soaring more than two hundred feet into the clear highland sky.

Saturnino unlocked his door and stepped into the anteroom of the three rooms he occupied. To his right he had set aside the quarters for his bedroom, an old mattress on the floor and the few necessities. To his left was a small room that served no purpose for him except that it led to a tiny kitchen where he cooked and ate. The third room opened straight off the entrance and was long, running the length of the others. It had three tall windows that overlooked Licenciado Verdad and faced the baroque facade of the former Temple de Santa Teresa la Antigua.

At the door of this room he stopped and began taking off his shoes. He placed them side by side just inside the door. Then he removed his sports coat, folded it neatly, and placed it beside his shoes farther into the room. Next he removed his trousers, folded them neatly, and placed them beside the sports coat still farther into the room. Next his shirt, folded and placed beside the trousers, then his shorts in the same manner, until he had created a trail of clothes leading to the center of the room, where he stood naked, facing the west wall to the left of the door. The long empty room was dimly lighted by the coppery patina reflected off the dull, overcast sky.

With slow deliberation he approached the west wall, where a long stone shelf was now visible extending along most of the wall. Hanging along the shelf's front edge were strings of obsidian disks and circular mosaics polished so finely their mirrored surfaces caught the spectral glow from the windows and scattered it to every corner of the room in a prowling swarm of nebulous sparks. On either end of the shelf were terra-cotta pots overflowing with marigolds, which spilled onto the shelf and lay in withered heaps upon the floor, their bright yellow color strangely altered in the eerie light. Other pots along the shelf held dead ashes and smelled of the resiny incense, copal, and tiers of candles had spilled so much wax on the stone shelf that long claws of it hung down like pale stalactites. All around him in the dark margins of the room he could hear the sluggish, scuffing movement of saurian priests, preparing.

Trembling with excitement, he drew nearer to the shelf, his bare feet feeling the dead marigolds, the brittle splatters of cold wax, until he stood with his face almost touching the shelf, close enough to smell more than the dead copal, more than the wax, more than the marigolds, but the other things too, the fuggy odor of the eleven leathery lumps the size of prunes lined up along the edge to the last one, much larger, less withered, still retaining a semblance of its original shape. Twelve, an even dozen. The symbolic lives of eleven capuchins and Isolda Bodet.

Chapter 26

"WHY DIDN'T YOU TELL ME THIS?"

Haydon was leaning against one of the coral pillars. When he had walked out of the studio Isabel had remained momentarily, giving instructions to Celerina to take Amaranta back to her rooms, and then she stepped out onto the loggia to join him. She moved over beside the stone balustrade, faced him, her back also against one of the beveled pillars, and plucked a geranium, a gesture that seemed calculated to give her a few seconds to collect her thoughts. The rain had stained the outside of the pillar behind her.

"I am not sure," she said, and swept the hair back from her face with one hand. "When Juan called and told me you were coming, I certainly had no intention of doing it this way. I knew what you were wanting, to talk with her about your father, about them. I was sorry for you, for what you were going to learn."

"You mean about Amaranta's condition, or about my father's yearly trips to see her?"

She shook her head and looked out to the palms and the light rain in the courtyard. She couldn't hide her embarrassment. "I don't know. All of it, I guess. Everything."

"You deliberately led me to believe I would be able to talk to her," he said.

She looked at him. "I didn't tell you that you would be able to learn anything from her. I put you off as much as I could. I said you could talk to her, which, technically, you can." She stopped. "But, yes, I deceived you. I don't have any excuse for it. It was a cowardly thing. I was dreading it."

"But why?"

She shook her head, her green eyes sad, a little weary.

"Did Lockhart tell you about Saturnino's death threat?"

She shook her head again. "No, he didn't tell me that. He said only that you were wanting to know about their relationship."

"Did he discourage you from talking to me?"

"No." She gave him a puzzled look.

Haydon looked through the open French doors into the studio, seeing a corner of one of the large easels and part of a cluttered work table with a jar of skewed paintbrushes. The long room with its stretches of bare wooden floor seemed more empty now than before, as if through his inquiries he had effected the release of the spirits of Amaranta and his father, as if they finally had departed, leaving behind only the past and secondhand memories of what it all had been like.

But even though he realized now that there were many things he would never know about his father and Amaranta, he knew, too, that some of his questions still could be answered. He had to accept the silence of the dead and the lost, but as far as he was concerned the living still owed him some explanations.

He looked at Isabel. "You told me that Saturnino didn't know about the affair, my father's trips here."

She nodded, watching him.

"Then whatever his reason for wanting to kill me, it isn't a distorted connection between me and my father's adultery," he said. He turned and looked into the courtyard. The dove-colored light of the rainy afternoon was quickly deepening into shades of perse. "It has to be related to events much earlier, perhaps before he was born."

Isabel continued looking at him, but he could see from the shift in her eyes that her thoughts were casting back.

"Do you know of any other time aside from those meetings when my father and Amaranta were together? Was there any other communication of importance?"

"I'm not aware of any."

"There was an argument sometime in those early years," he said, watching her, "between my father and Lockhart. What was that about?"

Isabel frowned at him again, and shook her head. "I don't know," she said. "I knew about it, but I learned of it only after I met your father. During those first few months following that meeting, Amaranta was more willing to talk about her past than ever before. From that time until the time she began to lose her mind she told me most of everything I know about those days. I asked her if Juan was aware of their affair. She said no, that once, way back, your father and Juan had been the best of friends, but something had come between them. She wouldn't elaborate. After I got to know your father so well I asked him about it. He only said that they had had a disagreement, that it wasn't worth talking about. That was all."

"You never asked Lockhart about it?"

"No. He isn't the kind of man you can approach about something like this."

"And you said Lockhart didn't know about their affair?"

"No. I don't know how he would have found out."

He believed her, or believed what he read in her face.

"Something happened," he said.

"What do you mean?"

"I believe that whatever occurred between my father and Juan Lockhart, whatever it was, is the crux of all this. Maybe Saturnino stumbled upon something. Or something happened that got him started, something specific. His file on me began just a little less than a year ago. Until then he apparently had shown no interest in me at all. Maybe he didn't even know I existed."

Isabel folded her arms and turned away from him, facing the courtyard, where the rainy dusk had darkened the palms to silhouettes. The loggia had become a murky border, and Isabel's profile was lighted only by a weak glow coming from behind him through the French doors that opened into the second-floor vestibule.

"I'm sorry," she said. She spoke softly, and the slow rain clacking against the palms almost obscured her words. "This is horrible, all of it, and I'm ashamed that you have been dragged into it."

Haydon looked at her, and everything about her appealed to him—her emotional strength, which was inextricably bound with a strain of vulnerability that showed itself when she least believed it did; her physical beauty, which was extraordinary and which she carried with an unconscious reserved dignity inherited from her mother; her rejection of self-pity; her refusal to condemn in her own blood what others so readily censured.

He moved away from the pillar he had been leaning against and approached her. He didn't speak, though he suddenly felt a great sadness for her again, a great compassion for what she had seen in life and for what she had missed. She had endured a great deal, and he suspected she had sacrificed much more only to find herself in a position that she knew no one would have wanted to share with her. He remembered what Lockhart had said of her, using the endearing form of her name. "Chabela," he had said, "is a saint." There was more to her than he understood, and it was with considerable guilt that he acknowledged that not all of his feelings for her were so intellectually detached.

He stood close to her, close enough to see the regret and chagrin in her eyes, close enough to smell her scent and to feel the acute ache of sexual arousal that was rendered even more intense because he knew she was aware of it too. She did not look at him, but he could sense that she was waiting for him to touch her, to speak, to give her the opportunity to turn around and face him, and in that act to disintegrate all the barriers of propriety and feigned incognizance and mutual deception that had kept them apart until this moment.

"Señora." Celerina's voice was low and apologetic, coming across the dark loggia from the French doors of the vestibule. "*Es teléfono, señora, para el señor.*"

Isabel looked at him.

"I didn't tell anyone I was coming here," he said. "It'll be Lockhart." He turned away from her and walked toward Celerina's silhouette in the doorway. He followed her inside, where she showed him the telephone on a small table near the stairs.

"This is Haydon," he said, and turned to look out to the loggia, where he barely could see Isabel's dusky figure where he had left her, looking into the courtyard.

"I want to talk to you," Lockhart said. He did not identify himself, and his voice was curt.

"Fine," Haydon said. "When?"

"As soon as you can get here."

"Give me half an hour."

"I'll be waiting," Lockhart said, and hung up.

Obviously he had either gone to Saturnino's himself or had learned about it in detail from someone he had sent there as a result of Isabel's call. Either way, it had loosened his tongue, and now he either wanted to tell Haydon something or he wanted to ask him something. Haydon thought it a little curious that he did not mention the incident and that he did not ask about Isabel.

Returning to the loggia, he approached Isabel, who had not moved from the pillar.

"He wants to talk to me," he said. "I'm supposed to go to his place as soon as I can."

"What did he say about . . . Saturnino?"

"He didn't mention anything about that."

Isabel was silent.

"Have you talked to Paulo and Celerina?"

She nodded. "I told them who you were, what you were, and I told them that Saturnino was in trouble and was dangerous. I didn't elaborate, but I did go over the things you told me to have done. Paulo has replaced the lamp, and has arranged for a security firm to provide a man twenty-four hours. He will sit inside the drive gates, which he will keep locked, and watch the outside courtyard from there. As for the dogs, he was having some trouble finding exactly what we needed, I think."

"If he can't find trained guard dogs then borrow some from friends. Anything that will bark will do."

There was a brief silence. "You should have told me about the monkey," Haydon said. "How long has she had one?"

"For years. He's always resented them, hated them."

"I wish I had paid more attention to the carcasses in his apartment."

"I looked," she said. "They all had been cut open."

"And what does that mean?"

"For him? Who knows. In the Aztec traditions the heart of a human sacrifice was offered to numerous gods for various reasons. The primary reason, however, the one that gave rise to all the others, was that the sun, having been created by the self-immolation of one of the creator gods, was from that time forth in continual need of blood sacrifices in order to keep it moving in its course across the sky. In order to prevent darkness from overwhelming the world, the sun had to be fed every day with the 'precious water' of human blood. That's the essence of it. But he's twisted all that around somehow.

There's no way of knowing what kind of sense any of this is making in his mind."

"Do you have a gun?" he asked. "Any kind?"

"No. And I don't want one," she said flatly.

There was silence again. The rain had stopped, and even though it was dark around the loggia, he could feel a grainy mist drifting in, making his clothes limp again and bringing the slight chill of night. In the dusk he could see her eyes, though he could not discern their color. But it didn't matter; he was close enough to sense it. She was facing him now, as he had wished her to be only minutes before. He didn't know what might have happened if Celerina hadn't come through the vestibule to call them, but he knew now that he could not move, and that she would not. It seemed that both of them had decided it was not the time or the place.

"I have to go," he said.

"Yes," she said. "I know."

HE HAD REFUSED THE OFFER OF HER MERCEDES, HAD REFUSED THE short ride down the cobbled Calle Frontera to Plaza San Jacinto, where the taxis stood in a line in front of the Fonda San Ángel. Instead he had walked on the uneven stone sidewalk, passing in and out of the pools of yellow light thrown by the widely spaced streetlamps, hugging close to the high wall that followed the curving street down from the Plaza de los Arcángelos. A few establishments were still open in the plaza, a pharmacy, a couple of taverns, a variety store; the interiors of the old colonial buildings looking dingy and somehow secretive.

Haydon crossed along the eastern edge of the plaza and approached the taxis, all of which, he was relieved to see, were large Fords or Chevrolets. He took the first one, told the driver where he wanted to go, and crawled in, watching the plaza closely as the driver squeezed his way along its northern side and turned right to Rivera and then left to Galeana, where he started the slow bumpy climb up the narrow cobblestoned street toward the Periférico expressway. At the top of the hill they saw the expressway lights, and within moments they were accelerating quickly, moving into the sparse traffic headed toward downtown.

Haydon turned sideways on the backseat, stretched one leg

out in front of him, and watched the traffic behind them. The driver was not a talker and was absorbed in a boxing match on the radio. They were just passing Molino and approaching the clover leaf at Avenida San Antonio when Haydon spotted the car. It had maintained a sensible distance, allowing other cars to feed in and out between them, but the driver ultimately had tipped his hand. Obviously afraid of losing them on one of the exit ramps, he had revealed his inexperience by switching lanes every time the taxi driver switched, which turned out to be a giveaway, because for some reason this driver wandered all over the expressway, causing the tail to believe he was preparing to take any number of exits. The tail ran their exact pattern five or six cars behind them. It was easy to spot, even at that distance.

"Go through the cloverleaf at San Antonio and head west," Haydon said suddenly. The driver simply nodded, cut across traffic without signaling, and hit the exit ramp for the west bound loop on the cloverleaf. The tail made the same spectacular sheer and followed them under the Periférico, heading west on a wide boulevard that ended abruptly by intersecting with a smaller but still well-lighted street. To their left was the entrance to a cemetery, Panteón Guadalupe.

"Take a right," Haydon said. "Then left." He didn't have to tell the man to hurry; his nonchalant manner seemed in reverse ratio to his appreciation of speed. After they had traveled several blocks Haydon said, "Any of these streets to the right." He was still looking back, watching the dark car gain on them.

The tone in his voice must have alerted the driver, who began to glare at him in the rearview mirror.

"Hey, I thought you wanted to go to Bosque de las Lomas."

"That's right," Haydon said, watching out the rear window.

"This is not going to get you there."

"Someone's following us," Haydon said. "I wanted to see if he was trying to catch me or simply see where I was going."

"Following you?" The driver gave up the mirror now and looked over his shoulder. "What the hell is this?" He had slowed as it dawned on him he was involved in something, and through the rear window he saw the dark car—which Haydon could now tell was a large BMW—roar up behind them, weaving back and forth, its intentions unclear.

"What is this?" the driver blurted nervously. "What's he rying to do?"

"I don't know," Haydon said, reaching behind his back and pulling out the Beretta.

"What the hell are you doing?" the driver yelled. "No, no, no . . . no guns, no guns." He slammed on his brakes and the taxi skidded along the gravel on the shoulder of the street. Haydon looked up, realizing for the first time that they had worked their way into one of the slums. "Get out! Get out!" the driver was yelling. "You got drugs? You in drugs? Get out!" He had turned around and was on his knees in the front seat, waving his hands wildly.

"No. Police!" Haydon yelled back, watching the quickly approaching BMW and looking around at the driver at the same time. "Police!"

"Get out! Get out!" The driver was getting frantic. "Police don't take taxis," he yelled. Then his eyes widened suddenly as he saw the BMW slide up behind them, its lights on bright, and then they both heard the pop! pop! and saw the muzzle flash beside the driver's window, the solid chunk! chunk! as the slugs hit the taxi.

"My God! My God!" the driver screamed.

"Get down! Get down on the floor!" Haydon yelled at him. He felt naked in the fixed headlights of the car behind them, knowing that the right-caliber bullet could easily cut straight through the trunk, straight through the padding in the car seat.

Pop! Pop! Pop!

"My God! I'm going to be killed!" the taxi driver screamed, grabbing the back of the seat with both hands and shaking it violently, making the whole car rock. Then suddenly he lunged at the door, threw it open, and jumped out running. Pop-pop-pop! The taxi driver's torso seemed to outrun his legs and he was thrown forward, his arms flung out as if to embrace someone as he made a belly dive onto the asphalt, landing on his face and neck first, skidding facedown, his brains flying out ahead of him so that he slid over them, scooping them up with his chest and stomach.

Jesus Christ!

Haydon threw open the rear door and quickly crouched in the door well. He fired six steady, evenly spaced shots into the

BMW's headlights, knocking out only one, but giving himself enough cover time to wheel around and jump into the taxi' opened front door. Jamming the accelerator to the floor, he jerked the gearshift down, and the taxi whined and lurched forward, swiveling wildly half on and half off the pavement and throwing gravel and caliche onto the BMW. Finally gaining the pavement and control at the same time, he concentrated on the configuration of the streets hurtling past the headlights never knowing when the wrong turn would bring him to a dead end. Occasionally he would get a glimpse of a sign— Saturno, Venus—and then he was on a fast, winding street named Chicago, the taxi screaming as if it were going to explode. The paved streets played out and the taxi hit the dirt streets with a jarring whump. Though the recent rains had eliminated the dust that normally would have boiled up behind him and given him some protection, he was still in luck, because either a light fog had moved in or they had moved into it as they advanced farther into the slums that rose into the foothills. When he turned around he could clearly make out the single headlight bouncing and wobbling on the rock-strewn streets. In front of him his own panning headlights picked up flashes of long corridors of shanties, abandoned cars, contentious dogs that chased after him, and, as he careened around corners, the surprised wide eyes and gaping mouths of half-naked children standing before their cinder-block shacks watching him fly by like a night demon.

The BMW came on, even gained on him, and once, glancing around, he thought he saw a third set of headlights burning through the thickening fog. He had nine shots left. He kept turning around to gauge the BMW's distance, doing most of the driving with his left hand, sometimes using the one holding the Beretta also, glancing over his shoulder, then peering over his headlights, his shoulder, his headlights, fearing one of the kids would step out or an old man, the single headlight miraculously gaining, five car lengths back, mad to drive blinded by the heavy fog like that, and then when it happened it was not a child but a horse, no, a mule, and he hit it square in the hindquarters, wheeling it around so that its head came into the car on the passenger side, screaming through the exploding glass, just the head going on into the backseat by itself, Haydon slapping at the steering wheel, the

car spinning around and around but not turning over because
of the lubricating muddy glaze, but spinning so that he didn't
know where the BMW was because of the disorienting fog and
he had no idea where anything was except the front of the car.

Then he was dead still.

He heard people yelling, his one headlight picking up
eddies of swirling mist. People yelling all around him as if they
were circling the car, though he could see nothing but swirling
fog through the shattered windshield and fog pouring in
through the hole left by the flying mule's head which he now
thought of in the backseat and the blood which he could now
smell as well as the mulish odor of damp hair. He scrabbled at
the door and forced it open and fell onto the wet earth,
crawling fast over rocks, because they would be coming to the
car and he had to get away from it no matter what direction.
People yelling, his head spinning. Then from his right—a
surprise that it was his right—a car roaring up and sliding—
two headlights!—men yelling, everyone talking at once. He
thought he heard his name, knew he did. Pop! Pop! Pop! The
same weapon that had gotten the taxi driver. Pop! Pop!
Coming from his left? The searing rip of a semiautomatic—a
Mac-10 or a Walther—coming from the two headlights on the
right. Pop-pop! from the BMW. The Mac-10 again, and then
silence. From where he was lying flat against the rusty ridges
of a corrugated tin shack, he could hear and sometimes catch
glimpses of figures running back and forth through the dense
gray glow in front of the two headlights, then the one headlight
visible now shining away from him but the mist falling past it,
men standing in front of it.

"Señor Haydon!" A man's voice. "Señor Haydon. This man is
dead. It is okay." Pause. "My name is Eloy Palacio. I work for
Señor Lockhart. Are you all right? We were following you."

The man was walking back and forth in front of his headlights, his voice clear, then faint as he spoke in different
directions. A dog had begun barking furiously somewhere in
the tumbling fog.

"Señor Haydon! This man is dead now. Please show yourself. I am supposed to escort you to Señor Lockhart. We do not
have much time. The police. Please hurry."

Haydon stumbled to his feet. "Over here," he heard himself
choke out, and even as he did it he felt that it was a mistake.

He had no idea who the hell the man was. The guy could say anything, could have been anyone. "Over here," he said louder.

"Señor Haydon. Are you all right?" The man came toward him even though Haydon was sure he did not see him. "Are you all right? Where are you?"

"Here," Haydon said, standing and stepping away from the shack. He smelled raw sewage. People running everywhere. He kept the Beretta off safety, his muscles quivering.

Then the man was beside him. "Señor Haydon, please. Hurry." He took Haydon gently by the shoulder. "This way, over here."

As they moved toward the taxi Haydon saw the scene as if he were coming upon an automobile accident, the headless carcass of the mule driven into the hood of the taxi, the BMW sideways to it sitting fifty feet away, women and children standing around the BMW looking down on the ground.

"Wait," Haydon said, pulling away and heading for the BMW. The mesmerized onlookers parted as he approached, and the dog suddenly decided that Haydon was the one who needed to be barked at. Ignoring the dog, he walked up to the front fender and bent over the contorted figure lying under the opened front door. At first he couldn't tell; the blood and mud created a formidable mask. He grabbed the body by its legs and began dragging it around to the single headlight, the dog crouching down close and following him, barking at him, at the body, then a loud whump! and a yelp as someone kicked the dog, and then Haydon was being helped by a man in a suit, then two men in suits, and the voice of Eloy Palacio was saying, "Okay, okay, but hurry, hurry." Two of the men lifted the body by the shirt at its shoulders, grunting, trying to keep their hands out of the blood which was still seeping out of the ears and nose, and as they twisted him up into the headlight beam Haydon recognized the sharp features of Napo Cuevano.

"You know him?" Palacio was speaking quickly.

Haydon nodded, and the men dropped the boy with a squishing sound onto the rocks and then took Haydon by the arm and ran with him to the car with two headlights. Haydon was hurried into the backseat with one of the men while Palacio got into the front passenger's seat with the other man behind the wheel. The car started up with a winding whine and lunged into the fog, scattering the people, the fog and mist boiling up around them to sift back down on the shaken bystanders, on the children, the dogs, the decapitated mule, and the handsome bloodied face of Napo Cuevano. In a light daze, Haydon slumped in one corner of the backseat, the Beretta still in his hand dangling down between his legs. He felt the momentary exhilaration of being propelled away from the fog and chaos and death, through the cleansing night air pouring in from the window.

"Where the hell are we?" he heard himself ask. "Where is this?"

"Just a slum," one of the men said. "A *colonia* in Obregón called Paraíso."

Paradise.

Chapter 27

SINCE THEY WERE ALREADY IN THE SOUTHWESTERN PART OF THE
city—too close to Lockhart's to make the expressways a
convenient alternative—the driver took a closer but more
serpentine route to Bosque de las Lomas. They skirted the
northernmost neighborhoods of Obregón and then doubled
back south along the rim of Chapultepec Park and through the
poorer districts on the border between Obregón and Hidalgo,
finally turning north again on the outermost leg of the Paseo de
la Reforma where it rambled through the wealthy sections in
the foothills.

Although neither Palacio nor his two companions paid any
attention to Haydon's Beretta, he was too apprehensive to put
it away. He simply flipped the safety on and laid it on his lap
as he slumped against the door and watched the landscape fly
by. Christ. He had not believed the kid was that marginal, had
never dreamed he would be capable of something like that. It
didn't make sense. Surely Saturnino wouldn't have hired Napo
to kill him after he had so carefully lured Haydon to Mexico
with the apparent intent of killing him himself. And if Napo
was merely supposed to be following him, why did he turn the
surveillance into a hot pursuit and then a rabid gun battle?
Had Haydon humiliated him that much? Had it done that
much damage to his machismo? Maybe that had been at the
root of it, but Haydon was sure that cocaine had emboldened
him, had pushed him over the line. The manic car chase and
the senseless shootout were isolated from the larger web of
things, a coke-dream fantasy lived out with cinematic panache
by a foolish kid who didn't understand the special effects of
reality.

For a while now the car had been climbing steadily, and
occasionally Haydon would get glimpses of a sheer dropoff and

then city lights far in the distance below them. The fragrance of rain-dampened pines and eucalyptus filled the car, and the air grew lighter and crisper. It seemed that they were indeed on their way to Lockhart's, which was pure good fortune. It had been a moment of poor judgment when he had revealed himself to Palacio, and if he wasn't getting into deeper trouble than he had just gotten out of, he gave himself no credit for it.

No one spoke until they turned off the main pavement onto the private drive and Palacio used a hand radio to notify the guards at the gate they were on their way up. Now the paved drive grew even steeper and the car slowed considerably to make the switchback turns, the headlights swinging out over black space, then slamming back into the forested mountainside or one of the stone arches that spanned the drive. At last they approached the gatehouse and drove through to the front of the white marble house. The car pulled around the fountain and stopped.

Everyone got out of the car but the driver, who took the car away as Haydon put away his Beretta and followed the other two men to the front of the house. The second man stopped by the long, softly lighted colonnade with its potted fan palms. Haydon continued with Palacio to the front door, where Palacio rang the bell and they waited. This was the first time Haydon had had a chance to see the Mexican's face. He was quite handsome, with an immaculately trimmed mustache and a neat haircut. He seemed to be in his early thirties, muscular and calm, with the passive face of a professional hired gun. Haydon already had seen enough of his abilities to appreciate his skills.

As before, Lockhart opened the door himself, and stared a second at Haydon with his cloudy blue eyes.

"Are you all right?" he finally asked, backing away from the door for Haydon to come in.

Haydon nodded and stepped into the foyer.

"Lucio." Lockhart raised his voice only slightly, and a short stocky Indian in simple white peasant's clothes appeared from one of the two major hallways. "Lucio, will you please take Mr. Haydon to a guest room so he can clean up?" Then, turning to Haydon, "Is that fine with you?"

Haydon nodded. "I would appreciate it."

"Fine. Whenever you're ready, come down to the living room."

As Haydon turned to follow the Indian, Lockhart began a quiet conversation with Eloy Palacio.

In the guest room, which was on the second tier of the four-level house, the bath was almost as large as the bedroom itself and overlooked one of the valleys that fell away from the ridge upon which the house was built. It was entirely of white Mexican marble.

Haydon was surprised to see in the bathroom mirror that the right side of his face and suit coat were splattered with a spray of blood which could only have been from the mule. He removed the coat, which smelled of the red mud of Paradise, and then his shirt, and proceeded to lather his arms and face with soap and warm water. He rinsed off and then repeated the process, finally rinsing with cold water. Bracing both hands on the white marble, he leaned his dripping face over the sink and looked at the water disappearing into the dark hole of the drain. His arms were trembling. He thought about the taxi driver. What kind of misery had been dealt his family tonight? They had lost everything. Everything. And Cuevano's parents? How were they supposed to understand what had happened? He doubted that there was any hope that what had happened in the fog on the muddy streets of Paradise would ever be explained, or understood, by anyone. Mexico City was full of mysteries; it was the City of Mysteries. He reached for a towel and dried his face.

Juan Lockhart waited for him on the lower level of the living room, in the same muted light they had talked in two nights before. But the city far below them on the other side of the crescent wall of glass was less visible tonight, shrouded in a drifting fog that permitted only brief glimpses of the glittering lights.

Lockhart was standing at the liquor cabinet filling two glasses with ice as Haydon approached him across the marble floor. He was wearing a lightweight brushed-silk sports coat the color of straw, with ecru linen trousers and a white shirt open at the neck. For some reason Haydon saw considerably more gray in his sandy hair than he had noticed before.

"You'd like a drink?" Lockhart said, turning and looking at Haydon.

"Gin and soda," Haydon said. "Lime if you've got it."

"I've got it." Lockhart nodded, immediately working on the drink. When it was ready he turned around and gave it to Haydon, picked up his own drink, and went to one of the heavy ivory-colored armchairs within the circle of furniture. He waited until Haydon had done the same and then he sipped his own drink.

"I spoke with Palacio," he said. "He told me you knew the man."

"I had met him," Haydon said, and he told Lockhart about the encounter the night before.

Lockhart shook his head, watching Haydon as if he expected to read something in his manner.

"He was probably one of Saturnino's students," he said. "I would bet on that. Saturnino is unscrupulous. He slept with the women, and used the men for all sorts of things."

Haydon gave Lockhart a sharp look.

"Nothing sinister in that remark," Lockhart said quickly. "I simply mean that he saw his students as instruments of convenience at his disposal, for his career, for his personal pleasures. He is simply a user."

Haydon nodded. He didn't completely understand, but it wasn't something he had a burning desire to go into.

"What about the disaster in Coyoacán?" Lockhart said suddenly. His expression had grown hard, even challenging.

Haydon knew better than to lie to him. Lockhart probably already knew more about it than Haydon would ever know.

"What about it?"

"You've been followed since the night you were here," Lockhart said. "My men saw the whole thing in the Plaza Río de Janeiro with you and this young man who was killed tonight. I know you went to Saturnino's, that you let yourself in with a key, that you left, that you stopped at a telephone and probably called the police—you really should have called me instead. I want to know what the hell happened there."

Haydon was too tired to be surprised; he told Lockhart everything, in detail, about why they had gone to Coyoacán and about what they had seen there. When he finished, the Scotsman's face was rigid. He was shocked, and he didn't pretend to hide it with a false play at sophistication. It wasn't his nature.

"Jesus Christ Almighty." He sat his drink on a table and slowly rubbed his hands together to dry the moisture from the sweating glass. He was frowning at Haydon.

"Didn't your men see her?" Haydon asked.

"No. They didn't know anything was amiss when they saw you come out of the house. They just assumed you had searched the place. Then Chabela called—I assume you were there—and by the time they got back over to Saturnino's the police had arrived and wouldn't let them in. They would only say that a woman had been killed, that's all."

"Have you made any effort at all to find him?" Haydon asked. It was a straightforward question that, whether Lockhart noticed it or not, signaled a change in Haydon's attitude toward everything that had happened.

"Yes, actually, I have," Lockhart said. "No luck. None. In fact, I think I must have talked to that girl. Palacio had checked the Coyoacán house late Saturday night, after you were here with Gaston. I sent him right over. Saturnino was gone. Palacio said he didn't find anything in the house about you. Said there wasn't much there, though he did tell me about the weird room with the statue and the dead monkeys. After that I thought the best thing to do would be to have Palacio follow you. That way there was the chance he could prevent . . . something from happening. Looking for Saturnino would have been futile in this city. A man can disappear here if he wants to, forever. Sunday I called over there and got a woman on the line who said Saturnino had left for Cuernavaca and she was house-sitting until he got back sometime next week. Oddly, I didn't believe the part about Cuernavaca, but I did believe she was house-sitting. I just assumed he had lied to her about his whereabouts, but it didn't occur to me that she was lying to me too. Probably she was simply covering for him."

"Maybe he did go away, and then returned," Haydon said.

Lockhart shrugged, and reached out and got his drink again. He sat back in his chair, looking at the collection of black pottery sitting not far away. "I don't know, but I'll bet I talked to her. I'll bet that was the girl." He sipped his drink and shook his head. "Jesus Christ."

Before Haydon had a chance to speak, Lockhart continued.

"You met Amaranta." He lifted his eyes to Haydon from the black pottery.

"Yes. You might have told me."

Lockhart shook his head again. "No. I don't know how she handled it, but Chabela did a better job of it than I would have."

"It wouldn't have required much cleverness," Haydon said pointedly.

"Sorry. I didn't think it was my place." Lockhart was cool. He wasn't used to being spoken to in even a dubious tone of voice. "What did you think of Chabela?"

"I liked her."

"Yes." Lockhart rolled the glass between the palms of his opened hands, thinking. "What are you going to do now?"

Haydon looked at the older man, trying to think of the best way to nail him down, to get past the cool superiority that would have to be breached in order to get at the heart of the questions he wanted to ask.

"I am convinced," Haydon said, "that whatever reason Saturnino has for wanting to kill me, it has nothing to do with me. It has something to do with what I represent in his mind. It has to do with my father's past, with his relationship to Amaranta, and probably something to do with you."

Lockhart looked at Haydon without the smallest twitch in his face to give away his thoughts.

"For starters," Haydon said, "I want to know the reason for the split between my father and you."

Lockhart studied him with blue eyes that seemed to pale even more as Haydon watched them. "And what if I won't tell you?"

"I realize I'm out of my element here in this city," Haydon said. "But I've reached the point where I'll do whatever I must to get some answers."

"You may not be able to do enough," Lockhart said.

"What do you mean?"

"Amaranta has all the answers."

"I don't doubt that. But I don't believe she's the only one."

"You may not like the answers."

"I understand that," Haydon said. "Am I supposed to believe that you're holding back on me because you're concerned for my feelings?"

Lockhart allowed a sour smile to cross his mouth. "No," he said. "You shouldn't believe that."

"Then you should know that I am very determined regarding this," Haydon said. "But it would be an embarrassment to both of us, Mr. Lockhart, for me to be put in a position in which my response to your question could be interpreted as a threat. I don't think we should take it that far."

Lockhart's eyes were leveled at Haydon, the sardonic smile faint, but unmistakable. "That was smooth," he said. "You might have been Webster sitting there. It was something he would have said. He would have been proud of you." He turned his eyes away, toward the broad sweep of windows overlooking the misty Valley of Mexico.

"We were not exactly the same age," he said. "Your father and I. Though that kind of thing doesn't make any difference except when you're very young. I am seventy-five now. I was two years younger than he. Amaranta was exactly between us, in more ways than the three of us wanted to admit.

"In 1934 when Webster came to Mexico City to work for my father at Royal Dutch Shell, my family very quickly 'adopted' him. Webster's arrival was, for us, fortuitous. We had just lost my older brother in a riding accident, and all of us seemed to find it emotionally convenient to have Webster step in about that time and take his place. He was someone to fill the void. For me, especially, he was a lifesaver. Even though my mother was Mexican and I had lived almost all of my life in Mexico, I never really felt entirely at ease, never really 'Mexican.' I have known some Mexicans I have considered my social and intellectual superiors, and of course, being an Anglo I found it natural to feel superior to most Mexicans . . . but I never felt their equal. Still don't. Most of the young people I socialized with were from the same social stratum as myself, educated at good schools all over the world, wealthy and influential families, but they were mostly Mexicans. I always felt like an outsider no matter how graciously they treated me in their homes, at work, or socially. Because of this I had been extremely close to my older brother, and when I lost him I was devastated. Then came Webster, congenial, urbane, kind—all the right adjectives—someone with whom I could once again let down my guard, in whom I could confide, who I could be reasonably sure would understand. At least he always made me feel that he did."

Lockhart sipped his drink, looking at Haydon over the glass. He seemed to be steeling himself.

"As I said, Webster was two years older than I, but he always seemed . . . much older. I don't know, perhaps it was because he had had the experience of bucking his family traditions early on and that had given him a special confidence in himself, a kind of bravery to face the world, or perhaps he simply was born with an older soul—there are people like that, you know, who seem innately to understand more deeply about life and death than other people. Whatever it was, Webster seemed far older than his years, and I was somewhat in awe of him. Respected him enormously, grew to have a . . . great affection for him." Lockhart looked down into his glass. "And I believe he felt something for me, too. I think we were exceptionally close."

He stopped and seemed to think about that for a moment before continuing.

"I was the one who introduced him to Amaranta. It didn't take me long to realize, of course, how naive I had been. You see, it never occurred to me that first night that they would have any attraction for each other. I simply wanted to show him that I traveled in heady circles, that I knew glamorous people, showing them off to him, showing him off to them, the whole crowd of social nitwits. That particular crowd." Remembering, he swirled the ice in his tall glass. "It was actually months before I heard about their relationship. Webster never told me he was seeing her, and I think *that* was the beginning of the end for us. The fact that he never told me. Why wouldn't he have told me?" Lockhart asked, looking at Haydon. "We confided in everything, or so I thought, and here he had kept this entire relationship a secret. I didn't know for months, and I didn't know why he hadn't told me. I still don't, or rather, he never told me why, but now I think I know."

Lockhart emptied his glass and stood. He hesitated before walking over to the liquor cabinet, where he began making another drink. It seemed to take him longer than it should have, and then when he was finished he stepped over to the crescent of glass and looked out into the Valley of Mexico. The fog had lifted a little now and the lights were visible as if through a filtered lens, each speck of light throwing off faceted sparks, millions of lights, billions of sparks colliding with

others until they became a haze, as if the valley were dusted
with light. Lockhart stood with his back to Haydon, and
suddenly Haydon felt as if he were an intruder, as though by
simply watching this old man remember a painful past he was
somehow breaching a code of social decency.

"Do you realize," Lockhart said slowly, his voice slightly
altered as it was thrown back off the glass, "that I am talking
about events that occurred over fifty years ago, and which
still . . . move me. And I have spent a lifetime practicing
self-control."

Haydon didn't respond; no response was desired.

Lockhart turned around and looked at Haydon from the
windows. His thoughts were already falling back over the
years.

"I was only one of dozens of young men who wanted to be
special to Amaranta. I had dated her some . . . no . . . I
had been out with her on a few occasions. She had granted me
that. She had granted many of us that. I'm sure you have heard
countless stories about her by now. There's really no reason for
me to contribute others. And really, it would be useless
anyway. Nothing could make you understand what she meant
to us in those heady days of our youth.

"Well. Their affair was scintillating, both for them and for
those of us who heard of it and listened to its rumors and
myths. Webster never changed toward me, not even minutely.
We remained the best of friends. But he would not discuss his
relationship with her, not even in the smallest way. It was a
universe, you see . . . yes, it was that large for him, it was
that rich . . . a universe for only two people. Like gods they
created their own world, and they protected it with a vast,
empty galaxy of silence. It was remarkable, I swear to God it
was remarkable. None of us had ever seen anything like it.
And none of it, not one intimate moment, was observed by
anyone other than themselves. It was all the more extraordinary because Amaranta, this wild and dashing and demonstra-
tive woman whose whole life had seemed to be a dazzling
performance, adhered to this strict privacy in their affair. Their
relationships with other people continued on as usual, but
their involvement with one another was inviolate."

Lockhart took a few steps toward Haydon, his eyes fixed on
him with a glimmer of uncertainty.

"And then the serpent entered paradise," he said. "I have no idea what happened, if there was fault or not, and if there was, whose it was. I would wager a fortune they didn't know either. But it began to be imperfect, strained. It didn't happen quickly, but over many months, and in between the pain they had begun to cause each other there were lengthy returns to paradise. The rest of us watched from a distance, as if watching a shadow play, not knowing really what was happening behind the screen of their privacy, but observing its effects. Webster grew taciturn, Amaranta more . . . extreme. It got very bad."

Lockhart walked past the liquor cabinet, set down his glass, and came back to his chair and sat across from Haydon, never taking his eyes off him. He crossed his legs slowly, his arms lying on the arms of the chair, his face suddenly ashen.

"One day she called me," he said, seeing the memory now, not Haydon. "She called me and asked me to come to her house in San Ángel. I went. I thought at last I was going to learn something about them. I thought that Armaranta finally had grown desperate, needed to talk, was going to spill everything out to me."

Lockhart's demeanor was calm, but it was obvious his mouth was dry and it was getting difficult for him to speak.

"She gave me a specific hour to be there," he continued. "And when I arrived, there was a note pinned to the door telling me to let myself in and to come up to the studio. I did. I knew where everything was, I'd been to so many parties there. As I walked through the house it became apparent that no one was home, no maids, no one. I went up the stairs and walked across to the studio door, which was open, and walked in. Amaranta was at the far end of the room at one of her easels painting, the back of the easel facing me so that I saw only her skirt beneath the canvas. When I came in I spoke to her, because I was afraid she hadn't heard me, and she leaned around and smiled at me, and motioned for me to come over.

"As I approached the easel she stood and raised both arms to pull back her long hair. She was naked from the waist up . . . her arms raised . . . her breasts . . . the look in her eyes, those green eyes. I knew instantly what was going to happen, I knew instantly. She reached out and took my hands and backed to the bed, which was only a few steps away. She took my hands and put them on her breasts. I started to speak—I can only give myself that much credit, that I started to speak. Over the years I've remembered that moment thousands of times, but, really, I don't even know what I was going to say. I cannot be sure that I was going to protest, but I might have been. It doesn't matter. She stopped me; I let her stop me. I remember every minuscule movement, what she did and what I did as she undressed me. I remember the sequence of the movements. I remember the color of the light around us and the sound of the cicadas outside in the summer heat, her smell, the way her skin felt, and the fact that even as I was looking at her I knew that I would never, never as long as I lived, get enough of the sight of her, of her shapes and hues and proportions . . ."

Lockhart's voice grew husky, and Haydon had to concentrate more closely to understand him.

"We were there a long time . . . without speaking." Lockhart nodded. "Without speaking. I tried to, but she put a finger on my lips. I tried again and she said, 'No.' We lay there, her legs around me, holding me there. Because he came around on the loggia I didn't hear his footsteps until he walked in through the French doors. I tried to move—her legs tightened. I saw the change in her green eyes as she looked past me and I knew what I would see as I turned around, her legs still wrapped around me, holding me. He didn't look at me, but at her, and she at him. His eyes didn't even flicker at me. You see, even though I had physically, literally, come between them I didn't really exist at all as far as they were concerned. What had happened was actually between just the two of them. I mattered only as . . . as a symbol, I suppose.

"Webster turned and walked away. Amaranta watched him go, her eyes remaining fixed on the empty doorway, unblinking. Not a muscle moved in her face. Her legs relaxed and I got up, but she simply lay there. In despair I quickly dressed, overwhelmed by the realization of what I had been an accomplice to. Amaranta didn't move, didn't even cover herself, simply lay there, staring at the doorway. Like a dead woman. Numb with self-hate, I turned to leave her and almost stumbled over the painting on the easel which all this time had been facing the bed. It was an unfinished portrait of Webster, all of it very rough except for the eyes. The eyes had been completed with startling detail."

Lockhart stopped. Somewhere during his narrative he had uncrossed his legs, and now he was sitting back in his armchair wan and debilitated, for the first time looking like the old man that he was. At that moment Haydon was trying to imagine his father's face, but he couldn't, not the face of the portraits or the face of the older man he had known. The image simply would not come into his mind.

"He never spoke to me again," Lockhart said. "That was the end of it."

They both remained silent, Lockhart with his bitter memories, Haydon trying to imagine the effect that scene must have had on his father, trying to fit the shock of that moment into its proper place in the new history of his father that he was uncovering. Then he said, "He went to Britain."

"In two weeks he was gone."

"Did he see Amaranta before he left?"

"No."

"But eventually he did become reconciled with her."

Lockhart's expression could only be described as stoic. "Yes," he said. "Eventually."

"How did that come about?"

The faint sour smile returned to Lockhart's ruddy Scots face, a smile of irony. "It was because of me," he said. "I brought them together."

"What?"

Suddenly the smile vanished and Lockhart pulled himself forward in the chair. He looked at Haydon, his face taut, and then he stood.

"I've something to give you," he said, walking across the room to a cabinet. He took an envelope out of a drawer and then returned and handed it to Haydon. It was sealed.

"This is a copy of a document that I believe will explain some of Saturnino's motivation, if you give it some thought. But don't open it now, please. Take it back to your hotel, read it. We'll talk again."

"But I want to know the answer to my last question," Haydon insisted. "I've got to know what started their . . ." He stopped.

Lockhart looked at him once again with that strange, now

familiar smile, as if he knew how Haydon would have finished his sentence.

"About what I've told you tonight," he said, the smile fading and something else overtaking his face, something supplicatory. "Chabela doesn't know that . . . story, and she mustn't."

Haydon nodded. He rose from his chair and immediately saw Eloy Palacio standing in the upper level of the living room waiting for him.

"Eloy will take you back to your hotel," Lockhart said.

Haydon held the envelope. "You've known all along about their annual meetings, haven't you?"

Lockhart's glaucous gaze did not communicate a response.

"Good night, Stuart," he said, and turning aside he walked back to the crescent of glass and stood with his back to Haydon. In the upper part of the room Palacio motioned to him to leave the old man alone.

Chapter 28

HAYDON DID NOT OPEN THE ENVELOPE IN THE CAR. DURING THE RIDE
back to his hotel through the rainy streets he went over
Lockhart's story again and again, replaying the episode in the
studio and recreating the movements and thoughts of each
character as if he were blocking out a scene in a drama. Time
after time Amaranta stood from behind the easel, raising her
arms to her hair, revealing her naked breasts; time after time
she lay back on the *lit en bateau*, drawing Lockhart with her;
time after time he imagined her enigmatic seduction, his lust,
their intercourse; time after time he saw his father walk
unsuspectingly through the loggia doors . . .

As the car passed through the dark forest of looming
ahuehuetes in Chapultepec Park, he tried to second-guess
Lockhart's confession. His father was dead, Amaranta was
beyond revealing such things, the secret of that afternoon
could have remained a secret forever. And yet he had revealed
it to Haydon with very little persuasion at all. Juan Lockhart
did not seem to be the sort of man to have been haunted by his
conscience, though his telling of the incident clearly had been
a wrenching confession. But there was something else. Somehow it seemed to Haydon that Lockhart's recounting of that
fateful afternoon had been more in the way of a prologue than
a conclusion. He squeezed the thick envelope of folded pages,
and mentally hurried the car along the Paseo de la Reforma,
past the palms, past the *glorietas*, toward the soaring golden
angel of independence.

Eloy Palacio told the driver to circle the Angel monument
and let Haydon out on the corner of Río Tiber next to
Brennan's, which was adjacent to the María Isabel. Haydon
got out of the car and thanked them, and followed the curving
sidewalk past the newsstands and around to the front of the

hotel. It seemed as if it had been a week rather than only this morning since he had walked out these same doors to go to San Ángel.

Once in his rooms he tossed the envelope on the table next to the windows and began to undress. He wanted to bathe before confronting the information in the envelope, hoping the shower would help order his mind, which was churning with the day's events and the new revelations that had kept him tense and had given him a lot to think about. He would have liked a long time alone in which to sort it all out, but he had the feeling that kind of time was something he couldn't very well afford.

After his shower he ran a comb through his damp hair, slipped on his robe, and sat down at the table. He looked out the window, at the city lights fading away into the fog, at the Reforma below bathed in a green mist. Then he reached for the envelope, tore open one end, and dumped the papers onto the table. There were only three pages, stapled together, a legal document, an agreement. He turned to the last page and looked at the signatures and the date. It had been signed on March 8, 1943, by Amaranta de la Sierra and Everardo Sarmiento, and had been witnessed by Gaston Arreola and Webster Haydon.

Though the document was written in legal language, the essence of the agreement was this:

Amaranta de la Sierra was acknowledging the fact that though she was unmarried she had just had confirmed by Dr. Eduardo Monroy that she was two months pregnant. Not wanting to marry the father of the child, but being aware of the necessity of maintaining conventional appearances out of concern for her parents and family, Amaranta de la Sierra was consenting to marry Everardo Sarmiento in order to provide a father and a name for the child.

Señor Sarmiento, in consenting to such an arrangement, agreed to accept paternity of the child and never to divulge the fact that he was not the biological father. He acknowledged that he did not know the identity of the child's biological father. In agreeing to accept all paternal responsibilities for the child, Señor Sarmiento was being granted legal guardianship over fifty percent of Amaranta de la Sierra's financial assets, which he was free to treat as his own. The legal description of those assets was itemized in the document. Sarmiento also was required to leave all of those assets plus any financial gains acquired from the investment of those assets to Amaranta and/∼r the child in the event he should predecease them.

However, if it was ever revealed by any of the signatories that Sarmiento was not the biological father of the child, then Sarmiento would forfeit all legal rights and access to said assets and to all adjoining profits which he might have derived from his investments of same. Additionally, Amaranta would then make public the factual circumstances of her pregnancy, and take the appropriate legal action against the biological father.

As legal documents go, it was brief, but it was also one of the strangest conditional contracts Haydon had ever seen. And it contained astonishing implications as well as raising a number of significant questions.

First of all, it had been signed by his father a year after his parents had moved to Houston. What was he doing back in Mexico City, and why was he asked to witness such a contract when he and Amaranta hadn't spoken in over five years? Why was Arreola involved? Why hadn't Lockhart—by this time, supposedly, her lawyer—witnessed it? By binding all the signatories to secrecy, didn't the contract imply that only they knew the circumstances of the pregnancy? And did that also mean that they knew the identity of the biological father? Obviously the agreement was designed to prevent the biological father from revealing his identity on pain of prosecution. But on what grounds would he be prosecuted? And how would he know about this unless he was shown the contract?

Haydon suddenly froze. His eyes settled on his father's signature at the bottom of the document, a signature that was familiar to him and that he had instantly recognized with its thin, elongated letters, a style which it seemed he had learned from an old-fashioned book on decorative handwriting. He remembered Lockhart's words: ". . . a document that I believe will explain some of Saturnino's motivation, if you give it some thought." Haydon felt his heart pounding, hammering against his chest, and a strange coolness washed across his face. Could it be that the biological father knew exactly the conditions of the contract because he was one of the signatories? Is that what Lockhart had meant? Was this grotesque ordeal founded in an even more grotesque secret that had been kept quiet for over forty years?

He put his elbows on the desk and ran his fingers through his hair. How could he believe this? How could he believe that his father would have allowed his own son to be reared by a man like Sarmiento? Perhaps his affair with Amaranta could have been forgiven as a rash mistake, the pregnancy an unfortunate result, but the solution, the contract, was something altogether different. The contract—if it had been his father's idea, or even if it hadn't been and he simply had agreed to its terms as the biological father of the child—had been a calculated immoral decision to which his father had had to recommit himself every day of his life because it was something he could have stopped at any point. Had he actually allowed others to live out such a twisted charade on his behalf? Had Amaranta loved him that much? Had Webster Haydon been guilty of that kind of cowardice?

It was a sordid story, as Isabel had said, and Haydon didn't want to believe it. Perhaps it was true, as Gabriela had insisted, that Amaranta had been cursed with her beauty, that it never had brought her anything but misery. Or maybe Arreola was right when he had said that she was simply cursed with bad luck. But whatever the truth, and the truth here was proving both elusive and grim, if Haydon's suspicions were borne out, Amaranta's life was not the only one that had been cursed by her beauty.

He stood and looked out to the city obscured by rain and fog and night, metaphors for everything he had encountered since the arrival of the first photograph. Only a week had passed since he had stared at that first portrait of his father, a man he hadn't even recognized and, as it was turning out, a man he hadn't even known. Thinking of this, Haydon realized that subconsciously he had always assumed that his father's life—or at least that part of it with any real significance—had begun with Haydon's birth, that everything that had come before had been so remote in time as to make no difference to the life they shared as father and son. He remembered that hot summer afternoon again, when his father had gazed at him from the shadow of his library across the bright green heat of the lawn and their eyes had met and he had waved from the shade of the lime trees—and his father had stood stock-still, refusing to acknowledge his innocent gesture. He remembered his own embarrassed confusion and then the bleakness that had overcome him at this act of stoic rejection. He remembered feeling that his father had thus conveyed to him an unspoken sign about their relationship, a sign which his boy's mind could not fathom but which had left him covered by a pall of isolation that had paralyzed him and made him think of death.

Did that strange moment in his youth have anything to do with his father's own youth, with his days and nights in this rainy Valley of Mexico? Did it have anything to do with a woman other than his mother, or with a son other than himself? And if it did, did his father's reprehensible acts in this other life invalidate the life that Haydon had known with him? Did it rescind the goodness he had known from his father, the kindness, the wise counsel, the compassionate understanding, the firm guidance, the shared love? How was Haydon supposed to feel about his own past in light of his father's past? What was he supposed to believe about any of it? Everything had been recast. It was as if he were a boy again, suddenly realizing through the shocking insight of a single moment that there was a vast complexity to life that in the comfort of his innocence he never had imagined; and once again it was from his father that he was about to receive instruction.

Haydon stepped away from the window and picked up the telephone, then stupidly realized he didn't have Lockhart's number. He knew there was no need to call information. He looked at his watch; it was only nine o'clock. He dialed another number, the line disconnected, he pushed the button and dialed again; after a great deal of static the number began to ring. The maid answered and Haydon introduced himself and asked to speak to Gaston Arreola. It was a few moments before Arreola picked up the telephone.

"Stuart!" he said. "*Qué dice?*" He sounded genuinely happy to be hearing from him.

"I've got the contract, Gaston," Haydon said quietly.

"Contract?" Arreola didn't understand, and then in the next instant Haydon could tell that he did.

"The one signed in 1943. Amaranta, Sarmiento, my father, and yourself."

"Ah, *hijo*." Arreola's voice was suddenly heavy, even weary, a groan. "Where did you get that paper?"

"Lockhart gave it to me a couple of hours ago."

Arreola was quiet.

"Did you hear me?"

"Yes, Stuart, I heard you. Did he tell you about it?"

"No. He wouldn't let me read it until I had left his place. Now I can't get in touch with him, because I don't know his number, and I assume it's unlisted."

"Yes, it is."

"Have you spoken with him today?"

"No."

"Then I need to talk with you, Gaston. A lot has happened, and I've learned a great deal from Isabel. Saturnino has killed a woman at his home in Coyoacán, a very gruesome murder, and I'm sure he's going after his mother as well as me. I've got bits and pieces of this, Gaston, but now I want to know everything. I want you to tell me everything."

Arreola did not respond immediately. There was a pause, then, "You have seen Amaranta?"

"Yes."

Silence.

"Gaston?"

"Yes, Stuart. I understand. Can you come here? I think you should come here."

"When?"

"As soon as you can make it."

"I'll get dressed and come straight over," Haydon said. He hung up, thought a moment, then picked up the telephone again and called Nina. He would tell her nothing, only that he was fine, that he had learned a lot, and that he would probably be coming home in a couple of days.

SATURNINO LAY NUDE ON HIS BACK, HIS ARMS AND LEGS STRETCHED out, the rough wooden floor abrading his shoulders and buttocks. Raising his head, he looked between his spread feet and saw the rock altar glowing with lighted candles, the marigolds brassy in the golden glow, spilling over the shelf and into heaps on the floor, the aromatic smolder of copal. He put his head back on the floor again and watched the slowly spinning points of light on the ceiling and dark walls, the countless tiny scintillae reflecting off the polished obsidian disks and mosaics. He felt as if he were floating in a dark sky of shooting stars, that the Lord of the Night was with him, he who was known as Night and Wind, that they rode on the bony-backed Night Mares, whistling down the cobbled streets of Tenochtitlán, everyone fearful of them, everyone afraid, their wooden doors bolted, the crossroads deserted as ill-starred places, even the waters in the narrow canals afraid to make the sound of lapping, the tides afraid to obey the moon in the Lake of the Moon in Tenochtitlán.

He turned his head to the tall windows that looked onto Calle Verdad, where the thin coppery light tried obsequiously to worm its way into the darkness of the Lord of the Near Vicinity. He stood and went to the window, stood before it in the coppery light, and then stepped up on its low, deep sill. He spread his arms and legs the width of the window and braced them against the frame, facing Calle Verdad, facing the baroque facade of the former Temple de Santa Teresa la Antigua, the ornate colonial building now tilting to the east as it settled into the ancient lake bed of Tenochtitlán, Mexico City, facing the *calmécac* where the youth acquired authentic faces from the wisemen priests. Behind him, through the walls and the centuries, were the Temples of Chicomecoatl, of Xipe, of Xochiquetzal, the *tzompantli* where the skulls of the sacrificial victims were hung in tiers, thousands upon thousands upon thousands supported by two flanking walls made of skulls cemented together, thousands upon thousands, the Metropolitan Cathedral, the neoclassical La Mitra, the Churrigueresque El Sagrario. Suspended between copper light and candlelight, between temple and church, between canals and cobblestones, he awaited the end of the Fifth Sun when Tezcatlipoca would steal away the sun and the dream of this life would be ripped asunder like a veil and the monsters of everlasting twilight would swarm out of the western sky rattling and whistling and keening to devour the inhabitants of earth and bring on the end of time.

Later, in the bare cell of his bedroom, he turned on the recorder where it lay on the floor beside his mattress, and listened to the telephone messages. There had been three. The gate guard at Lockhart's—twenty-five dollars given and twenty-five promised—had called to say that Haydon had arrived with three of Lockhart's men. It was six thirty-seven. Stupid Napo had not called. The guard at Lockhart's had called a second time to say that Haydon had departed with two of Lockhart's men. It was eight-fifteen. Stupid Napo had not called. The low-level desk clerk at the María Isabel—fifty dollars given, fifty dollars promised (excessive because it was a four-star hotel and their employees disdained such things . . . unless the money was excessive)—had left a message that Haydon had come in and gone up to his room. Alone. It was eight thirty-five. Stupid Napo had not called. A waiter at the Champs Élysées had not called. Others had not called. But it didn't matter now. This was a good time. This was the way he wanted to do it.

Leaning across the mattress, he dragged the cardboard box toward him. He dumped out the reports from Swain, the newspaper clippings, the photographs, the scraps of paper with scribbled notes, and at the bottom of the box the document that had enlightened him when he had found it in the false bottom of the tortoiseshell cabinet in the old woman's bedroom. He was sure Chabela had not seen it, Chabela didn't imagine false bottoms and secret compartments; she didn't look for them, and she didn't find them. But he had.

He had spent a good deal of time over the past two years roaming through the pink house in San Ángel. The first time had been a whim. One day after so many years of not going there at all, he decided he wanted to see it again, alone. The Sunday outings when Celerina and Paulo would take the old woman to church and then to spend the afternoon with friends in Jardines del Pedregal had long been a tradition of which he was aware. One Sunday when he was sure they had gone, he drove over from Coyoacán, parked in Plaza San Jacinto, walked up to Plaza de los Arcángelos, and waited on the stone benches among the bougainvilleas and pines, guessing that Chabela would take the opportunity to get away for an afternoon. And he had been right. After he watched her car come through the arches and drive away, he walked along the cobblestones and under the arches to the house. Chabela didn't always leave, of course, but she did often enough that when he felt the urge to prowl he didn't have to wait many Sundays for the opportunity.

Since that first afternoon he had spent many hours walking among the quiet corridors and tranquil rooms of the pink house, moving among the pale day shadows, passing through the muted light, studying the paintings he hadn't looked at closely since he was a boy, seeing pieces of furniture he had forgotten, the Italian desk in the *sala*, a chest, a table of Honduran rosewood, odors of childhood that flooded his mind with latent memories, the forgotten shape and color of a vase, the way of afternoon light across a staircase, the soughing of the mourning doves in the *zapotes*, the occasional waft of eucalyptus, the sultry way the palm fronds hung from the Guadalupes, the shape of the shade in the loggia. For a long time he would come only to walk, to see, to smell, to remember, to remember far, far back in that distant country of the past when memory took on the same amorphous life as dreams and sometimes the borders failed and they became inseparable.

And then one day he was standing beside a cupboard in the large living room watching the light change across from him where the windows opened into the courtyard, his thoughts tacking to and fro through the long waters of memory, when he absently opened a drawer next to his hand. The old wooden boards of the cupboard drawer were bare, but something, a single, solitary thing, had rattled to the back of the drawer. He pulled it out farther, almost all the way, and found a small, dull red stone, nearly square, resting in a back corner. He recognized it, a special stone. He remembered it clearly, a dimple in one side, a rhomboid, its edges blunted by time, a tiny caramel thread running diagonally through its center. His eerily precise recollection of this object was totally unexpected. He remembered having the stone, playing with it, going weeks with it in his pocket because it had become something that kept him alive and if he lost it he would die. He remembered putting it on the marble top of his bedside table at night, remembered making sure it was the last thing he saw as he turned out the lights because if he hadn't done that he would die in his sleep, remembered kissing it whenever his mother left home at night because if he didn't she wouldn't return, remembered . . . everything about the stone except how he had gotten it, and how he had lost it. He stood beside the cupboard and stared down into the drawer with as much amazement as he would have viewed a resurrection from the dead.

And then he looked at the living room as if through different

eyes and suddenly he saw the rose house of San Ángel as if it
were a vast and lavish treasure trove waiting to be plundered.
That very day he began a methodical room-by-room search of
every drawer, cabinet, nook, and crevice in the entire house,
and it was not long before he decided that not only were there
things in the old house that would bring him memories so
vivid as to be hallucinations, but also that the house held
enormous and complex secrets. He decided there were hidden
places, and he became obsessed with finding them, and he
prowled the house for a year of Sundays, probing, searching,
tapping, prying, opening, seeking with an excitement, a sweet
and tremulous anticipation, that was wholly addictive.

He found no such places . . . until he found the only one,
and the document.

IT RAINED THROUGHOUT THE ENTIRE WORLD. AND IN THE HOUSE-
with-five-courtyards the rain fell on the right arm of Saturnino
Sarmiento de la Sierra as he walked along the balcony with
iron railings and made the five turnings down the stone steps
through the lingering odors of fried onions and hot tortillas and
urine and old stone. He carried his umbrella in his wet right
hand and gripped the deep pocket of his raincoat with his left,
feeling the long bulk of the butcher knife wrapped in a
protective sheath of newspaper, and the lump of the handgun.
With the turning at each balcony he shed a hundred years,
through the voices of Indian women in darkened stoops,
through the sweet brume of marijuana, through sadness and
lust and hope and despair, down through five hundred years to
the courtyard, where he paused and looked up through the
surrounding galleries, through the falling rain of centuries,
rain so far away that the drops he saw would never reach the
stones where he stood.

Turning into the darkened corridor that led to the street, he
was careful to stay away from the walls, from the sleeping
lumps, the damp and desperate lost, but kept his eyes on the
burnished cobblestones of Calle Verdad at the end of the
darkness. He came into the light, turned up the collar of his
raincoat, opened his umbrella, and stepped out into the rain.
He turned right and proceeded along the wide sidewalk
through the splashing rain to Moneda, where he again turned
right, the rain dribbling off the scalloped edges of his umbrella

as he passed between the walls of the red *tezontle* stone of the
National Palace and the old Archbishop's Palace, heading for
the Zócalo and the godly stones of the Metropolitan Cathedral.
When he got to the vast expanse of the Zócalo, he stood and
stared across the gilded stones, through the immense lighted
sky of drifting, glinting copper rain.

The Volkswagen taxi left the southeastern corner of the
Zócalo and puttered down the narrow Calle Pino Suárez
through the old colonial district until the street turned into the
broader San Antonio Abad and a little farther the even larger
Calzada de Tlalpan that ran straight as an arrow through the
rain into the southern *delegación* of Coyoacán. They turned
west on Quevedo through familiar streets of the northern part
of the district and into Obregón, slicing through the gloomy
Parque de la Bombilla, where the gray granite monument to
General Álvaro Obregón protected the revered relic of his
severed arm, a heroic sacrifice for the Revolution. Every block
brought him closer, across Insurgentes on La Paz, across
Revolución, climbing the steep street to the old colonial Plaza
San Jacinto.

The plaza was dark and empty; nothing moved but the
leaves shivering under the pelting downpour. He was the only
one on the street, the only one on the curving, climbing
Frontera, a slow, steep walk in the rain, oblivious to the
rivulets that hugged the low joints of the cobblestones,
glistening underneath his soaked shoes. His shoulder bent to
the weather, he turned into Privada Frontera, the small,
angular alleylike street that took him to the Plaza de los
Arcángelos. He crossed to the center of the tiny plaza and
stepped into the paved paths under the dripping pines and
banks of bougainvillea whose brilliant blossoms were reduced
to monochromatic black in the night. He looked down the
short drive to the two stone arches. He looked at the pale glow
of both streetlamps flanking the arches, the water tumbling off
his umbrella and splashing a circle around his feet, soaking his
shoes and the lower part of his trouser legs. Both streetlamps.

He moved to the far side of the plaza and walked on the gray
stone sidewalk that followed the wall around to the arches.
When he got halfway around the curve he realized there was
no way he was going to be able to walk under the arches
without also walking through the spill of light from which the

curving wall was now protecting him. He stood in the steady rain, thinking, then turned and retreated across the plaza the way he had come.

Seen from above, as on a map, the rose house was at the end of a little cobblestoned drive that was too small even to have a name. The drive came to an end in the middle of a piece of land isolated from other streets and bordered by Árbol, Juárez, and Miramón streets, and the Plaza San Jacinto. The houses behind the high walls that faced onto each of these streets had large properties that extended out into the piece of land behind, so that the backs of several large estates joined together and were separated by the traditional high walls while their entrances all radiated in different directions and opened onto the different streets.

During the time he had been secretly prowling the rose house, Saturnino had remembered from childhood this conjoining of property walls, and that it was possible to gain access to the rose house from several of the adjacent estates. One of these properties was by far the best for this purpose because of its location, and he had used it on numerous Sundays when he felt the little Plaza de los Arcángelos was too busy with art students and lovers and sunning old women. This estate fronted Calle Miramón and was not far off the Plaza San Jacinto, its high terra-cotta wall turning and climbing with the cobblestoned street to its entrance gate around the curve. Where the wall began, a narrow wrought-iron gate had been set into the corner under a scallop-shell lintel. Immediately inside was a thicket of underbrush, but the rear wall of the estate ran straight through it to the back of the property, where it also served as the rear wall of Amaranta's land.

Now ascending the slick stones of Miramón, Saturnino thought only of the two dogs, a golden Labrador and a cur of no distinction, who lived behind the gate. They were friendly animals and quickly had grown familiar with his surreptitious entrances and trips along the hidden walls, gamely following him through the brush as if he had belonged there. But now it had been over eight months since he had done this and he wasn't sure they would remember his scent. As he approached the wall, which made an abrupt step up from the one adjoining it on the street, he worked the latch quickly and stepped into the gloomy underbrush, folding his umbrella. He waited a moment in the darkness, hoping the dogs would be under the shelter next to the house and would not even hear him, or smell him, moving through the soggy thicket. He really didn't even need to see. Putting his left hand lightly on the wall, he held his umbrella close in front of him to protect his face from the vines and branches and proceeded along the wall. Occasionally his shoes sank in the spongy earth, but mostly it was rocky soil beneath the wet mat of twigs and leaves. It seemed a longer walk than he had remembered, but he welcomed the odors of damp vegetation and sometimes the spicy smell of woodsmoke from the surrounding estates.

When he finally reached the junction of the rear walls without attracting the dogs, he counted himself extraordinarily lucky. With face and hands dripping from the wet brush, he began searching the corner for the random series of stones that projected from the wall and that he had used for steps to climb to the top. It took him a while to find them, and when he did he was frustrated to find them glazed over with a slick coat of moss. He wasn't sure he could get a firm footing. But he started up, pausing at each ledge to scrape his shoes over the tops of the stones until the slimy moss was worn down to the stone. It was slow going, but he finally reached the top and was able to look over into the grounds of the rose house. Through the *zapotes* and eucalyptus trees he saw the lighted second story, the dim glow in the studio, the old woman's bedroom, Chabela's, the wall at the back of the courtyard. After a moment's hesitation he went over the top and dropped into a stand of plantains.

As soon as he hit, he heard a low woof not far away, then quickly two more, heard them running and moaning deeply, something between a worried growl and a whine of curiosity, and then the two dogs plunged through the broad watery leaves and jumped up on him, licking him, muddying him, the Labrador and the cur, happy to see him, smelling nasty, a whirl of wet coats, muddy paws stepping all over his feet, their wet tails slapping the broad leaves of the plantains.

Chapter 29

REFRESHED BY HIS BATH AND WEARING A CLEAN CHANGE OF CLOTHES, Haydon sat in the taxi with the contract in his breast pocket and stared out the window at the passing lights. Since both Juan Lockhart and Gaston Arreola lived in the same district of Bosques de las Lomas southwest of Chapultepec, the taxi ride was almost an exact reversal of the trip he had made just an hour before. Now, however, he was seeing the streets and the night with different eyes. In a matter of an hour he had changed into a man with a different history, and therefore a different perspective. At the moment the past dominated his thinking, and the present—Houston, Nina, the pending question of the lieutenant's position—were as remote as distant time.

For a moment, when they had to stop near the Monumento Diana Cazadora, he saw his reflection in the taxi window. He shifted his eyes. For once it was not introspection that compelled him, but rather imagination as he tried with distressingly little success to project himself into his father's youth, to try to understand why he had done what he had done, why his decisions had been so contrary to all that Haydon would have expected of him. In addition, Haydon was trying to sort out his own feelings about Saturnino. How in God's name was he supposed to feel about such a startling discovery?

By the time the taxi had reached the winding Oyameles high in the foothills, the fragrance of damp pine and eucalyptus filled every breath that Haydon drew. The taxi driver turned off the main street and they approached Arreola's home, a traditional Mexican-style hacienda that lay on a low rise behind a small landscaped park filled with giant ceiba and camphor trees.

Haydon could see the lights of the house through the trees as they rounded the park and started up the gently sloping drive. Even though they were expecting him, Haydon thought the place seemed unusually bright, and he peered through the taxi's windshield, trying to see if there were other cars under the pillared covered drive at the front. As the taxi approached, Haydon saw Arreola's rotund frame striding forward, head tilted back as he squinted into the taxi's headlights, his coattails flapping as he waved at the taxi to stop even before it had gotten under the shelter. A couple of men were with him, two of his "assistants," a driver, a door-opener, whatever they were called, members of the small—and sometimes not so small— entourage that wealthy Mexicans always seemed to have hanging about them, one of them in fact already opening the rear door of Arreola's big Mercedes. Arreola was agitated, shifting his weight nervously from foot to foot under the bright lights, reaching out in Haydon's direction as the taxi pulled to a stop and swiveling his right hand in a rotating motion in a signal for Haydon to hurry as Arreola's second assistant opened the taxi door while Haydon scrambled for the money in his wallet.

He paid the driver and stepped out of the taxi. As its rear door slammed behind him, he frowned at Arreola's dancing agitation.

"Stuart, Stuart, get in, get in!" Arreola said, already lowering himself into the Mercedes's rear seat. The taxi pulled away and Haydon ducked into the rear seat on his side of the car. Arreola's driver slammed the door and climbed in behind the wheel. With the two assistants in the front and Arreola and Haydon in the back, the Mercedes shot out of the drive and down into the park.

"What's the matter?" Haydon blurted at Arreola, who was bracing himself with a stiff arm against the back of the front seat.

Arreola was shaking his head. "It's Saturnino. Juan called . . . just now, three minutes ago. Isabel had just called him and Saturnino's in the house . . . in the studio with Amaranta."

Haydon was suddenly weak. "What do you mean, 'with' her?"

"She tried to call you," Arreola said, not answering his

question, his elbow resting on the window frame as he rubbed his forehead. His voice was breathy. "You were on the way . . . so she called him."

"What's the situation? Is he threatening her?"

"I don't know." Arreola grabbed the strap hanging from the doorjamb as the Mercedes leaned into the curves of the falling street. "I don't know."

Haydon didn't know which question Arreola was answering, or if he was answering both of them. Haydon looked at him, and the old man seemed to be in pain; his agitation had almost made him incoherent.

"I have no idea, no idea, how this will end," Arreola said. "This is the worst thing, the *worst* thing!"

"Did Isabel say anything else? Are they alone?"

Arreola shook his head, his large frame leaning forward, his eyes glued on the street flying by in the glare of the headlights, every nerve in his body seemingly bent on urging the Mercedes through the night streets, across the northern district of Obregón. The two men in the front seat appeared calm, but the Mercedes was straining.

Suddenly Haydon was swollen with anger, the anger of frustration and helplessness. He was furious with Arreola, with this agitated old man sitting beside him who had persisted in the arrogance of secrecy, who had cast aside doubt for a blind faith in his own rectitude, who had been haughty in his confidence in hidden things, believing that concealment was the preferable thing for all concerned, even when pushed to the point of deception. And Lockhart, too. They both had been warders of old histories, fearful of their charge, and fearful of passing on the keys to another generation. It all had been a terrible mistake, believing they were the only men who could deal with darkness.

Haydon looked away, out his window where the night rippled past in a jittery dance of grays and umbers and half-perceptions. He thought of Isabel, knew that when she saw Saturnino she must have thought of the blonde in the Coyoacán garden, how she must have imagined herself in that context, how horrified she must be, how he wanted to be there for her, how he wished he could have spared her this, the brackish taste of terror. None of it was working out the way he had thought it might, and then he supposed it must be much the same with Arreola. Surprise, even after decades of knowing how bad it was, fighting the nausea at the realization that it could be even worse. He needn't blame the old man. How could one really be expected to get the jump on life? Men were not gifted with that kind of foresight, that kind of wisdom.

They approached San Ángel from the Periférico expressway, from the opposite direction of the Plaza San Jacinto, and soon they were on Frontera, going down rather than up the narrow cobblestoned street. The fall was gradual, but when they reached the alley-like lane of 2a Privada Frontera the Mercedes turned sharply upward and climbed with a straining roar up the steep grade between the close colonial houses to the Plaza de los Arcángelos.

There were two cars parked at the skewed angles of a hasty arrival in the courtyard in front of the rose house. Both were Lockhart's. Two men were standing between the cars looking up at the lighted windows on the second floor. Arreola's men jumped out of the car and opened the rear doors as they shouted at the two Lockhart guards about the disposition of the situation in the house. Even as Haydon and Arreola hurried through the wrought-iron gate set in the wall they were told they would be met inside. They met another one of Lockhart's men in the small courtyard, and he ushered them into the house. They hurried through to the main living room and then to the stairway. Eloy Palacio met them at the bottom and talked to them as they climbed: Saturnino was holding a gun at the señora's neck . . . there were only the four of them in the empty studio, Saturnino would allow no one else in . . . except them . . . he knew they were coming . . . he was waiting for them . . . he seemed a little agitated . . . wasn't demanding anything . . .

Arreola huffed and heaved himself up the stairs, his breathing powerful and labored. Haydon's heart was hammering. He wanted to see Isabel, to see that she was all right, and he wanted to see Saturnino.

At the top of the stairs they hurried across to the door at the end of the studio, and Palacio stopped.

"This is as far as I can go," he said. He stepped back.

Haydon approached the door, hesitated, and went inside. Everyone in the studio heard his footstep and turned around, all of them, sitting in a cluster halfway down the long studio in front of Amaranta's portraits of Webster. It was a peculiar scene in the dimly lighted and cavernous old room, which was so wonderfully bright and spacious in the daylight but had hardly been furnished with adequate illumination for the evenings. The tall windows were thrown open, as were the French doors on the loggia, the openings surrounding the small gathering in the center of the room like a backdrop of ominous observers at a secret meeting. Amaranta and the capuchin sat in one of the cross-frame armchairs in the middle of the vast wooden floor, the old woman proud and straight-backed and beautifully mindless, the monkey perched on her shoulders, hunched and keening, casting quick, furtive glances all about, the eyes and mind for both of them. Behind her was Saturnino, standing and holding a gun to her neck as Palacio had said, his disheveled demeanor offering a foreboding air to the picture the three of them presented, a rigid portrait of queer formality.

Sitting side by side and facing them, Isabel and Lockhart also occupied armchairs, Lockhart's long legs crossed at the knee, though he was alert, not slouching. Like her mother, Isabel sat with a straight back, her hands in her lap. She had been crying.

From this tableau of perfect tension Haydon singled out the electric gaze of Saturnino, who stared solemnly at him across the empty space of the studio. Haydon said nothing, but remained motionless, sensing that the protocol of the moment required him to wait for Saturnino to speak. But he did not seem so inclined. No one moved. Silence. Haydon waited. Saturnino did not take his eyes off him, and Haydon had the feeling that the other man was indulging himself in much the same way one savors an entire glass of water without taking a breath after a long, painful thirst.

"They told me you were coming," he said at last. "After all this time . . ."

Haydon found Saturnino's voice strange, at once weary and tense. He did not attempt to raise his pitch to cover the distance between them, but his words were clear and distinct.

"And the old man," he said. "Tell him to come in, too."

Haydon nodded, and glanced at Isabel. Lockhart's face was stony. He turned to the doorway, but Arreola had heard the command from where he was standing and stepped inside.

"Gaston," Saturnino said.

"Hello, Nino," Arreola said, with the grave demeanor of a man who had come to officiate an execution.

"There are two more chairs over here," Saturnino said, nodding at the workbench behind Isabel. "Just two more." He tilted his head for them to come over.

Haydon and Arreola approached the tense quartet, and Haydon could see the little capuchin's petrified, goggling eyes, its infant's arms tightly gripping Amaranta's neck. The old woman wore a peaceful, ethereal expression, almost a smile, as she looked at Isabel.

Arreola took the first chair and dragged it around beside Isabel, leaving Haydon to put his next to Lockhart. He deliberately placed it at a bit of an angle to enable him to see everyone's face. The tension was palpable, and Haydon felt from the stiffness of Lockhart's attitude that Saturnino's nerves were strung very tightly.

He looked at Saturnino, and only now noticed the thick cord that was looped around Amaranta's neck securing the barrel of the handgun. He couldn't tell the make or the caliber, but of course it didn't matter. Saturnino was sweating. He wore a well-traveled dark blue suit that looked as if it had been slept in, wadded and wrinkled where his arms bent. A blotch of yellow glowed on his upper chest where a battered marigold was pinned to his lapel. Glancing to the floor, Haydon saw part of Saturnino's left shoe, a muddy heel, and the cuff of soiled trousers.

Saturnino worked his lips, pursed and relaxed them as if they were chapped and bothering him.

"About your men, Juan," he said, looking suddenly at Lockhart. "I suppose you've got them in the dark out there, on the other side of the loggia, with the cross hairs on the back of my head. But you don't know about reflexes, do you, Juan? There's an unknown there. Who knows what my fingers will do in that last . . . moment, huh?" He shrugged, the sweat glistening on the sides of his nose. "I don't know either. And when they finally shoot I probably won't find out. But that won't matter, will it? Either I will have, or I won't have." He tried to smile, but his mouth didn't quite make the right shape.

He looked at them. "This is unfortunate," he said. "I suppose it will end badly now. If I could have done what I wanted to do it would have been different. But this is the end of it, I can see that. Now there are only a few ways it can go, a limited number of ways."

He looked at Haydon as if Haydon were the one to whom he owed an explanation. "Isabel came to check on the old woman. She heard us talking before she opened the door. She ran to her room and made the telephone calls, thinking someone could stop it from happening, I suppose." He glanced at her for confirmation, but she didn't respond. "Yes, I suppose, and then she came back to the bedroom and . . . came in. Just like that. She told me Juan was coming, that he was calling Gaston. I assumed you would end up here too. Paulo was already outside with a shotgun . . . I was here to stay. So I devised this." He indicated the handgun and cord. "And suggested we move to the studio, a more appropriate setting for the finale. Still, I wish I had been allowed to work it out . . . satisfactorily. I had planned it for so long, as you know. I was almost there."

Heard them talking? Haydon didn't move, but he glanced at Isabel, whose eyes were riveted on her brother. They sat there like participants in a séance, the few of them, a small group of adherents who believed against reason that Amaranta would speak something revelatory, something significant. A sibylline utterance that would deliver them all from the impossibility of their situation.

Saturnino gazed at Haydon, the sweat glistening on his forehead, his mouth unsteady, looking haggard. He was more heavyset than Haydon had imagined him, thicker, settling into middle age. A professor of anthropology, a man who could take the hearts out of eleven monkeys and a woman. Who could imagine what else he was capable of doing? And now that he was closer, Haydon could see that Saturnino was fidgeting, quick little movements, sometimes thrusting his free hand out to the side with a little jerk as if he were adjusting his shirt sleeve under his coat.

"I would have thought we would look more alike," he said after a moment. "I had imagined we did, looking at the photographs. You can't always tell with photographs, though. Still, I don't see any resemblance at all."

"No," Haydon said. "I don't see any resemblance either."

Saturnino looked surprised, and then a fleering smile moved

over his face as if he were amused at Haydon's impertinence in speaking without being asked to do so. Then his expression hardened and he said, "Resemblance. You don't have any idea what I am talking about, do you?"

"You're talking about our being half brothers, about our having the same father."

Saturnino almost staggered, as if Haydon had leaped to his feet and slapped him. He started to speak; his mouth opened and closed without a sound. He swallowed, and suddenly he turned on Arreola. "You son of a bitch," he said with a shudder.

Isabel whirled around at Haydon, her eyes frozen. He couldn't imagine what she was thinking. Only Lockhart and Arreola remained motionless, both looking at Amaranta as if daydreaming.

"He didn't tell me," Haydon interjected. "I've known since my father died. His copy of the contract was among his papers. I didn't do anything about the discovery. I don't know what I could have done anyway."

"What contract?" Isabel was still looking at Haydon. Her eyes were swollen, but surprise had dried them. "*What* contract?"

Looking blanched and pasty, Saturnino glared at Haydon. As they stared at each other in silent confrontation, Haydon slowly realized that Saturnino had wanted to reveal the enormous secret to Haydon himself. He had been denied a long-awaited assuagement.

"Please!" Isabel's voice was anguished with confusion and anger.

"In 1943 your mother signed a contract," Lockhart said unexpectedly, his voice measured and lawyerly. "It has caused a great deal of confusion." Without looking at Isabel, his eyes still on Amaranta, he proceeded to explain the essentials of the conditional contract, not glossing over either Amaranta's cold machinations or Everardo's blatant venality. It was a cogent recitation of the facts, a chilling account for a child to hear of her parents, even if one was as familiar as Isabel with their lifelong unorthodoxies. When he finished, no one spoke; nothing could be heard but the keening capuchin stroking Amaranta's throat.

Isabel simply stared at Lockhart, not speaking and, clearly, not wanting to relate to the facts she had just heard and the dialogue that had passed between her brother and Haydon.

"No, it didn't make any sense to me either," Saturnino said, reading her face and casting another irritated glance at the capuchin, which was plainly nervous at having Saturnino behind it. As the creature clung to Amaranta, caressing her, rubbing its simian face against hers, stroking her hair as if comforting her, it kept glancing back over its shoulder, sometimes putting its hands on the cord as if concerned about it, fearing it on behalf of its mistress.

Saturnino wiped his forehead on the arm of his suit. "Not at first. At first the only thing I could think of was that that cretin wasn't my father after all. I was thrilled to know I didn't have an ounce of the bastard's blood in me, not a single gene, even a recessive one. It wasn't as twisted anymore, not as sick, what he did to me, because . . . he wasn't my father after all. There wasn't the defilement, you see. That was very important, the defilement."

As he talked his squirming became more prominent, and Haydon began to worry about an accident with the gun. He looked at Lockhart and was surprised to see the elder man staring at Saturnino not with the sharp, clear expression of animal fear or repulsion or hatred, but rather with what seemed to be a profound sadness, as if he already knew the denouement and did not fear it, or dread it, but mourned the pity of it all.

Saturnino raised his eyebrows. "But then . . . then I wondered, who *was* my father? Who?" His eyes widened theatrically and he looked at each one of them, exaggerating the point. "Who had given me to Everardo Sarmiento? With her consent, of course. Always. It seemed more callous, in fact, than what Sarmiento had done, to have given a child up to that kind of fate and to stand by and watch it happening year after year, for a lifetime. Well, it wasn't too difficult to reason that out; it was instantaneous. He had showed up every year with the regularity of her menstrual cycles." He shot a look at Isabel, who stiffened noticeably at the reference. "Christ! You thought you were the only keeper of secrets? I have a mind encrusted with them. I discovered their shabby little charade while I was still a student at the university. It only contributed to my disgust at her. I put it all together. The stories she had

told, the things I knew, the portraits, their nauseous obsession
with each other, this long and mawkish minuet of theirs, as if
they stood apart from the rest of the world . . ."

The capuchin keened and worried with the cord around
Amaranta's neck, glancing at Saturnino, its shoulders hunched
as if it were expecting a blow. Amaranta stroked the creature
in return, made soft suckling noises as it absently probed her
lips with its dark Lilliputian fingers, then again snuggled into
her neck. For a moment Saturnino looked down at them with
an undisguised revulsion, then he collected his thoughts and
continued.

"I came to hate Webster Haydon with a more precise
loathing than ever I had for the brutish Sarmiento. Here
was a refined man, a strikingly handsome man . . . a truly
shameless man . . . so I had two fathers and . . . a thousand mothers—God only knows where the *true* Amaranta was
in that amalgam of Amarantas—" Saturnino was increasingly
distracted, everyone sensed it, tensing, anticipating. "One of
them simply discarded me like a spiritual abortion . . . one
of them persecuted me . . . one of them loved me with a
twisted, uncertain affection and then it was only twisted and
then it wasn't even that . . . not even that . . ."

He was foul with perspiration, his eyes blinking rapidly as if
he were fighting to avoid passing out, his shoulders snatching
this way and that, the cord around Amaranta's neck sometimes
tightening as his hand jounced the gun so that she was noticing
it now, sometimes slightly flinching but without concern,
unaware of any danger or, really, of anything at all. The
capuchin keened and cheeped, sensing Saturnino's heighten-
ing agitation, its own nervousness responding in kind as it
began to try to comfort Amaranta with childish fingers that
patted her and cosseted her, nuzzled and caressed her, all the
while a distracted hand tugging at the tightening cord, while
Amaranta responded to its pampering with her own apprecia-
tive fondling and suckling noises.

Suddenly attracted by the sounds of their interplay, Saturnino stopped and fixed his goggling eyes on their affection,
on their caresses, their concern and mutual comfort. Everything stopped.

Haydon saw the next brutal act in Saturnino's eyes the
instant before it happened. Swiftly, expertly, cleanly, like a

man who had done it many times before, Saturnino grabbed the capuchin's curling tail, which was poised over the pistol at Amaranta's neck, and jerked the animal screeching from its embrace, slinging it powerfully in a high arc over his head as the creature's high-pitched and sustained scream made it seem like a whistling toy on the end of a string, and then violently slammed it down on the studio floor with a sickening force and the sharp, resounding crack of death.

Isabel jumped to her feet with a sudden, sickened shriek. Arreola grabbed her and held her, staring wide-eyed at Saturnino, knowing as they all did that anything could happen now, that Saturnino's nerves were unraveling right before their eyes like the strands of a rope stretched taut beyond its limits. Amaranta did not move, did not look around and see what had happened to the capuchin, which was not quite lifeless in the pool of its own mess on the floor, but her face had changed and she stared at the weeping Isabel with a vacant expression that almost achieved concern. Saturnino never came close to letting go of the gun, his eyes now darting crazily over all of them, trying to see if any of them would be foolish enough to do something, sweat pouring off of him, his jaws clenching, his mouth grimacing, waiting to see what was going to happen, not having any idea himself except that he was exploding.

Haydon tried not to imagine the way it was going to end.

Slowly, calmly, Lockhart turned to Arreola, who had managed to get Isabel into her chair again, and said, "When it's over, tell them everything."

Arreola, shaken, his arm still around Isabel, was looking over his shoulder at Lockhart with an uncomprehending frown.

Lockhart spoke more deliberately. "Afterward, tell them everything, Gaston. All of it."

This time Arreola heard and understood, or at least understood part of it, and nodded.

Saturnino was watching the two of them, breathing hard, almost hyperventilating from the tension and the exertion, but not understanding it any more than the rest of them.

Again slowly, carefully, so that Saturnino would not misinterpret his actions, Lockhart unfolded his long legs and eased out of his chair and went to his knees on the floor in front of Amaranta. He knelt before her like an aging knight.

"Amaranta, forgive me," he said, his words pained and private, shutting everyone out but the two of them. "Your disdain was justified . . . my cowardice . . . years of it . . ." He placed his left hand over the two of hers that lay in her lap. "But you cannot deny that I loved you . . . the only good thing in me, that I loved you . . . more, more than him, but you could not have known . . . it wasn't in you . . . to understand it." She looked down at him uncomprehendingly, an empty emerald gaze.

The tenderness of the scene was shocking, almost blasphemous so close on the heels of Saturnino's outburst of awesome ferocity. The now motionless body of the capuchin was only a few feet away, and Juan Lockhart was on his knees begging forgiveness and pledging love before a mindless old woman of great beauty and lifeless green eyes. In this unreal setting Haydon's attention was attracted to a single moth that had come in through the open windows and was flitting unsteadily in the dim air above Lockhart's bent head while the old man continued muttering softly like a pious man of faith before the silent image of the Virgin, prayers and supplications, and the moth dancing crazily above his head like an Absurdist imitation of the Divine Presence, and then the resumed and uncontrollable weeping of Isabel, and Saturnino turning to look at her and at that instant Lockhart's hand going into his suit-coat pocket and in one smooth, graceful motion rising from his knees and his hand coming out of his pocket and going up to Saturnino's forehead as if to bless him and Saturnino's eyes leaving Isabel and coming around to meet him and the deafening explosion, the brilliance of the explosion and Saturnino's surprise, his hands flying up and back and out to keep his balance and the instant of silence and then the sound of his body hitting the wooden floor as loud in its way as the capuchin's and Lockhart already striding toward the French doors to the loggia stopping just outside and perfectly framed in the double doorway in the edge of the stained light and the same arm coming up to his yawning mouth and another explosion sounding odd and hollow among the columns that surrounded the courtyard and the fan-shaped fronds of the Guadalupe palms.

HAYDON REMAINED IN MEXICO CITY UNTIL AFTER THE FUNERALS.

Saturnino Sarmiento de la Sierra was interred on a bright clear morning near the lacy shade of a ceiba tree in the Panteón Jardín in the Colonia Flor de María not far from San Ángel. It was not a large funeral. He hadn't many friends, and of the few he had, only one or two cared enough to come. There were two colleagues from the university, the kind of quiet men who still retained enough of a sense of civilization's proprieties to know when duty dictated their presence at funerals and weddings and christenings. There was a cluster of young men and women, students, Haydon guessed, who he believed had come out of curiosity—the happenings at the house in Coyoacán had caused quite a stir, although many people had disregarded the grisly details of the story as being the products of the overactive imaginations of gossip mongers. It was an ironic stroke of good luck—something Saturnino had not much experienced in life—that few believed the truth. There were flowers, but only marigolds, a thick saffron cape of them scattered over his grave as bright as dusted gold beneath the downy coral blossoms of the spreading ceiba. Isabel, showing her mother's mettle as well as her penchant for the unusual, shocked the Catholic priest officiating at the grave-side ceremony by having portions of a Náhua funeral poem read at the end of the service:

> Will I go like the flowers that perish?
> Will nothing remain of my name?
> Nothing of my fame here on earth?
> At least my flowers, at least my songs!
> Earth is the region of the fleeting moment.

Do men have roots, are they real?
No one can know completely
what is Your richness, what are Your flowers,
Oh Inventor of Yourself!

I will have to go down there,
to our-common-place-where-we-lose-ourselves,
nothing do I expect.
I leave you,
given over to sadness.

I will go away forever,
it is time for crying.
Send me to the Place of Mystery . . .
I, the Prince of the Sad Omen,
will go away forever.

Juan Lockhart Chavero-Casas was buried the next day in the early afternoon in the grand Panteón Civil de Delores at the heart of Chapultepec Park. As all who had witnessed his death agreed, it had been a tragic accident, and so he had not suffered from the church's discrimination against suicides. The funeral cortege had been large, the dark hearse and black limousines winding through the crooked lanes underneath the brooding and centuries-old *ahuehuetes*, the whole affair played out in a peculiar light created by the sun filtering through a choking layer of fuscous smog. In this unreal glow the long queue of black-suited mourners followed the plain mahogany casket along the narrow paths, the puffs of smoke from the singing priest's swaying censer hanging in the still air, through files of burial stones and ranks of tombs, past iron-fenced lots set aside for Jews or Masons or Moslems, past crypts and vaults and catafalques to the marbled garden of the Lockhart family plot. There the politicians and bureaucrats, the lawyers, entrepreneurs, and oil barons, the great and the grand (the president of Mexico had come to the cathedral, but had slipped rather noisily out a side door with his entourage before the huge church began to empty for the slow and stately procession to the cemetery), watched as Juan Lockhart was lowered into the grave beside his elder brother, who had preceded him by fifty years and who now would remain forever younger.

Isabel and Amaranta had attended both rites, accompanied by Celerina and Paulo. Saturnino's funeral had been little more than a local affair in San Ángel, but Juan Lockhart's requiem mass had been attended by the *haut monde* of Mexico City and Amaranta's appearance had been duly noted in the city's numerous newspapers, many of which printed photographs of her veiled figure arriving or leaving the cathedral or at the cemetery in Chapultepec.

Haydon had been at both funerals, too, standing at Isabel's side in the morning, but keeping his distance in the afternoon, camera-shy and unwilling to become a part of the spectacle. Besides, he had a lot to think about, and he could do that much better as an observer. With these two disparate interments, the long story of his father's affair with Amaranta had come to an end at last. But it was a complex story, and even its conclusion was not what it appeared to be.

In the moments following the second shot, Lockhart's and Arreola's men had swarmed into the studio, where there followed a few hectic minutes of confusion while the nervous, bewildered, and gun-waving bodyguards tried to sort out what had happened. Both of Lockhart's actions had been a total surprise to everyone, including his men. It had happened so unexpectedly and quickly that none of them had been able to reach him in time to stop his suicide. Had it not been that the snipers—who had indeed been stationed out in the dark loggia with their rifles trained on Saturnino—had seen everything, Haydon thought there would have been serious trouble with Eloy Palacio, whose frustration at having failed to prevent Lockhart's death was driving him to distraction. Everyone was shaken.

But the murder-suicide had galvanized Isabel, and at her command Celerina quickly took Amaranta away to her rooms. She immediately had Paulo bring white sheets for the bodies, all three of them, and then called a hasty conference with Arreola, Haydon, and Palacio at one end of the room to discuss the best way to handle the police, who would have to be notified. Finally it was decided that Palacio would summon a police captain from the central city *delegación* of Cuauhtémoc who long had been indebted to Lockhart, and rely on him to see that the incident was entrusted to an officer in the *delegación* of Obregón—which had jurisdiction—who would understand the situation and conduct a discreet and perfunctory investigation. In the meantime everyone but a few guards went downstairs and Isabel went straight to the kitchen to make coffee. It was to be a long night.

It was after two o'clock before everyone had gone. The police had come and taken photographs, they had conducted apologetic and cursory interviews, and the bodies had been taken away. The studio floor and the loggia tiles had been scrubbed by Paulo with Macbethean thoroughness, and finally the last of Lockhart's men had driven out of the courtyard and away through the tiny Plaza de los Arcángelos. Quiet settled over the rose house once again, leaving Isabel, Haydon, and Arreola alone in the *sala*. They were drained and exhausted, but sleep was out of the question. Without being prodded, Arreola knew the moment had come for the explanations. All the actors were gone now, except Amaranta, who in her own way was as far beyond them now as if she too had died. Lockhart's last words had to be explained, and there was no longer any reason for silence.

Like all of the young men in Mexico City's society circles of the 1930s, Juan Lockhart had been infatuated with Amaranta. But in the late summer of 1936 when she singled him out to play Brutus in her sexual assassination of her relationship with Webster Haydon by carefully planning their tryst to be witnessed by him, Amaranta also destroyed Lockhart. From that afternoon forward he was haunted by her, he found no peace anywhere. Hounded by his conscience for his betrayal and eaten from within by his lust for Amaranta, Juan Lockhart became a man bedeviled. Thunderstruck at having suddenly lost his best friend because of his own foolishness, he also found himself shunned by Amaranta, who, repulsed by her own actions, wanted nothing more to do with him. Within a month Webster Haydon had moved to England without having spoken to either Amaranta or Lockhart. Ashamed and isolated, Lockhart began a long emotional decline which eventually seriously affected his health. For a period of time he took a leave of absence from his father's firm, unable to concentrate on his work.

After nearly six months, Lockhart decided to sail for England himself, seeking to rid himself of his bad conscience by a face-to-face confrontation with Webster Haydon in which he would beg forgiveness. But when he arrived in London, his old friend refused even to see him. Devastated, Lockhart returned to Mexico and began the slow process of putting his life back together, trying to forget Webster Haydon as well as Amaranta.

Then early in 1938, Webster returned to Mexico City from England to work with the Mexican government in organizing a nationalized petroleum industry as a result of President Cárdenas's expropriation of all foreign oil holdings in Mexico. He brought with him a wife. For a year or more Amaranta was able to rein herself in, careful to avoid Webster, because she knew that was the way he wanted it. But eventually, because they circulated in the same social circles, it could not be avoided any longer. They saw each other for the first time in nearly two years at an opening-night exhibition of paintings at the Palacio de Bellas Artes. Neither spoke, but their eyes met unexpectedly. Fired by this chance encounter after so long an absence, Amaranta began a campaign to meet with him secretly, sending messages by couriers, pleading with him in letters that she suspected he never read, proposing secret rendezvous in churches or small out-of-the-way plazas or parks where he never appeared, and, in several instances, even confronting him personally at night after having waited for hours outside his offices downtown. But he never spoke with her, nothing more than a coldly correct greeting as he turned away.

In the meantime, Juan Lockhart had taken Webster Haydon's marriage as a signal that he was free to make his own advances to Amaranta, and just as in Amaranta's case with Webster he was met with nothing more than cold disregard. But, still burning with the memory of that one encounter with her in her studio, he was far more aggressive, and much more reckless. The manner in which he threw himself at Amaranta began to be the talk of their society friends, and Juan Lockhart became a parody of the foolish, spurned lover. The more she rejected him, the more outrageous became his behavior, the more he wanted her. It was an absurd triangle, one that created a great deal of pain and, eventually, disaster.

Just after Easter in 1943, Webster quit his position with the

Mexican government and moved to Houston, where he proposed to establish his own law practice specializing in international law, believing, correctly as it turned out, that his specialized experience with the Mexican petroleum industry would work to his advantage in the then burgeoning oil fields of Texas and Louisiana. Between Thanksgiving and Christmas of that year his business took him back to Mexico City for the entire month of December. It was during that time that he finally gave in to Amaranta's entreaties, and secretly met with her. The meeting was an emotional one in Amaranta's studio in San Ángel, but there was no liaison.

Lockhart, still being spurned by Amaranta and having heard of Webster's arrival in Mexico City, had suspected Amaranta would try to contact Webster again, and had him followed. When he learned of their meeting, he was enraged. That same night, after making sure Amaranta was alone, he forced his way into the rose house and confronted her. There was an argument, a struggle followed, and he raped her. He held her captive all that night, having his way with her numerous times, crazy with anger and his own pent-up desire. In the gray dawn hours of the next morning, he slipped out of the house and left San Ángel.

In a decision that seemed to run counter to her personality, Amaranta told no one. Instead she calmly met with Webster several more times during his last week in Mexico City. It was from this time, this brief week before Christmas when all of Mexico City was aglitter with holiday lights, that their annual meetings had their beginning. It was then that a bond was formed between them—Webster would say later that the bond always had been there, but it was only then that they realized it—that found its matrix in something deeper than the physical attraction that seemed to have dominated their relationship up to then. Webster returned to Houston.

Then two months later, in February 1943, Webster received a cable from Amaranta asking him if he could arrange a trip to Mexico City as quickly as possible. She urgently needed to talk to him. When he got there he went straight to San Ángel, where he found an alternately distraught and coldly calm Amaranta who informed him that she had just learned that she was pregnant. She then proceeded to tell him of the circumstances that led up to her rape by Juan Lockhart. After talking with Amaranta for hours and learning of her plans—which would eventually result in the strange conditional contract with Everardo Sarmiento—Webster Haydon returned to the city with a single purpose in mind. He went straight to Lockhart's bachelor home, which at that time was a large hacienda-style house on Calle Horacio in the elite *colonia* of Polanco. Persuading Lockhart's young maid to let him walk into Lockhart's library unannounced, Webster strode into the room. Paralyzed by surprise, Lockhart stood still as Webster stalked across to him and without saying a word, knocked him to the floor. Then he fell on him in a blind rage, unleashing a wrath fed by years of resentment at his betrayal, and beat Lockhart senseless. He probably would have killed him if the maid's screaming hadn't attracted the attention of one of the gardeners and Lockhart's driver, who after a considerable struggle managed to pull Webster off the unconscious Scotsman.

No one ever understood why Amaranta didn't abort the pregnancy, or why she chose to marry Everardo Sarmiento, of all the men she could have had. But that was the way it happened, and such things cannot be foreseen or even imagined. Who would have dreamed, for instance, that Saturnino would one day meet his death by the hand of his own father?—the same man who had violently given him life had violently taken it away.

THE DAY HAYDON WAS TO LEAVE MEXICO CITY, HE SENT HIS LUGGAGE ahead to the airport and made one last trip south to San Ángel. The taxi driver turned down the long, sloping grade of tree-lined Insurgentes Boulevard, which stretched out before them and disappeared into the nicotine haze of morning smog. Haydon sat quietly in the backseat breathing a confused mixture of automobile exhaust and the cloying fragrance of cherry Lifesavers, which the taxi driver was eating like peanuts, crunching them energetically one after the other instead of letting them dissolve in his mouth.

Soon after they crossed over into the *delegación* of Obregón, the driver turned right and cut across Revolución on La Paz, leaving behind the modern boulevards as he slowed to a crawl on the cobblestones below Plaza San Jacinto and began climbing into the old colonial village of stone buildings and small shops sunken a few steps below the sidewalks of the steep streets. The plaza was busy, and they had to wait a few moments behind the silent electric buses powered like old trolleys by rods connected to cables above the street. After a crowded exchange of passengers between the plaza and the buses, they lumbered out of the way and the taxi eased around the park to Frontera and began the ascent. The air was much cleaner here, away from the low environs of the inner city, and when they turned onto a still-narrower street the sunlight broke through the morning clouds and threw splashes of early light across magenta banks of bougainvillea that crested the tall curving walls.

In the tiny Plaza de los Arcángelos surrounded by the pastel walls of houses, the morning shade still prevailed except on the tops of the tallest eucalyptus and poplars, whose crowns were already burning with descending fire. Two eager art students had set up their easels near the old fountain, painting the falling water from opposite sides, the light changing quickly all around them.

Haydon got out of the cab and paid the driver, who left him standing at the edge of the plaza looking toward the stone arches that led to the outer courtyard of the rose house at the end of the short drive. The upper floor of the house stood out above the blue morning shadows, powder rose in the clean light. For a moment he remained there, trying to see the old house as if he were a stranger seeing it for the first time, as if he knew nothing about it except the raw architectural aesthetics which it presented to everyone. But it wasn't any good. It was a feat of imagination beyond his abilities. The rose house had become too much a part of his life, a symbol of something too intimate to be regarded objectively.

He found her in the studio, of course, sitting at the far end on the *lit en bateau*, perfectly centered between the two winged mahogany sphinxes. The studio was bright with morning sunshine, and as he walked down the length of the long room he passed through great hazy shafts of it falling through the tall windows. As he approached the midpoint in the room, he could not help but notice the faint umber stains on the wooden floor, which could not be removed totally, even by Paulo's earnest efforts. They were there to stay, like tangible, unforgettable memories. He could not count the number of times such marks had driven Houston families from their homes. Continuing to live within the same walls, being reminded day after day of the exact location where someone they had loved had met a violent death, was something they literally could not live with. They moved away. But here, in an older society where the ages of many homes were counted by centuries rather than decades, such tragedies were absorbed within the greater history of the family. Many things happened in these houses, which seemed often to make them microcosms of the society at large. The thick walls took it all in, the tragedy and the happiness, the beginnings and the endings. It was all a part of the inheritance.

Finally he was standing in front of Isabel, looking at her green eyes and the dusk of her skin through the simple cotton dress with all the emotional energy and naiveté of an adolescent. But he saw more than her loveliness, and he felt more than an adolescent would recognize or understand.

"You're leaving," she said. She knew he was; he had told her over the telephone that he wanted to say goodbye.

He nodded. "I've got some time, though," he said.

She smiled. "But not enough."

He shook his head. "No, not enough." He knew what she meant. For them there was never going to be enough time; half of it was gone the moment they met.

Her smile faded, and she stood and put her arm through his as she turned him around to face the length of the studio. It was a gesture that made his heart ache.

The sun streamed through the windows in ranks of orient light, seeming to levitate an easel here, a cluttered work table there, a cross-frame chair farther on. She took him a few steps into the room, leaning close to him as naturally as if they had done it for years, with a comfortable intimacy that he knew she expected him to understand.

"I am grateful that we met, anyway," she said, slipping her hand down to his, lacing her slender fingers through his. "Now we know, even if it is only to understand that it never can be different for us. Still, to have met, to know how it is . . . between us, that is a very rich thing, isn't it?"

He couldn't bring himself to reply. He wanted her to keep talking, never, never to stop, because all she said was as familiar to him as his own thoughts, as if she knew his every emotion regarding her, responded in kind, and spoke for them both. In doing so, it seemed, she treated their dilemma with greater grace and honesty than did his silence.

"There is so much of you here," she said with a subtle change in tenor. "As much of you as there is of me. It would be a mistake, I think, if you planned never to return."

They moved slowly through one of the shafts of light, through suspended dust motes and floating flecks of gold, toward the center of the room, as Haydon inhaled deeply of the rich odors of oil paints and resins and Belgian linen canvas. They stopped and looked across at his father's portraits still leaning against the wall between the open French doors.

"Even he could not stay away forever," she said.

There was silence a moment, and then he said, "I'm not sure it would be wise."

Her shrug was almost imperceptible except for the press of her breast, soft against his arm. "Perhaps not," she said. "Who knows? In this house, as you have seen, we know little of wisdom."

"I know less of it now than I did," Haydon said.

"Do you think of him badly?" she asked, as both of them looked at the portraits. "After all this?"

"No, I couldn't," he said, remembering Arreola's warning that if he insisted on looking into Amaranta's life he would discover that he would find not answers, but only more questions, as if he were peering into a deep well where there were two kinds of darkness, or perhaps a mirror. "But maybe I understand him a little better, or at least will come to. He was even more complicated than I had believed. I didn't know him very well after all. It makes me wonder how much more there is, how much more I don't know."

He thought she held his arm a little tighter. "Is it necessary to 'know' more? Maybe you think he used poor judgment."

He wasn't sure what she meant.

"Why do you suppose he kept these things from you, these secrets?" she asked. "You already have discovered more than he wanted you to know. Perhaps he knew that discovering facts about another person's life is not the same as understanding them. That there is a point at which information is only information, and nothing more."

"Yes, maybe," Haydon conceded. "But at least I'm closer than I was to understanding what he was really all about."

Isabel slipped her arm from his and moved over by one of

the portraits, the one in which Webster Haydon was sitting on a rock wall in white summer clothes with the lavender ridges of the Sierra de Tepoztlán in the distance. She looked at the portrait a moment and then turned to Haydon.

"Do you really think you can 'understand' this young man, why he felt the way he did about the woman who painted his portraits, and how he felt inside when he touched her and smelled her and tasted her? To tell you the truth," she said, dropping her eyes to the picture again, "I hope you are wrong. You should not be allowed to know those things, to truly understand them. They are mysteries that do not belong to you, only to him, and to her."

Haydon stood there and looked at Isabel and the portrait, and time played tricks with his perception. He saw the emerald-eyed Amaranta older than she had been when she painted the portraits, but younger than she was now, and he saw his father, younger than himself. He no longer knew what he believed about his father, beyond the fact that he would never again be able to think of him in the same way that he had before. He hoped that time would help to clear his mind, for, despite what he had told Isabel, he was a long way from reconciling the man he had known with the man he had discovered during the last seven days.

Perhaps Haydon's father had been anticipating a moment like this when, on that warm spring night many years earlier, the two of them had stood on the terrace of their home and Haydon had delivered the sad news that a family friend had just been arrested for the murder of his mistress. Haydon had been vicious in his condemnation of the man, but his father had cautioned him. It was wrong, he had said, to pass judgment on another man with such surety. No man could ever fully understand the actions of another, nor be sure that he himself would never act as foolishly. Such men were to be viewed with compassion, and with the humbling knowledge that none of us can ever really understand the mysterious inner workings of the human heart.

He knew Isabel was right, that his desire to know should have its limits, that there were times when memory had to be its own reward, even when its hue was richer or paler than the truth from which it came. It had to be enough. In the end it was all he had.

ABOUT THE AUTHOR

David L. Lindsey is the author of *Black Gold, Red Death; A Cold Mind; Heat from Another Sun;* and *Spiral*. He lives and writes in Austin, Texas.

MERCY
by David Lindsey

Here is a special advance preview of David Lindsey's chilling new novel, *MERCY*, which will be available as a Doubleday hardcover in May 1990, at your local bookseller.

MERCY

CHAPTER 1

Thursday, May 11

Sandra Moser paused in the broad entryway of her home, a rubber band in her mouth, her arms raised to the back of her head where she was gathering her blond hair in a ponytail. She was wearing a pink bodysuit over white leotards. When she had her hair pulled tight, clasped in one small, pink-nailed hand, she took the rubber band from her mouth and wound it several times around the hank of hair. As she did this, pulling at the loose hair of the ponytail to tighten the band, she listened to the television in the family room across the hallway where her children, Cassie, eight, and Michael, six, were eating hamburgers on TV trays with the family maid.

She had already kissed them good-bye, receiving inattentive, routine "'byes" from them, commensurate with her routine trip to aerobics class. But now she paused again, listening for Cassie's thin, muffled cough. The third grader had received the first of her series of spring allergy shots earlier in the day, and Sandra was hoping they had not waited too long. Cassie was prone to chronic sinus infections when the mold-spore count was highest. Tugging at the tight leg of her bodysuit cutting into her groin, she wondered if she should take Cassie's temperature before she left. The kids laughed at something on television, their small voices, nearer, louder than the canned laugh track, and Sandra decided to wait until she returned later in the evening.

Grabbing her monogrammed athletic bag from the closet near the front door, she noticed her husband's umbrella hanging against the closet wall. Andrew refused to take it with him. It just cluttered up the car, he argued, always getting in his way. Besides, he simply never needed it. He parked in a covered garage and walked to his office through the tunnels. She would remind him of the times he had been drenched—it had happened three times in the last three months—but he would shrug off her cautionary examples as "unusual." Andrew did not entertain the unusual.

She took the umbrella off the wall and leaned it against the small Chinese table in the entryway to remind her to put it in his car when he got home. It was absurd for him not to carry it with him, especially in the spring. Making a mental note to call Gwyn Sheldon about a fund-raising idea for the children's academy—she thought of it because Gwyn's husband had an umbrella with a handle like Andrew's—she hurried out of their two-story Georgian home nestled in the thick pinewoods of Hunter's Creek, one of several townships clustered together in west Houston and known as the Memorial Villages. The Villages ranked near the top of the list of the nation's wealthiest suburbs.

A fresh spring rain had moved through the Villages only half an hour earlier, making the woods fragrant and washing the city clean in the dusk. Sandra inhaled deeply of the damp evening smells as she tossed her bag into her dark-blue Jeep Wagoneer and climbed behind the steering wheel, flipping on the headlights. It was just now getting dark enough to use them. She started the Jeep, fastened her seat belt, wheeled the Wagoneer around the island of magnolias in front of the house, and drove quickly along the drive bordered by a white fence covered with brambles of pyracantha. When she reached the street, she waited for a car to pass as she checked her watch. It was seven-forty. Her aerobics class began at eight o'clock, and Andrew was at a weekly business meeting until ten.

Hurrying along the winding street she came to the major north-south artery of Voss and turned left. Within a mile or so she would come to Woodway where she would need to turn left again to go to Sabrina's, an athletic club that catered to the already sleek bodies of the women of the Villages. But Sandra Moser did not turn left at Woodway. Instead, she breezed past the intersection and turned left at the next street, San Felipe, and pushed the Wagoneer east through the high-dollar neighborhoods of Briargrove and Post Oak Estates and Tanglewood until she made her first right turn onto the fashionably posh Post Oak Boulevard. Now known as Uptown Houston, the Galleria area was the largest suburban business district in the nation. It's newest pearl was the Pavilion, Saks Fifth Avenue, a multimillion-dollar complex of elegant shops separated from the boulevard by a phalanx of sixty-foot palms that glistened in the light mist that was now moving in on heavy air from the gulf coast fifty miles to the southeast.

With the lights of the office towers and high-rise condominiums reflecting back at her from the glistening, black boulevard, Sandra Moser whipped the Wagoneer into a median turn lane and quickly cut across traffic to the Doubletree Hotel, a flat-faced structure with an inset glass-curtain wall in its center section that fell to two overlapping half-barrel arches that were also made of glass and formed the hotel's porte cochere. She did not stop for the uniformed doorman who stepped to the curb to open her door, but continued past him and drove around to the parking garage gate. She took a ticket from the buzzing dispenser, which opened the gate, and entered the garage, having to drive up to the third level before finding an available parking space. She snatched her bag out of the Wagoneer, locked it, and walked to the elevator which took her back down to the lobby.

At the registration desk she presented a counterfeit driver's license and told the concierge she wanted to pay in cash. The license was a document that had cost her a significant amount of money as well as considerable trouble. Those among them who were married had to worry about those kinds of things—their wire was stretched tighter, their balancing act a little more delicate than the others'. But it had been worth it. It had served her well for over two years now. She asked for a room facing the boulevard on the highest floor available. After signing the registration forms and paying, she declined the help of a bellboy and walked straight across the cavernous lobby to the elevator, her high-cut bodysuit and stylish figure turning heads. Sandra Moser was a beautiful woman.

She found her room on the eighth floor not far from the elevator and slipped the rectangular magnetic card into the slot above the handle, heard it click, and shoved it open. She did not turn on the lights, but tossed her bag and the card on the bed and walked straight to the curtains and opened them. A little to her left a sweep of buildings rose up above her, their lights glittering in the mists like a rainy sky of winking eyes peering at her in the opened window, their vantage points the envy of even the most demanding voyeur savant. And across the shiny boulevard the palm trees of the Pavilion stood dripping in a surreal desert of green sand.

Sandra Moser walked to the telephone and placed a call. She spoke only a few words and hung up, then walked back to the window. Standing in front of it, she reached up and began taking the rubber band from her ponytail. But her hands were shaking; the rubber band was too tight. It snapped, startling her. She raked her fingers through her hair and tossed the rubber band aside and shook out her hair. She took a deep breath. The room was clean, did not smell of cigarette smoke. It was new and clean.

From this moment on it would be different from all the times before. Until now she had been learning. It had been a long apprenticeship, hampered by her own anxieties and psychological impediments. She might never have come to this point at all if she had not had help, if she had not been coached and coaxed and brought along with patience and understanding. She had reached that stage where she would have to give herself up completely, or never know what it might have been like to understand something few people would ever know. It was that simple. It had been explained to her, but she had known anyway, instinctively. The body was the gateway to the mind. She almost had done it before, almost had crossed the threshold, risking her identity until she had grown intoxicated on nothing more than the other's breath, that feather of one's essence that no one could ever alter or destroy.

Her hands were trembling even more now as she pulled off her bodysuit and tossed it out of the way. And then she peeled off the leotards, freeing her body from the tight, embracing web, her skin feeling tingly, alive with millions of tiny, sensitive fingers. Standing naked in front of the plate-glass window, she let them look at her, let them glitter and wink at her. It was electrifying to have finally made the decision to acquiesce, and for a full week she had been distracted with anticipation. The curtain was about to rise on her repression.

There was a firm knock at the door and she flinched. For a moment she didn't turn around, but remained, nude, facing the night of greedy lights. It really was too late. She picked up the magnetic card from the foot of the bed as she walked by it on her way to the door. For some reason unclear even to her—she had never done it before—she didn't open the door, but knelt and slipped the card into the sliver of light as if she were pushing it out into that promised and anxiously anticipated dimension. Then she backed away slowly, listened to the card slide into the slot and click, listened to the double click of the turning door handle, and watched the sliver of light widen into a harsh brightness burning around the silhouette like a blinding white aura. Then the flood narrowed to darkness again, the light returned to a sliver on the floor, and the figure stood somewhere in the dark passage.

She waited with her back to the room again, facing the window, listening to the sounds of a small leather valise yielding up its contents behind her in the dark room. Almost immediately she caught the thick, musky odor of lipstick and oils, followed by the tinny chinking of buckles, the brittle rustling of new tissue paper, the muffled clacking of ebony wood beads, expelled breath, a waft of "Je Reviens." She had planned all this, choreographed these smallest details of sounds and smells in their proper sequence. Not only was she trembling because these things accommodated her imagination, but she was delighted that every detail of her design was being followed. By prearrangment she controlled the events about to happen and she knew they would continue inexorably, no matter how she pleaded for them to stop. But she could not control her trembling. The rain, it seemed, was coming through the glass.

Like a No play it took hours, or seemed to, though it was impossible to know. Time quickly had lost its capacity to be measured. And there was talk, an agitated monologue, a hypertensive soliloquy in which she recognized the familiar disquiet of her own restrained arousal. Even though they had talked it through before, every act and scene, every syllable of dialogue, every postured movement of the hand and tongue and pelvis, there were surprises—of intuition and sensation, the mutual, unspoken decision to sustain the prelude of erotic tension.

Eventually she lay on the bottom sheet of the bed, everything else having been stripped away and thrown into a corner, her arms and legs extended, her wrists already secured. She listened to the gabbling, felt her right ankle being secured. Sometimes she understood, sometimes she didn't, as she struggled against her body's insistence to hyperventilate, though she knew that it was in the act of her surrendering that she controlled the sequence of the play, and achieved a dimension of experience never before realized. As she felt her left ankle being secured, she took long, deep breaths. Trusting was vital. She remembered: the body was the gateway to the mind. She had never concentrated so hard in her life. When the last buckle was snapped she suddenly felt lighter than air, as if she had been released rather than bound. In that instant she understood that total helplessness, total surrender, was like a black feather, floating, falling into a vast, dark emptiness.

The choreography was followed precisely. She cried and writhed and fought the bindings; she begged for it to stop; she pleaded. But it continued, past what she thought she could endure, past the pleasure she thought she would gain from it, and into something beyond, as had been promised. She rolled and tossed upon the waves of pleasures she had never imagined, she swooned in the troughs and rode the high, rolling curls of sensations she had not dreamed. Sometimes, through it all, to stay in touch with reality she looked to the rain on the window, fixed her eyes on the stippled, fracted light that formed a complete wall of Brownian motion behind the figure above her. As the tempo increased they approached once again that moment of experiencing each other's breath, that feather of one's essence that no one could alter or destroy. And then she was heaved upon a dark tsunami, a long, swelling high from which she looked down into real fear. This was it. She was too high, too far, reality was frighteningly small and still receding. She pleaded for it to stop, and it didn't. It was worse, much worse, and for a moment she panicked, almost slid into incoherence before she remembered the safe word. "Mercy," she gasped, and waited to be saved. "Mercy! Mercy!"

But everything disintegrated in a flare of mandarin red.

The first blow broke her jaw.

And she felt herself being bitten and chewed.

She was stupefied. "Mercy."

The second blow snapped the cartilage of her nose.

She listened in horror to the gibbering that was faster than comprehension, faster than lips could form words it seemed, and suddenly she was called by a name she had never heard and was accused of things she had never done.

"Mercy."

Another blow, and the incredible, dumbfounding

sensation of being bitten, the teeth everywhere on her, no place sacred.

She gulped desperately at the blood that poured into her throat from the back of her nose and tried to see through eyes bleary with shock. This was wrong, all wrong. She heard the clicking sound of a buckle and then something slithered under the back of her neck and she felt the naked knees on either side of her chest. The belt was thick, like a high collar, and as it slowly tightened, her ears filled with a rushing roar and her heart hammered, rocking her as if it would explode. Then she went deaf and her heart seemed less insistent. She began to drift. She had almost left her body, almost achieved that blessed separation, when she was cruelly brought back through the roar and the hammering and the pain and the unimaginable sorrow of her ordeal.

Then the belt was tightened again.

Time had no meaning apart from her coming and going through these sounds and sensations that filled the verge of consciousness. It all had gone wrong, all of it, this and everything, even the years rolling back over memory. She had granted someone the authority to toy with her life, neither allowing it nor denying it, perversely bringing her back again and again, gabbling faster than comprehension, faster than lips could form words, calling her by a name she had never heard, accusing her of things she had never done.

Only the rain was virtuous, and it was through the rain that she drifted for the last time.

Now there are two great ways to catch up with your favorite thrillers

Audio:

Kinsey Millhone is...

"The best new private eye."   —*The Detroit News*

"A tough-cookie with a soft center."   —*Newsweek*

"A stand-out specimen of the new female operatives."
                                    —*Philadelphia Inquirer*

Sue Grafton is...

The Shamus and Anthony Award winning creator of
Kinsey Millhone and quite simply one of the hottest
new mystery writers around.

Bantam is...

The proud publisher of Sue Grafton's Kinsey Millhone
mysteries:

☐	27991	"A" IS FOR ALIBI	$3.95
☐	28034	"B" IS FOR BURGLAR	$3.95
☐	28036	"C" IS FOR CORPSE	$3.95
☐	27163	"D" IS FOR DEADBEAT	$3.95
☐	27955	"E" IS FOR EVIDENCE	$3.95